OF QUEENS AND DRAGONS
QUEENMAKERS SAGA XI

BY
BERNADETTE ROWLEY

ACKNOWLEDGEMENTS

Deep thanks must go to my beta readers and biggest fans,
Nic Page and Rachel Cass.
Their generosity in being my first readers for
Of Queens and Dragons and their enthusiasm for my words are
inspirational. Thanks also to these ladies for their critical feedback
during cover creation.

To Duncan Carling-Rodgers for his assistance during the
Of Queens and Dragons edits and for the formatting.

To Dar Albert for her stunning cover.

To my husband, Michael, my sons and their ladies for their unending
love and support and for sharing the disappointments and triumphs
of a writing life.

TITLES BY
BERNADETTE ROWLEY

(in suggested reading order)

Princess Avenger - Queenmakers Saga I

The Lady's Choice - Queenmakers Saga II

Princess in Exile - Queenmakers Saga III

The Lord and the Mermaid - Queenmakers Saga IV

The Elf King's Lady - Queenmakers Saga V

The Lady and the Pirate - Queenmakers Saga VI

The Master and the Sorceress - Queenmakers Saga VII

Elf Princess Warrior - Queenmakers Saga VIII

The People's Princess - Queenmakers Saga IX

The King's Blade - Queenmakers Saga X

Of Queens and Dragons - Queenmakers Saga XI

TABLE OF CONTENTS

CHAPTER ONE

VARD Anton met the eyes of the battle leaders in the crowd. "Commanders, marshal your forces and keep watch on the enemy during the hours of darkness."

He couldn't bear to say more. He turned and entered the hospital, weighed down by the loss of his leader. The king lay on a table, a sheet pulled over his body, leaving his face visible. He looked peaceful in death.

Queen Adriana, and the ladies Merielle and Alique, stood by the table while two women waited in the corner.

Vard went to Adriana. "Please accept my condolences, My Queen."

Adriana took a deep breath. "Thank you. Beniel showed you the letter before he passed?"

Vard nodded. "He did, though I can't believe he was serious."

"He was *deadly* serious, Vard. And I supported his decision." She lowered her voice. "You are the only one who can do this. The transition must be seamless, especially as we are in the middle of a war. It was the only course of action to take."

Vard looked to the heavens and shook his head. "It will cause a scandal. No one will think I deserve this." He met her gaze, and she flinched. "The military leaders will be furious, the admiral included."

"Let me deal with Nikolas," she hissed, "and the others." She turned to their companions. "Lady Alique, Lady Merielle, please leave us for a moment." Once the ladies and their attendants had departed, Adriana continued.

"I don't think we should make the contents of that letter public until the war is over," she said. "You are the King's Blade and will step into the role of ultimate leader now he is gone. If there is dissent, I will quell it. After the war, we will make the succession public."

Vard nodded. "I agree. That will give me time to accustom myself to the idea." *As if I could ever get used to being king! Alecia is going to… there isn't a word suitable for what Alecia will do when she finds out.*

Adriana grasped his forearm. "You will be a good king, Vard, but first we must defeat the *Sis Lenweri*."

He nodded. "Yes, one thing at a time. I must go. Will you be fine alone?"

"I'm going with you."

Vard hesitated, but nodded. The last thing he needed was the queen sticking to him like glue. An idea occurred to him. No! It was too ridiculous to countenance.

"I'm off to the meeting room in the battlements. I'll have food brought there. You're welcome to attend."

Adriana gave him a curious look. "It is nice to be given permission to attend my own briefing, but as you wish."

When they arrived at the meeting, all were in attendance, including Nikolas Cosara, General Formosa, various captains of the army and cavalry, Ruven Magbalar, and Isiloe.

The king's seat was vacant, although Vard had wondered if Formosa would have the audacity to pre-emptively seat himself there. Vard walked to the chair, pulled it out, and indicated the queen should seat herself. There was a shocked silence as she did so.

"Thank you all for being here," Vard said, "and for your efforts in the field today."

There was a general murmuring and nodding of heads.

"I wish to take this time to reflect on the life of Beniel Zialni, King of Thorius. As we each do this, let us be silent."

Vard bowed his head, bending his thought to the times he had spent with the king recently. Though they didn't always see eye to eye, he had formed a deep respect for his king. He had been a decent husband and a loving family man who had felt profound grief at the passing of his younger brother, Alecia's father. Vard believed the loss of his brother had literally broken Beniel's heart. But when needed, the king had been fierce, as demonstrated in the battle with Faenwelar. Vard was convinced Beniel would've been the victor if the high prince hadn't fled with his minders.

"Thank you," he said. "I'm sure you have fond memories of King Beniel. His efforts on the field, despite ill health, were astounding."

Cries of "Hear, hear!" echoed around the room.

"But now we must turn our attention to the continuing war, as the king would've wished."

Adriana nodded. "I urge you all to put your mourning aside and ensure Beniel's death leaves a lasting legacy in Thorius."

The room broke out in enthusiastic clapping.

"Casualty reports please." Vard said, when the room had quietened.

Nikolas stood. "Cavalry losses were minimal, perhaps one in ten total deaths or injuries. I'll have more accurate figures when I meet with my sub-commanders. Some of the horses were burned at the end of the dragon fire." His jaw clenched as though horse losses impacted him as deeply as losing his men.

Nikolas gave way, and Formosa stood. "Infantry losses were higher. Around two in ten deaths and three in ten injuries, many of which were burns. We didn't have enough protection for everyone and some were caught out of the trenches. But it could've been worse."

Adriana spoke up. "We lost some of the stretcher bearers in the fighting, women and some children included. Lady Merielle should be mentioned honorably. She took it upon herself, when the reports of deaths came in, to take her horse and fight to protect those fetching the injured."

Vard nodded. "She did a wonderful job."

Nikolas's eyes blazed aqua fire. "And that will be the last time she does that!"

Vard fixed his gaze on the admiral who glared back at him. He shrugged, accepting there would be more said about the brave lady's exploits.

The city administrator gave a report as to the disposal of the deceased including the enemy dead who hadn't been taken away by their own soldiers.

"How is the hospital coping?" Vard asked Adriana.

"They have been inundated but I garnered more help from the nobility, including some of the ladies, who have made excellent nurse helpers. I had to commandeer two more buildings for housing the injured, one of them devoted to burns. Lady Alique has been miraculous, but she is ready to drop."

"My Queen," Vard said, "could you arrange some relief for the health workers? I know it has been a terrible day for you personally but, if you could see to that detail, I'd appreciate it."

Adriana nodded.

"On to the coming battles," Vard said. "We severely dented Faenwelar today, personally and his force. If we press hard, tomorrow should see us victorious."

Cheering and clapping greeted the announcement.

"We must be vigilant of the dragons. I want you to return to your units and ensure that a fresh coat of flame inhibitor is applied to all the shields and anything else we are using to protect ourselves and the horses. Debris is to be cleared from the trenches overnight, so we have clear and tidy ground in the morning. All weapons are to be fetched from the field, cleaned and sharpened. I'll give orders for the smiths to work through the night if necessary. And I'll personally tour the battleground overnight."

Formosa cleared his throat and stood.

"Yes, General?" Vard asked.

"Aren't we ignoring the real and present issue?"

"And what would that be?" Vard asked.

Formosa stared at him as if he had gone mad. "The death of the king? Surely that detail changes everything. There must be a handover of power. We must speak to the guardians of the heir and seek their orders before we resume fighting."

"And how do you suggest we do that when they're a minimum five-day march away?"

Adriana stood, forcing Formosa to sit. "There is no need to check with the Guardians or change our plans. Beniel gave his instructions before he died." She closed her eyes and clenched her jaw. "He trusted Vard and all of you to see this through. As King's Blade, Vard will continue in his role of commander-in-chief until we conclude this war."

She sat, folding her hands on the table.

"But, Your Majesty… I *can* still call you 'Your Majesty', can't I?" Formosa said. "After all, with the king dead, it's uncertain what your title should now be."

Several chairs scraped as people got to their feet. All stared at Formosa. Vard was gratified to see him discomforted.

"I meant no disrespect," Formosa said, holding up his hands. "I was merely …"

"General Formosa," Vard said firmly, "the king issued his orders just prior to his death. They were a written declaration as well as verbal, given with Queen Adriana's approval. It would be insanity to suspend the fighting while advice is sought. We'll press our advantage and defeat Faenwelar. Then we'll have the time to attend to the other details."

Formosa slammed his hand on the table. "Those 'other details' are rather important, don't you think?"

"Not more so than securing the safety and freedom of this kingdom. There'll be no further discussion on the matter."

Vard fixed the general with his death stare, and the man nodded.

"If you don't mind, King's Blade," Formosa said, "I have matters to see to." He left the room, slamming the door.

Several of the other leaders left after him until only Vard, Queen Adriana, Nikolas Cosara, Ruven, and Isiloe remained, along with James Tomel who had been so quiet Vard had again forgotten he was there.

"He will cause more trouble, that one," Isiloe said.

Vard was inclined to agree with her.

Ruven nodded. "Ramar Isiloe and I will keep an eye on the general, if it please you, King's Blade."

James cleared his throat. "Liaise with me, Ruven," he said. "I have people who can help you."

Vard nodded. "Very well, James. Thank you, Ruven." He nodded at Isiloe.

"Just exactly what were the king's orders?" Nikolas snapped. "Forgive me for asking. I know you closed the subject, but something tells me there's more to this than the king giving his blessing for us to defeat Faenwelar on his behalf."

Vard allowed Adriana to answer.

"Beniel wanted us to press on exactly as we are. He appointed Vard as commander. You are all to follow his orders."

"And you agree with this?" Nikolas asked.

Adriana nodded. "I do. Vard is absolutely the right man for the task. He is widely respected. You are to defer to him in all things or I will have something to say about it."

"My Queen," Vard said, "there's no need to put the cart before the horse. I foresee no trouble from the commanders."

"Oh, you don't?" Nikolas said. "I wouldn't be so sure."

"*Nikolas!*" Adriana exclaimed.

"Don't worry, cousin," Nikolas said. "Anton is a fair enough leader. I'll let him know if I don't agree with his commands, otherwise I'll hold my tongue. I can't speak for everyone else though." He bowed and left them, as did the others.

James approached. "I'll be about my information gathering, Lord Anton."

Vard nodded. "Report back to me at midnight."

As James left, Adriana placed a hand on Vard's arm. "Are you sure giving him this freedom is a good idea? Beniel wouldn't like it."

"We need him, especially now. Nothing will go wrong."

He escorted the queen to the waiting carriage, and they rode back to the castle.

"I'm going to need you more than ever, Vard," Adriana said, turning to face him. "I can't believe he is gone."

"You're strong, Adriana,' he said. "You will find your new place in this world and go on."

She was quiet for a time. "What do you mean, 'find my place'? I thought it was obvious what Beniel wanted. He wanted you to wed me."

Vard jerked toward her. "Wed you?"

She clutched his arms. "Yes! Don't you see how perfect it would be? There would be continuity of rule with me at your side. We could have a family, a son to continue in your stead."

"Stop!" Vard said, holding up his hand. "What you describe is a fantasy. Beniel meant no such thing when he made me his heir."

She shook her head. "We discussed it, Vard. He would make you his heir and you would marry me. It's what he wanted."

Vard couldn't believe what he was hearing. "You're not jesting?"

"No, Vard!" She pulled him close and kissed him on the lips, melting against him, her arms sliding up his chest and around his neck.

Taken by surprise, Vard initially did nothing to stop her advance. It was like he was outside his body watching the scene play out. Then he came to his senses and gently disentangled himself.

"You're overwrought, My Queen," he said. "Here—we've arrived. Let me help you down and get your maids to put you to bed. I prescribe a large goblet of wine before you retire."

He helped her from the coach and led her to the entry.

"You'll see, Vard. It will be perfect. *We* will be perfect."

"Hush now. Go with the footman and your ladies will attend you."

He watched as the queen ascended the stairs, a shiver climbing his spine at what she thought might happen. His world had just become even more complicated.

He returned to his chambers to wash and change and found James Tomel waiting for him.

"I thought you were out gathering information," Vard said.

Tomel followed him into his rooms. "I was, but on the way to my first meeting I got intelligence which concerned me. I grabbed a horse and hurried straight here." He hesitated, then turned and closed the door. "Is your man about?"

Vard opened his senses but discerned only the two of them. "We're alone. Out with it. What did you hear?"

"General Formosa is already spreading a rumor about you and the queen. He's insinuating an inappropriate relationship between you, even suggesting you may be responsible for the king's death."

Of all the possibilities, Vard had never imagined this could be the news James had brought him. "How did you hear this?"

"Without revealing my source, it was overheard in a tavern between the general and one of his cronies. I couldn't identify which one from the description. Will you move against them?"

Vard shook his head. "Not yet. I have Ruven and Isiloe watching Formosa, and will advise them of the line he is spinning."

If Formosa was aware of the contents of the letter, it would play straight into his hands. Luckily, his cousin Alique had pronounced the king's death, but Vard was certain the general wouldn't be above incriminating even his own cousin if the benefits to him were great enough.

"I must get the doctor to examine the body," Vard said, "and do whatever tests are needed to judge a cause of death. That way we have a defense when Formosa comes against us."

James cleared his throat. "My Lord, is there any truth in the rumor the general has started?"

Vard speared him with the force of his gaze. "Of course not! I'm devoted to Alecia and I was loyal to the king. I'd never betray either of them. You can wipe that thought from your mind immediately."

"I had to know. But you must stay distant from the queen and not be seen with her from now on. Appearances are just as important as reality."

Vard drew a deep breath and nodded. "I'll think on what you've said and make sure I'm never alone with Her Majesty. Thank you, James. That was valuable information. You may go."

Vard rubbed his forehead as he closed the door behind James. Evil rumors were just what he didn't need now. He'd have to advise the queen. Perhaps that would convince her how silly her idea of a future together was.

For now, it was time to get a good look over the enemy encampment and the hawk was just the creature to do that. He locked the door, stepped to the center of his sitting room and began to form the image of the hawk in his mind.

The hawk slipped through the narrow gap in the stone wall of the keep, perched on the sill to measure the wind and current strength, then launched itself.

It sped out over the beach and ocean below and turned north to head back over the forests. Though its eyes were not specifically designed for night action, there was enough moonlight to detect what it needed to observe.

The battlefield was silent and still although there was some action close to the city wall and in the trenches. Patrols marched the circumference of the walls and on top of them, calling to each other as they met. The hawk was careful to stay outside of arrow reach and was soon close to the forest where the enemy camped.

The forested slopes north of the city produced drafts of warm air that allowed the hawk to stay aloft with little effort. It glided over the tops of the trees, its eyes on the ground below. The first movement it spied turned out to be a hare and the bird almost dived through the branches for a snack. But the human link to the avian brain jerked it back from its baser instincts and forced it to continue searching.

Soon, it spotted elven sentries and then the camp came into view. It was spread out through the forest and far up the hill; not a single organized camp, but many small ones centered on a large pavilion made of animal skin. *Faenwelar*. The word dropped into the bird's brain and it shook its head. It landed on the roof of the tent, out of sight, and observed the elves nearby.

Many sat around campfires, talking quietly, while others had rolled themselves into blankets and slept beside boulders or their horses and ponies. Yet others were sharpening swords, knives, and arrow tips. Once the bird tired of scanning the mundane tasks, it tuned into a voice that came from the tent.

"My Prince!" the voice said. "We must complete our task here, not head for Brightcastle. Just one more day should be enough. It is said the human king collapsed after you left the field and that he is dead. The news came from high in the kingdom army. They could be leaderless and easily defeated."

Another voice huffed. "I doubt the king died, and if he did, the kingdom army has any number of gifted leaders and strategists. They could be more successful now, not less." A pause. "No! I think our only chance is to meet up with my son and conquer Brightcastle. It is the prize I have always sought and is less defensible than Wildecoast with its high sea wall. We should steal away during the hours of darkness. We can be on our way before they realize and give chase. It could give us half a day lead."

"I wish you would reconsider, High Prince."

"All will be well; besides, I have already given the order to the commanders. We move out in half an hour."

The hawk took flight from the roof of the tent and climbed carefully through the tree branches until it made its escape from the forest canopy. Once out, it took a circuit of the full extent of the encampment, and, indeed, saw elves and gear being readied for departure.

It turned for the east wall of the keep, careful to avoid the eyes of the sentries on the wall.

Once Vard transformed to human from the hawk, he straightened his clothing and went in search of the queen. It was the last thing he wished to do, but he had no choice.

She opened the door at his knock, her sleepy eyes brightening upon seeing him.

"Vard!" she said, taking his hand and pulling him into her room. "I'm so glad you came to see me." She led him over to her chaise longue and pushed him down on it then sat beside him, too close for comfort.

"This isn't a social visit, Your Majesty," Vard said. "I have news of the elves."

To her credit, her drowsy gaze cleared, and she fixed him with all her attention. "What news?"

"I took a tour of the northern forest and happened to see them preparing to break camp. It will be quite an effort with the number of them, not to mention their injured, but I heard sentries talking of Brightcastle as their destination."

She released his hand and slumped back against the lounge chair. "We must stop them before they do that!"

"We can't stop them altogether, Majesty. Even now, they'll be on the move. The best we can hope for is to harass their force all the way to Brightcastle. It's a risky move on Faenwelar's part. I don't quite understand it, but he does have support in Brightcastle in the form of his son and the rest of the force, not to mention the dragons."

"Yes, yes," the queen said, distractedly. "What do you suggest?"

"Well…" Vard hesitated. "The king's funeral must wait. We have no time for it now. Place his body in the crypt and we'll attend to it when we return."

She closed her eyes and blew out a long breath. When she opened her eyes, she nodded. "When do we leave?"

"I had planned on leaving you here, Your Majesty. You're skilled in managing the day-to-day issues of a large city and can supervise the injured. You are also grieving. It might help you to stay with your king."

Utter devastation swept her face. "I could never abandon my people. What would they say, or Beniel for that matter? He would never allow his armies to fight without him."

"My Queen, you're not in charge of the Kingdom Army, I am. You can do nothing to help and may even hinder our cause if you insist on traveling with us." He thought of the rumors already circulating. "I command you to stay in Wildecoast and ensure the city is safe for us to return to."

The queen's mouth dropped open. "You command me!" Her eyes narrowed. "I think you have it the wrong way around."

"Did King Beniel not name me heir?" Vard asked. "Does that not give me the right to make commands?"

The fact was he couldn't allow Adriana to accompany him. Not after hearing of the rumors. Granted it would be good to have her voice behind him during the campaign but not if that came with whispers that undermined his leadership.

Her eyes widened. "Yes…" she said hesitantly, "but I had no idea you would use your new position to shut me out. I thought we could lead together."

"You thought I'd come meekly along with you? That I'd marry you as well? Is that what Beniel really wanted to happen?"

"When you say it like that, it sounds dirty," she snapped. "Beniel never actually said he wanted us to marry. It was not discussed. But I got the feeling he wouldn't object if it happened."

Vard gripped her upper arms gently but firmly. "Adriana, you have made up these plans in your head with no encouragement from me. Don't blame me for my reaction. You know Alecia holds my heart, but you've steadfastly refused to consider that. I can't marry you and I can't take you with me to Brightcastle. There are already rumors spreading about the two of us. It won't take much for the nobles to start wondering if the king's death was really an accident."

Adriana gasped and placed her hand to her throat. "They wouldn't! Would they?"

Vard raised his brows at her. "Just stay here and all will be well."

"You can't do this to me, Vard! We are a team. Beniel would have wanted you to seek my help."

"The king wanted me to take his place as leader, not as your husband. He knew my loyalty to Alecia."

Adriana interrupted. "That loyalty is misplaced! She doesn't love you enough to be by your side or she would be here right now."

Vard feared that was true, but he couldn't allow the queen to strike a blow. "Alecia has her own aspirations to fulfill. Our time will come."

Adriana's eyes blazed green fire. "You are a fool if you believe that. *I* am ready to support you now."

She was nothing if not persistent. He allowed a phase into the wolf, just enough to change his eyes, and stared down at her. "Forget these fantasies of you and me, Adriana," he growled. "I've explained why they won't come true, and I don't intend to explain again. Your task is to look after the people of Wildecoast until I return. I'll send word as I can."

Vard released her trapped gaze, hoping the mild compulsion he had used would be enough to keep her from trouble. He turned and left the queen's suite, closing the door with a click.

Vard sent scouts into the forest and surrounding countryside to observe the departure of the enemy. They confirmed the march's direction to the west. Faenwelar and his troops were indeed heading to Brightcastle. He sent several ravens off to warn the Guardians, and a team of his rangers on fast horses in case the birds failed to arrive. Then he advised Nikolas Cosara, General Formosa and the other leaders of the enemy's retreat.

It was still dark when they met in the small castle audience hall. This time Vard seated himself on the chair that would normally be taken by the king. Several raised their brows, but no one said anything.

Once they were all seated and had started an early breakfast, Vard stood.

"I imagine most of you know by now that the enemy has decamped and are heading west to Brightcastle."

"I have my foot soldiers standing by to follow, King's Blade,' Formosa said. "They'll carry enough food for the journey and the supply wagons will follow as fast as they are able."

Vard nodded. "I thank you for your speedy response, General." He turned to Nikolas. "Admiral?"

"The cavalry is ready, Lord Anton. They'll leave as soon as I give the word. How much lead does the enemy have on us?"

"Several hours, perhaps more considering elves can move more quickly than we can and have greater stamina."

Nikolas nodded. "It will be a tricky juggling act to stay close or catch them without exhausting our army and cavalry."

"That it will. Admiral, I want you to leave one unit of cavalry here to defend Wildecoast and take the rest. Follow the enemy, leaving as soon as you can. Try to catch up with them, but don't engage unless they turn on you. Take support wagons and personnel as well as spare mounts."

Vard turned to the rest of those gathered. "Once the cavalry is on its way, the infantry will depart under General Formosa's leadership, along with the supply wagons. All individuals are to carry as much with them as will last at least five days. I'll be moving as needed between my rangers, the cavalry and the infantry. There should be no need to change plans unless the enemy turns and attacks. They may do this to weaken us before they assault Brightcastle." He looked at each of them. "If they attack, we'll defeat them."

Ruven stood. "King's Blade, what task do you have for the *Lenweri?*"

"You'll move as swiftly as you can to keep up with the cavalry in case of enemy attack. Some of the fighting may be in the forest where you're most comfortable. Also, if there is dragon attack, your archers will be handy."

Ruven nodded. "If you will excuse me, I will make final preparations before we depart." He gestured for Isiloe to go with him, but she declined. He frowned and left.

"Isiloe?" Vard asked.

"I wish to support Lady Alique if she is to travel with us," Isiloe said. "My sister will take on my command."

Vard was surprised at her request. "I'd like to know why."

"The lady is precious to Kain Arenil. I offer my *Lenweri* guard to protect her and her patients. The last time she took to the road in a battle, she almost died. I would not have her husband on my tail because I failed to protect her."

Vard was unsure how to respond to the request. He needed Alique on the road with them and wanted her protected. But Isiloe was one of the best *Lenweri* fighters, and he was unsure if guarding Alique and her staff was the best use of her skills.

"Ramar Isiloe," he said, "I don't wish to have you in a position you feel is beneath you."

The diminutive elven woman drew her shoulders back and her ice blue eyes met his. "If I felt the position was beneath me, I would not have offered. This is about family. Also, I will still be available to advise and fight where needed."

Vard nodded. "Of course. I'm sure your presence will be a great help to our healer. Thank you. You may go, Ramar Isiloe."

She bowed and left, as did most of the attendees. Vard was left with Nikolas and James Tomel.

Nikolas approached him. "What of my wife? Will she remain in Wildecoast with Lady Esta?"

Vard had been waiting for this question. He drew a deep breath and faced Nikolas.

"I can't keep your wife in Wildecoast, even if she wished to stay here."

"She doesn't," Nikolas said. "She has some idea of actually fighting."

"Did you see her in the last battle? Merielle is an accomplished warrior and extraordinarily strong."

Nikolas raised his chin, a proud light in his eyes. "She is. When I met her after the battle, she had transformed. However, as much as I can tolerate her protecting the stretcher bearers, I don't think I can deal with her placing herself at risk in the heat of battle."

Vard thought of Alecia, and a pain stabbed his heart. This was exactly what his beloved wished to do. Ride into war, except she wished to be at the head of the kingdom army. He shook his head.

"You could forbid her to go, Lord Cosara. She *might* obey you."

"I was hoping you could give her a direct order, King's Blade. Keep her chained to the stretcher bearers, or better yet, leave her behind in Wildecoast."

"I could do that, but I'm not going to."

"No," Nikolas snapped. "I didn't think you'd agree. You *do* owe me a favor, you know."

"I wondered when this issue would raise its ugly head."

"I could've had you tossed out of Wildecoast or even into prison. I didn't because I didn't want to do anything that could harm the war effort."

"And you think that undermining my authority now is wise?" Vard asked.

Nikolas scraped his fingers through his hair. "I don't know. The things I've heard since the king died…"

Vard raised a brow. "Go on."

Nikolas scowled. "Where's the queen? I thought with the king dead she'd be more visible. Instead, all we get is you."

"The queen is in her chamber as far as I know. She won't ride with us. Instead. she'll stay and protect Wildecoast."

"Are the rumors true?"

Vard stiffened. "What rumors?"

"That the king named you as heir and that you and the queen will marry and rule Thorius."

"I'm not going to discuss rumors with you now. The king is dead, and we'll miss his leadership acutely. However, I was his blade and I intend to follow his last instructions and defeat the *Sis Lenweri*. Once that is done, you and I can discuss our differences. In the meantime, let me promise you that I don't intend to marry the queen."

Nikolas examined his face for long moments before nodding. "That assurance will do for now." He bowed and left without another word.

James Tomel came forward. "Well done. I see a bit of him as Katrine's sister is Merielle's friend. Nikolas Cosara isn't an easy man to deal with, especially where his wife is involved."

"He and I have had a couple of confrontations in the past," Vard said. "However, he seems the loyal type." He focused on James instead of staring through the door Nikolas had just closed. "What news do you have?"

"I've installed several of my people in positions close to Josef Formosa and Cosara. We'll hear if there's any further gossip." He paused. "Did you really persuade the queen to stay here?"

"I did. She wasn't happy, but I convinced her it would only add to rumors if she went to Brightcastle."

"It certainly is best if she stays away. Her role is tenuous with the Guardians taking control in future. How do you see that playing out?"

"I think we need to get this war won first before we worry about that."

"You're probably right. Do you require me to travel with you?"

Vard still hadn't decided. "Where's Lady Star?"

"She has holed up in the forest west of here with her hounds." A shiver went through him. "I don't like those beasts."

"They may mean the difference between winning and losing this war," Vard said. "On the other matter, King Beniel wanted me to keep you with me, so you had better come to Brightcastle. You can keep Samael company."

"If you insist. He's not bad for a pirate."

Vard smiled. "See that you're packed and ready to go and get my man to pack my things as well."

James bowed and they left together.

CHAPTER TWO

ALECIA had visited Hetty in her new lodgings and they were now seated before the fire in her sitting room. It was a modest addition to one of the noble houses close to the palace and contained a bedroom, sitting room and kitchen as well as a bathing room. Even though it was smaller than Hetty's cottage on Firedrake Alley, it was much more luxurious.

The reason Alecia had installed her there was its proximity to the castle.

As she gazed into the fire, Katrine Tomel's face formed in the flames. There were trees in the background as if Katrine were in a forest before a campfire.

"Hello, Hetty," Katrine said, her voice strained.

"What's happening, child?" Hetty asked. "I need to know how the war is going."

"You should receive ravens soon, telling of Faenwelar's latest move. He has left this place for Brightcastle."

"I knew it!" Alecia said.

Katrine paused. "Is there someone else there?"

Hetty shifted so Alecia could come closer. "Alecia Zialni, Katrine."

As she watched, Katrine stiffened. "I have terrible news."

Alecia's heart leapt. "It's not Vard!"

"No, no! Vard is perfectly fine." She paused then went on. "I'm sorry, Princess. It's the king. He has entered the halls of the dead."

"Uncle Beniel dead?"

He *couldn't* be. They needed him. Even though he'd wanted an arranged marriage for her, Uncle Beniel had always been kind. Now he was no more.

"What happened?" Alecia asked.

"I'm not sure. He fought Faenwelar, and the high prince fled. Next thing the king was dead on the battlefield, though I'm told he wasn't badly wounded. I can't get much information about it."

Though she tried to fathom the ramifications of her uncle's death for the kingdom and the war effort, Alecia was reeling from the loss of yet another family member. "Who's in charge?" she asked.

"All is confusion here, but I think, as King's Blade, Vard has command of the kingdom forces." Katrine huffed out a breath. "Of all the terrible things that could have happened, the loss of the king is the worst. I fear Vard won't be able to pull everyone together as King Beniel did."

Alecia's mind worked furiously to understand what this might mean. Vard in charge! And Ramón and Benae would soon take command of the kingdom, though that would likely wait until the war was over.

"How did the fighting go today? We must have won the day if the enemy is on the move."

"We did indeed," Katrine said. "The dragon was used early, but we were ready for it. There were terrible burns and many casualties, but it could've been much worse. Our people are exhausted. The last thing we need is a forced march to Brightcastle. I think it's a deliberate tactic to weaken us, as the elves are naturally more resilient."

"Where is the king's body? Was he buried?" Alecia asked.

"The king lies in a chamber underground and will be buried when the war is over. Rumor is that the queen won't travel with the army, but stay in Wildecoast."

Alecia closed her eyes. "Aunt Adriana will be devastated. Her world has come crashing down."

Hetty patted her hand. "The queen will survive as she has in the past." She gave Alecia a meaningful look. "This is no time for mourning, Princess. We have a war to win."

Alecia drew her shoulders back and focused once more on Katrine. "We'll need your help to defeat Faenwelar, Katrine. Are you prepared to defend Thorius against the *Sis Lenweri*?"

Katrine flinched. "While I might wish to stand aside and protect my powers and my hounds, there's a reason for my gifts and the advent of the beasts. They follow me, and they're a formidable weapon which the *Sis Lenweri* have no answer to. I'll fight for Thorius, and so will they. I only hope and pray I can live a normal life afterward."

Hetty snorted. "Your life has never been normal, girl."

Katrine frowned. "I have a husband and a family I wish to keep. I'm not like you, living as a hermit. Any notice I attract will affect James and Esta."

"You should have considered that before you made your recent choice to wed," Hetty snapped.

Katrine shook her head. "I love him."

Alecia knew how that felt—the push and pull of a great love and a powerful goal. The two didn't always align. She wondered what Vard's newfound power would mean.

Would it cause even greater animosity between them? If faced with a choice between Vard and becoming queen, which would she choose? And she had Iona, her child and Vard's, to consider in that decision.

Alecia shook her head. "Those matters must be dealt with after the war. Much may change. But I'll do my best to foster tolerance for magic practitioners in the kingdom as long as I have any influence."

Katrine nodded, and the two shared a look of understanding.

"What else can you tell us?" Hetty asked.

"The kingdom army is leaving for Brightcastle as I speak to you. That's all I know. Expect Faenwelar's forces within four to five days. Are your preparations complete?"

"Almost," Alecia said. "At least now we can concentrate on defending Brightcastle."

"I must prepare to leave," Katrine said, and, with a swirl of her hand, her face disappeared from the fire.

Alecia sat back, rubbing her arms as a chill swept over her. She took a moment to send a prayer to the Goddess that her uncle would be welcomed into the afterlife.

"I wonder when Piotr will make his move," she pondered.

"I thought we may have seen him before now," Hetty said. "He's been sniffing around Wildecoast for some time, and even courted Esta Aranati."

"Really?"

Hetty nodded. "It was thought then that he wanted an excuse to be close to the court."

"Surely as nephew to the king, he didn't need another reason?"

"The king suspected him of the attack at your father's funeral; even your father's death was blamed on him at one stage by some."

Alecia glared at Hetty. "Let us not discuss my father's death. I don't wish to get angry with you and Ramón all over again." She thought for a moment. "What do we do now? I can't burst in and tell Ramón all of this. He and the commanders will either not believe me, or be suspicious of my sources."

"We have at least four days to prepare, perhaps less if the *Sis Lenweri* from Amitania attack first. I advise we try to get a good night's sleep, and hope that the ravens bring the news on the morrow."

She nodded. "Yes, that's the best plan. I don't want to draw attention to myself just yet. Uncle Beniel's death brings too much uncertainty into the future of the kingdom leadership. At least with him there, I knew who I was dealing with. If Ramón and Benae are handed leadership of Thorius or, Goddess forbid, Piotr pushes his claim, I could be in trouble."

"What do you intend to do about your suspicions of Solomon's parentage?" Hetty asked. "Have you confronted the Guardians yet?"

Alecia shook her head. "I've been reluctant to reveal my suspicions lest it trigger a chain of events I don't wish to deal with. I don't want Piotr anywhere near the throne."

Hetty nodded. "I can see that."

"But I worry that exposes Solomon to danger. If I were to reveal he had no relation to the throne, he'd be safe."

"And the Guardians would be neutralized," Hetty said.

"Leaving Piotr as heir now that Uncle Beniel has passed, and I have no male children," Alecia said. "It's so unfair! I can rule as well as any man!"

"Shhhh!" Hetty said. "The walls have ears, especially in the manors of the nobility. You never know who's lurking around the corner, close enough to hear. We can't let this get out. For now, it's better that Solomon is named heir. At least that places Piotr a step further away from the throne."

"But Hetty," Alecia said, quietly, "that also puts him at risk. Don't you think it unfair if the child is harmed? He is so exposed."

"All is fair in love and war, my girl."

"Well, I don't agree. He may not be my brother, or related to me at all, but I love him, and wouldn't see him harmed."

Hetty pulled her closer. "I never said the road to the throne would be easy, my dear. I would counsel you to keep quiet about Solomon for now. His protection will be increased once the Guardians learn the king is dead."

Alecia had a sudden thought. "We need to protect him this night, Hetty. What if assassins are sent because the king is dead, and no one here knows to increase Solomon's security? It might be too late tomorrow!"

Hetty's eyes widened. "You're right. What can we do?"

Alecia stood and drew Hetty up with her. "I'm going to visit Ramón. They must double the guard and move Solomon to a different chamber until we can be sure he's safe."

Ramón wasn't difficult to convince once Alecia told him about the latest news from Wildecoast. He knew she was still in touch with Hetty, even if he didn't know she was living right under his nose. And Benae wasn't about to take any chances with the safety of her son.

She had Solomon moved to her chambers immediately, and Ramón joined them. Several of Benae's female guards were assigned to her sitting room to stand watch over the heir. With the numerous tunnels running through the walls of the castle, the risk of assassins appearing from secret passages was high.

But no matter all the security precautions, Alecia still worried. She had her ladies move into her sitting room to guard Iona, even though her daughter shouldn't be a target for an assassin working for Piotr. And she asked Vard's father, Lyam, to patrol the hallways of the keep. She smiled as she recalled Vard had performed this same task when they had first met. Back then, she had resented his presence in the passage outside her room, but knowing Iona's grandfather stood guard calmed her anxious heart.

After a night of broken sleep, Alecia rose, dressed, and scraped her hair into a semblance of order with Millie's help. Full of nervous energy, she headed to the audience hall, noting Lyam standing guard in the shadows at the end of her corridor.

Breakfast had been served there in readiness for the morning meeting of battle leaders, but the room was empty. She crossed directly to the sideboard and poured herself a strong tea, selecting a plate of pastries as well. She sat at a small table and drank half the tea, then took a bite out of a buttery crescent roll.

"Good morning, Alecia," Ramón said as he entered. "I hope you slept well?"

She surged to her feet. "Do you have further news?"

He frowned at her. "All is well this morning, thanks to your suggestion of last night. None of us got much sleep what with the extra guards and the worry." He examined her face. "You didn't get much either, did you?"

She shook her head. "I worried all night, and when I wasn't worrying, I was trying to take in the news from yesterday. It changes everything."

"Yes, it certainly does." He fetched himself breakfast and sat at her table.

Alecia finished her tea, then poured another and sat down. "I've been thinking. You can say you received a raven even if you haven't yet. No one will know. We must prepare for the advent of the *Sis Lenweri* from Wildecoast."

He nodded. "I was thinking the same. We only have four days to prepare, and the other enemy group will be here before that. It appears Brightcastle will be the staging ground for the biggest battle the kingdom has seen for centuries."

She met his troubled gaze. "It would be easy for an assassin to sneak in under the cover of all that chaos and kill your son."

"I won't let that happen. I'll have him moved to the lower reaches of the castle during the day when the battle is raging. What will you do with Iona?"

Alecia sighed and closed her eyes. She opened them to meet Ramón's intense blue gaze. "I really don't know. I'll think on it. Somewhere without hidden passages would be wise. The lower rooms of the castle *would* be ideal." She shivered. "Even if they do bring back horrible memories..."

Ramón reached across and squeezed her hand. She smiled at him just as Benae entered. The beautiful brunette paused, staring at their joined hands.

"Good morning," she snapped, sending Ramón a pointed look. She continued to the sideboard and poured herself a tea, then took a sugary roll.

Ramón stood and walked to her, kissing her on the cheek. "Join us, my love," he said, leading her over to the table.

"There hardly seems room for me," Benae said, staring at Alecia. "Did I interrupt something?"

"We were just discussing the best place for the children. Ramón suggested the lower rooms of the castle," Alecia said with a shudder. "They hold terrible memories for me."

Benae nodded. "That's understandable. You were imprisoned there by Jiseve. I still can't believe he did that to his own daughter."

"Well, he did," Alecia snapped. "But I forgave him—only I didn't get a chance to tell him that."

Benae frowned. "And I understand you blame me for that. I can't think of anything else I can say to convince you I'm innocent. Jiseve's death was an unfortunate accident, though your father *did* contribute to his own death."

Alecia glared at her. "How do you figure that?"

"He was taking herbs for impotence! The doctor thinks they could have affected his heart. If someone had known what he was doing, perhaps he could've been saved."

Alecia sat back in her chair and folded her arms. The whole chain of events was so sordid, especially if Benae had been unfaithful with Ramón.

No wonder her father had been under so much stress. He had put pressure on himself and Benae to conceive quickly, having realized she didn't care for him.

Alecia could so clearly see how it must have been.

Jiseve would have been overjoyed to have a beautiful young wife. He gave Ramón the task of taking his fiancé to Wildecoast for a wedding gown fitting, not knowing the convoy was at risk. Only Benae and Ramón had survived. Perhaps the trauma had even brought them closer.

Then more drama had occurred in Wildecoast when a storm had nearly drowned Benae. The two had been found sheltering in a hut, and she had heard from the servants that her father's attitude to both Benae and Ramón dramatically changed soon after their return to Brightcastle.

She just *knew* they had betrayed Jiseve. If her father had started to abuse Benae, *their* behavior had triggered it. He had been pushed too far and snapped.

Alecia looked down. The hand which grasped the teacup shook violently.

Ramón again reached out, but this time he grasped her forearm. "One day you'll see it wasn't Benae's fault. Until then, please try to put it out of your mind. We need to work together to save the kingdom—you, Benae and I."

Alecia pulled her arm out from under his hand and leaned away. Her gaze flicked to Benae and then back to Ramón.

"I'd really like to believe you mean that."

Now Uncle Beniel was dead, there was no reason why she couldn't pursue the throne, and damn it, that was just what she was going to do. There would be no trio of happy workers, at least not after the war was won.

There would just be Queen Alecia Zialni.

There was a knock on the door, and a footman entered. He approached Ramón and handed him three notes. Alecia held her breath as the servant left, and Ramón unrolled the parchments. He cleared his throat.

"It's from Vard Anton." His voice held a ragged edge as it always did when he mentioned Vard. "*It is with deep regret that I inform the Guardians of Brightcastle and its citizens that King Beniel Zialni died on the battlefield this day. May his spirit enter the halls of the Goddess, and may her light shine upon us all.*" Ramón paused, his jaw muscles tensing. "*The Kingdom Army won the day, but the enemy has decamped and is headed for Brightcastle. Please prepare for war on your doorstep within four days. Wildecoast forces will be in the field in pursuit of the* Sis Lenweri *by the time you receive this missive. May the Goddess protect you.*"

Ramón took a deep breath, Benae reached to take the papers from him, and Alecia slumped in her chair.

Vard was coming!

It was just as her dream had indicated. Brightcastle would be the site of the final battle with the *Sis Lenweri,* and she and Vard would fight alongside each other. They would defeat the enemy, she would take up the mantle of queen, and she and Vard could be together again.

This time, it would be forever.

CHAPTER THREE

KAIN and his small army approached Brightcastle from the northwest. He hoped to arrive before Gorin's force did, but he feared he wouldn't. They had too many injured, and the days of forced marching had exhausted those who were fit.

Rasalar remained unchanged, lying on her pallet dragged by two ponies, her face pale and breath shallow. Julli and Tuthariel had done their best, but all they could do was keep the elder clinging to life long enough to reach Benae.

Ramar Morlynn trotted up on his horse. "Prince Arenil! Our scouts have seen the towers of Brightcastle. The battle has not yet begun. They have spotted the *Sis Lenweri* a half day from the city."

"It's too damned close for comfort," Kain said. "We needed at least a day to rest before fighting."

"The enemy will be just as tired as we are, My Prince," Morlynn said. "The Brightcastle soldiers will be fresh and allow us to rest before we come against the *Sis Lenweri*."

"I hope you're right, Morlynn." He wasn't in great shape himself. If he didn't take a break now, he'd drop from the saddle before long. The horses could also do with food and a drink. Kain signaled for the force to stop and dismount. "Spread the word. We'll rest here for an hour and eat, then remount and push as hard as we can for Brightcastle."

* * *

Gwaethe and Jacques had pressed their tired army as hard as they could, but still struggled to keep pace. The dragons had successfully harried their progress, flying close enough to make them wary, but far enough away that their arrows were useless.

Gwaethe ground her teeth in frustration, but they took the moments when the beasts hovered over their army as a chance to rest and eat. It became a regular pattern of nervous stops with extra scouts monitoring the skies for signs of a fire attack, and forced marches when the beasts disappeared.

Jacques believed the news of the black dragon's death had reached Gorin's army and the *Sis Lenweri* were wary of losing another. At least wary until they could bring the beasts against the kingdom forces in the final battle.

A hand on her arm brought her out of her musing, and she turned to find Jacques beside her.

"It's time to mount up." He helped her to her feet. "The scouts believe we're only a day from Brightcastle. The *Sis Lenweri* are a half day closer."

She shook her head. "This has been one of the most frustrating marches I ever endured. If we could fight them, at least we would feel we had accomplished something."

Jacques placed his arm about her shoulder as they walked to the horses. Usually, she avoided these displays of affection in front of her soldiers, but today she needed the comfort. She leaned into his side and breathed in the scent of her man. How had she ever managed without him? He was her strength when she had nothing left to give.

He helped her mount her golden stallion, and, when he would've moved to his own horse, she gripped his hand. He gazed up at her, a smile on his face and affection in his blue eyes.

"What is it, love?" he asked.

"Thank you for all you have given me," she said. "There has not been one moment of regret since we married. You are my rock."

Jacques squeezed her hand. "Believe me, it's no chore to be married to you. You're the center of my world, and I wouldn't have it any other way."

She smiled, her heart lighter for the moment. Jacques mounted his horse, and they moved out, side by side.

* * *

Vard trotted through the open forest west of Wildecoast, James beside him and Samael in front. He could smell the slight taint of fear in James. The emotion wasn't for himself, but for his wife, Katrine. She was somewhere ahead with her hounds. Meanwhile, Sam's emotions lay bound under a veneer of calm optimism—which was his normal state.

They had left Wildecoast in the early morning, hot on the heels of Faenwelar's force. Even so, the enemy had several hours start. The cavalry was up ahead, led by Nikolas Cosara. Foot soldiers, some of whom were fortunate enough to have a mount, or ride in a wagon, were in the middle of the force.

General Formosa commanded the infantry, which obviously grated on him. He no doubt believed he should command the entire army.

The support wagons brought up the rear, including the food and medical wagons.

Vard was concerned for Nikolas, who rode with half a mind on the safety of *his* wife, Merielle. Cosara had forbidden her to be involved in the coming battle for Brightcastle, but they couldn't afford to decline any offered help. The red-haired lady had fought exceedingly well in the last battle and deserved her place in the force. When she came to Vard and begged to be allowed to fight, he had reluctantly agreed and ordered her to stay by him. It was another thing Cosara would make Vard pay for later.

He tried to keep his mind off Alecia and Iona by concentrating on the people under his command. Better that than be distracted by anxiety over his family's safety, or Alecia's reaction when she discovered he was now heir to the throne. That last didn't bear thinking about.

He was convinced it would spell the end of their relationship.

But, first, they needed to win the war against the *Sis Lenweri*. To do that, the entire kingdom and all its disparate people and leaders must work as one.

They could do this, in fact, they must. Vard wouldn't contemplate any other outcome. He caught up to Sam and nudged him on the foot.

"I'm heading up to do some scouting. Can you keep this group on track and watch Lady Cosara until I return?"

Sam appeared to shake himself from introspection. "Of course."

"Keep your mind on the job, Sam. We can't afford to lose concentration. The enemy could launch a rearguard action, or an ambush. Stay alert. Ride with James."

Sam nodded, and Vard trotted into the forest to the left of the trail.

Once into the trees, his wolf senses found a game trail heading in the right direction, and he trotted his horse along it. When the forest got too dense, he dismounted and tied his horse to a tree, then shifted into the wolf.

In wolf form, every sense was heightened. Vard took it all in. He tuned into the closest pack and asked them if they'd seen the hounds. They had, but were unwilling to give him details. The night hounds disgusted them. He convinced them of the urgency of his request, and they gave him directions.

Vard loped through the trees on a narrow game trail, his nose beset with the scents of rabbit and grouse. He reveled in the freedom of this form even as he stayed wary of his surroundings.

Finally, he observed Katrine's camp and her hounds. He morphed back into his human form and entered her clearing.

He bowed. "Lady Star."

She stood. "There's no need to bow, Lord Anton. We're at least equals, and I suspect you'll soon far outrank me."

Vard fought puzzlement. What was she referring to? Did this sorceress somehow know of the king's decision? She couldn't. It must be something else she meant. He shook his head.

"How fare you and your hounds?"

She placed her hand on the head of the closest beast, a massive brown female. "We are well. My hounds are eager to teach the enemy another lesson. Would you have any objection if we harried the hind ranks and picked off a few *Sis Lenweri*?"

Vard smiled. "That's an excellent idea. I've observed the terror your creatures inspire, even in the *Sis Lenweri*." He paused. "I ask only one thing."

Her brows rose slightly. "And what's that?"

"Please take care. James would be desolate, should you be injured."

She smiled. "How is my James? I presume he isn't taking kindly to your role over him. Or has that died with the king?"

Vard tilted his head. "Out of respect for King Beniel, I'll continue to be responsible for James until we win this war. He has more freedom, but not complete. I must be seen to be doing the right thing. Too many would enjoy removing me from a position they believe is above me."

Katrine's jaw tightened, but she nodded. "So be it. I trust you and hope James's name can be cleared. I feel responsible for his plight as I convinced him to speak up. And he was trying to protect me in part when he hid the presence of the dragon."

"Fear not, Lady Star. I'll do everything I can to clear his name, including petition the queen."

"Who has no power now that her husband is dead! Everyone knows queens have little influence in this society unless they are married to the king. All I can foresee is danger ahead."

"Again, let us get this war won, then we can sort through the rest."

She nodded. "If that's all, I'll take the hounds and begin reducing enemy numbers."

She turned, clicked her fingers, and the hounds leapt to their feet, whining and growling, their eerie crimson eyes casting around for the threat. Katrine spoke to them in a foreign tongue and mounted her horse, riding off with the hounds through the forest.

Vard hesitated. He wanted to scout further ahead to see exactly where the *Sis Lenweri* were. The hawk form was his most vulnerable but, on this occasion, the most useful. Was it worth the danger? *Yes!*

He began forming the image of the hawk in his mind. In seconds, the transformation was complete, and he took to the air. His body trembled with adrenaline born of the proximity of peril. Something in the hawk's brain rebelled at the need to risk everything this day.

The scent of danger floated on the breeze. Night hounds prowled below. He couldn't count, but they were many, and there was a human with them who made him wary. Instinctively, he knew she could hurt him.

He swerved to the north to create a safe distance from them and climbed into the sky until all below was far distant. Here he found warm upward drafts to carry him, sparing the energy which was quickly depleted.

Urgency spurred him on, though he didn't understand why. In the distance, the sun glinted off many things. He flew faster until he floated over a crowd of beings, some on horseback and others on foot, heading rapidly west.

Something deep inside made him take notice of the numbers, though his bird brain rebelled against such things. Finally, he scanned the entire area, looking for other forms of danger. The beings below couldn't hurt him—he was too high—but another bird or …

A shiver ran through him, a warning of dire peril. Something *different* was nearby. He climbed still higher, hoping to spot the danger, and angled to the left in a slow sweeping glide. He was almost finished his lazy circle when he saw it—the biggest bird he'd ever encountered.

The giant was golden and hadn't seen him. On its back sat a rider, no, two riders. The hawk shuddered when one of them gestured at him and pointed his weapon. He didn't hesitate. but dropped into a dive, his wings folded against his body, carrying him away from the trajectory of the deadly dart. Out of the corner of his eye, he watched the projectile fall harmlessly.

He pulled out of the dive and flew in rapid zigzags toward the east. One more dart flashed across his path before he was safe. He retraced his flight to the site of his transformation then found the horse.

Vard's heart pounded as he pulled himself onto his mount. That had been too close. Perhaps it had been foolhardy, but they had gained valuable information. He now knew where the enemy was and how large the force. The kingdom army was further behind than he'd hoped. And the golden dragon would come against Brightcastle. He wheeled his horse and galloped east to rejoin his people.

* * *

Kain Arenil caught sight of the towers of Brightcastle Keep as the last rays of the sun slipped behind the trees at his back. The sparkling quartz lit up for a moment before disappearing, only there long enough to tell him he had arrived. He drew a sigh of relief. Now if only they could snatch a day of rest before the battle began.

A scout rode up. "Prince Arenil, *Sis Lenweri* forces are close on our left flank. They almost captured two of us. We had no idea they had spread out so far."

"What did you do?" Kain snapped.

"Those who attacked us are dead, but Ferol has a deep cut to her arm. I do not think she will fight for some time."

Kain shook his head. "Did any of them escape to raise the alarm?"

"I think not, but there is always the possibility."

"Spread the word down the line. We must enter Brightcastle as swiftly as we can, before Gorin's *Sis Lenweri*."

The scout nodded and spurred his pony down the lines, calling as he passed. Kain raised his arm to signal the column to speed up. His second in command caught up with him.

"I do not like this, Kain Arenil. The enemy is too close. If they choose to attack us now, we would be exposed. The injured need to be protected, and many of the soldiers are dead on their feet."

"Tell them to get moving, or they really will be dead. We need to make it into Brightcastle before Gorin's force cuts us off. I'm going to take the first half of the force and hustle them into the city. But be careful. There'll be traps and pitfalls to avoid on our way in."

The second nodded and galloped off. Kain trotted back to find the guard of the captured dragon lord. When he came upon them, he approached, ignoring the jibes of the prisoner.

"Guards, bring the prisoner forward. I want him in the keep. We can't afford to let the enemy take him." With those instructions, Kain turned his horse and galloped forward, reaching the front of the line and passing them, his personal guard forming a line behind and to the side in a semicircle. They wouldn't be happy that he was in front, but they would have to deal with that.

Some hard riding later, and with their horses blowing, they reached the northwestern edge of the Brightcastle wall and slowed their pace. Although they should be expected, his elven force could be mistaken for the enemy. He drew his horse to a halt and selected four soldiers to come with him. Despite his care, he was close to riding into a camouflaged first-line trench that he only recognized when he was two paces from it. He flung up his hand and stopped his companions. They waited, his guards with bows drawn and arrows nocked.

Someone called down from the top of the wall. "In the name of the Guardians of Brightcastle, state your reason for approach."

One of Kain's guard rode forward. "Prince Kain Arenil of Selinore requests entry into Brightcastle for the purpose of aiding the kingdom against the *Sis Lenweri*."

"How do I know you're friendly?"

"We come in peace. Have one of your elven allies within the walls vouch for us at the southern gate. We'll make our way there."

"So be it!"

Kain signaled for the rest of his force to follow, and they rode along the outer wall to the southern gate. It was the largest gate into the city and the most vulnerable to attack. When they arrived, the heavy wooden gates, which had been reinforced with iron, were closed. Dozens of guards with loaded crossbows stood along the adjacent walls.

He ground his teeth in frustration, but understood the need for caution. However, with each minute that ticked by, Gorin's force crept closer.

Finally, an elven leader, whom Kain remembered as Reese, appeared beside the armed guards on the wall. He raised his hand to Kain, then turned and spoke to the guards. The gate slowly opened. Kain spurred his horse through, pulling to the side to speak with Reese, who had arrived at the entrance.

Reese saluted. "Well met, Prince Arenil. We have been eager to see you. The *Sis Lenweri* force is only a few hours away."

"That's closer than I'd like," Kain said, dismounting. "Our force is in two sections. I wonder if you could send some wagons out to help with the injured. Otherwise, they may be trapped outside the walls."

A slight frown creased Reese's brow. "I am not sure that will be possible, My Prince. The enemy force is close, and I don't have the authority to send a rescue party."

Kain drilled the elf with his eyes, but Reese didn't back down. "Rasalar is out there, Ramar. If you can't send human forces, at least round up some elves to help."

Reese again saluted. "I will do what I can." He whistled to a few elves close by, and they jogged into the city. Kain watched them go, hoping there was something that could be done. When he again focused on his force's entry, a human captain stood before him.

"Prince Arenil, I'm Captain Estevot of the Brightcastle Army. We're glad to see you. As word of your arrival came several days ago, we've made room for your elves in several halls along the western wall of the city. You have apartments in the keep should you wish to use them."

Kain examined the captain. He liked leaders who got straight to the point. "Thank you. I'll stay with my guard, but I appreciate the offer of a chamber. Perhaps I can use it for sensitive meetings."

Estevot bowed. "As you wish. I'll get one of my aides to show you to your lodgings." He turned to go, but Kain stopped him.

"Captain, I wonder if you can help with the matter of getting my injured into the city. They're in the second half of my force, and our people are struggling to move them quickly. Some wagons would be welcome."

Estevot turned back, his posture stiff. "I'd like to help, Your Highness, but I'm sure you understand I can't place my people at risk with the enemy so close to our walls."

Kain took a step forward. "I thought the purpose of this war was to protect both our people. I expect you to work cooperatively with me to the advantage of both."

Estevot's jaw tightened, and his frown deepened. "I assume you'd help if you were in my position, Your Highness?"

"You can be assured I would. And I expect no less from you."

Estevot shook his head. "I'm sorry, but no. Besides, Reese has already pledged his aid. I'm sure that will be sufficient."

"Well, I'm not," Kain said through gritted teeth. "I don't wish to pull rank—"

"You can't!" Estevot snapped. "I'm the Brightcastle Army Commander. I have the final say."

"Is there anything I can do to help?" a feminine voice asked.

Kain turned to find a flaxen-haired noble woman striding up to them, her grey horse trailing behind her. Princess Alecia Zialni. He was sure he heard a groan from Estevot.

Estevot bowed. "Princess, there's no need for you to trouble yourself with this matter. I have it in hand."

Kain examined her while her attention was on the captain. She was tall, the top of her head past his shoulder, and had an arresting presence. She wore a splendid cloak in the Zialni colors, reminiscent of the battle queens of old. Kain noticed she carried herself with more confidence and assurance than when he had last seen her in Selinore.

His eyes wandered beyond her horse to the four women who accompanied the princess. Two of them had been in Selinore with her. The ladies were almost as impressive as Alecia and, by the comfortable way they handled their horses and weapons, were a force to be reckoned with.

Kain waited for the princess to turn her attention to him. When she did, her lilac eyes demanded *all* his attention. Alecia Zialni had a presence that even he couldn't ignore.

He bowed. "Princess, I'm delighted to see you again."

She curtsied, and, upon rising, a smile lit her face. "Well met, High Prince of the *Lenweri*," she said. "Although these aren't the best of times, I thank you for being willing to fight alongside us. You could've fled to Amitania, but you came here."

"Princess, the *Sis Lenweri* must be defeated once and for all. Then we can turn our attention to bringing the two elven factions together in peace. There's no point in any of us hiding from the facts. I hope we can work cooperatively to accomplish common goals." He looked at Estevot who glared at Alecia. *So, he wasn't a fan of the princess.* "However, there *is* something you can do to help."

Estevot cleared his throat. "I have this in hand, Princess. You've no need to trouble yourself."

She cast a glance at the captain. "So you said, but I was sure I heard raised voices." She raised one pale brow at Kain. "Can I help, Prince Arenil?"

Kain inclined his head. "I was explaining to the captain that my injured are in the second half of my force. I need help to get them to safety before the invading army arrives. He seems to think he doesn't have the authority to order wagons for me."

Alecia smiled. "Captain Estevot must answer to the Guardians. I, however, happen to know Ramón and Benae well and am happy to supply permission for the wagons. Indeed, I'll organize them myself. My ladies will see that your injured are made comfortable."

"Thank you, Princess."

"You must call me Alecia, and I'll call you Kain."

He nodded. "So be it. May I come with you to fetch the wagons?" He turned to his second and gave instructions for the men with them.

Estevot wore a deep frown when next Kain met his eye.

"There is a war council planned for later today, Prince Arenil," Estevot said, stiffly. "I'll see you are advised of the location and time." He bowed and stalked away.

Kain made a mental note to smooth the captain's ruffled feathers as soon as he could. Shrugging off the awkward scene with the Brightcastle leader, he joined Alecia and her ladies.

Alecia made the introductions to Cretia and Kenna, who hadn't met Kain. When he saw the frankly appreciative looks of the ladies, he was glad of his married status. They looked positively predatory. He turned his attention back to Alecia.

"I assume the wagons won't fit through the western gate?"

Alecia smiled. "I've had some wagons specially made, pulled by one small horse or pony. They can take two injured lying down or four seated and fit through the narrow city gates." She turned to Arelle and Kenna. "Ladies, please take charge of Prince Arenil's wounded. Commandeer all the help you need to get the injured into the city. They must be taken to the infirmary to be examined." She turned back to Kain. "Do you have a healer with you?"

He nodded. "I have Alique's assistant, Julli, and my elven healer, Tuthariel."

"*Two* healers! Benae will be pleased. It will certainly take the pressure off, if only temporarily. Once the fighting starts, we'll be back scrambling to stay ahead of our chores."

"You're close to Benae?" The question was out before he could help himself. "I'm sorry. It's none of my business."

"It's no secret I've had my problems with her. After all, she married my father, and that often creates animosity." A wave of grief slid across her face, and he changed the subject.

"I can't thank you enough for your help. I was in a tricky situation back there."

"Not at all, Kain," she said, pulling up at a stone mansion. Arelle opened the gate, and she and Kenna walked their horses up the graveled drive while Alecia, Lin, and Cretia prepared to take their leave. "I'll leave you with my ladies and whoever they round up to assist. I've other tasks to see to. Call on me if I can be of any further help."

Kain smiled. "I'll keep that in mind."

"Perhaps we'll speak again at this afternoon's war council," she said.

"I look forward to it, Alecia."

She smiled and nodded, then wheeled her horse and trotted up the street, her ladies on either side of her.

"Prince Arenil is a dish," Cretia said, casting a glance behind them as they departed the elven leader. "If he asked me, I might be willing to lose my maidenhead to enjoy a night in his company."

"He's married," Lin said, "though I don't disagree with you. Those thighs, that chiseled jaw, and the way he fills out his elven garb… I wouldn't mind climbing on board for a ride." She made a low growling noise in her throat.

Alecia snorted. "You're both speaking utter crass rubbish. I expect better." She lowered her voice. "Kain Arenil isn't interested in an affair with either of you, no matter how attractive you are. He's married to a stunning noblewoman for whom he'd die. I don't wish to hear any more comments like you just made."

Lin huffed. "Princess, you're no fun. I'm rethinking being your second."

"Kain Arenil isn't eligible, so let that be the end," Alecia snapped.

Cretia piped up. "We were only joking, and you know it."

"You were only *half-joking*, and you know *that*. You ladies have been growing increasingly bawdy, and I've been meaning to mention it." They arrived at the keep and handed their reins to grooms who rushed out from the stable.

Despite the words Alecia had just uttered, Lin eyed the man who led her horse away and, damn him, the man smirked at her. Alecia frowned at her second, who threw up her hands.

"It doesn't hurt to look!"

While Cretia laughed, Alecia stalked toward the entrance. "Come along. I'm late for a meeting with the Guardians, and then I must see Iona."

Ramón's face wore a stormy frown as Alecia related her meeting with Kain.

"I really wish you'd leave these things to me," he said. "Someone should've summoned me immediately Prince Arenil arrived."

"I'm sure he'll make his way to the keep as soon as he settles his people, Ramón," Alecia said, glancing at her ladies who stood on either side of the door. Ramón frowned at them as if he wished they weren't present.

"And there was no need for you to interfere with Estevot's handling of the arrival. Again, you have overstepped."

Alecia drew herself up. "Oh, how things have changed between us," she said. "You would never have spoken to me thus before I fled this castle. Now you think you can order me around."

She told herself to stay calm, but it was difficult when Ramón treated her with such … such… contempt! Even Benae wouldn't stoop so low. At the thought of the woman, there was a knock at the door, and Benae entered. She cast a sidelong glance at Alecia and hurried across to her husband, whispering in his ear.

Ramón scowled at Alecia. "I believe Kain Arenil is outside, asking where he can find you, though I'm not sure why he'd need to see you again so soon."

Alecia lifted her chin, then reminded herself she had nothing to prove. "I organized wagons to transport his wounded. Perhaps he wanted to discuss that with me."

Ramón frowned. "Perhaps. Regardless, he can come in and speak with me." He waved his hand at the footman who stood by the door.

Alecia took his moment of distraction to approach Benae. "Prince Arenil has many wounded with him, Benae. I'm sure he'd appreciate your help with them."

Ramón cast Alecia a harried glance as he greeted Kain.

Benae stood with her hands folded before her, her emerald velvet gown hugging her curves. She wore her silver tiara as if to remind everyone of her status. Alecia fumed and waited, striving to appear unflustered and suspecting she'd failed.

"I'd be glad to inspect the elven wounded, if Prince Arenil requests it," Benae said. "I wouldn't want to step on his healers' toes."

Kain left Ramón and swept Benae a bow. "Princess, it's my great honor to see you again. The times we've met in the past have been too brief."

Benae smiled and inclined her head, for all the world as if she were a queen and Kain a lowly lord, instead of a contender for elven king. Alecia ground her teeth, but remained silent.

"I'm honored to host you, brother-in-law," Benae said. "I trust Alique is well?"

Kain frowned. "As for that, I can only hope. She's supporting the Wildecoast war effort. Speaking of that, I'd be grateful if you could help with my injured."

"Are there any who need urgent care?"

"Ramar Isiloe's mother, Rasalar, has been unconscious since the battle. There are several others who hover between life and death."

Benae stiffened. "Then I'll gather my things and tend to them immediately." She nodded to Alecia and kissed Ramón, then got instructions from Kain before departing.

Kain watched her go, then faced Ramón. "Your wife is a devoted healer, Lord Zorba."

Ramón smiled. Nothing pleased him as much as praise of his wonderful wife. "I trust you won't overtax her, Your Highness. She'll have much to do in the coming days and weeks." Ramón studied the other man, as if taking his measure. His demeanor couldn't be called friendly, and Alecia wondered if Ramón approved of Kain's marriage to his sister, Alique.

"I'll see she doesn't exhaust herself," Kain said. "I have two talented healers, so it's just the more complicated cases she'll attend." He looked around the room. "Estevot mentioned a war council. Is this where it is to be held?"

"The members of the council will arrive soon. Please make yourself at home, and I'll call for food and drink." Ramón turned away, and Kain joined Alecia.

"How well do you know Lord Zorba?" Kain asked her.

She smiled. "Very well indeed, though lately he has changed much; grown into his manhood, so to speak."

"And his wife?"

"She's an excellent healer; second to none."

"That wasn't precisely what I asked."

Alecia paused. She didn't know this man well, and he *was* married to Ramón's younger sister. He could well be after information about her own ambitions. On the other hand, she must forward her own tilt at the throne, and, with Uncle Beniel dead… Her heart cracked at the thought. She had truly loved her uncle, almost as much as she had loved her father. Now they were both dead.

Kain frowned. "I didn't mean to upset you, Princess, though I thought it an innocuous enough question."

She sighed. "Your question reminded me that my uncle is dead."

Kain froze. "*What*?! The king is dead? When did this happen?"

Alecia's heart dropped to her stomach. "A day or so ago. He died on the battlefield."

Ramón joined them. "I had no way of letting you know as you were en route from Selinore."

Kain stared at his boots, brows furrowed. "This changes everything. Who oversees the Kingdom Army?"

Ramón stiffened. "I've yet to hear. I imagine Josef Formosa is leading it, even though Vard Anton was the King's Blade. As a commoner, Anton would hardly retain a position of authority once King Beniel died. And he has come so recently to his post."

"And you think Formosa can win this war?" Kain asked.

"Clearly *you* don't," Ramón said.

Kain stalked away to the end of the room. Alecia watched with appreciation as he gathered his composure and strode back to them. "And what of you, Zorba? As Guardians, you and your wife have some appreciable say over the conduct of this battle."

"The king placed us in this position when Prince Zialni died," Ramón said. "As Guardians of Brightcastle and the heir to the throne, I imagine we have the ultimate say."

"Over my dead body," muttered Alecia under her breath. She was just far enough away that only Kain heard her. He gave her a sharp glance.

"What did you say, Princess?" Ramón asked.

The arrival of the other members of the war council saved her from replying. Kain frowned at her before taking a seat at the front of the room, near Ramón's throne. Ramón, too, glared at her before turning to welcome the others. Alecia ushered Lin over, and they took seats at the front of the chamber.

"What happened?" Lin whispered.

"Prince Arenil has only just learned of the king's death."

"Ooh," she said. "And he wasn't best pleased?"

"No, he wasn't," Alecia said. "Seems his confidence in the Kingdom Army has taken a hit."

"If I could bring this meeting to order,' Ramón said loudly, his gaze resting on her. "As you all know, today will see Gorin's army arrive on our doorstep. We're ready for him and his *Sis Lenweri*."

There was a general murmur of agreement. Alecia tightened her lips.

"Today, we welcome Prince Arenil of Selinore and his army, fresh from their victory on the tabletop which included the downing of a dragon."

There was boisterous applause, and Kain rose and bowed to the gathering.

"I invite Kain Arenil to say a few words."

Kain strode to the center of the space and stood with his hand on his sword hilt.

"Thank you, Lord Zorba. It is with great relief we find ourselves in your keep after many days on the trail and a hard-fought victory over the *Sis Lenweri*. Even so, we're more than happy to support you in your battle against Gorin's force."

He waited as applause broke out once more.

"My sister, Princess Gwaethe Arenil, and her husband Jacques Vorasava, follow Gorin's passage toward us. Thus, we possess the enviable position of having our enemy trapped between our combined forces."

Captain Estevot interrupted. "How is the Amitanian force composed, Your Highness?"

"It is roughly half-human and half-elven, thus combining the best of the two fighting styles. I believe we'll have the advantage as the battle will occur on open ground, and you've had the time to prepare."

Estevot nodded. "What of the dragon threat? You've fought the beast. What tactics can we employ?"

Kain paused, and Alecia watched his jaw clench. Clearly this topic made him uncomfortable—but why? He was a hard and capable fighter, and an experienced leader.

"It's a tricky beast and guided by elven riders, perhaps elven lords, if legend is to be believed. We have one rider in your prison, as I speak. There's verbal communication between beast and rider. Dragons are sentient beings, and can reason and think. I also believe they harbor quite a deal of malevolence toward their enemies."

"You haven't answered my question, Prince Arenil," Estevot said, arms folded across his chest.

Kain raised one brow and swallowed. "We downed the beast with a well-placed arrow to the eye, but my first shot failed, allowing the dragon to get too close. Boney ridges, above and below, protect the eye. I was on a flat-topped hill, thus able to get a better angle to miss the ridged protection. The castle walls would present such a vantage. You must have your best archers there with whatever weapon they're most proficient with."

Estevot nodded. "What about the ability of the dragon to breathe fire? How do you protect from that?"

"As to that," Kain said, "we've been lucky. The trees protected us while on the run. Then, on the ridge, the mist was so thick, it hindered the dragon's sight more than it did ours. We had shields for protection and rocks to get behind, but we were lucky with the mist."

Alecia had been watching Kain closely, and suspected he wasn't telling the full truth. There was something about his vanquishing of the dragon he wouldn't or couldn't share. She wondered what it was. Had Estevot seen what she had? Used to hiding the truth in her own life, perhaps she was more used to seeing it in others.

"So, we must pray for mist?" Estevot asked.

Kain fixed him with a hard look. "We must use all the tactics at our disposal and be constantly inventing more."

Estevot sat back, satisfied for the time being.

"Thank you, Prince Arenil," Ramón said, and Kain returned to his seat.

Ramón continued. "I've heard little from the Kingdom Army since they departed Wildecoast, except to be assured they're hounding Faenwelar's *Sis Lenweri* all the way here. The elves have several hours' start on them. Vard Anton has been responsible for the correspondence thus far, but I have no confirmation who's leading the army."

"What of the king?" Estevot asked. "And the queen, for that matter?"

"The body of the king lies in state in the Zialni crypt until such time as there can be a proper service. The queen has remained in the city."

Estevot stood. "Then we have a ragtag army of part-time leaders to help defeat the *Sis Lenweri*? And a battle for control of the throne when we're done? Perhaps even before?"

His command of the audience impressed Alecia, but Ramón held up his hand, and Estevot snapped his mouth shut.

"Talk like that won't help, Captain. We have an ample sufficiency of leadership talent to defeat the *Sis Lenweri* threat."

"From where I stand, Lord Zorba," Estevot said, "we have no king, and therefore no clear leadership. We don't even know who oversees our major armed force! The command of our elven allies is solid, but ours is anything but. Vard Anton is untried in battle, and so is Josef Formosa. As far as I can see, the only man with a proven command background is Kain Arenil, once commander of the King's Army."

Estevot's words caused a great stir in the hall, and Alecia's heart thumped wildly. To Ramón's credit, he didn't panic. He waited for relative calm to descend and spoke again.

"Captain, you command Brightcastle forces with the help of Ramar Reese, and now Prince Arenil is here to give you support. Soon we'll have Jacques Vorasava and his wife to add to our command reserves. As long as we work collaboratively, we'll be a force to be reckoned with, dragons or no dragons."

Alecia stood. "Lord Zorba is correct. We have plenty of talent and more on the way. We have plans in place. In fact, we couldn't be better prepared. Now is the time to stand united, not to fight amongst ourselves."

She stared down Estevot until he nodded and sat, then she let out a quiet breath.

As she took her seat, Ramón met her eye and smiled. Her speech had had two effects. The first was to calm the hall and present a united front, and the second was to lull Ramón into thinking she had ceded power to him. Good.

She could understand Estevot's anxiety, but he'd cause disquiet by voicing his concerns. She glanced around. The members of the council were nodding and smiling, even if they were grim smiles.

"And now," Ramón said, "please see me before you leave if you have any concerns about your various preparations. I expect Gorin's force within six hours. The city's bells will ring the moment the enemy is sighted."

Alecia and Lin stood and prepared to leave. She had several chores on her list before she could snatch a couple of hours' sleep. Her heart stabbed her at the thought that she might not get to put Iona to bed.

Lin whispered in her ear. "That was a pretty speech you gave at the end, Princess. I almost think you believe it yourself."

"I *do* believe it," she hissed, grabbing Lin by the arm and leading her into the hallway. "We need to present a united front if we're to win this war. After all, that's the first goal."

"And the next?" Lin asked, as Cretia joined them.

"You know damned well what the next goal is. I don't intend to repeat it here."

Alecia prepared to hurry them outside when her name was called. She turned to find Kain Arenil waiting for her.

"What can I do to help, Kain?" she asked. Her companions stepped back, allowing her to speak with Kain with a semblance of privacy.

"Perhaps nothing," he said. "However, I'd like to speak with you. I have rooms in the keep, though I don't know where."

She smiled. "I can show you to them, and we can have a quiet word if you like."

His brows rose. "I'd hate to trouble you."

"I have some duties to attend to, so it would only be for a few minutes. Would that suffice?"

"It would indeed."

Alecia motioned for her ladies to follow. She guided Kain to the central staircase and up to the west wing where he'd been allocated a chamber. A carafe of red wine, a loaf of bread, and some cheese lay upon the table in the sitting room. A fire burned in the hearth.

Kain glanced around, then strode to the table and poured two glasses of the thick ruby wine. Alecia asked her ladies to wait outside, then closed the chamber door. She accepted a glass from Kain.

"To your good health and the success of the kingdom, Alecia," he said, raising his glass to her.

She smiled and nodded, sipping the wine. "What did you wish to speak with me about?"

He drew in a deep breath. "I wish to know your assessment of Ramón Zorba."

"He's a good man," she said quickly, and noted the narrowing of his eyes.

"But?" he asked, his gaze focused as if to draw out all her secrets.

She wanted to squirm, but future queens did no such thing. "I owe him my gratitude and loyalty."

"And yet?"

She wanted to yell at him to stop. Instead, she placed her goblet on the table and walked across the room, trying to give herself time to answer.

Kain continued, his voice low, "The man appears to have come from virtually nowhere to lead Brightcastle and influence the next king of Thorius. I simply wish to know your impression of his worthiness and ability."

Alecia sighed. "He's a good man, but untested in battle and tactics." She kept her suspicions to herself about Solomon's father. After all, she might be wrong. "He brought me back from exile, and, for that, I'll always be thankful. My uncle the king obviously saw something worth this promotion. Lord Zorba has grown much in stature, ability, and self-belief in the last year."

Kain made a snort. "Why don't you just say what you really think? Does he deserve to be in the position he holds, and does Princess Benae?"

Alecia's heart hardened at the mention of Benae, and she knew it would show in her eyes. "If I must answer," she said, "then I don't believe either of them deserves the positions they've been given. I only hope it doesn't lead to us losing the war." She met his hard dark gaze. "*I* should oversee Brightcastle. As Jiseve Zialni's firstborn, *I* should now rule in Brightcastle and ascend to the throne of Thorius."

Kain looked surprised at her proclamation, but not as startled as she had expected. His brows drew down, and his hands found his hips.

"There hasn't been a ruling queen in Thorius for hundreds of years. What makes you think *you'll* be the next one?" he asked.

A tiny spark of excitement lit in Alecia's belly. This was her chance to convince someone with power of her worthiness. She squared her shoulders and met his gaze.

"As the child of the previous heir to the throne, I'm the next logical choice for kingdom ruler. Besides, I know I can do this."

She took a step toward Kain who wore a smirk. She wouldn't allow that to put her off.

"I can fight, and I could lead men into battle. I notice the small things that make a difference. I'd be a kind ruler, not the tyrant my father was. Since my teen years, I've tried to fix the wrongs he inflicted on Brightcastle."

Passion infused her as if she had a direct channel from the great Queen Izebel herself. "If not me, then who? Solomon is too young for decades yet, and his guardians are untried as rulers. Over my dead body will I allow Piotr to rule the kingdom. There is too much suspicion over his possible role in my father's death and the attack on the king at the funeral."

Kain nodded. "I agree. Piotr must be avoided. But what makes you think you'd be accepted?"

She squared her shoulders, and Kain's eyes fell upon the war cloak she wore. "Don't I look the part? I've worked months to prove my worthiness to the people and the nobles. Granted the king wouldn't consider it before, but now he's dead…" Her voice wavered.

"I can see you had deep feelings for him," Kain said.

She smiled. "At times, I felt closer to Uncle Beniel than I did to my father. He was more approachable. But in the end, he still traded me to Lord Finus and expected me to do my duty. He approved of the plan my father came up with." She shuddered at the memory of her lecherous fiancé.

A large hand grasped her shoulder, and she looked up into dark eyes, warm with compassion. "And the child you bore? Don't you fear that the populace will disapprove of a single mother as their queen?"

She glared at him. "Let them suggest my daughter is something to be ashamed of, and I'll soon set them straight."

"Is there no possibility that Vard Anton will marry you?"

"Make an honest woman of me, you mean? I don't need any man to stand behind me, though I admit I'd like him in my life. I must gain the throne on my own, and this is the time to do it." She hurriedly went on. "I don't mean in the middle of the war, but I can use victory over the *Sis Lenweri* to gain the support I need." She stopped, feeling this was the time to broach the topic. "Would you support me as Queen of Thorius, Prince Arenil?"

She clasped her hands before her. "Think of it! You'll be king of a united *Lenweri,* and I shall be Queen of Thorius. We can support each other. I could use your advice in battle."

Alecia could see the cogs ticking over in his mind. How would he decide?

She could do this; she knew with absolute certainty that she could help win this war and then rule the kingdom. If she could cover herself with glory, then enough people might support her. She wouldn't be the first ruler to win the throne on the foundation of a war victory. But first they must win!

"Well, Kain? What do you say?"

"As to advising you, Princess, that I'll certainly be happy to do. For the other, let me think on it, and I'll decide after we win the war."

Alecia nodded, excited and more certain than ever she would rule Thorius after they vanquished the *Sis Lenweri.*

CHAPTER FOUR

GORIN'S force arrived at dusk, sparking a mad dash to ensure they completed all the preparations. It was late before Alecia sought her bed, and she had only been asleep for two hours when Hetty shook her shoulder.

"Princess, the attack has begun!"

She was instantly wide awake, though an ache immediately formed a tight band around her skull. "Where's Iona?"

"The maid has taken her to the lower room along with Prince Solomon. They'll be well guarded, and I'll stay with them."

Alecia clutched the old woman to her breast and hugged her fiercely. A tear squeezed from her eye as she realized she hadn't been able to farewell her daughter.

"Have a care, child," Hetty said. "I'm not made of stone!"

Alecia released her and laughed. "I'm sorry. Give Iona a kiss for me, and one to Solomon as well."

"Now, child," Hetty said, "you'll not be getting maudlin. All will be well, and I'll be seeing you for supper."

Hetty bustled away, leaving Alecia temporarily frozen in place, knowing her next move would take her into uncharted territory. She had never been in battle before. Now it was time to test herself where it mattered.

She dressed in a rich red gown with divided skirts for riding. They wouldn't hurt for fighting either. Intricate silver embroidery decorated the bodice and sleeves, as well as encircling the waist. A maid arrived to tend her hair, and, in minutes the girl had created a practical style that would carry a tiara and stay out of her eyes. She slipped into soft black riding boots and reached for the red, silver, and black Zialni battle cloak.

The maid clasped her hands to her face. "Princess," she said, tears pooling in her eyes, "you look like you stepped straight from a tapestry. You'd awe Queen Izebel herself."

Nerves squirmed in Alecia's gut. While she was glad to have elicited this emotion, it was a lot to live up to. "Thank you," she said.

The girl curtseyed, and Alecia collected her sword and longbow. She also slipped five knives about her person. The knife was her second favorite weapon after the sword. She wouldn't be killed for a lack of arms.

She met her ladies in the hall, all four of them dressed for war. Linnet wore a pale green gown divided for riding. As a countess, she had deemed it unseemly to be seen on the battlefield in breeches. Alecia didn't think it unseemly, but she wished to make an impression. An elegant gown seemed the best way. She could hardly wear a tiara and breeches.

The other ladies had donned their breeches and appeared comfortable in varied shades of gray, green, and brown. All wore similar cloaks, less fancy than hers, and all carried multiple weapons. Their smiles were tight, brows creased, and jaws clenched.

"Fear not, my ladies," Alecia said, "you'll soon be too busy for nerves."

That was what Vard had always said. The few skirmishes she'd been involved in had proven his words to be true. The anticipation was usually worse than the reality. Fighting carried you to a different place where fear relaxed its grip on the mind and body.

They hurried to the stables to be met by stable lads with their horses. In minutes, they exited the small northern castle gate, which was heavily guarded.

"Princess!" one guard called. "Should you be out here?"

"Where else would I be?" she asked.

The young man stepped in front of her horse. "I've been given no directive about ladies on the battlefield, Your Highness. I'm sure Lord Zorba wouldn't be happy to see you here."

"Where is Lord Zorba?" she asked.

"He has accompanied Captain Estevot and Prince Arenil to the front lines to assess the situation."

"Then that's where I shall go," Alecia said. "My ladies will accompany me, so I'll be quite safe."

Even in the darkness, Alecia spotted the whites of his eyes. He was probably imagining all chances of future promotion fade if he allowed her to take the field.

"And before you speak another word, Corporal," she said, glancing at his insignia, "please note one thing. You'll have to arrest all of us if you wish to stop me. Now step aside unless that's what you plan to do."

She heard a gulp from the young soldier. He turned to look at his comrades, who took a step back from him.

"As you wish, Princess," the corporal said, his tone one of weary resignation. He joined his fellow soldiers, and Alecia clucked to her horse and carried on through the gate.

After clearing the portal, she pulled up and surveyed the battlefield. The *Sis Lenweri* had formed up, their foot soldiers in front and several lines of mounted elves behind. An eerie silence hung over the field, the only sounds the restless clop of horses and the snap of flags in the moderate wind.

Ramón and his co-commanders were at the far north of the kingdom lines, facing the enemy. She urged her horse toward him, ignoring the cries of soldiers along the way. Good, they all recognized her. All the better for proving her worth at the conclusion of the battle—assuming she *did* prove her worth.

She shook her head. Now wasn't the time for pessimism. She wouldn't allow these self-defeating thoughts to take hold. As she grew closer, her ladies following behind, Alecia realized Ramón and the others spoke with Prince Gorin. How utterly strange, she thought, as she assessed the enemy prince and his honor guard.

She felt the force of the elven prince's gaze before she saw him. His sneering face could just be seen in the moonlight.

"And this must be the fabled Princess Alecia," he said, his white horse shifting under him. "I see that the kingdom army allows its women to fight as the *Lenweri* do."

Ramón spun to face her. "Get back, Princess. You shouldn't be here."

"*You* are here," she said. "The Zialni name needs representation in this battle, and I'm here for my father and uncle."

She looked at Gorin. "You must be the fabled Prince Gorin," she said. "It's good to know my enemy. That way, I can be sure I kill the correct elf."

His laugh rang across the field, and she felt its chilly authority. "Believe me, Princess—if we meet in battle, *I* will be the victor. There is no way any elf would allow himself to be defeated by a kingdom woman. Go back to your castle and prepare to surrender."

Gorin's tone and words made her blood boil, but Alecia wouldn't respond to his jibes. "I suggest you follow your own advice and quit the field."

"Brave words," the elven prince said. "I can't help but wonder if you can follow them with action. I give you one last chance to stand aside and open your gates, as I have offered your *brave* commanders and the *Lenweri* half-blood. Failing that, my army will annihilate yours."

She swallowed the fear his words brought. Gorin's army might vanquish them, but if they opened their gates to the enemy, they'd have no chance of freedom. That was an outcome she wouldn't accept without a fight.

"Be gone from these lands, Gorin," Alecia said. "They belong to myself and my people. I won't surrender them."

Ramón yelped beside her, and his head whipped toward Gorin at her words. She didn't know what had upset him and didn't care.

"As you wish, human princess," Gorin sneered, wheeling his horse and charging back to his lines, a mere two hundred yards to the north. His entourage followed on his heels.

Alecia signaled her ladies, and they trotted back toward the keep. She may have just invited warfare with the *Sis Lenweri*, but she wouldn't sit on the front lines and wait for an arrow through the head.

She heard Ramón and the others following her as the rows of infantry and cavalry opened for them and closed with their passing. Their soldiers appeared magnificent in the light of the torches, their faces taking on a hard and determined look with the enhancement of the flickering shadows.

"Princess Alecia!" Ramón called as she reached the trenches closest to the keep. Ramón trotted up, his face appearing carved from stone. *What now?*

"Yes, Lord Zorba?" she asked, falling into his formal choice of address.

"I don't appreciate you interfering with that meeting!" He snapped his mouth closed as if he was worried angrier words would slip out. "I'm the Guardian here and in charge of this campaign, not you!"

The other men who had been with him moved away to give them privacy.

"Are you sure you wish to have this discussion here, Lord Zorba?" Alecia sat her horse, back straight and head held high.

"I do. I must ask you to cease your infernal meddling. And if you think I'll allow you to take the field and fight, you can think again. I'll have you locked up if necessary."

She went cold inside, deep inside where she had locked away the scars—the ones sustained from her father's treatment of her. That this man would suggest abusing her this way stole her breath; at least it did for a moment.

"I am Alecia Zialni, niece of our recently departed king, and you will *not* treat me as a criminal. I'm staggered you'd even suggest such a thing knowing my recent history."

He flinched, and she knew she'd scored a point. "I'm merely trying to make you see sense. I know you're capable, but I *will* ensure your safety. If I must lock you up to do so, then you can join your daughter and… Benae's son."

He'd been about to say "my son". She knew it!

"I won't allow you to lay hands on me and neither will my ladies. In the name of our friendship, you must let me participate in this war."

He swallowed hard, and his eyes moved to his surroundings as if seeking an escape. Then his gaze hardened. "What are you doing here, Anton?"

Alecia hauled her horse in the direction Ramón stared and a dark figure on horseback rode several steps forward. *Of course it isn't Vard, but his father!*

"I would ask the same thing, Lyam," Alecia said.

Lyam's gaze switched to her, but his smile didn't soften his flinty gaze. "I made a solemn promise to my son that I would protect you, Princess."

Alecia huffed. "Of course! You are another man who would control me."

Instead of answering, Lyam turned to Ramón. "Guardian, I will shadow the princess and her ladies and see that no evil befalls them."

"I don't know you at all, Anton," Ramón sneered. "How can I trust you with Alecia's safety?"

Lyam shrugged, the gesture reminiscent of Vard. "What choice do you have? At the very least, I'm an extra sword on the field. You can't stop me from taking part, and if you try, you'll regret it."

Lyam's words were sober and full of conviction.

"You threaten me?" Ramón asked.

Lyam's eyes flared. "No."

"Just work with me, Ramón," she said. "I *can* be of help. You're not responsible for my safety or answerable to anyone for it. You've appointed yourself as my caretaker, and I neither want nor need it." Surely he could see she had enough protection with Vard having appointed Lyam to watch over her?

He heaved a great sigh. "If I allow this, you'll work with me, not against me. You'll follow orders and go where I place you?" His eyes flicked to Lyam. "You too, Anton."

Damn the man! When would he ever learn? But if she didn't allow him some concessions, he'd try to prevent her fighting altogether. She nodded.

"I must be able to see you at all times, Princess. Also, your ladies and Anton must stay with you. If I leave your side, one of my commanders will take my place, and you'll obey them. I reserve the right to add to this list of rules as the battle progresses."

Alecia closed her eyes as each of the conditions settled upon her. She bit her lip to keep from gasping or snapping back a response. *You must agree for now!*

As he finished, she nodded. "I so agree."

Her ladies snorted as one, and she turned her gaze on them. They were either angry on her behalf, or thought her agreement false. They knew her well. Lyam merely sat his bay mare as unmoving as a rock.

"Come ladies, we'll ensure our preparations are complete. It will be a long day."

Lyam moved alongside her as they rode back to the north wall. "We have had little time to speak these last weeks, Princess." His voice sounded so much like Vard's that it played tricks on her mind. But she must remember this wasn't Vard.

"It is my great regret that I don't know you better, Lyam," she said. "I hope I don't cause offense when I ask you to keep your distance during battle. I don't need another mother hen clucking around me."

Lyam chuckled. "I've watched you train, Princess. You are skilled, but in battle you can never have too many friends watching your back. I won't get in your way, but I *will* be there when you need me." His eyes flicked to her four ladies. "The same applies to your companions."

Alecia nodded, wondering how Lyam's "help" would impact her during battle. She didn't wish it to appear she had a bodyguard or to be reminded that Vard was fearful for her. She wished for no distractions at all.

They moved closer to a vacant piece of wall where a brazier burned and dismounted. Lyam nodded and rode away. Alecia checked her saddle and weapons, as did the others.

"The hide of him," Lin said, yanking her girth tighter. Her horse always blew himself out when the saddle was first placed. It always needed tightening later. "Who does he think he is? No wonder Princess Benae resents you. He clucks around like you belong to him."

"Shhhh!" Alecia said. "No need to make things worse. In the past, Ramón oversaw my safety and old habits die hard. *That's all*. I once thought it sweet, but it's getting more annoying by the day." She stubbornly refused to mention Lyam again. Perhaps she might be able to ignore his presence if he kept his word.

"It wouldn't be an issue if you had a husband,' Kenna said, sitting on a stone and sharpening her sword.

"Well, I *don't* have one!" Alecia said. "Let's stick to discussing tactics. We'll stay by Ramón's side and save his stubborn neck a few times. That should placate him."

Arelle looked skyward. "The man is as close to a master swordsman as I've seen. What makes you think he'll need saving?"

"Do you have a better idea?" Alecia asked.

"Let's all calm down," Cretia said. "We'll get ourselves killed if we go into battle with hot heads."

Lin nodded. "She's right. I think Alecia's is a good plan. We stay close to Zorba and help where we can. Also look out for each other and try not to get injured or killed."

Arelle huffed. "Well, that goes without saying."

A horn blew in the enemy ranks and dread ran through Alecia. She sent a quick prayer of protection to the Goddess and mounted her horse. "That's the *Sis Lenweri* call to arms. If you're ready, we'll find Ramón."

The rest of the ladies mounted, and Alecia led them between the trenches, toward the battle, Lyam several paces behind. Cries already came from the front ranks of foot soldiers and pikemen. She flinched as a blood curdling howl preceded a loud clash of metal on metal. The battle had been joined.

She pulled up and scanned the ranks of cavalry that waited beyond the last trench. Men jogged on foot past her horse, cursing at having Silver and the other mounts in their way.

"There he is!"

Alecia spurred her horse forward, moving at a brisk trot between the trenches, turning left across the front of the most northerly trench until she reached Ramón and his personal guard. None of the other Brightcastle commanders were with him, as they had their own sections to control.

"Princess." Ramón's clipped tone eloquently expressed what he thought of her presence. "You and your ladies stay behind my men. That way you may stay in one piece." He flicked her a quick look before returning his attention to the battle before him.

Alecia scanned the action rather than reply to his insult. The Brightcastle force was doing well. Their shield wall was so far intact, at least in the section she could see. Their force was even pushing the enemy backward.

"Yes!" she cried, eyes riveted to the action. Deep within, something moved, filling her with excitement. If only she could be amid that fight. *You'll be there soon enough.*

The line of men swayed back and forth, and then the shield wall splintered. Elven warriors broke through, voices screeching in victory. Seizing her chance, Alecia urged Silver forward, her battle-trained mare eager. She was halfway to her goal before any of her ladies caught up. Lyam sped past like a one-man army, engaging the first soldiers through the breech.

Lin swore. "I thought we agreed we'd hang back and keep Zorba safe!"

Alecia ignored her and pushed forward to engage the elven soldiers who had poured through. They were on foot, and she had the advantage of height. She lay about with her short sword, hacking at the enemy from above, first to one side of Silver and then the other. Kenna and

Cretia set their horses either side of her and a little to the rear, both as a protection for her and to clean up any enemy she missed. Lin and Arelle worked on each side, in front of Alecia. Lyam fought ahead of them, cutting through the enemy like a knife through butter. Their teamwork was death for the *Sis Lenweri.*

Soon they were all grinning wildly. The breech was closed, the shield wall back in place. Dead and wounded *Sis Lenweri* and a few Brightcastle defenders lay on the surrounding ground. Alecia raised her sword, and men and women hidden in the trenches dragged the dead and injured away, raising lanterns to identify and examine the fighters.

Alecia shuddered as her battle rage left her. It was one thing to attack someone in the heat of battle and another to see the fruits of your sword work.

She shook off the shock, then reached for her flask and took a swig of strong brandy. It warmed her through.

"Come, we should return to Ramón. I'll be in enough trouble without him having to search for us." She turned and trotted Silver back toward the keep, looking amongst the cavalry for Ramón. She found him having a field dressing applied to his forehead.

"What happened to you?" he snapped, wincing as the medic tied the bandage.

Alecia smiled. "I could ask you the same thing." She pointed to his head. "How did that happen?"

"Another breech at the same time as the one you rode off to," he growled. "I thought I told you to stay with me?" He fixed Lyam with a cold stare.

Alecia raised her brows at her ladies. "If we hadn't acted, the shield wall wouldn't have stood. I can't always get permission from you, Ramón. None of us is injured."

"This time," he said. "Stay with me and my men, and you may continue to be fortunate."

As the sun crested the horizon, a man on a large black pony cantered up and stopped in a spray of dirt. "Lord Zorba, they've broken through on the right flank. The captain asks for reinforcements." He saluted, turned his pony and sped back the way he had come.

"Come on."

Ramón kicked his horse after the scout, and Alecia followed behind Ramón's guard and cavalry.

When they arrived, their front lines were in disarray. The shield wall had collapsed, and the foot soldiers were locked in combat with the taller and faster *Sis Lenweri*. Elves on horseback had swept through the breech and attacked the Brightcastle soldiers with devastating results.

Alecia saw one man's head cleaved in two by a vicious downward stroke from a screaming elven warrior. He saw her looking and kicked his pony toward her.

"To me!" she cried, and spurred Silver at the enemy. They met in a shoulder-jarring crash of swords. The maniacal glee with which the elf fought unnerved her. His eyes glowed in the faint moonlight. Clearly, he could see better than she, but Alecia wouldn't give the enemy an inch. She was vaguely aware of her ladies engaged in their own battles to left and right, and Lyam moved like a ghost, intercepting the enemy with magical ease. She had lost track of Ramón.

Alecia had the advantage of height as Silver was much the taller horse, but the elf was stronger. As she fought him, she realized he was no blade master. Neither was she, but she had superior sword skills to this elf. Elation fizzed along her limbs, lending her extra strength. She aimed a two-handed swipe at the enemy, sweeping left to right and down in a chopping motion. The blade cleaved deep into his right leg and jarred on bone. She tightened her grip on the handle and pulled.

The elf screamed, transferring his sword to his left hand, and clapping his right palm over the wound in his leg. He bled profusely, but Alecia had no time to readjust before her enemy spun his horse and sent a vicious backhanded slash at her. She swayed out of the way. Her movement made Silver sidestep to the left. Safe for the moment, she backed up a couple of paces and cast her gaze at the elf just in time to watch Silver inflict a savage bite to the rump of the elven steed.

The elven pony squealed and leaped forward into the midst of another skirmish where Captain Estevot dispatched his rider. Alecia groaned at the sight. Why did it have to be him who killed her combatant?

She shook the thought from her head and looked around. The battle had abated for the moment. The shield wall in this section was restored, albeit with fewer men. They needed reinforcements and quick. She swung Silver and spurred her toward a messenger waiting on his pony.

"Send for reinforcements," she said. "One hundred now and another hundred in an hour. And I need more cavalry. Another sixty should do it. Find Prince Arenil. We could do with elven backup."

The young man saluted and spun his horse back toward the keep. From further behind the lines, Alecia now had the chance to survey the battle. Their front shield wall was still relatively intact, with just a few minor breaks where cavalry reinforced the rupture.

The kingdom lines were getting thinner while the enemy ranks just seemed to grow. Cavalry waited behind the infantry, ready to ride into the breach if needed.

Then out of the north came a thunderous shriek like a giant bird. Ice water ran through Alecia's veins at the sound. It came again, echoed by another further to the west. As she peered northward, two specks became visible, getting larger by the second.

"Dragons!" Alecia shouted, pointing north at the sparkling green and red monsters. It was clear by now what they were, even if they were only vaguely defined. A gout of flame left the mouth of the green beast. "Take cover if you can! Shields, capes, trenches now!"

Others echoed her screams. The fighters in the shield wall ignored the cries. Caught up in the battle for their lives, the advent of dragons was less important. So too the cavalry who merely rode closer to the infantry, perhaps hoping the fire wouldn't be loosed on the *Sis Lenweri* and their proximity would save them.

Alecia glanced toward the keep and saw the reserve fighters and cavalry making their way to the battle lines. She trotted toward them, sensing her ladies with her. One of them groaned. Kenna? She had no time to check yet.

She pulled up before the commander of the reserves. "Sergeant, I fear this isn't the time to take the field. Dragons are on their way. Take cover in the trenches until the danger is past."

The man frowned, looked north, and his eyes widened. "There *are* dragons!" His hardened gaze swept the trenches and the battle lines. "We'll take cover in the northernmost trenches and join the men when the danger is past."

Alecia nodded and pulled her horse to the side as the men filed past. The cavalry split their ranks and half rode to each flank, hoping to escape the dragon fire. Alecia gulped down her fear. The men hadn't hesitated to take the field, even with dragons threatening. Shields up and cloaks wrapped around them, they moved into position.

Alecia then turned to her ladies. All looked the worse for wear but were tired and disheveled rather than injured. Except for Kenna. She was pale and had a thick field bandage wrapped around her right upper arm. Alecia came alongside her.

"Get yourself to the infirmary now! You've lost a lot of blood. Find Princess Benae. Cretia! Go with Kenna and come straight back."

Kenna opened her mouth to protest, but Alecia glared at her. Cretia grabbed the reins of Kenna's mount and led her toward the gate that was the keep's northernmost access point. Lin and Arelle faced their mistress.

"What do we do now?" Lin asked, her voice hoarse from screaming at her enemies. "You don't have enough protection. You can't fight."

"Watch me,' Alecia said, spurring her mount back to the front lines, wrapping herself in her cloak and bringing her shield up. The dragons which were near enough to see the riders on them now. Lyam sidled closer.

She spotted a break in the shield wall to the east and charged at it, collecting cavalry on the way, and hoping her theory that the dragons wouldn't torch the *Sis Lenweri* soldiers was accurate. Soon, she was too busy to think of anything but the next slash and duck. An icy rage burned through her, and she felt taken over by the spirit of a deadly warrior. *Izebel?* She laughed loudly, and her opponent, a slender *Sis Lenweri*, gaped at her. Likely he hadn't seen too many human warrior princesses. He didn't gape long. Alecia's next attack breached his defenses and sent him tumbling from the saddle to be trampled under Silver's feet.

Silver was a marvel. The mare had been a gift from her mother, almost as if she knew what Alecia would need one day. She had not fully appreciated the horse's battle training before, but she relished it now. The mare took delight in inflicting damage and death wherever she could. Anyone who fell from the saddle faced being viciously trampled, and the horse knew which were enemy and which were allies.

Alecia patted Silver's neck, and the mare nodded her head up and down as if to say, "Of course I'm a wondrous warrior horse". Alecia laughed and turned her mare to find the next fight.

By now, the dragons were almost overhead, the green beast closest, and the red further to the east. There were two riders on each, both holding a bow and arrow. How they could aim considering the movement of the mount under them, Alecia didn't know.

Their target appeared to be the area of the allied trenches and the rear portion of the battlefield. Off to the west, Alecia prayed she'd be safe, but felt guilt that there were so many in the fire's path. She was gratified to see the southern end of the field almost deserted. The soldiers would shelter in the trenches under fireproofed canvas, the recipe for which Hetty had created with the help of the royal seamstress. There was more to the dressmaker than met the eye.

A great gout of fire leapt from the maw of the green dragon, aimed at the kingdom cavalry in the center of the battlefield. Alecia flinched as the blaze roared over them. Because the dragons were flying north to south, if they wanted to avoid their own fighters, the range of their fire sweep was restricted. Should they turn and come from the east or the west, the devastation would be greater, as they would be able to target the entire length of the kingdom's fighting lines.

The flames killed more than a few, and singed riders and horses scattered after the fire ceased. Unhurt riders nearby dragged wounded soldiers onto their mounts and galloped with them for the keep, while other soldiers led injured horses away.

Alecia's cheeks were wet with tears, and her heart bruised from the slaughter. The picture was much the same when the red dragon attacked the eastern ranks.

It wasn't just the injuries inflicted by the dragons, but the terror they caused. No one wanted to be roasted alive, and most cavalry riders cared more for their horses than they did for their woman. To witness what the fire did to the soldiers it struck was to take a deep blow to the spirit.

She shook her head. The dragons were gone for the moment, and it was time to attack.

The field came alive with men and women, climbing from the trenches and joining the melee, or helping to get medical aid to the injured. The cavalry reinforcements poured in from the relative safety on the wings and plugged the holes in the shield wall.

Estevot and Ramón urged their men forward. It was as if the dragons had added urgency to their cause, and, indeed, the enemy were being pushed back.

Alecia retreated to the western edge of the battle to observe it. Beyond hope, the allies were doing well. She watched as Kain Arenil led his elves into the fray, most on foot, but some mounted on ponies and small horses. All carried swords, bows, and arrows. She frowned as she wondered how they'd attack.

There must have been five hundred *Lenweri* on the field. They had divided into two forces, one led by Kain riding up the west flank, and the other led by an elf in tatty locks leading his eastern group.

Once in position on each flank of the battle, they attacked the enemy cavalry lines in a pincer move. But it was risky, Alecia thought. If they moved too far into enemy territory, they could be isolated and picked off one by one.

As the *Lenweri* mounted forces engaged the enemy elven cavalry, it became easier for the kingdom foot soldiers to break through the enemy lines, at least on the edge of the battle.

"They're going to need help!"

Alecia kicked her horse into motion. So much for sticking close to Ramón and impressing him with her skills! But Kain was important to Thorius. He must be safe at all costs, and she'd help to make it so.

By this time, Cretia had returned. She joined Lin, Arelle and Lyam as Alecia dashed for the edge of the western battle wing.

As they arrived, it was chaos, with one of the kingdom soldiers attacking Kain as though he were the enemy. She rode Silver at the man, pushing between him and the elven prince.

"Princess!" the soldier cried.

"That is Prince Arenil, our ally, soldier," she said. "Back off and do your job. Didn't you see the white bands around the arms of the *Lenweri*?"

The soldier ducked his head. "My apologies, Princess."

Kain nodded to her and, wheeling his horse about, charged into the fray once more.

Alecia stayed close to Kain and her ladies to her, with Lyam guarding them all. They fought where needed, and monitored the battle further down the line. Twice Alecia intervened when Kain Arenil was attacked from the side or behind. They made progress, pushing their way in from the western edge, and cutting off the enemy from their own cavalry.

The *Sis Lenweri* around them became more frantic until reinforcements arrived from the center of the battlefield. Then Alecia spied Prince Gorin over the heads of the mounted enemy before her.

No wonder! He rode a magnificent white charger which looked as if it had been kingdom bred. His eyes turned in her direction, and he smiled. A chill ran through her.

The *Sis Lenweri* prince looked fit and fresh whereas she felt as if she'd been fighting for a week. Would he make his way over and engage her, or would he consider her beneath his mighty notice? Well, he'd already seen her, so perhaps she wasn't.

Fight, you ninny!

Before her, a kingdom cavalryman fought off two mounted enemy and turned to face another. Exhaustion lay like a cloak on his shoulders and already another enemy had turned to target him.

Alecia nudged Silver forward and intercepted the oncoming enemy, cutting her sword across and intercepting his blade. The *Sis Lenweri's* black gaze turned to her and narrowed as he took in who had thwarted his attack. He turned to engage her, and there followed a vigorous battle where she only just managed to deflect two deadly sword strokes.

Her enemy was the most skilled warrior she had come across that day. He seemed to anticipate all her moves.

"To me!" she cried.

Lin appeared on the other side of the attacker, and her horse bit his thigh savagely. The elf doubled over with the pain and shock of the horse's assault.

Alecia bashed him on the temple with the butt of her sword, and he toppled off his horse.

Lin snatched the reins of the elven horse and motioned Alecia to follow.

She didn't argue, close to toppling off her horse with weariness. They took refuge on the edge of the battle, Lin's wary gaze ensuring no one approached without their notice.

Lyam joined them. "You need rest, Princess."

Lin nodded. "I saw Gorin just now, and he was working his way through the battle toward you. You can't fight him in this state."

She frowned at her friend, reluctant to leave the field. But fatigue dragged at her. Glancing at the sun, she realized she had fought for the better part of eight hours. She needed food and rest.

She nodded. "Where is Ramón? I must let him know I'm leaving."

Lin shook her head. "Why? He already thinks you answer to him."

"If he can't find me, he'll think I've fallen. I can't do that to him. Besides, I don't want him to be distracted from the enemy."

Now it was Lin's turn to frown, but she couldn't fault Alecia's logic. "Fine, we'll look out for him as we return to the keep."

They whistled Arelle and Cretia, and all five made their way from the field. On the way, they engaged more enemy as they came across heated skirmishes.

Finally, they arrived back at the northern gate, albeit with three wounded mounted behind the ladies and another on the elven horse they had captured. They hadn't seen Ramón, but had tasked a messenger with finding the lord and explaining Alecia's plans.

A mess and field hospital had been constructed in the castle forecourt. They pulled up nearby. Grooms ran to take their horses and orderlies the injured, while Lyam bowed and took his leave. Alecia spied Benae working in the hospital. She sighed and hobbled over to her.

"How goes it?" She placed a hand on Benae's shoulder. The woman looked terrible—tired and disheveled as Alecia had never seen her.

Benae pushed the hair from her eyes and looked at her. "You appear to have been dragged through a muddy field with sharp sticks."

"You don't look much better," Alecia snapped. She ached all over and bled from numerous but insignificant nicks and scrapes.

"Sit down over there, and I'll tend your injuries."

Alecia huffed. "I don't need your help. I'm simply here to check on you and get some food and rest."

Benae stood up and turned from the patient she was bandaging. "Those cuts could fester. They need cleaning. Sit over there." She took in the other ladies. "You can join her. I'll have food and drink brought." Benae turned away, and that was that.

Alecia staggered over to a bale of straw and sat heavily, muttering about stubborn women. Benae could hardly afford to make a big fuss over a few cuts. It embarrassed Alecia that she would be using the woman's valuable healing talents.

A bowl was brought for each of them, along with a clean towel. They washed their hands and faces, and dried them.

"That feels good," Lin said, draining a goblet of watered wine.

"Sure does." Cretia winced as she scrubbed a cut on her face. It started bleeding again, making her appear gruesome. "I've never been so weary. I could sleep for a week."

"We rest for an hour, eat, and have our wounds tended. Then we go back," Alecia said. "We can't afford to be weak. Thorius won't win that way."

Lin slid closer and lowered her voice. "And we can't afford for you to be killed, or have you forgotten?"

Alecia drew in a deep breath. "Of course not, but our first goal is defeating the *Sis Lenweri*. Without that, nothing else matters."

Benae returned with Tyra, her blonde maid, who often helped her mistress with healing. The girl tended to them, gently cleansing wounds and helping suture the deeper ones. Benae laid her hands on each of them, murmuring soothing words. When it was Alecia's turn, she swore she felt a tingle in her cuts and bruises. Afterward, she felt a little less pain. A green paste was applied to each of the cuts whether stitched or not. The deeper ones were bandaged.

"None of you should return to the field until tomorrow," Benae said, finishing the last bandage. "There's significant risk of wound breakdown with activity, and Cretia and Arelle have lost much blood. They'll be weakened for some days."

"We can't afford the luxury of rest," Alecia said. "Every sword counts, especially until Gwaethe gets here. We shall rest another thirty minutes, and then return. How is Kenna?"

Benae shook her head in dismay but answered. "Kenna is resting. I'll send her back to you only when I'm satisfied she's well enough to sit a horse."

"We didn't see Ramón," Alecia said. "Has he been injured?"

Alarm flared in Benae's eyes. "He hasn't been brought in. I'm sure if he had fallen, I would've been told."

Nonetheless, Alecia thought the woman still appeared uncertain. She reached out and patted her shoulder. "Thank you for your care. I'll keep an eye out for Ramón." Just at that moment, attendants carried three gravely wounded soldiers in, and Benae was called away.

"How does she do it?" Lin mused, almost to herself. "It must take its toll."

Alecia watched as Benae smiled at the injured. The first she laid hands on had a deep wound to the chest. She closed her eyes for long moments, her hands over the injury. When she opened them, the man breathed easier. She pointed to another tent which Alecia assumed was a surgery of sorts.

Alecia mused on the scene before her. Having seen Benae in action, she was surer than ever before that the woman used magic in her healing.

It took courage to do that in plain sight with the fear of magic so prevalent. Even the recipient of a magical cure could eventually turn on their benefactor if the incentives were great enough.

Alecia shook the thoughts from her head and turned to her ladies. "Let's go up on the wall before we return to the battlefield. They finished their food and slowly made their way to the stairs which led up to Brightcastle's defensive wall. From that vantage point, looking across the trenches to the battlefield, Alecia could see the extent of their task. She also found Ramón.

He smiled as she approached, her ladies hanging back to give her privacy.

"I wondered where you were," he said. "I've had officers marking your position all morning, once the sun was up. And then you vanished. A messenger finally found me and told me you had quit the field."

"Thank the Goddess," Alecia said. "I didn't want you distracted, but I couldn't see you when we left."

Ramón sobered. "I hope this means you've given up the folly of fighting."

She stiffened. "You still don't understand. We need every sword, and I intervened several times when our men were backed against a wall. Ask Kain Arenil if you need proof. I'm not quitting the field. I just needed food and rest."

"Well, you'll have tightened up now and will feel every stiff muscle. That's when your body will let you down. It's too risky to return."

"I'll be careful," Alecia said, through clenched teeth.

"You don't have a careful bone in your body, Princess!" Ramón snapped.

She took a mental step back—something she wouldn't have done several months ago—and turned to survey the battle. On both sides, numbers had been significantly depleted, though the kingdom force was the smaller. Thorian cavalry was a larger force than the elven one, but the *Sis Lenweri* had hundreds if not thousands of foot soldiers. She hadn't thought they'd fight unsupported for so long.

When will the Amitanian army arrive?

"I was thinking the same thing," Ramón said beside her.

She realized she must have said it out loud.

Alecia studied the country beyond the Sis Lenweri, eyes scanning for evidence of another force of soldiers. They have to be close. She looked so hard, she started seeing things moving where there were only trees. At least she saw no dragons.

"There!" someone said beside her.

Ramón Reese had approached, and now had his arm out, pointing north. Alecia followed his direction and at first saw nothing. Eventually, she spotted the glint of sunlight on metal, then movement. Over the next twenty minutes, they became certain that Amitania had finally arrived.

"They will attack the rear of Gorin's force," Reese said. "He will be trapped between us." The *Lenweri's* dark eyes were lit with glee.

Alecia took a step back from the wall as Ramón stared into the distance. She motioned for the other ladies to follow her as she quietly and quickly descended from the wall. She didn't breathe until she was at its base and marching toward the stables.

"He's going to be furious with you when this is over," Lin said, giggling.

Alecia sent her a dirty look. "This isn't a laughing matter. If Guardian Zorba was more reasonable, I wouldn't need to use tricks to achieve my goals. Ramón may be in charge here, but he'll have to get up mighty early in the morning to best me."

At her words, all the ladies broke into raucous giggles, causing those around them to stare. Alecia hushed them as they entered the darkness of the stable. Honestly, she didn't understand these women sometimes.

After a heated debate with the master of horse about taking their mounts back out to the battle, Alecia emerged on Silver. Lin kept her bay mare, and Arelle the elven horse she had acquired in their first fight months ago on the way to Amitania.

However, Cretia gave her brown a rest and instead mounted the horse Lin had taken from the elven blade master. The black stallion was also clearly kingdom bred, full of spirit and a little smaller than the normal kingdom war horses. Despite his fiery nature, he responded to the rein, and Cretia declared she'd have no trouble with him.

Privately, Alecia thought Cretia hoped her war horse might fight for her like Silver and Lin's mount did.

Though not a common occurrence, some trainers taught their mounts to bite the enemy and trample them. Not all horses could be taught, and sometimes the biting was turned on their owners when not in battle.

Ramón waited for them outside the northern gate. Lyam lounged against the wall nearby, wary as a snake ready to strike.

"I don't suppose I can talk you out of returning to the fray," he said, his brows raised at Alecia.

She shook her head, even though her body screamed at her to be sent to bed. She shook her head again just to convince herself.

"No, we're committed to the cause, and will make our mark on this battle," she said, nudging Silver forward. She surveyed the field, dismayed to find the ranks of their soldiers thinned even more. The orderly lines of pikemen and cavalry had erupted into screaming, slashing groups of mounted and foot soldiers. Her resolve wavered in the face of it.

"Come with me," Ramón said. "I've called for fresh troops. We'll see if we can restore some order to the rabble."

He trotted toward the battle, the ladies following in his wake and Lyam bringing up the rear.

CHAPTER FIVE

"A T last!" Gwaethe said, reining in her golden stallion. She stood in the stirrups and could just see the back ranks of Gorin's force and his supply wagons. "Now let us see who the victor is."

She knew her voice was cold, for Jacques sent a startled look in her direction.

"Indeed," he said, raising his arm into the air, then swinging it forward. "I hope we're not too late. That force must be much larger than Brightcastle's."

Gwaethe kicked her horse into a canter, eager to engage with the enemy elven force. At last, she might come face to face with Gorin, the elf whose visage adorned her nightmares and waking dreams. She gritted her teeth at the torture, both real and imagined, she had endured at his hands.

"Please don't let someone else kill him," she muttered.

Their battle plans had been set days ago, so there was no need to stop and discuss tactics. Jacques's signal had set the plan in motion, and their soldiers would move into their positions, preparing their weapons as they did so.

Half of their mounted units were to divide into two groups, one for each flank of the enemy. En masse, they would sweep left and right, attacking the sides of Gorin's force and pushing forward as quickly as they could. The foot soldiers would keep moving up the center. Reinforcing them were the other half of the cavalry, divided into three units. Gwaethe had charge of one, Jacques another, and Theoden Leovaris the third.

As she advanced, Gwaethe thought how appropriate it was that their combined leadership represented human, *Lenweri,* and former *Sis Lenweri.*

Theoden's crossing to their side had truly been a blessing, and she thanked the gods daily that she had rescued him from Faenwelar's dungeon. They would prevail, and she would ensure the *Sis Lenweri* faction never rose its ugly head again.

Their soldiers were tired, but had done everything they could to prepare for this battle while on the march. At least their mounts were in good condition, having been walked or led as much as possible. They had brought good high energy food for the horses, but could only carry so much grain, and it was running out.

Gwaethe's stomach growled as she had the thought. She had gone hungry many days, but they had enjoyed a hearty meal each night when they had stopped near midnight. She shook her head. The last week was one she would happily forget. Only Jacques had made it bearable.

She knew he worried for her in battle, but it was all she knew. Her people had long been persecuted. That she had chosen a soldier's life was no surprise. And Orionkael had needed her to be the leader Kain would have been, had he been raised by his birth father. She knew a pang of loneliness. She missed Orionkael and regretted that he had never known his son. He would have been proud of Kain.

She drew up in a stand of trees and her guards gathered around. The scouts trotted up.

"Princess, we will not have the element of surprise," a short elf with tangled long locks said. "They have been waiting for us and have a separate force ready to engage."

"How is it composed?" she asked.

"Mainly cavalry. They have held their archers back to deal with us. It will be perilous on the approach. The dragons have appeared only once, but it would not surprise me to see them again."

Gwaethe nodded. "Thank you." She turned to her group. "Spread the word. Shields up and look for dragons."

Her words warned her force of archers and also alerted her dragon defense force to prepare their bows. She felt for her weapons and calmed as she touched them.

As she kicked her stallion forward, her guard made a ring around her. She had the center right position, Jacques the center, and Theoden the center left.

She sent a quick word to Kain that she was on her way and focused on her goal.

* * *

The enemy had pulled all their supply wagons into a wall and used them as cover to fight behind. It wouldn't serve them for long, but it gave them an early advantage. Jacques raised his arm, and the archers sent their flaming arrows into the structures as the first enemy darts pierced their front lines. This would be bloody.

He thought of Gwaethe instinctively, but then pushed her from his mind. He couldn't fight *and* worry about her. His wife was a gifted soldier with good people to guard her. She'd survive, and he could only hope he too would live through the coming storm to be reunited with her.

Minutes later, he was among the blazing wagons, one of the first to penetrate the enemy lines. Exmund was by his side, deflecting enemy blades and fighting like one possessed. It was desperate and deadly.

As he hacked and defended, attacked and sliced, Jacques tried to keep a piece of his mind apart to observe the surrounding fight. That way, he could instinctively adjust his orders to respond. Part of his mind also responded to Exmund, both noting his partner's moves and watching his back. It was a dicey juggling act, but he stayed alive, only taking a slice to his ribs, and one to his cheek.

If the casualties amongst the riders were minimal, the same couldn't be said for the foot soldiers. They fell at a steady rate, and Jacques became concerned they were losing more men than Gorin was.

The enemy fought with a savagery that bordered on desperation, a feeling he was experiencing as well. Something had to give, or they'd sustain too many losses.

He looked to the right in a momentary lull and spotted Gwaethe, mounted on her golden stallion, sword flashing in the weak sunlight as she served death to her adversaries. The leader of her personal guard, Syndra, fought mercilessly at her side, and Jacques nodded. His wife would be well as long as she had fighters like Syndra around her. He turned his attention to those nearest him and found a space had opened.

"To me!" he cried, galloping forward, Exmund swearing in his wake.

"Hold up, My Lord!" Exmund said. "You'll get an arrow through you, exposing yourself like that."

Jacques reined into a canter until Exmund caught up. "I wanted to take advantage of the gap before it closed," he said, looking back to see two dozen of their force had followed him.

He could still see Gwaethe, now a little to the rear. Easy enough to get help if they were surrounded. He wanted to find Gorin and kill him if he could. Trouble was, he didn't know if the prince would be in the thick of the battle or protected in the center.

"I see a standard up ahead, My Lord," Exmund said. "It could be Gorin."

Jacques looked to where his aide pointed. Sure enough, there was a white flag with a green dragon one hundred paces away.

"It could be him," Jacques muttered. "Let's head over there and make it a little hot for the green dragon lord."

He urged his horse forward and his band followed, elves and humans working together to protect each other as they made their way south. The fighting became hotter as they neared the center of the enemy forces, and when Jacques next looked behind, *Sis Lenweri* surrounded him.

"Keep moving south, and we won't get boxed in permanently," he called. The sun was setting, and a cool breeze whipped across the battlefield, sending a shiver down his back.

Exmund looked around, a deep frown on his forehead. "What's your exit strategy, Sir?"

They were about twenty paces from the flag Jacques had been working toward. It didn't belong to Gorin, but another elven lord. The *Sis Lenweri* who fought under the standard wore bright green tunics with silver embellishments and scaled leather forearm and lower leg guards, painted green. They fought well, and Jacques tried to skirt around them, hoping to spot Gorin and take him out of the fight, thus weakening the resolve of the *Sis Lenweri*.

Unfortunately, a force of twenty green dragon fighters saw Jacques and his men and elves before they could avoid notice. They immediately charged, short swords at the ready.

"We have longer weapons, comrades," Jacques cried. "Our greater reach will win out." And that was all he could say before the green dragons were upon them.

"To me! To me!" Jacques cried.

They bunched up, turning their horses, rumps in and heads out like the spokes of a wheel. A whistle sounded from the right, and then another from the left. Gwaethe had noticed the attack, and she'd help if she could, as would Theoden.

They met the attack head on, charging out of formation when they needed to and back in when their enemy was defeated. The longer swords of the allies injured many of the enemy horses, which served to take their riders out of the fight, or at least made them fight on foot. It was blood-thirsty work, and Jacques's soul bled every time a horse suffered. The poor beasts had no choice. That said, some of the elven mounts were battle trained and could fight almost as effectively as their riders.

Jacques received a savage bite to his thigh as his mount sidestepped out of the circle. He slapped the flat of his blade against the neck of the enemy horse, which reared and dislodged its rider. The downed elf jumped up, grabbed his horse's reins, remounted and galloped away, likely to get help.

"Stop him!" Jacques screamed and in the next moment, the fleeing elf toppled off his horse, an arrow through his neck. He turned to see Syndra sling her bow back over her shoulder before she redrew her sword and killed one of the green dragon enemy.

The numbers of green dragon fighters had dwindled, but their leader remained untouched. He sat on his horse, watching the chaos around him and only intervening when needed. He met Jacques's gaze and nodded.

"Human Lord, what is your name?" he asked, holding up his hand when his soldiers tried to surround Jacques.

"I am Jacques Vorasava," he replied. "Who are you?"

"Hah!" the elven lord said. "You are the human dog who has mated with the *Lenweri* princess, Gwaethe Arenil." He looked Jacques over. "I wonder what she sees in *you*."

"You didn't answer my question." Jacques rode closer and stopped five paces from the green lord.

The elf looked down his nose at Jacques and finished a leisurely inspection which made his skin itch. There was something *off* about this one.

"I am Cordaneil nar Veilan, trainer of dragon riders and blade master of the *Sis Lenweri*."

Jacques's gut tightened with anticipation. He had trained night and day over the last four months to be worthy of his role as Gwaethe's battle commander. Though not a blade master himself, his skills were formidable, and the challenge of fighting a master was one not to be missed.

"Nar Veilan, I challenge you to a sword fight in which none can intervene until the result is decided. If you agree, we shall fight on foot, and the winner will be the first to draw blood."

The dragon lord sneered. "If I deign to fight you, it will be to the death, human."

Jacques hesitated. Having come from a noble family, it was rare for a sword fight to end with death for either of the combatants. However, this was war. He nodded.

"Accepted."

Nar Veilan dismounted and swept his arm out in a circle to those nearby. "Stand back and do not interfere."

Those on the side of the allies looked to Jacques for confirmation, and he nodded.

"Don't be distracted by our personal fight, but heed those around you," Jacques said, dismounting and removing his cloak. "Intervene if any try to end our duel before its natural conclusion."

His force nodded and moved their horses to create a barrier to interference.

Jacques faced off with the dragon lord.

The elf was heavier than most and a little taller than he was. Jacques estimated they were evenly matched in reach and weight. The result of their clash would depend on speed, agility, and skill, the latter which was likely to be in Nar Veilan's favor.

Jacques adjusted his balance, feet apart, mind clear of all extraneous matters, and focused on his opponent. The elven lord was still, gaze narrowed and fixed on Jacques, as if he could predict his moves by sheer concentration.

Jacques knew this would be a monumental challenge, but his mind shied away from predicting the outcome.

Down that path lay ruin.

He gripped his longsword in both hands, flourished it, spinning the blade, and turning his body in an arc in order to warm up and get his mind in the fight. He knew it put his opponents off, but it also gave them a chance to study his movements. Jacques had found it a helpful way to start a fight—if he had the chance.

Nar Veilan's eyes widened at the display before snapping his surprise back under control. Jacques allowed himself the merest twitch of the lips at his opponent's surprise.

So far, so good.

The green elven lord attacked, slicing his sword down and across his body, its lethal edge sliding toward Jacques's shoulder with startling speed. If he hadn't been moving in the right direction, he might've been taken by surprise, but his sword stopped the elven blade a hand's width from his body, and he threw his weight behind the parry, forcing his opponent off balance. He aimed a sweeping slice at the lord's exposed lower legs, but Nar Veilan recovered in time to turn the attack away.

Jacques immediately cut his sword at Nar Veilan's head and was blocked again.

The elven lord was quick on the defense, but what about his attack?

He grunted and cut his blade at Jacques, to left and right, then left and right again, Jacques engaging with powerful blows of his sword, then countering with lower cuts aimed at the knees of his opponent.

No matter where Jacques attacked, Nar Veilan defended easily and launched counter attacks that Jacques defended only with increasing difficulty. He was being drawn into more desperate maneuvers and getting tired. This had to end—and soon.

Jacques attacked with an aggressive series of swipes, then parried Nar Veilan's last defense, moved in closer, and swept his opponent's heels from under him when the lord was off balance. He went down with the tip of Jacques's blade at his throat.

Jacques stared down at the elven lord, who glared back at him.

"This is a fight to the death," Nar Veilan said, his lip curled. "Finish it!"

Jacques was undecided about what to do. His code of honor decreed he let his opponent live, but this was war, and the dragon lord a key strength of the *Sis Lenweri*. Taking him prisoner wasn't an option in the middle of a battle. Kill him, and it would be a significant blow.

Jacques sighed and pressed the weight of his body to the tip of the blade. It sank into the lord's throat. The sneering features relaxed, and the light in his eyes died.

There was a scream from the assembled *Sis Lenweri* as they attacked with renewed vigor after the death of their leader.

"To me! To me!" Jacques cried, desperate to recover his horse, but mounted *Sis Lenweri* surrounded him. None of his honor guard had moved quickly enough to reach him. He grabbed Nar Veilan's sword from his dead fingers, preparing to swing two blades and keep the riders at bay. It wasn't much of a defense, certainly not against an arrow, but it was the best he could do.

Jacques began swirling the two blades around his body, slowly revolving in the hope he could see where the first attack would come from. In the end, it came at his back, but luck ensured he deflected the blade of his enemy before it could cut deeply.

It stung across his side as he twirled, and his second blade sliced the elf's head from his shoulders. Thank the Goddess for ponies! But for the beast's shorter stature, he wouldn't have had the reach.

He pushed the spasming body from the saddle and vaulted up, dropping the elven blade as he did, and grabbing the reins. He charged forward, not enjoying viewing the world from the shorter horse.

All around was chaos as his soldiers fought to reach him. The cut on his left side dripped a steady life-leaching flow. He needed it stitched and soon. Seeing a gap, he kicked the pony through it and into a pack of elven foot soldiers, relieved so see they were *Lenweri* by the white bands on their arms.

He rode into their midst, and they advanced, shields held before them, swords glinting in the last rays of the sun.

"I'm glad to see you!" Jacques said, pulling his pony to a stop and glancing over his shoulder. His guard fought for their lives, still unable to come to him. Then he looked again at the elves around him, noticing there were no females among them. That could be chance, but....

Two elves grabbed his reins, and another two pulled him out of the saddle, pushing him face down in the mud.

"Stupid human! Did you never think your white bands could be used thus?"

They all laughed. "Prepare to die," another said."

They let go of him, and he rolled over. He'd meet his end face to face, not stabbed in the back.

A pity he wouldn't see Gwaethe again in this life...

The *Sis Lenweri* closest to him lifted his sword to run him through—then staggered and dropped. In the space left by the fallen enemy, Gwaethe appeared, bow drawn, her honor guard and Exmund with her. In seconds, all the enemy foot soldiers around him lay dead.

Jacques pushed himself up. "Excellent timing, Princess," he said, taking the reins of his horse from Exmund.

She rolled her eyes. "Do not place yourself in that position again, husband. We are not fighting in your honor-bound homeland, but with ruthless elves who value nothing but winning."

Jacques climbed into his saddle. He bowed to her. "Thank you for your rescue. Now I must seek the healer before I bleed to death."

Gwaethe's eyes widened as she spied the blood dripping from his side. "Exmund, see to your master," she commanded." I should gather our people before darkness falls. We must regroup and form a plan for night fighting."

She whirled her stallion and trotted to the southwest, shouting for her force to join her.

Jacques turned and headed northeast to their camp. Suddenly, he was too weary to think properly. He concentrated on staying in the saddle and welcomed Exmund's presence beside him.

"What do you think, Exmund?" he asked. "Have we won the day?"

"We are even, I think, Sir, though Nar Veilan's death was a blow to them. I hear he was their most experienced dragon trainer." Exmund paused, and then continued. "Whatever Princess Gwaethe says, you did well, Sir."

* * *

Gwaethe gathered her people to the east of the enemy force. They had struck a blow at the rear of the *Sis Lenweri*, but the battle still raged at the front. They had to move further up or slide past somehow.

Faenwelar would come at them from the east. If she could advance before then, she could block him from joining forces with Gorin's soldiers.

"It is too risky, Princess," Syndra said. "We will be squeezed between the two *Sis Lenweri* forces."

"Perhaps we can use the males among us to confuse the *Sis Lenweri*," Gwaethe said. "I've had our people collecting armor from the fallen enemy. If we dress our males in that, they can infiltrate the enemy posing as their own soldiers and do untold damage. They may even make it all the way to Gorin himself." She paused to consider. "That would make me regretful, though—that bastard is *mine* to kill."

"Forget your vendetta," Syndra said, as she drew her sword over the sharpening stone. "It will only lead to your risking death, and you are too valuable."

Gwaethe stood and approached her. "I need to do this, or his face will haunt me for the rest of my days. His death is all I dream of."

"It's a mistake," Syndra said.

Gwaethe's temper threatened to get the better of her. She breathed deeply, trying to get it under control. When she was calm again, she spoke.

"You are not my counselor, Syndra. From now on, only speak to me when I ask for your opinion."

Anger smoldered in Syndra's eyes, but she remained silent.

Syndra's sword gliding over the whetstone put Gwaethe's nerves on edge, so she called some of her guard to her, and they mounted their horses.

"I'm going to find Jacques," she said, riding into the night.

Gwaethe found her husband sitting at the fire beside the medical wagon, looking relaxed. Although she was glad to see him hale and healthy, anger simmered in her gut at the risk he had taken. Having witnessed the last stages of his fight with Nar Veilan, she had been certain he was doomed when that circle of riders closed in on him.

"I see you are feeling better," she said, sitting beside him. Her hand moved of its own accord to touch his injured side, feeling the thick bandage there.

Exmund brought her food. "Are you hungry, Princess?"

She nodded to the young sergeant and took the offered stew. "Was it you who tended to him then?"

Exmund nodded. "I wouldn't allow anyone else unless it be Lady Alique or Princess Benae herself. I may not be the finest healer, but I have Lord Vorasava's best interests at heart."

"A 'jack of all trades', that's you, Exmund," Jacques said, his voice sending shivers up her spine.

How long had it been since they had lain together? A week? Longer?

At this rate, she would *never* conceive, though Jacques didn't expect them to be blessed with children. Still, her own half-brother was proof that relations between the two peoples did sometimes result in children.

Gwaethe smiled up at Exmund. "I can't think of anyone I would rather entrust him to. You have proven your worth time and again. Take your rest. Tomorrow will be another long day."

Exmund bowed and left them alone, sitting on their log, staring at the fire.

"I meant what I said about you not taking part in duels again," she said. "It's unwise and unnecessary. You were lucky to win, let alone escape the aftermath."

"It seemed like a good idea at the time."

"And you have been longing to test yourself against a blade master, which Nar Veilan was. Are you satisfied now?"

He stared into her eyes. "I almost spared him."

Terror leaped up and seized her heart. "That would have been fatally foolish!" She stood and lay her empty bowl on the log, then paced up and down before the fire. "Can I not trust you to look after yourself for even half a day?"

He stood and came to her, wrapping his arms around her. "But I *didn't* spare him. You don't need to lecture me." His blue eyes shone down on her, stirring love that she felt she must dampen. "Think what you'll do to my credibility if you're overheard."

She shook off his arms. "You are not taking this seriously. I must have your promise that you will do whatever it takes to return whole to me, otherwise how can I fight this war?"

She began pacing again, batting away his hands when he tried to restrain her.

"Gwaethe." His voice was commanding this time, brooking no dissent. When he used that tone, it reminded her that he too was a leader and used to being obeyed. "Stop pacing and come here."

She kept walking for a little longer before returning to him. After all, as a princess, she wasn't required to instantly obey her husband.

He took her hands in his. "This is war. People die. We must both come to terms with the possibility of one losing the other in this conflict." He fixed her gaze. "I'd never place chains on you. You must fight as you see fit, and I must hope you are skilled and lucky enough to survive. Just as you should trust that I'll do the same."

As he stared at her, she wondered how she could ever survive if death took him from her.

But he was right. She could not constrain him, nor should she.

"I will pray each day to your Goddess and to my own gods that you will be safe, my love."

"And I'll do the same," he said, leading her back to the log.

They sat, arms around each other, enjoying the closeness of the moment until Gwaethe could delay no longer.

"We must make a new battle plan."

"How goes it?" Jacques asked, playing with her fingers.

"When I left, there was still fighting at the front between the Brightcastle forces and Gorin's. When we pulled back, the *Sis Lenweri* rear advanced, but, by now, surely the enemy will have made camp for the night."

"There's no guarantee of that. They see almost as well by night as by day. It would be to their advantage to fight on."

"Except," Gwaethe said, "they need rest. And I think they will take it." Her dark eyes met his. "I have an idea, one suggested by the trick the *Sis Lenweri* played on you. I've had *Sis Lenweri* helmets and armor collected from the battlefield. Some of our males will disguise themselves in them and infiltrate the enemy, taking out key commanders during the night hours."

Jacques's eyes flared in the fire. "Brilliant! Have you enacted this?"

She shook her head. "I have some individuals in mind but wanted to discuss it with you. It could turn the tide of this battle. We could also employ it when Faenwelar's force arrives. That is the other topic I wished to discuss."

"Go on," Jacques said.

"Most of my fighters are now camped to the east of the battlefield. We can proceed to the south on the morrow. It will take us perhaps a half-day to skirt the eastern flank of the enemy and join with the part of Kain's force that has occupied that side. Or we can stay behind and harry the rear of the *Sis Lenweri* as we have today. If we move up the eastern flank, we risk being caught between Gorin and Faenwelar when he arrives."

Jacques rubbed his chin with his thumb and forefinger. "And the western flank seems to have also been occupied by Kain's people. Why don't you consult your brother? He must be in the thick of things even as we speak."

She grabbed his face and kissed him long and hard. She almost forgot where they were until his hands caught her elbows. He gently pried her lips from his.

"As much as I'd like to continue this, my love, you need to speak to Kain sooner rather than later."

Cold reality dimmed her desire, and she sighed. "You are right. Let me see if he can speak."

She closed her eyes, clutching the ring that allowed her to communicate magically with her brother.

Kain Arenil, can you hear me? We must talk.

She instantly felt awareness through the bond they shared when they used the jewelry to connect. There was also irritation.

Why must he always be angry when I try to speak with him? She saw it as an unwillingness to fully accept her. But he *had* stepped into his role as elven prince, so perhaps she was being unfair.

Gwaethe, where are you?

His gruff response ruffled her.

We are camped to the northeast of the enemy. I am making plans for the morrow and would like your input.

Are you sure there's no way the enemy can intercept our communication?

It is safe.

Then tell me your ideas.

My people will infiltrate the enemy masquerading as Sis Lenweri, mainly during the night, and kill their key personnel. It may only be successful for one or two nights. And beware! The enemy wore white armbands and used this tactic against Jacques today. He barely escaped with his life.

Excellent idea. We had contemplated it ourselves but sustained heavy losses during our flight from Selinore and most of those suggested for the role are archers, desperately needed for that during the day. I can't use them all night and then expect them to shoot straight.

Leave the Sis Lenweri infiltration to us, Gwaethe said. *I have a question for you. What are your plans for the morrow? Where should our forces attack the enemy?*

There was a pause before he answered. *Intelligence tells me the second Sis Lenweri force should arrive late tomorrow, or perhaps early the next day. If I reunite my Lenweri and concentrate on the western flank, and your people attack the eastern, we could severely deplete Gorin's force before Faenwelar arrives. Do you have enough personnel for that?*

It will be a stretch, especially as I wish to continue our attack on the rear of the enemy, Gwaethe said, her mind furiously constructing and discarding battle plans. *However, with the help of our sabotage activities overnight, I think we can make this work. The more we dominate before the next force arrives, the better we shall be.*

Take care though, Gwaethe. You must not get caught between the two forces. Be ready to withdraw later in the day tomorrow.

I hear you. What of the dragons? What are your plans?

We've had two fly over, and lost men and horses. We intend to draw the fighting closer to our trenches and the castle walls, so we have more defense. Our archers are stationed on the walls, so we can shoot both enemy soldiers and dragons.

Vivid images of fire-breathing dragons and men dying in trenches swamped Gwaethe's mind, and she slumped for a moment. Jacques's hand landed on her shoulder, its warmth penetrating the layers of her clothing and reminding her she was not alone.

I wish you success, luck and safety, Brother, she said, withdrawing the contact before he could answer.

"What troubles you?" Jacques asked, his hand continuing to massage the tight muscles of her neck and shoulder. "Was it bad news?"

She shook her head. "No more than expected. It just dawned on me the magnitude of our enemy, with dragons to contend with and our force so splintered."

"Their force is fragmented, too," Jacques said, turning her to face him. "And we have right on our side."

"Right doesn't always win out. If you ask Gorin and Faenwelar, they believe the same thing!" She allowed her head to slump so the top of it rested on his chest. "When will we ever be truly free to love and laugh?"

Jacques raised her chin with gentle pressure under its point. "Head up, my love. We will decide this in a matter of days, and then you and I will secure a romantic getaway. I may even take you to visit my parents."

She smiled. "Doesn't sound very romantic, if you ask me. I was thinking of a week alone in that hunting lodge of yours."

"Now you're talking." He leaned forward and kissed her, passion in his cobalt blue eyes. "I love you, Princess Gwaethe Arenil."

"And I you, consort," she said, laughing as his body snapped backward. "One day, we must find you a proper title."

"All in good time, my dear," Jacques said, pulling her back for another kiss.

CHAPTER SIX

KAIN ignored the curious looks of the ladies, including Princess Benae, who were currently patching his wounds. His talk with Gwaethe had been hugely profitable. Perhaps he should revise his attitude toward this form of communication.

His gaze swept the makeshift hospital in the keep's forecourt and fell upon Benae.

She commanded the place like a general would a battlefield. He could use a dozen like her in his command.

She had to be exhausted. As far as he knew, she'd been at this from before dawn to now, when it was nearing midnight.

"Princess," he said. "You need rest. Anyone can see to me. I urge you to repair to your quarters and sleep."

Her intelligent green gaze narrowed on him. "You're critical to our cause, Prince Arenil. I would not allow your care to fall to one unskilled. Some of those wounds are deep and may fester if poorly managed."

She continued to supervise the bandaging of his wounds, especially those which had been stitched, then lay her hands over the injured areas and closed her eyes. "I'll pray over you now."

As she did so, the faintest tingling echoed in his arm and leg where the most serious wounds lay. He could be imagining it... the Goddess knew he was exhausted... but he didn't think so. After the prayer,

Princess Benae stepped back, staggering as she did so, and Kain stood to steady her. He felt far less tired than he had before her attention.

"Go to your bed, Your Highness," he said. "Your job here is done."

An old noblewoman approached and took Benae's arm. "Here Princess, drink this mulled wine. It will warm and restore you." The woman looked at Kain. "Thank you, Your Highness. Princess Benae will be with me. I'll see she gets her rest."

He nodded and watched as the woman led Benae away, seated her on a bale of straw, and made her drink the wine. The princess argued with the older woman, but it had no effect. He smiled, but then Princess Alecia blocked the view.

"Kain, how are you?" she asked, limping up to him.

"I could ask you the same. What happened?"

"Nothing that will slow me down. I've just come from the tactics meeting. Your suggestion of drawing the enemy toward the trenches has been accepted."

"I should've been there," he said. "I have more information to impart to them. My sister has contacted me and advised of her location and plans. They align with ours."

Alecia placed her hand on his shoulder, but her empathy failed to calm his frustration.

"It was imperative you get your wounds tended to," she said, softly.

He pointed his chin at the noblewoman who was tending to Benae. "Who's that older woman with the princess?"

Alecia's brows rose, and she turned to look where he indicated. "Oh, that's Lady Henrietta. She's my advisor. Why do you ask?"

He shook his head. "There's something about her that makes me itch." He frowned deeper and shook his head, trying to dispel the unease the old woman imparted. He grunted. "It appears Princess Benae finds her a nuisance."

"She would do well to listen to Lady Henrietta. Benae has pushed herself too hard this day. How can she hope to survive if she continues to disregard her mortality?"

Kain switched his gaze to Alecia. "And when will you decide if Princess Benae and her husband are friend or foe? You as good as say to me you don't trust her, but then push me into her hands for healing. I don't understand."

Alecia's clear lavender gaze fell upon him. She had something special about her that touched him, that signaled she was honorable and true, though she held secrets aplenty.

"Benae cares deeply for her patients. You're in expert hands. It's only her leadership credentials and her honesty I query, and I'm right to do so since she occupies the place I'm owed by right of birth."

"This again!" Ramón Zorba had approached unobserved and heard Alecia's last words. "I came to speak with Prince Arenil, but find I've been beaten to it." The Guardian's narrowed gaze fell upon Alecia, then he glanced at Kain. "You appear the better for a rest, Your Highness."

Kain inclined his head. "I have word from Princess Gwaethe." He explained her location and covert plans for the night, as well as the quarters they would each target the next day. "I think it will work well, until the *Sis Lenweri* arrive from Wildecoast."

Ramón nodded. "I'd like you to attend the strategy meeting just before daybreak, Kain. You can explain your tactics then, however, I don't see any issues. In the meantime, take your rest." He looked around at Benae. "I intend to take my wife off to her bed. She's dead on her feet."

He bowed to them and stalked away, intent on prizing Benae from her seat on the straw.

Alecia turned back to Kain. "Perhaps you should stay in your quarters in the keep tonight." She looked over his shoulder at the four elves who lurked in the keep's shadow near the servant's entrance. "I can have pallets made up for your guard, so they can stay in your sitting room."

Kain stood, stiffening muscles screaming at him to take the princess up on her offer. It had been a long day.

"I don't think my guard would be at ease in the keep, and I should return to my lodgings. I want to check on casualties and discuss tactics for the morrow."

Her eyes clouded with what appeared to be concern. "That will give you, at best, two hours of rest, Kain. You can't treat your body like that and expect to survive this war."

He stared down at her. "If I were you, I'd follow my own advice and take rest, Alecia. I'm sure your daughter needs you even more than the kingdom does."

He bowed and signaled his guard. They made their way out of the keep forecourt and down the street, another dozen members of his guard joining them outside the keep grounds.

* * *

Alecia shook her head at the stubbornness of men and went to fetch Hetty. She found her friend arguing with one of Benae's healers over what herb was better in the poultice she was making.

"Come along, Lady Henrietta," Alecia said. "We both need our rest." She took Hetty's arm and led her into the keep, climbing the staircase to the wing where her room lay.

"These young things have no idea about proper healing," Hetty grumbled.

Alecia sighed. "I may not agree with Benae in many things," she said, the aches and twinges making themselves felt as she pushed herself up the stairs, "but the woman knows her herbs and healing. Leave it alone."

Alecia's body screamed for rest, and her heart longed to hold her daughter. But Iona would be asleep in the lower reaches of the keep, well-guarded along with Solomon. She couldn't disturb her now. Perhaps she would have time to visit her in the morning.

They entered the chamber to a welcoming fire in the grate and a meal of bread, cheese, and wine set out on the low table in the sitting room.

Alecia threw off her cloak and hung the heavy garment on a hook before removing her boots. What she wouldn't give for a hot bath. She'd just have to settle for dinner, a fire, and a glass of wine.

Hetty followed her lead, and they were soon halfway through their repast. Food helped ease some of the tiredness from Alecia's body, but she must seek her bed soon if she was to perform at her best tomorrow.

"How do you fare?" Hetty asked, her dark eyes taking inventory.

She sighed. "I'm doing as well as can be expected. Just as our army is. I'd say we're even with Gorin. And Gwaethe and Jacques's force should really make themselves felt over the next twenty-four hours."

"And then?"

"Faenwelar will arrive with the Wildecoast force hot on his heels. Hopefully, Vard will have done some damage to Faenwelar on the way to us."

"And *then*?"

Alecia flew to her feet. "Would you stop saying that? How should I know? Somehow, we must ensure we vanquish the *Sis Lenweri*, so they never again pose a threat." She fixed Hetty with the look she used when trying to convince soldiers of her worth. Somehow, it didn't feel as potent when Hetty was the object. "We'll win, Hetty. I'll make sure of that. And then I'll take on the role I was born to—no matter what Vard, Ramón, or any of them have to say."

Hetty smiled and nodded. "You'll need every bit of that determination and a lot more. I want you to remember those words when the doubt creeps in. And it will—many more times than you can imagine."

Alecia nodded and turned to stare at the fire. "There's one thing I'm concerned about. Those blasted dragons. Kain has dealt with one, but there are three more. We're lucky they haven't played a more dominant role. I can only think the dragons or the lords who ride them are unwilling to risk themselves for the *Sis Lenweri*, or that they've been trying to spare their own soldiers. Regardless, it surely can't last. At some point, perhaps when it appears the enemy is losing, those beasts will attack, and we must be ready."

She fell silent, thinking of a recent dream she had had. Archers had aimed exploding arrows at their foes. Had it been a true dream? Or just her vivid imagination?

"Hetty?" she said, still forming the plan in her head. "Do you know anything about exploding powder?"

Hetty huffed. "What on earth are you talking about, girl?"

Alecia knelt before her old friend. "I've had a dream. Soldiers on battlements were shooting arrows loaded with a tube of something with a burning wick. When the arrows landed, the tubes would explode with devastating effects. Do you know of anything which could do that?"

Hetty's eyes narrowed. "I have an old recipe that uses charcoal, sulfur, and saltpeter, which might do what you say. But it would be dangerous. The combination is unstable. It might kill people just mixing it."

Alecia's heart raced with excitement. "But just think! If we could roll such a mixture into a light casing and set a wick in it. Depending on the length of the wick, it could go off at the perfect time to kill or maim one of those dragons."

"Now isn't the time to be experimenting, Alecia. We need tried-and-true tactics."

"How can we have proven tactics against a beast we've never seen? We must try this. On the morrow, I want you to set about procuring the ingredients, and, under your supervision, we'll make this exploding powder. Then watch how those dragons like it when we shoot it at them!"

Alecia went to her rest, almost too excited to sleep. Luckily, exhaustion dragged her under within moments of her head touching the pillow.

The next morning found Alecia late to the leader's conference, held before dawn in the small audience hall. Breakfast was served and the talks beginning as she walked in with Lin and Hetty. All fell quiet as she and her ladies seated themselves.

Ramón nodded to her and some of the army commanders stood until she had settled. She looked around the hall but failed to see Kain.

Dammit! She needed him to support her crazy scheme, for that's what the commanders would think it. Perhaps even Kain would be skeptical.

Ramón was assessing their losses and gains from yesterday's battle.

"All in all," he said, "I believe we took fewer losses than the *Sis Lenweri*, though our wounded numbers are high. At least half of them won't fight again in this war. However, I'll devise ways for them to help where they can."

Estevot stood. "Very good, My Lord. I was wondering where Prince Arenil is this morning. You invited him to this council, did you not?"

Ramón nodded. "I did. I'm sure he'll be here. His Highness is carrying at least two injuries which may prevent him from fighting today."

As he said those words, Kain strode into the hall with barely a limp despite his leg injury. "Good morning," he said, bowing towards Alecia. "I'm sorry I'm late. I took a tour of the battlefield this morning and got drawn into a skirmish." He smirked as he said the words. "It was difficult to drag myself away." He moved to stand beside Ramón.

"Oh?" Estevot said. "So how goes the war this morning?"

"There have been significant developments overnight," Kain said. "Gwaethe Arenil's operatives have infiltrated the enemy camp and killed some of the *Sis Lenweri*'s key people. These include another of the dragon lords and Prince Gorin's second in command."

There were loud exclamations at this news, and Estevot stepped forward. "How do you know this?"

Kain smiled. "I'm in close contact with my sister. She advised me last night that she'd try this trick and also that her husband had been deceived by *Sis Lenweri* wearing the white bands. He is well, but she warned us to be watchful of the same stunt being played against us. It was what gave her the idea of disguising some of her people as the enemy and infiltrating their camp. She was gathering armor yesterday to help with the disguises."

Ramón laughed. "Your sister is full of good ideas. Will you convey to her our thanks, Your Highness?" He turned to Ramar Reese. "Devise another way of differentiating your people, Reese—perhaps the addition of an emblem to the armbands would work. Just make sure it can't be easily copied."

Reese nodded. "If I might be excused, I will attend to this immediately."

"Do you have other news, Your Highness?" Estevot asked.

Kain cleared his throat. "Gwaethe's force is stationed to the northeast. It's planned that her people will attack from that quarter while ours will continue our northwestern concentration. As discussed yesterday, we'll also lure the enemy further south, closer to the trenches and the walls of the keep. It will take our cavalry out of play to a certain degree, but they'll still be effective on both flanks."

Alecia stood, interrupting Kain. "More importantly, it will mean our archers can attack the enemy soldiers and perhaps the dragons if they're used."

Estevot snorted. "If we see the dragons again. There's a reason they're holding back. Hopefully the dragon lords or the dragons themselves have rebelled. Perhaps the loss of the black dragon has made them cautious."

"That's possible, Captain," Kain said. "However, I wouldn't discount them yet. I plan to install our best archers on all the walls of the keep, not just the northern wall. If we can lure the enemy just a hundred paces closer, we could harm them greatly. If any of the dragons fly close enough to the keep, there's a chance there as well."

Alecia had remained standing amid curious stares from some attendees, including Ramón. Though Ramón was probably more anxious than curious.

"I have an idea."

She was sure she heard Ramón groan, but it could've been Estevot.

"I think my idea will make the arrows more effective at killing and maiming."

Estevot folded his arms. "Princess Alecia, I must protest."

She widened her eyes. "You don't wish to hear an idea that could give us an edge against our enemy?"

"I'd like to hear what she has to say, Estevot," Kain said, "if you don't mind."

Estevot threw his hands in the air and sat down.

Alecia smiled at Kain and moved to the side of the room where she could see her audience. "There's a substance which, if ignited, would cause a minor explosion. If we could wrap this powder inside a parchment tube and strap it to an arrow behind the head, with a wick that could be lit by a taper, then the powder will explode sometime later, depending on the length of the wick. It would be tricky to get the balance right. Also, the length of the wick would need to be judged, so it didn't ignite the powder too soon."

She looked around to find stunned expressions from almost every attendee, including Lin, with whom she hadn't shared the idea. They recovered quickly and scowls settled on many faces.

"It *could* work," Kain said, slowly. "But why not use gunpowder such as the navy uses in its cannons?" He turned to Estevot. "Do we have gunpowder available?"

Estevot shook his head. "Not in Brightcastle. If this strategy is to be applied, we'll need the princess's fabled powder." The man wore a slight smirk and Alecia worked hard to maintain a pleasant expression. *Damn him!*

"Where would we get this powder?" Kain asked Alecia.

She smiled. "I can get my hands on some."

Kain nodded. "We wouldn't wish the projectiles to fall on our own people or go off before we released them. But if we could get it right, it could cause damage to a dragon more easily than trying to shoot an eye."

"Are you willing to take ownership of this idea, Prince Arenil?" Alecia asked. "I'll have my archers join forces with yours, and they can work together."

Kain nodded. "Morlynn can take control of this project. He can supervise the construction of the incendiary devices and the practice. Thank you for your input, Princess."

Alecia sat down, and Lin leaned over to whisper in her ear. "That was brilliant, Alecia, but next time make sure you tell me. *I'm* your advisor, and I see from her lack of surprise that Lady Henrietta knew."

Hetty raised her chin. "Perhaps I'm just better at hiding my emotions, Lady Linnet."

Lin's jaw tightened, but she remained silent.

Alecia looked up to find Ramón frowning at her.

What's his problem now?

He cleared his throat and addressed the room.

"Yes, I thank Princess Alecia for her idea and give permission for Your Highness to develop the weapon. Now, I wish to discuss what will happen later today, that is, the arrival of the second enemy force. Faenwelar's army is said to be larger than Gorin's. We must impart whatever damage we can to Gorin while we can."

There was a brief discussion on strategy, and a plan to reconvene in the early afternoon. Most of the war leaders strode from the room once dismissed, grabbing food to take with them. Alecia was preparing to do just that when Ramón hailed her.

She stopped and bid Hetty find Iona and Solomon, then turned back to Ramón. His eyes held a certain tension she didn't usually see when she was the subject of his interest.

"How is Benae this morning?" she asked.

Ramón ran his hands through his hair, and then forced them down to his sides. "She was up before the dawn and down to the infirmary." His jaw tightened. "She works herself too hard, and I'm worried about her." His gaze snapped to Alecia. "Just as you cause me concern. Where did you get the idea for the arrows?"

She regarded him casually. "Does it matter? Who can say where inspiration may come from? I just woke up one morning with the idea in my head. I think it can work with a little trial and error."

"Are you trying to make me look incompetent?" he snapped.

She frowned at him. "No! I'm trying to do everything I can to win this war, just as we all are. Do you wish for me to keep my ideas to myself? Or perhaps I should just act on them without telling the leaders? Would that be better?"

Damn him! This war wasn't all about Ramón and his ego. Yes, she'd use the conflict to advance her cause, but the future of the kingdom was too important to play power games with.

He frowned deeply at her, his blue eyes troubled. "Of course, I don't want that! I'm just trying to understand you. Most ladies wouldn't be thinking up battle strategy and creating new weapons."

She quirked one brow at him. "You know me better than that! I've long been a woman of action. It's not in my nature to sit meekly and allow the men to make the decisions and take all the risks."

Ramón considered for a moment. "I suppose you're right. Benae isn't so different. She just shows her courage in different ways."

As to that, Alecia wouldn't comment. She nodded. "If that's all, I'll take my leave."

"Alecia!" Ramón called, as she made her way to the door. "I'll look out for you on the battlefield."

She stiffened but nodded and left the room.

CHAPTER SEVEN

VARD walked from the adjacent forest back to camp, his mind full of strategy and doubt. But there was no room for uncertainty this day. Rational plans would see them through to the start of the next stage of their conflict with the *Sis Lenweri*, specifically Faenwelar's force. By the end of the day, the enemy would arrive at the Brightcastle battlefield with Vard's force at least three hours behind.

His mind fleetingly lingered on Alecia and Iona. How would his love respond to the conflict on her doorstep? He was certain he knew, and it terrified him. But his father would risk his own life to keep Alecia safe, and Vard held onto that thought.

He found James Tomel waiting for him when he entered his tent.

The man bowed, his brow creased, and a muscle twitching in his jaw. "Lord Anton," he said, "when did you last see Lady Star?"

"We spoke briefly last night."

"How was she?"

"Lady Star is a remarkable woman and her charges equally so. She'll survive this war if anyone can."

James took a deep breath. "I ask you to let me go, so I can watch over her."

Sam Delacost barged into the tent. "I want to go with him. It's what Esta would wish."

Vard raised his hands. "Gentlemen, do you hear what you're asking? This is a war. As much as we'd like to protect our families, it's not usually possible." They couldn't argue with that, considering he had no way of protecting Alecia and Iona.

They both started talking at once, and Vard threw up his hands to halt the tirade.

"I've been in the forest scouting since before daylight, and I intend to fill my belly. You can join me and talk as we eat, but… one at a time." He turned and poured tea from the pot on the rough table. After a large mouthful of the hot brew, he buttered two slabs of bread and layered them with honey.

The food did wonders for his temper, and, as the other men followed his lead, Vard sat back and sipped his tea.

James went first. "I'm not doing much tied to your apron strings, Vard. I can be much more use protecting Katrine." He lowered his voice on her name, so it wouldn't carry beyond the tent. "She's valuable to our cause, after all."

Vard swallowed a bite of bread and took a large slurp of tea. "What makes you believe she *needs* protecting? Lady Star's more able to defend herself than most women I know."

"That's true, but there's always a chance of injury and death in war, even for the best warrior. And Lady Star will be a target because of her hounds. From what you say, they've been inflicting grave losses on the *Sis Lenweri* each night."

Vard nodded. "That they have, and your words are true."

"Well," James said, "I can stay by her side and watch her back. You know I won't leave her until the risk is over. Your promise to the king will be honored."

"My promise is dust, anyway. It died with the king. I was merely trying to avoid the anger of the military leaders and nobility. Now they have the war to distract them, I think they'll have other priorities." He failed to add that, as the new king, he could pardon James if he pleased.

James nodded. "Then you'll grant me this boon? To protect my wife?"

"It will be dangerous, James," Vard said. "*You* may lose your life. What will I say to Lady Star if that happens? She'll have my hide!"

He grinned. "Yes, she will, so I'll have to make sure I survive, so you can keep your skin."

Vard nodded wearily. "Go find her but be careful. If you can send me reports twice daily, that would be appreciated."

James stood, his face sober. "You won't regret this, Vard."

Vard smiled. "I will if you get yourself killed."

James nodded, shook Sam's hand, and departed.

Sam turned and fixed Vard with an unusually serious look. "I'm not joking about wanting to go with James. We're married to sisters, and my wife would want me to do everything in my power to keep Katrine safe."

Vard cleared his throat. "Use her alias, if you please, or lower your voice. The woman risks much by aiding us."

"I'm sorry. Passion overtook my caution. It happens a lot. But think how much safer she will be with two of us watching her."

Vard shook his head. "Stop right there. I'm not letting you go with him. You're too valuable as a fighter. What is it with you men who have married the Aranati sisters? You've both incurred the king's wrath and lived to fight another day. Don't push your luck."

"You let James go."

"What else would James do? He's not a fighter, he's an intelligence man." He saw Sam was about to launch into another plea and held up his hand. "You're not going, and that's my final decision. See that our horses are ready and send a man to pull down this tent. I don't wish to be late to the party."

Sam pursed his lips. He gave Vard a look that promised he had not heard the last of this.

Vard prayed James and Katrine would be safe, but he wasn't about to allow Sam to join their group. The man was too damned valuable as a fighter.

As the ex-pirate stalked from the tent, Vard prayed to the Goddess that he wouldn't lose too many good men and women before they won the war.

Vard rode at the head of the force, talking to Merielle. Sam and Nikolas were nearby. It seemed everyone wanted something from him.

Except General Formosa.

The surly military man had been studiously avoiding Vard since departing Wildecoast. It would've made him nervous, except he had a spy in Formosa's camp who would inform him of any mutinous talk—which there would be if the man got wind of what King Beniel had done.

"But I don't wish to ride up the front," Merielle was saying, a code for "she had no wish to be near her husband." It seemed Nikolas Cosara was too protective and cramped her style. "I want to move where I am most needed. Surely you can see that is the best use of my skills?"

"Lady," Vard sighed, "I can't allow you to venture out without a guard. Keeping you close to me and the admiral is the best way of ensuring you aren't killed!" Impatience was sapping Vard's good humor. "Now, please follow orders and find your allocated position."

She scowled and turned her horse away.

As she left, Cosara took her place.

Vard looked heavenward, pretending to check the skies when he was really seeking expression for his temper.

"Thank you, Anton." Nikolas said.

Vard's head snapped to look at him. "Pardon?"

"Thank you for not granting my lady's request. She'd be too exposed."

Vard grunted. "Lady Merielle is a valuable fighter. And she'd attract more attention than any of the men should she rove as she wishes. The *Sis Lenweri* would pick her off in a moment. She's too inexperienced to realize there are rules she needs to follow."

Now it was the admiral's turn to grunt. "She has always had trouble with rules. When I met her, she had broken her family's rules, and she's never stopped since."

Vard's ears pricked. "Oh?"

"Never mind," Nikolas said. "What do you think this day will bring?"

"The scouts say Faenwelar's force will arrive at the battlefront toward dusk. If they're smart, they'll make camp and attack during the night or just before dawn."

"Do you believe that's what will happen?"

Vard shrugged. "Who can know? The elves are a strange race, and the *Sis Lenweri* the oddest of the variants. Even Ruven doesn't know."

"Doesn't know or won't tell you," Nikolas said.

Vard slanted a look at him. "That will be enough of that talk. I've spent a deal of time with Ruven, and I'm pretty good at judging a person. I trust him."

Nikolas raised his brows. "And you estimate we're three to four hours behind Faenwelar?"

Vard nodded. "We won't be fighting today, but we'll stay flexible in our preparations. Tell your units to ensure their weapons and armor are ready, and they rest their mounts by walking them when they can."

"Of course," Nikolas said. "How did you do it?"

"I beg your pardon?"

"How did you convince the king you were worthy of the trust he placed in you? On the balance of your experience and achievements, there's no way you should lead this force. And yet here you are."

"That's not really your business."

Nikolas tilted his head to the side. "You're a man of certain… talents… Did you compel him? No wonder he was so suspicious of magic."

Vard made his voice cold. "Admiral, I'll answer this once, and then you're never to ask me again. I did *not* compel the king. If you're looking for the reason he trusted me, look no further than the queen, and my relationship with their niece. Perhaps I proved myself in ways others did not."

Now it was Nikolas's turn for a frigid look. "I'll expose you one day, and then you won't be able to dig yourself out of the muck you'll be in."

He kicked his horse forward, moving up to where some of the cavalry commanders rode. Vard was left on his own—just how he liked it.

* * *

"To me! To me!" Alecia screamed as she fought off the attack from a *Sis Lenweri*. By the elf's insignias, it was another senior soldier, perhaps a Ramar. Was she being targeted?

She blocked a savage cut and swept the blade high before spurring Silver forward out of range while she caught her breath. Her shoulder burned with fatigue, and she wondered again if she could beat this foe.

He fought with an icy determination that unnerved her. Alecia's technique relied on speed and passion to bring out her best, but her endurance suffered. She swept her gaze to the elf she had just avoided and was relieved to see that Lin had engaged him. Ramón trotted up to her.

"Off the field. You need a rest. Go and see how the archers fare." He looked at Lyam. "Anton, guard the princess with your life."

His order infuriated her, but she was aware enough to see he was right. He swept in and engaged her earlier opponent, now Lin's, while Alecia extricated Lin, Arelle and Cretia. The five galloped for the keep, imparting some damage on the way. They were laughing by the time they rode through the narrow northern gate.

"It's going well today," Lin said, dismounting.

"That it is, My Lady," Lyam said, his eyes serious, "but the princess takes too many risks." Lyam turned to Alecia. "How will I explain to Vard, my failure to protect you, should the worse happen?"

Alecia sobered and placed herself in the man's position. Lyam had saved her skin more than once today as she fought like a woman possessed.

She stepped closer and took his hands, an action which made him stiffen. "I truly appreciate your efforts to ensure my safety, Lyam. I hear you and will give more consideration to the risks I take." She dropped his hands and Lyam nodded, bowed and stalked away.

A wave of weariness hit Alecia as she watched him disappear. Would he report all this to Vard? But she believed Lyam was the type to leave the past in the past. He had conducted himself with dignity, leaving her to behave as she saw fit on the battlefield—up until that small protest. He was a good man and had shown her nothing but respect. She would do her best to minimize the risks to herself.

Grooms led their horses off, and they found food and a place in the shelter of the wall to eat and drink.

Alecia retraced the battle in her head. It had been in full swing by the time she and her ladies arrived, the *Sis Lenweri* fighting with a savagery more intense than yesterday.

She didn't understand the tactic, since the impending arrival of Faenwelar's force should have meant Gorin's soldiers would delay confrontation as much as possible, conserving their people until reinforcements could arrive.

She shook her head. "Do you think it strange that Gorin should fight so hard when he could conserve his strength and wait until Faenwelar arrives?"

"I've been wondering about that," Cretia said. "Perhaps they wish to finish us, so they can concentrate on the Wildecoast army."

"But, with the Amitanian allies present, there's no way they can win," Lin said, taking a long pull on her watered wine. "We have the superior numbers."

"Only just," Alecia said. "Princess Gwaethe was planning some covert attack overnight. I wonder if her action created this reckless attack today?"

"I bet that's it!" Cretia said. "She's canny, that one. What was she going to do?"

"I don't know," Alecia said, wary of the information getting back to the enemy.

She stood, stretching out tired muscles for a few moments before heading to the steps up to the wall. The other ladies groaned and followed her.

"You know, ladies," Lin said, "I liked it better when we could please ourselves and didn't have to follow the princess around."

"So did I," Arelle said, "Surely she can look after herself by now?"

Alecia smiled. "Of course, you liked it when no one knew who you were, and you led lives of drudgery and hardship. Anyway, I thought I was looking after you, not the other way."

The ladies rolled their eyes, and all four would've dissolved into laughter had there not been soldiers watching. Alecia had a reputation to uphold, after all.

They stopped at the top of the stairs and scanned the expanse of the four walls, then toward the city below. There was a low hum as hundreds of souls fed the war machine with their labors. But Alecia's attention was drawn by a line of archers set up at the northern end of the eastern wall. She walked closer and caught the attention of her Ramar Reese. He raised a hand to halt her, finished what he was saying to an elven archer, and walked across to join the ladies.

"Your Highness, happy I am to see you uninjured," Reese said, taking her hand and bowing over it. "Ladies." He smiled at her companions and bowed.

"How goes it, Reese?" Alecia asked.

He rolled his shoulders in the fluid way the elves performed every movement. "We have determined the size of the powder sack which can be carried by the arrow and also the positioning to give the best balance. Now we have set up straw bale targets and are lighting and firing the missiles. So far, they do not explode until they have lodged in the bales a full twenty seconds."

Alecia clapped her hands. "Very good! Isn't that better than going off in mid-flight?"

He nodded. "Of course, yes. However, it will be beneficial if we can get the measurement just right and can vary the length of the wick depending on the distance of our targets."

Lin frowned. "It sounds tricky. Has anyone been hurt?"

Alecia's heart throbbed with shame. She should've thought of that question!

"Only a few minor burns, and one of my archers may lose the sight of one eye."

Alecia gasped. "Where are they? I must get Benae to see them straight away."

Reese put his hand up. "Peace! The warrior has seen Princess Benae, and she has done her best. She remains optimistic she can save the eye."

Alecia swallowed down a small cry of relief. *Really!* She had to toughen up and remind herself of the inevitability of casualties in war.

If *she* were willing to accept the risk, then why shouldn't this injured elven archer? Reese certainly was.

"I won't disturb you further," she said. "Let Kain, er, Prince Arenil know if you need more saltpeter, casings or wicks."

Reese bowed, and Alecia turned away, walking to the north wall and looking out over the battle. They had lured Gorin's force a little closer to the trenches, and, so far, there had been no dragon sightings.

"What're they doing?" she breathed. "Where are the dragons, and what strategy are they pursuing?" Suddenly, she itched to get back to the battle. "Ladies, we need to find our mounts and get back down there."

Lin had gone still, and she grasped Alecia's arm, her fingers digging in until they caused her pain. She faced east and at first Alecia didn't see what had caught her friend's attention.

Then a speck appeared in the sky, getting dramatically larger with each minute that passed. "It's a dragon; gold, I think," Alecia said, swallowing a sharp burst of fear at seeing the beast.

She reefed her arms from Lin's grasp and hurried back to the soldiers on the wall.

"Ramar Reese!" she called. "Incoming dragon. Prepare to defend the keep."

Her words ignited a flurry of activity as archers prepared their missiles, and attendants stoked the fires and packaged more explosives. Their quick fingers moved carefully to wrap the volatile mix in the paper, installing wicks of varying lengths. Other workers made sure tapers were ready to light the wicks when required.

"Princess!" Reese called. "You should be first to shoot! This was your idea. Come! You may use my bow."

Alecia froze at the thought of confronting the beast. It was already so close that she could hear its strange wild cries and see the red spurt of its fire. It could torch her!

Or I could stop standing like a frozen princess and defeat it...

Once decided, she stepped forward and took the bow, listening as Reese fine-tuned her handling of his bow. It was larger than hers but made of lighter wood. The arrows were so well balanced that she hardly noticed the parchment wrapped package strapped behind the head.

As she drew back experimentally, the bow dipped only a little, and she could easily adjust.

"You need to aim a little higher to compensate for the added weight at the head, Princess. Sight your target and then adjust it higher, about so." Reese helped move the bow, so she could see. "We estimate one hundred and fifty paces will be the ideal distance, but a more powerful archer might succeed at two hundred."

Alecia drew a long and calming breath. "The beast will be so close."

"Its fire can hit at least fifty paces from its maw," Reese said, "and at the speed it flies, there is little room for error. It is perilous in the extreme. But these arrows do not need to kill, just maim." He grinned, a wicked glint in his eye. "I cannot wait to see what the beast makes of exploding arrows."

He raised his hand and attendants hurried over with large shields which they propped against the wall nearby.

"If you miss, you will have time for two more attempts. Then you must take shelter behind the fire shields."

Alecia nodded and took herself back through the steps as the flying nightmare loomed nearer. She was vaguely aware of Lin stepping closer, clutching her bow, and asking Reese for pointers. The woman was an excellent shot, and her cool temperament was ideal for the task.

Alecia aimed her arrow at the dragon as it flapped toward her, trying not to think of the beast, but only of a target. She focused a little higher than the golden head, adjusting for the weight of the arrow, the apparent speed of the dragon, the light wind blowing from the west and… her mind was dizzy with calculations. She let instinct rule.

Alecia motioned to the taper boy, drew in a deep breath, let it out all the way, then nodded. The wick lit, she drew back the arrow, sighted, and released.

Rolling her shoulders to remove tension, she watched the flight of the arrow as it fell short, exploding before it hit the ground. The dragon and its riders were oblivious.

"Try again, Princess," Reese said, handing her another loaded arrow. "Same wick and trajectory, just draw back further… to your ear."

She remembered Vard's words all those months ago and nodded.

Lin's arrow had missed too, but she was already sighting and sending another missile at the dragon. It looked so much bigger now.

Alecia nocked an arrow, drawing back to her ear this time. She waited for the wick to be lit, let out her breath, and released. She was a little off her line. The arrow missed the dragon but caught the first rider on the shoulder. There was a minor explosion, and the rider tumbled from the beast, his tunic on fire.

The flight of the dragon slowed, and the beast hovered in midair, its huge sparkling wings beating. An enraged scream issued from its mouth, along with a burst of flame. Alecia saw her chance and reloaded her bow, choosing an arrow with a shorter wick.

She nocked, drew back to her ear, and let fly, the dart soaring straight at the dragon's head. At the last moment, it swung away, and the arrow hit the side of its neck, exploding immediately.

A tremendous cheer came from the archers on the wall, all of whom had been ready to take the beast down if Alecia and Lin missed. As she observed the dragon, it turned northward, screaming its rage as it went. The flame it sent forth was safely discharged over the forest.

The second rider slid into place in front of the wings, beating at the spots of burning scales and powder to extinguish them. She almost felt sorry for the pain she had caused the creature, but it was its life or theirs.

Reese turned to her. "Well done, Princess. That was excellent shooting. It will be some time before that beast attacks again."

"Agreed," Lin said. "Our little experiment has been a success." She cast her eyes in the direction of the dragon, now a speck in the distance.

The battlefield had fallen silent momentarily as combatants from both sides watched the display. Then a loud cry rang from the field and the clash of weapons resumed.

Alecia watched the fighting. Their side seemed renewed by the shooting of the dragon. "Perhaps I've angered it, and it will return with renewed vigor. We can't believe one minor wound will scare it."

"That powder will burn wherever it touches, Princess," Reese said. "The rider will need to tend to his dragon, find a healer, and convince the beast this conflict is worth his life. It will be no simple thing."

She looked at him. "How can you be so sure?"

"Dragons are not dumb animals. It is said they possess a magic of their own, and an intellect at least equal to ours. They are rare and cannot afford to give their lives away lightly."

Lin was scanning the skies as she spoke. "I think Reese is right. When Prince Arenil killed the black dragon, it may have made the others more cautious. They've had the chance to attack in three theaters of war and have only mounted small sorties. They could decimate us but are afraid to expose themselves. Now they'll be even more afraid."

"Let us rather say they will be cautious," Reese said.

"That beast came from the east, from Faenwelar," Alecia said. "He's testing us, announcing his approach. I think he'll be surprised and angry at what has occurred." She turned to Reese. "Gather your archers and redouble your preparations. They must be ready to attack not only dragons, but our enemy. I intend to rejoin the battle and gain what information I can."

Alecia left the wall, her ladies following, and they reclaimed their mounts from the stable. As she trotted out of the gate and past the trenches, she felt more optimistic than she had in weeks. They would be victorious, and she *would* be queen.

CHAPTER EIGHT

GWAETHE had spent the day working her way from the back and the eastern side of the conflict toward the front. They had gained much ground, but she felt an urgency to inflict maximum harm on Gorin's force.

Of Gorin, she had seen nothing. Those infiltrating the camp had been told to bring him to her should they find him. They had seen no sign of the elven leader. Gwaethe wondered if he had fled the battle.

However, even though Gorin had not been apprehended, many other leaders, including the head of Gorin's guard, *had* been killed. Perhaps that was what had spooked the prince into hiding? And the *Sis Lenweri* fought today with a desperate savagery that had been absent the day before. Their discipline was lacking, and she believed the blows they had struck overnight were the cause. That and Gorin's absence.

She glanced at the western horizon and judged there was only three hours of light remaining. They needed to finish up here and retreat before the advent of Faenwelar's *Sis Lenweri*. Kain had been in contact earlier in the day after the golden dragon's wounding, and advised her that the high prince would arrive by dusk. Gwaethe had no desire to form part of his welcoming committee.

She grimaced at the thought of being wedged between the two *Sis Lenweri* forces. That would not happen.

She sat upon her horse on a low knoll in the center of the battlefield controlled by her forces. Syndra sat beside her on her ugly brown and white pony, whose withers were at least a hand shorter than Gwaethe's stallion. Having fought all day until the attack on the dragon, Gwaethe observed the battle for a time to assess their strategies. She also wanted to keep an eye on Jacques.

Her eyes swept the field, and she spied Jacques's banner one hundred paces to the west. It appeared Exmund was still with him. No distinctive *Sis Lenweri* uniforms appeared close to her husband, which usually meant no enemy elven lords were present. Her brow wrinkled. Where were all the enemy leaders? No wonder the *Sis Lenweri* tactics were disorganized.

"Where do you think the enemy leaders are, Syndra?" Gwaethe asked.

Syndra shrugged. "I have also been wondering about this. Perhaps they have fled the field and will meet Faenwelar to return with him."

"We would have noticed that, occupying the eastern edge of the battlefield as we do. Why would they leave their people to fend for themselves? Clearly, the leadership of the enemy is lacking. We did not kill *that* many elven lords overnight."

Syndra shrugged again. "Perhaps we did."

Gwaethe glanced at her companion, who had returned to surveying the battle below them. Jacques had vanquished his foe and was making his way toward her, fighting as he came. It gratified her to see him fit enough to fight like this after nearly losing him almost a year ago. She occupied herself by planning the next two hours and what she wished to achieve.

Jacques finally rode up a half hour later with Exmund in tow and his guard following, mopping up the few remaining skirmishes they had partaken in.

"Princess Gwaethe," Jacques said, bowing from the saddle. "I'm delighted to find you hale and hearty."

She smiled at him, noting the weariness on his face and the slump of his body. "A pity I cannot say the same for you, husband. You appear to need a bathe and a rest." Her eyes ran over him a second time, noting the various nicks and scrapes he'd suffered.

"Better off than I was yesterday. How goes it?"

"We were wondering where all the enemy leaders are. There are scant banners on the field apart from ours."

Jacques turned to study the battlefield. "I see what you mean. And the fighting has been undisciplined from the enemy today." He drew in a deep breath and winced. "Damned ribs. I think one may be broken."

A spike of fear struck Gwaethe. "You get that tended to before you puncture a… what does Lady Alique call them?"

"Lungs. Exmund strapped me up so tight I can barely draw breath, so don't worry."

She shook her head. "You should not be fighting if you think your ribs are broken. I know what can happen next."

He rode his horse closer. "Hush, Gwaethe. This is war, and I must fight. Would *you* remove yourself in the same situation? I know you wouldn't."

She set her teeth, determined not to agree—but he was correct. She would fight on no matter what. "Then perhaps you should do as I am doing and observe from afar. I think you have vanquished enough foes for today."

"All the Brightcastle leaders and Kain Arenil still fight, including Princess Alecia. Would you have me do less than them?"

Gwaethe swallowed fear and frustration at the remark. Everything and everyone conspired against her keeping him safe. She wished to know where he was when Faenwelar finally arrived.

"If you must return to the battle, keep an eye out to the east. Faenwelar's force will arrive inside the next three hours. I don't wish you to be trapped between Gorin and the new enemy force."

He nodded. "Agreed. I'll get back to it then. I want to squeeze the enemy further before it's time to retreat. We'll swing to the center and see if we can find an elven lord or two."

Gwaethe nodded. "I have a mind to form some wedges and drive them into the northernmost enemy soldiers."

He held up a hand. "I'll find you in two hours!"

He cantered off the knoll and joined his guard before charging back into the fray.

But, two hours later, as Gwaethe pulled her people from the field, Jacques still fought. It appeared he had formed a fighting wedge, with him at the point, and was pushing his way to the front of the enemy lines. The battle was furious all around him.

Gwaethe glanced to the east and spied the sun glinting off the weapons of Faenwelar's force.

She turned to Syndra. "I want one hundred of our best fighters on horseback. The rest should retreat."

Syndra nodded and started waving her arms around. Her actions sent the bulk of the *Lenweri* north, but the requested mounted elves awaited orders.

"Listen carefully. My husband is leading a wedge that appears to be trying to break through to our allies, or perhaps push the enemy closer to Brightcastle. Regardless, this maneuver needs to be completed soon, as the new enemy is almost upon us. You are to help me extract our force by pushing forward. Half of you will ride with me up the eastern flank of the wedge and the others with Syndra up the western side. We will make our own small wedges between Jacques's people and the enemy on each side. Good luck."

Gwaethe rode with a desperate need to fight her way to the head of that wedge and rescue Jacques, except he wouldn't think he needed rescuing. There wasn't time to think of anything except getting to him in one piece and getting them all out of there before Faenwelar arrived. All that kept her grounded was the thought that the rest of her people were safe in their camp to the north.

She almost laughed at the thought. *Safe!*

The wedge Jacques led was perhaps twenty riders deep, and she rode like a demon up its eastern side, forcing her way into any gap that presented itself, ruthlessly hacking away enemy resistance. At one stage, she screamed like a banshee and vaguely wondered if she would recover from this fit of madness.

The name that ran through her head was *Jacques! Jacques! Jacques!* Soon she was chanting his name under her breath, punctuating his name with a sword strike.

It seemed like only a few moments but must have been perhaps half an hour later that she found herself beside him. She would have laughed at the startlement on his face, but for a vicious assault from a *Sis Lenweri* warrior who was trying to take her head off.

The elf went down in a spray of blood, and Gwaethe screamed at Jacques.

"You need to get your people out! Faenwelar is almost here, and he will squash you like a bug." She blocked a blade and almost took the enemy's head off with the force of her counterstrike.

Jacques was fighting two *Sis Lenweri* who blocked his path, and she joined in, dispatching the one closest to her, only for him to be replaced by another. But the frontline was just a stone's throw away. Gwaethe spotted Kain and screamed at him. He didn't hear, and there was no chance to use the ring to speak to him. She screamed his name again.

Syndra had arrived on the other side of the wedge, and together the three of them plowed forward, step by step, their horses biting and kicking as they sought to create a path to their allies. Gwaethe screamed for Kain again, and, this time, he heard. She met his wild eyes over the heads of foot soldiers and through cavalry. He nodded.

"Don't lose focus now! Keep pushing!" she cried.

The strategy had forced the battle closer to the keep and now archers on the walls were firing into the ranks of the *Sis Lenweri*. Some arrows exploded near them while others were normal darts. An arrow lodged in Jacques's shoulder guard, and Gwaethe shouted at him.

"Push through! They will hit us." The archers' attack was being concentrated on either side of their force, but some missiles went astray. Kain broke through and gestured for them to follow him. He opened a path to the keep and their wedge followed, heading for the relative safety of the trenches. They pulled up between the last trench and the wall, and turned to watch.

The allies had retreated, mostly into the trenches, and watched as a thick fall of arrows, many with the lethal explosives, rained down on the *Sis Lenweri*. Elves and horses alike fell, and soon the retreat horn sounded, echoing across the battlefield, a mournful sound to match the decimation of the attack.

Gwaethe sat her stallion and sighed. "That was intense."

Jacques spluttered. "What were you thinking? You put yourself in grave danger."

"I'll thank you to mind your words, Jacques. I called the retreat, and you continued your wedge attack, necessitating me coming to your aid."

"And how many of ours did you kill doing that?" he hissed.

Gwaethe looked to Syndra.

"Perhaps a third of us will not return," Syndra said. "I will organize a search for the dead and wounded." She turned and rode away.

Many of the allies were picking through the battlefield while they could, helping the injured and retrieving bodies.

Gwaethe looked at her husband. "We will discuss this later in private." The tight lines of his jaw told her there would be harsh words between them, no matter how much they delayed the discussion.

"We've struck a heavy blow to Gorin's force today," Kain said, "no matter how it was achieved."

Jacques nodded, his movements abrupt. "And none too soon, if I'm not mistaken."

Gwaethe turned and walked to the nearest trench, furious at his words. He had failed to watch the enemy closely, and now he wanted to be the one to remind them all.

Well, there would be a reckoning between them that night, if they were given the chance.

She felt a presence near her and turned to find Kain. "It is a relief to see you well, Brother." Gwaethe clutched his shoulders and kissed each cheek lightly.

"And you, Sister," Kain said. "May I speak?"

She nodded.

"He's a warrior, Gwaethe. You can't tame his instincts as easily as all that. He's also a leader of men. You should commend him for bravery."

"You are as bad as he is," she hissed. "I told them all to watch the east and not to be caught. I called the retreat, and he either didn't hear or ignored it. He forced me to mount a rescue."

"Did he?" he asked. "Couldn't you have allowed it to play out without risking more fighters and yourself?"

She frowned at him. "Of course, I could have done that. And perhaps someone else could have made the rescue. But I am not that person, Kain. I am a warrior and leader as well. When I see my people under fire, I do not wait and see. I act."

"And when you see your husband in that situation, it's even more the case?"

She raised her chin. "You would be the same!"

He shrugged. "Perhaps. All I'm saying is that he made his choices, and you made yours. You could've chosen to allow his choice to run its course. You can't always rescue him."

Gwaethe allowed his words to make their mark and struggled with them. In the end, she decided he was correct.

She could have waited and allowed Jacques to bear the full weight of his leadership—some would say she should have done exactly that.

She took a deep breath and let it out. "You are right. I must take responsibility for my choices this day, and I will bear that in mind when Jacques and I talk."

Kain nodded. "Now, Faenwelar is almost here. Let's gather with the other leaders on the wall and decide strategy."

She, Kain, and Jacques joined Princess Alecia, Lord Zorba, Ramar Reese, Captain Estevot, and the heads of the army on the north wall. They stood looking east as hundreds of *Sis Lenweri*, mounted and on foot, came into view.

"The question is," Ramón said. "Will they attack after a day of marching, or will they make camp and start the assault at dawn?"

"They'd be foolish to attack now. Gorin's force was dealt a heavy blow today—"

"Gorin's banner," Gwaethe said, pointing at the head of the army where two banners flapped in the dying rays of the sun. One belonged to Prince Gorin, and the other was Faenwelar's. "That's where he was all day! He left camp to welcome his father, leaving his people to cope as best they could."

"Which wasn't very well," Kain said, folding his arms and staring at the enemy as though he could read their plans if he concentrated hard enough.

"We can't hope for a respite," Ramón said. "I'm going to plan for an attack now or during the night. I suggest you all do the same. Princess Gwaethe, I'd like you to move your force to the west in preparation to attack the enemy on three sides. They won't stand a chance."

Gwaethe nodded. "Jacques, let us move our people."

He bowed and accompanied her down the stairs to the wall and out the gate to their mounts. As they turned west to avoid the battlefield and headed back to their army, Gwaethe couldn't help but fear the coming days.

Even more so, she feared the conflict this war had brought to their marriage.

* * *

James and Katrine sat around their fire, sharing a skin of wine and a companionable silence. The flames crackled within their circle of stones, and the sleeping hounds made dark humps around them. Several of the beasts were on patrol in the surrounding forest. He was content that neither friend nor foe would surprise them.

"I'm sorry," Katrine said.

He glanced at her, puzzled. "Why?"

"I should never have convinced you to tell the king about the dragon. It changed everything for you, and I'm not sure how necessary it was."

He shrugged. "It matters not. With the death of the king, I'm a long way to resuming a normal life."

"Yes, it seems so." His love looked far away as she said those words.

"What troubles you, Kat?"

She tore herself from whatever scene she observed and focused on him. "Nothing. Everything. This war. The hounds. You and me. I can't yet see my place in this world. Perhaps when the war is won, it will become clearer."

"You're thinking perhaps of taking up Hetty's position?"

She shook her head. "I don't even know what that is. She's Princess Alecia's advisor, and that's very different from who she was before. How can a witch be an advisor when the practice of magic is outlawed?"

"Perhaps the Guardians don't know she's a witch. From what I hear, Princess Alecia is a law unto herself. She'd hardly be likely to tell the Guardians all her secrets."

"The Zialni family has a history of persecution of sorcerers," Katrine said, "but that may change with the death of the king. It depends on who gains power now."

"Yes, who indeed? It looks like a power vacuum to me. An infant and his guardians will hardly inspire confidence. And what are our alternatives? The adult nephew, Piotr?"

She shook her head. "King Beniel was determined to keep him away."

James sent her a sharp glance. For a woman who avoided court, she seemed to know much. "No allegation against him has ever been proven. It wouldn't surprise me if he is named heir."

"He won't be."

There was something Katrine wasn't telling him. What?

"Do you know something about the heir to the kingdom? If you do, you should tell me."

She shook her head. "It's only a feeling I have, that there are still too many players and numerous secrets being kept." She focused her silver-specked blue gaze on him. "You should be accustomed to secrets since that's the world you've inhabited for some time."

He took her hands. "There are no secrets between us now, my love. Tell me your suspicions when you can. I promise to do the same."

She smiled. "Let's take this time of peace to be together tonight. I don't know when we'll have the chance again." So saying, she drew him into her arms.

CHAPTER NINE

VARD patrolled the forest in his hawk form. It was times like these he wished he could morph into the owl, a true creature of the night, but this bird would suffice. He winged over the enemy encampment with its fires and sentries, noting the numbers yet again. It was a mighty force. He saw three night hounds skulking between the tents and sleeping bodies, heard the crunch of bone and muffled cries as their jaws closed over soft flesh.

If the hawk could have smiled, it would've done so. The campaign was proceeding well.

His keen gaze took in the hulking form of the keep where his heart lay, and he knew an urge to fly over it. It was too risky. His love would have to wait.

The bird turned back toward the camp, discovering the sorceress and her protector where they lay together, entwined under furs. The coals of the fire gave enough light to expose a smile on the woman's face.

The hawk's heart was sad as he flew back to his rest, merging into the man once he had alighted on a low branch.

Vard dropped to the ground and returned to camp, his head still fuzzy with the memory of the fresh rabbit he had consumed as the hawk. Samael was there, sitting beside Vard's fire, waiting for him. He looked up as Vard approached.

"You look strange," he said, staring into Vard's eyes.

"I always look strange after being on patrol," he said, truthfully.

"How is it out there?"

"Quiet, actually. The *Sis Lenweri* numbers have swelled. Some of Gorin's force have joined Faenwelar's camp."

Sam stared at the fire. "It won't matter. The numbers are the same no matter how they're distributed." He looked up. "Why would Gorin leave his force? Surely they could have done with his leadership today?"

Vard quirked a brow. "Missing his father's love? I don't know. Perhaps he wanted last-minute instructions? It makes little sense. One sentry said the kingdom allies won the day."

"I wouldn't doubt it," Sam said. "Any word on the gold dragon?"

"Nothing more. My guess is it limped off to heal."

"I'd love to know how our archers bested it."

"We'll know soon enough," Vard said. "What did you want, Sam? The hour is late. I need my bed."

Sam stood. "I heard Nikolas muttering about the heir today. I'm not trying to cause trouble, but I think his words will lead to nothing good. You need to talk with him."

"Dammit," Vard said. "I thought I'd addressed that issue. Did he say anything else?"

Sam looked uncomfortable. "I don't want to get caught between you and him. He's my half-brother, and you're my friend. I want to be loyal to both. Niko gave me a chance against his better judgement when no one else would."

"The way I heard it," Vard said, "the king didn't give him much choice."

"He still took me under his wing. I owe him."

Vard studied the blond man who had become a friend. "Don't worry, Sam. I'll speak with the admiral and put the matter to rest once and for all."

He wanted to tell Sam everything that had happened in King Beniel's last moments, but it would place his friend in the difficult position of having to keep a secret from his family. Vard couldn't afford to let his secret out, not yet.

But how would he settle this with Nikolas? If he didn't believe him last time, how would he convince him now?

Sam nodded and shook his hand. "I know you're good and true, and were loyal to the king. You'd not be involved in a scheme to marry Adriana and take over the kingdom."

Vard held his gaze as he shook his hand. "Thanks for the vote of confidence. It means more than you know. I'd never consider marrying Adriana. All I wish for is victory in this war and a return to peace. I'll do everything I can to achieve that."

"Exactly so," Sam said. "I bid you good night, Vard." He released Vard's hand and walked into the dark.

Vard sighed. When Sam found out the truth, he'd be angry. Or perhaps he'd understand why Vard had kept the news to himself. He hoped so, for Sam was his first male friend in a long time, and he had no wish to lose him.

On the morrow, if the situation arose, Vard would speak with Nikolas, but for tonight, sleep was calling.

Vard was up before light as the hawk, making a patrol of the land between their camp and Brightcastle. The enemy encampment already bustled with activity, as did Brightcastle keep. Soldiers crowded the east and north walls, possibly preparing more of the exploding missiles. He kept low, close to the trees, to avoid notice, ghosting on silent wings over the clearings where cooking fires burned.

On the way back, he noted that the sorceress's camp was already deserted. The forest was quiet except for the sentries and scouts from either side. Of the night hounds, he saw nothing. The beasts scared the hawk with their glowing crimson eyes and mouths dripping with saliva. Luckily, they were never likely to cross paths.

He returned to human form and was saddling his horse when Formosa and Cosara arrived. Both men appeared solemn and tense.

I wonder what this is about. As if he couldn't guess.

"Good morning, gentlemen," he said, pausing in his task. "It's a good day for a fight, don't you think?"

Formosa snorted. "We have something we wish to discuss, King's Blade. It can't wait until after the battle."

"Go ahead," Vard said, standing with hands on hips.

"We ask you to stand aside," Nikolas said, not bothering to hide his dislike for him. "The leaders of this army aren't at ease with you as commander. There are others better suited to the task."

"There are?"

Both seemed surprised at his response.

"Of course, there are!" Formosa snapped. "You're army-trained and an outstanding warrior, but much more is required. We propose a leadership team consisting of the admiral and I, both heads of our respective forces. You'll be next in the line of command for now, as the king wished."

"Good of you to follow the king's wishes, even in death," Vard said, quietly. "Do you think it wise not to have an ultimate leader with the final say?"

They would force his hand, these two. Nikolas he could stomach as commander, but Formosa? *Never.* King Beniel had placed Vard in command, and, by the Goddess, he was going to honor the monarch's wishes.

Nikolas shuffled his feet. He didn't like this joint command either, if Vard was any judge. "It should work well enough," he offered. "Besides, we're joining forces with Brightcastle and Amitania, so there'll be many other leaders. We'll merely be another two."

"Then why change things? If you don't trust me, I'll soon be merely another leader with those others you mentioned."

"Are you willing to step aside or not?" Formosa asked, hand on his sword.

Surely, he wouldn't allow this to come to blows?

"I think not," Vard said. "The king trusted me, placed me second to him in this war. I believe it wise for the status quo to continue at least until this conflict is over. Let that be the end of this discussion."

He turned to his horse and finished saddling the beast. If they left it at that, he wouldn't need to tell them just yet.

When he turned back to them, Nikolas and Formosa had moved away and were in a whispered discussion. He morphed partially into the wolf to listen. Nikolas wanted to leave it be. However, Formosa insisted Vard had to step down.

Vard waited, arms crossed, as their discussion came to an end.

Formosa stalked up. "I insist you step down. If you do so immediately, I'll allow you to keep your position."

Vard took a step toward him, and, to the man's credit, he didn't back away.

"Since you force my hand, General, let me inform you of something." Vard took a deep breath, hoping he was doing the correct thing. "As he lay dying on the battlefield, King Beniel showed me something. He removed a parchment from his pocket and made me read it." Vard then took out the parchment and held it up for Formosa. The general staggered back three steps, his round gaze rising to Vard's.

"I don't believe it! Cosara, read that and tell me I'm not hallucinating."

Nikolas stepped forward and read the letter Vard held. When he had finished, Vard folded the missive and replaced it in his tunic. "Now, gentlemen. I suggest you return to your companies and get ready to move out. This is the day we finish this war."

* * *

Alecia rose before the dawn. This might be the day she would see Vard again—and the day they'd win the war. Her blood bubbled with anticipation. She had thought she'd be scared, but this felt more like excitement. Everything she had worked so hard for since coming to adulthood may well be a reality after today.

She rang the bell, and her maid arrived with breakfast. She ate as the woman did her hair in an updo and carefully applied powders, kohl, and lip color. Next, she dressed in the scarlet and black tunic and trousers she had chosen for this day. Then came the jeweled headband in the Zialni colors tied firmly around her brow. She couldn't wear a tiara with breeches, but a war headband was appropriate and part of her plan to be noticed.

The finishing touch was to place the beautiful and queenly cloak about her shoulders. She thanked the maid and descended through the castle to the lower keep, where the children slept during the war.

She tried not to remember the days she had spent imprisoned there, not knowing if her life would be free or chained to the side of a lecherous lord. Vard had saved her in the end, but she believed she'd have found some way out of it on her own.

It was a very different kingdom she was now dealing with. So many of the old players were gone—her father, Finus, her uncle the king—replaced by the new guard, all ready to build a modern era in the kingdom.

First, they'd have peace, and then a queen—*her*—to rule them. Alecia swallowed hard at the thought.

She halted at the door to Iona and Solomon's chamber and drew a deep breath, centering herself, calming her thoughts and preparing to greet her daughter.

Without knocking, she opened the door and stepped through, stopping just inside the room. Someone else was there ahead of her.

"I should have expected to see you here," Alecia said, approaching the woman slowly.

Benae looked up from her sewing. "And I, you." She sat by the fire, a cup of tea beside her. "I thought to steal some peace before the day began."

Benae looked tired, as though she hadn't slept for days.

"I wanted to see Iona, to kiss her cheek, and tell her I'll return tonight after we vanquish the *Sis Lenweri*."

Benae's brows rose. "You're certain we'll win?"

"Aren't you? Ramón was confident."

"That's men for you," Benae said. "My husband hasn't been trying to save hundreds of gravely wounded men and women. It makes one pessimistic."

Alecia nodded. "I can see how that would be the case. If it's any consolation, I believe this will be the last day of battle. And I, for one, can't wait."

She crossed to Iona's cot, and warmth suffused her body as she gazed upon her daughter. She leaned over and ran a finger down her cheek, smiling as the little girl's lips curved in a smile. "Daddy will be here soon, my darling, and we may be a family."

"You still long for him, don't you?" Benae said from close behind her.

She turned to confront Benae. "I want him more than almost anything else in this world, but the timing must be right. Will it be the right time when this war is won? Perhaps. If it's not, then I'm willing to wait."

Benae's green gaze probed her, and she felt exposed, her true self laid bare, under the woman's scrutiny.

"For so long, I've been insecure because Ramón thought so highly of you. Even when we were married, he was still driven to find you and bring you home."

"It has always been Vard for me. Ramón has always been just a friend. Your husband has a strong sense of duty. He wanted me back where I belonged, with my people. Except now, I have no true place here. Not yet."

Benae's gaze had softened, but, at her last words, the beautiful healer's eyes flashed fire. "And you now think your time has come—to take your place?"

Alecia threw back her shoulders, taking full advantage of her superior height. "I deserve my position in this kingdom. My family is the ruling family."

"My son is part of that ruling family," Benae snapped. "That's why he needs to be protected. Or had you forgotten?"

"I forget nothing. Not one thing, Benae. But let's defeat the *Sis Lenweri,* and then we'll chat again." She didn't intend to reveal her suspicions on the eve of this critical battle. The wrong step now could prove fatal to her cause, and possibly even change the outcome of the war. There was no telling what small decision on her part might alter the future.

Benae's gaze narrowed at her words. "Speak the words you were intending to, Alecia. I would know what's on your mind."

Alecia shook her head. "I don't think so. Not now, but soon." She leaned over the crib and kissed her daughter's cheek, then took Benae's hand in hers.

"I wish you well this day. With luck, we'll celebrate together soon."

She met her ladies near the base of the steps that led to the north wall of the keep. All four were there, and she rejoiced they could be together again. Kenna had recovered some of her color, and couldn't be discouraged from joining them on such an auspicious day. They climbed the wall together, finding most of the army leaders there.

Kain nodded at her from his post near Ramón. They leaned against the northeastern corner of the wall, their heads slightly inclined, as though discussing a secret.

Alecia's shoulders tightened. *Kain might not support her after all!* Then she took a second look. Ramón had a map of the battlefield on a sheet of parchment, and Kain was pointing to various areas of it while Ramón made comments. Just discussing battle tactics then.

She dismissed them from her mind, and saw Reese striding toward her.

"Princess! Good morning. Will you spend more time on the wall today?"

She smiled. "I thought I might, at least at the start of proceedings. Are the archers in position?"

He nodded. "We have a full complement along three walls with adjacent firepits. When Wildecoast gets here, I will add their archers to ours." He was the most animated she had seen him. "I think we can win today, Your Highness."

"Let's not get ahead of ourselves, Reese."

"The princess is correct, Ramar Reese," Estevot said, joining them. "One step at a time and good planning will see us right. We must not assume the outcome."

Alecia nodded. "Just so, Captain. Where will you be stationed this day?"

"I intend to lead the Brightcastle Cavalry, Princess. The fighting will be fierce. Might I suggest you stay here on the wall where you and your ladies will be safest?"

His words were like a red rag to a bull.

"When have you ever known me to take the safest route, Estevot?" she asked, fire burning in her gut. "I'll be on the wall this morning, and we shall see where I end up later." She snapped her mouth shut before she could say too much. This man didn't deserve more explanation.

He nodded. "Very good. I'm glad you'll be out of harm's way."

At that moment, Ramón cleared his throat. "Gather round, good people." He waited until they stepped closer, and a servant handed them each a goblet of mulled wine. "Today we meet Faenwelar and send him to hell. Not much needs to be discussed, as our plans haven't changed. We'll attack the enemy from south, east, and west. Brightcastle and the keep forms the base in the south. The Amitanian and Selinore forces have the west, and soon Wildecoast will arrive to attack the eastern sector."

"I've had confirmation via raven that the King's Army is only a few hours away. It will be tight, but I believe we can hold until that force arrives."

"The King's Army?" Alecia asked. "We all know King Beniel is dead."

"Let's not split hairs, Princess. You know to what army I refer," Ramón said, glaring at her.

She raised a brow at him. Soon it would be the Queen's Army.

"Good luck be with you all, and may the Goddess protect you." Ramón raised his goblet. "To the allies and victory!"

They all echoed his toast, then raised their goblets and drank.

As they went their separate ways, the sun broke over the horizon, and Alecia saw the extent of their task spread out below them. Her ladies came to stand with her.

"Look at our enemy," Cretia said, her voice little more than a whisper.

Alecia turned to study them, disturbed to see the fear on all their faces. "You can't allow this into your hearts, my friends," she said, steel in her voice. "We always knew this would be difficult. Dwelling on the extent of the enemy will defeat us before we even begin."

Their eyes were on her now.

"Take a deep breath and envision our victory." She breathed in the cool morning air and closed her eyes. Alecia ran the picture of their ascendance through her mind, saw herself mounted on Silver, leading her victorious troops from the field while their enemies wailed—envisioned her crowning.

She would rule from Brightcastle, as did the queens of old.

Triumph in her heart, she opened her eyes and smiled to see confidence returned to her closest supporters. "That's better. Now I see women who can win this fight today. Let us go forth and take up our swords. We'll sweep the *Sis Lenweri* from the field, and none who challenge peace shall be allowed to live."

Her four ladies let out a cheer to the astonishment of the others on the wall, then made their way down the stairs to the stables and accepted the reins of their horses.

Alecia led her ladies from the northern gate to take up the fight to the enemy.

* * *

Vard pushed his army as hard as he dared. They must arrive ready to do battle, for he wanted this over today. Whatever the day might bring, they must deal with it. Any delay in their arrival could shift the tide in Faenwelar's favor. By now, the allies must be outnumbered on the battlefield.

Merielle and Sam rode beside him, and he was glad of their support. He hadn't as yet revealed the contents of the letter to them. No doubt they would have mixed feelings when he did. He still believed it was best to conduct this battle as Vard Anton, King's Blade.

The revelation had delayed trouble with Formosa and the admiral. They wouldn't take his elevation lightly, but at least they wouldn't interfere until Faenwelar was defeated.

He and the cavalry, along with as many foot soldiers as they could mount, were hurrying to the front of the force, intent on attacking Faenwelar through his back lines. Of course, the elven leader would expect it, but perhaps not as soon as they would arrive. Vard was determined to snatch an hour back from their previous arrival time—the time he had sent Ramón Zorba. He just hoped one of the three ravens he had sent had got through.

Alternating walk, trot, and canter, they advanced through the lines of marching foot soldiers who had been advised to clear a path through their center. They cheered as Vard passed, and he waved at them. Merielle got twice as many cheers as he did. He could tell the attention buoyed her.

Today, her dramatic scarlet mane was tamed by a tight plait and a dolphin's tail adorned her helmet. It was a strange insignia to include, but he didn't have time to ask of its origins. She wore chain mail on her torso, covered with light silver armor that shone with a greenish tinge. Vard was grateful that Merielle had donned the protection. She had been far too exposed on the battlefield in Wildecoast during her impromptu attack.

Vard shook his head. Merielle's hair and unusual insignia would make her a target, especially when the enemy realized her huge ability to inflict damage on them. He sighed. Nothing much he could do about it except keep an eye on her. He was sure Nikolas would also have detailed men to watch over her. If they were also waiting to knock Vard off his horse, let them come.

Who knew what the admiral's response to Vard's revelation would be? He shook the question from his mind and turned to the day's tactics. In an hour, they'd arrive at the front, and he could take back everything the *Sis Lenweri* had stolen from them, starting with peace.

* * *

Katrine had also dressed herself in light armor for the battle. Not that she'd be physically fighting, she hoped. No, her hounds would perform much of the combat this day. However, she'd need to protect them from the enemy, and that meant hurling her fireballs. And there was James as well.

Even though he was there to watch over her, she'd also be watching over him. The specter of the dragons crashed into her mind. A few well-placed fireballs might go a long way to scaring them off.

She'd be busy that day. Already the light armor, helmet, and chain mail chafed and dragged at her body. She stopped her horse and looked across at James. He shook his head. No hounds in sight then. Howls and inhuman cries rose from the country ahead, and she smiled. The attack was underway. She had sent all her beasts ahead in three groups, by far the largest attack by her hounds yet. Hopefully, unleashing all twenty-one at once would terrify the *Sis Lenweri*, sapping their strength before the real battle ahead.

She joined James. "I'm going to see what they're up to. Can you watch my back?"

He smiled. "Of course." He signaled to the scouts who had joined them that morning, sent by Vard. Goddess bless that man!

Katrine closed her eyes and reached out to the night hounds. They immediately filled her mind with images and terror. Through their eyes, she witnessed the attacks as they occurred. Their fangs ripped into *Sis Lenweri* flesh, tearing through throats and legs, killing and disabling with vicious efficiency. She shuddered as she saw one of their leaders cut down by two of her brutes.

She had done her best to instruct them to avoid harming the horses, and to concentrate on pulling down the leaders of the *Sis Lenweri*.

The hounds were difficult to communicate with when it came to understanding the differences between one enemy and another based on insignia. But she believed her best chance of making an impact was to attack the leaders. Perhaps even Faenwelar. That elf deserved to die at the teeth of her hounds.

She gasped and sagged in the saddle as pain ripped through her chest. James's arm curled around her. His worried voice cut through her distress.

"What's wrong?"

"I don't know," she gasped, then cried out as pictures of Silverdoom, a spear through his chest, flooded her mind. "It's one of the hounds. He's hurt." Agony flooded her again as another thrust penetrated the body of her champion fighter. "Arghhhhhh"

"Katrine! What can I do?" James asked.

She couldn't talk, couldn't think against the agony crippling her. She felt James pull her from the saddle, lay her on the ground, and drag her helmet off. And then the pain stopped abruptly. She rolled on her side, gasping as the aftershocks faded.

It was ages before she could catch her breath. Her horse cropped the straggly grass near her, and blew warm air on her face. She rolled on her hands and knees, and sat back on her haunches, the move difficult in her armor.

Taking a deep breath, she looked up at James. He handed her a wineskin.

"Are you well?" he asked.

She nodded. "I think so. That was intense."

"You can't go through that every time one of them gets injured."

James kneeled and pulled her against him. Not much of a hug in their armored suits, but welcome all the same.

She agreed; however, they couldn't stop their attacks. "I can't back out now and the hounds won't, anyway."

The scouts came jogging up. "Is she well, Master Tomel?"

"Yes," James said. "Get back out there, and let me know if there's danger."

As they jogged away, James studied her. "You won't survive that kind of pain, Katrine."

She raised her brows at him. "I can do whatever it takes. It's just pain, not injury."

"You forget I watched all that. Can you honestly tell me you could go through it again and again? The only reason you're somewhat recovered, I'd hazard a guess, is that your hound is dead."

Pain hit her again, but this time it was emotional, the loss of a friend. Her hounds now depended on her. She had placed them in a position where they could lose their lives. And they were so few. She had vowed never again to be responsible for their deaths. It just showed how little her word meant.

"And don't start beating yourself up over the loss," James snapped. "It's not your fault. Blame Faenwelar. We must do better, protect them better."

"How do we do that? At night they have protection, but, in the day, they're vulnerable."

"Then pull them out and send in targeted attacks. Use your magic instead. Learn from this."

James was right. It would do no good feeling this crushing guilt. The hounds wanted this, and, in some way, understood the risks. He was also correct that she couldn't face that pain each time they hurt a hound. Eventually, she'd die of shock.

Katrine closed her eyes and reached out to the hounds, asking them to complete their attack and withdraw. Then she replaced her helmet and mounted her horse. By the time they had ridden five hundred paces to the west, she had twenty hounds back with her, and the body of Silverdoom.

"We must bury him," she said, dismounting and removing her armor.

James followed suit and joined her. They found a shallow depression in the ground large enough to take the body of the fallen beast and laid him in it. Then they gathered rocks to cover the body. As they worked, the remaining night hounds sat in a semicircle, watching their progress.

Finally, her heart heavy, Katrine placed the last rock on the cairn. James pulled her into his arms. She gulped down the lump that rose in her throat and forced back the tears that threatened. Now wasn't the time for that.

"Thank you, James." She kissed him. "No matter what this battle brings us, I want you to know I love you more than I can ever express."

He smiled. "I love you, too. And I can't wait for us to start our life together when this conflict has ended."

She studied his face, so handsome it took her breath away. Would they survive this and get their chance at forever? Could she be the wife he truly needed? Her gut warned her life would always be turbulent, even with this wonderful man to care for her.

"One step at a time," she said. His face clouded at her words, and it saddened her that she should pull him down this way. She spoke over the grave, and James held her hand as they walked back to the hounds.

All the beasts had sustained slight injuries, some requiring sutures. James helped her clean all the cuts and scrapes, even though the beasts unnerved him greatly. Dawngaze snapped at him as he bathed her paw, and Katrine spoke harshly to the hound. Luckily, James wasn't harmed, and they completed their medical duties and resumed their trek westward.

This time, she kept the hounds with her, determining she would wait until the battle was joined and supervise the hounds as they fought. That way, she could help with a fireball or two as they battled the elves.

It wasn't ideal, but she couldn't risk any more losses, not yet. Never if she could help it. If she was being honest with herself, she didn't know if she could again endure the pain she had felt when Silverdoom was attacked.

Katrine and James, along with her hounds, trotted through the bush, their Ranger scouts alert for sentries from the army ahead. Several times, they sent a small group of hounds to take out enemy scouts, all with no loss to her precious beasts. Her body was recovering from the trauma of Silverdoom's death, but she couldn't afford to forget how it had affected her.

Finally, they had advanced as far as they could without engaging the *Sis Lenweri*. They made camp on a small rise and posted their scouts to keep watch. From their camp, James and Katrine watched the slow advance of the enemy and the battle raging before Brightcastle Keep. Katrine's link with the hounds fired her, urged her to attack and kill. But the mere thought of engaging the enemy and revealing herself made her heart pound and palms sweat.

Her husband's long fingers wrapped around hers, and she looked across at him.

"We'll be safe, Kat," he said, warmth in his gaze as he examined her. "I promise."

She smiled. "You can't promise such a thing, James. Once we enter this battle, we're vulnerable to fate, luck, *and* the *Sis Lenweri*. Even our own people could kill us accidentally. You can't say we'll be safe with any certainty."

He looked down at their joined hands. "We're part of the future of this kingdom. I have faith in us, in you. I even believe in your hounds."

She shook her head. "Brave words, my love. I'll try to keep them in mind."

He nodded, and they looked over the land to the west and waited.

CHAPTER TEN

VARD cantered at the head of his army, Merielle and Sam riding on either side, the cavalry at his back. He felt the stares of Nikolas and Formosa boring into his skull. Damn them, he could do this—defeat the *Sis Lenweri*, and bring peace to the kingdom. He would succeed, and they'd have to follow his lead. They were the only people besides the queen who knew he was now the king.

Perhaps he should've brought Adriana with him, so she could support his new position. But no—to do so would've been too great a risk.

Adriana was likely to say anything that suited her. She could have devastated his standing with the leadership by supporting the story that had spread about the two of them, let alone what she may have said to Alecia.

He almost groaned out loud. He pushed his lady from his head and concentrated on the country ahead. They should be close to the back lines of the *Sis Lenweri*.

He pulled his horse to a trot, and all those with him followed suit. He needed space, so signaled a halt, then rode a few paces ahead.

Closing his eyes, he pushed his senses out, trying to ascertain if Katrine or any of his scouts were close. A faint scent of horse and the unmistakable odor of the hounds drifted to him from two locations. The horses were off to the south and the beasts spread out a little way to the west. The horses were stationary, which meant they were waiting for him.

He put his hand up for the army to dismount and signaled his two companions forward.

"I think James and Lady Star are close," he said. "Let's meet them, and we can get the lay of the land before we attack."

Meri and Sam nodded, and they turned a little south, trotting through the low scrubby trees and past the occasional farm until they found the hillock where James and Katrine were camped. They hailed him from their lookout.

"Well met, Lord Anton," James said, waving. "Lady Cosara, Delacost." The last was said in a gruff tone, as if the once pirate still made him uncomfortable.

James still held a grudge against Sam for coming between Esta Aranati and his best friend, master goldsmith Reid Vetta. But that wasn't a topic for the moment.

"What news do you have?" Vard asked.

"We lost a hound in one of the recent attacks."

Vard noticed James's jaw tighten and Katrine's throat spasm. There was much they weren't revealing. Katrine had a close bond with the hounds. This loss would've cut her deeply.

James went on. "We decided they needed to be part of a wider attack, so opted to wait for you and go in together. That way, we can help defend them."

Vard nodded. "I see. I've spread the word that the beasts fight for us. I'll update the force that they're to look out for them and defend them where they can. Are you ready to resume your march?"

They both nodded.

"Faenwelar's *Sis Lenweri* have already engaged the Brightcastle defenders," James said. "We need to attack as soon as we can before they're overwhelmed."

Vard waved and spun his horse, cantering back to his force, Meri and Sam behind him. They were arguing.

"Merielle," Sam said, "I can't watch out for you if you insist on haring off in all directions. Stick close to me, and we'll fight together."

Meri made an indelicate sound through her nose. "I cannot make any assurances. When I fight, it is like an angry force takes over me. I cannot control what I do."

Vard partially morphed into the wolf, so he wouldn't miss what she said. Meri was a berserker, becoming a killing creature when the mood hit her. That was unexpected. He had trained her, should have realized what lay within, though, in reality, her true nature wouldn't have shown itself until her life was threatened.

"Well, don't turn on me in your berserk rage. I'm there to help you, not fight you!"

Clearly, Sam had come to the same conclusion.

"I will try to keep that in mind, though I feel you are safe from my hand."

"Ha! As if I'll trust that. One eye on the enemy, and one on you. That's how I'll have to fight."

They reached the rest of the army and resumed their march, breaking into a canter. To the south, on his left, Vard could just make out Lady Star and her hounds, along with James. He raised his left hand in a pre-arranged signal to his rangers, and they peeled off the southern flank, ready to protect Katrine and her hounds. Really, it was Katrine who needed the protection, especially when she threw her fireballs. Little would save her from being targeted when she drew such attention.

He raised his other arm and twisted his hand in another pre-arranged signal, then moved a little to the northern edge, but still in the center.

Ruven and the rest of the elves from Wildecoast joined him on their horses and ponies, their faces expressionless, dark eyes focused. They wore laminated wooden helmets and armor of overlapping leather, though what animal had supplied the material, he didn't know. Camouflage colors of brown, gray, and green may not help much on the battlefield, but if they fought at night, they'd be virtually invisible.

The *Lenweri* carried cross bows and short swords, except for those trained to shoot the dragons. They carried the long bows whose distances ranged up to three hundred paces. Vard could shoot a long bow three hundred and fifty paces, but the elves were new to the weapon and were yet to perfect it. Three hundred would do.

Ruven maneuvered until he was beside Vard, his elves spread out behind them. They were to be Vard's honor guard. He thought it fitting the leader of the human army should have an elven guard since they had come from Amitania and pledged themselves to protect the peace of humans and elves. This must be a truly united force, or there'd be continued conflict in future.

When Ruven came to him and asked to form his guard, he'd taken some days to consider it. His human commanders would be shocked. His heightened senses detected anger directed at him from the vicinity of the admiral and the general. Let them look daggers at him. So he was unconventional! It was to be expected. He'd use the people in his force as he saw fit.

Vard shook his head. There was more to do. With another arm movement, he sent his best cavalry to join Sam and Merielle. They'd need protection aplenty when the *Sis Lenweri* saw how Meri rallied fighters. He'd seen the way soldiers had drawn courage and ferocity from her example in the Wildecoast battle.

And so, the attacking force from Wildecoast assumed its most lethal form. Katrine and her hounds advanced on the extreme left, Merielle and Sam with their human guard center left. Vard and his *Lenweri* rode center right, and Admiral Nikolas Cosara and General Formosa with their best cavalry on the right flank.

Behind them came the remaining cavalry, then the foot soldiers with their shields and pikes. He had ordered the foot soldiers to mount any stray horses and join the conflict on horseback. The rest would form a shield wall and fill any gaps in the cavalry line. It was an unconventional attack plan, but Vard hoped their targeted killing of *Sis Lenweri* generals and other leaders, as well as the surprise attacks by Katrine's hounds, along with Merielle and himself would place the *Sis Lenweri* on the back foot, and they would never recover.

He could only hope. If a few things went their way, including being able to down at least one dragon, they just might win the war.

He morphed into the wolf just enough to take advantage of its sense of smell.

Yes, the *Sis Lenweri* back lines were only a few hundred paces ahead. Their scouts must have been decimated by the hounds and *his* forward scouts—at least, he hoped so.

Vard drew his sword and raised it high. Closing the visor of his helmet, he spurred his horse on. The front lines of his army surged with him, dodging small trees, and leaping bushes and rocks. The back ranks of the *Sis Lenweri* appeared, some mounted, many on foot. He tugged back from the wolf and used his hawk sight to assess their readiness.

The *Sis Lenweri* had expected their attack and were facing the east. Their foot soldiers had formed up at least ten elves deep, then a space, and the cavalry behind. They had split their force in half, it appeared. It was difficult to tell as Gorin's elves bordered their western edge. They must be confident to allow their combined army to be surrounded. Still, it appeared from this vantage point that the *Sis Lenweri* still had the superior numbers. *Just.*

Vard could only hope the allies had the greater leadership and determination.

They hit the shield wall of the enemy at a canter, their horses withstanding the spears of the *Sis Lenweri*. Vard's longsword slashed and hacked at the *Sis Lenweri* foot soldiers, and, all along the line, his people followed his lead. Their horses wore leather chest plates, but still some came to grief on the spear tips of the enemy. He was proud to see his unhorsed *Lenweri* picked up by their mounted peers and continue the battle, front riders slashing with their swords while the rear rider fired crossbows.

The *Lenweri* with Vard sprayed crossbow bolts into the enemy foot soldiers, aiming for the chinks in their armor. Some of his guard fell, but they took many of the enemy with them. His enhanced scent and hearing allowed him to sense danger and meet the covert attacks of the enemy against him. That, and Ruven, who stuck closer to him than a limpet on a rock. The elven leader had picked up a fallen comrade who fired his bow from behind the saddle.

Slowly, they made their way into the enemy ranks, inching closer to the cavalry where Vard knew the leaders sat.

None of the enemy commanders had joined their foot soldiers, and their voices called from horseback, urging their fighters to push forward. Perhaps they no longer had enough *Sis Lenweri* commanders to fight at the front after the night hound attacks.

Whatever the cause, cowardice or lack of numbers, it disgusted Vard that men should fight without their leaders amongst them.

* * *

Sam and his guard, along with Meri, hit the middle of the *Sis Lenweri* foot soldiers hard. He drove his horse back two rows until the enemy surrounded him.

With Meri at his side and his guard around him, he wasn't taking much of a risk. Meri would soon scare the elves with her berserker rage, and he had the best fighters with him.

He was agile and extremely quick with the sword. His vision was a little hampered by the helmet, but he was glad of it, and the chain mail and light armor that covered his body.

Not that he was invincible by any means, but the elves were more used to fighting in the forest, so he felt they had the upper hand. They had to cut through to the mounted enemy quickly before they lost too many of the cavalry. Personally, he wanted to leave the *Sis Lenweri* foot soldiers to their friends behind and reach the proper fight—the enemy cavalry.

And so, he fought savagely, sweeping left and right with his cutlass, shearing through limbs and necks, grateful for the years of piracy that had taught him his balance and ferocity. And Vard had helped sharpen those skills. Where he could, he aimed for a chink in the armor, somewhere like the armpit or neck, exposed for a moment, allowing him a deadly strike.

He kept one eye on Merielle, but she was absorbed in the battle, screaming at her opponents and often freezing them in their tracks. She never hesitated, slashing at them with a deadly, inelegant efficiency. Now they had drawn the attention of the enemy cavalry and movement in their ranks revealed archers at the ready.

"Meri!" Sam's shout caught her attention, and she glanced up while taking the head off an unfortunate *Sis Lenweri*. He pointed to the danger, and she focused on it, screaming in a note so high he barely heard it. The sound was a mere vibration on the edge of awareness, but the mounted enemy in its path clapped their hands to their ears. They slumped and fell from their saddles, blood pouring from their ears.

A *Sis Lenweri* almost impaled Sam as he struggled to gather his wits after the attack. He came to just in time to block the sword of a mounted enemy. Sweeping the blade away, he stuck the enemy through the neck. The elf fell from the saddle, and Sam reached over and whacked the pony on the rump, sending it back to his foot soldiers. The more mounted they had, the better.

Meri had resumed her attack with an ever-mounting pile of enemy in her wake. She was a little ahead of him, so he pushed forward.

Niko would never let him forget it if Meri died on his watch.

* * *

Nikolas fought with a cold fury that was cathartic. Lately, so much had been out of his control. This, at least, was a stage he understood, and a cause he truly believed in. He wished his cousin, the queen, was here to act as a figurehead. Instead, he had Vard Anton as his leader, a man who was now, supposedly, the king. His lips moved in a savage smile.

The man wasn't even human, or he didn't think he was. What human could morph into a hawk and fly away?

He took the head off a *Sis Lenweri* foot soldier and found himself facing the enemy cavalry. At last! He hated chipping away at men on foot when he was mounted. It felt wrong, gave him too much of an advantage. The elf before him was a commander of sorts by his insignia. The alien eyes glinted darkly through the weird helmet he wore. Nikolas clenched his teeth. How had Sam ever sailed with the blighters? They were enough to make his blood run cold.

The elf attacked, and Nikolas realized he fought an opponent with superior skills. Surprise swept him. Elves weren't used to the sword, so this one must have studied under a human tutor.

Nikolas wasn't a blade master, but what he lacked in technique, he more than made up for in strength. He shouted for those around him to watch his back and went in. Launching a savage flurry of blows, Nikolas caught a widening of his enemy's eyes. The elf was on the defensive, reeling under the crushing blows of Nikolas's cutlass. One thing he and Sam agreed on was this weapon. It was compact in close quarters, and large enough to inflict a fatal wound with a stab or a slash.

Nikolas grunted as he easily fended off the stylish blows of his opponent. The elf's short sword was an effective weapon, but his elaborate training wasn't necessary here. There was no time for elegance, just for killing. Despite his skill, the elf lasted only a few minutes before falling to a lethal stab to his groin. Blood pumped from his leg as he tumbled off his horse. Nikolas grabbed the reins of the riderless beast and sent it back to his men with a slap to its rump.

As he turned to face the next enemy, a scream rang out to the south, and his eyes flicked in that direction. Merielle had her face to the sky, arms outstretched, a sword in one hand and a wicked knife in the other. At that moment, it seemed the battle froze. While he marveled at the soldier his wife had become, he also shook with fear for her. He'd demanded to fight alongside her, but she had refused, claiming he'd suffocate her. *Damn right!* How could he set her free to live or die as she saw fit? He ached to fight his way to her, but so far it seemed she had the upper hand.

He snapped back to the present, and his very real fight. A little way to the north, Formosa fought surrounded by his cronies, all on white horses. They were close to breaking through the foot soldiers and taking up the long-awaited fight with the enemy cavalry. Formosa pushed forward, ahead of his honor guard, determined to reach a pack of mounted enemy.

Nikolas swore as he watched the general get cut off from his guard, and swung his horse for the leader.

Nikolas called for his men to follow and, hacking and stabbing his way, pushed through to rescue Formosa.

The general had engaged several of the enemy and was hard pressed, slashing at them to keep them at bay while his horse spun this way and that, following his leg movements.

Nikolas looked around, found the general's honor guard, and signaled for them to charge. Meanwhile, he slid in beside Formosa, blocking a wicked strike aimed at the general's throat.

"In a bit of a pickle, Cosara," he said, puffing. "Thought my men were behind me."

Nikolas grunted, sparing talk as he drove two of the mounted enemy back with the aid of his bigger horse and broader cutlass. He snapped one of their blades while his bay battle mare swung her rump to clear a space, neatly swinging back into formation.

By that time, the general's cronies had reached him, beating back the enemy, some of them firing crossbow bolts at the *Sis Lenweri*.

He looked round for Formosa and saw him slumped over the wither of his horse, blood dripping from a wound to the head.

Swearing, Nikolas urged his horse to Formosa's side and dragged the general over the saddle in front of him. He turned and, towing the general's white stallion, made his way back behind the lines of the Wildecoast army. He seized the first mounted soldier he saw.

"Take the general to Lady Alique as quick as you can, Corporal."

Having transferred Formosa to the corporal's horse, Nikolas passed the reins of the white horse to a foot soldier and turned for the front lines. He took a moment to observe the carnage and find his guard.

His men were spread over fifty paces along the front lines in a jumble of foot soldiers and cavalry from both sides. Spotting a hot patch of fighting, he headed for it.

* * *

Katrine pushed the bloodshed before her away and concentrated on finding her hounds. She had sent them out in four packs of five, concentrating on the foot soldiers, whose lines the hounds could easily penetrate. The only trouble was there were no leaders among the *Sis Lenweri* front line, or none that wore insignia. At first, her hounds had created chaos on the southern wing of the attack. The kingdom soldiers with them had cut through the *Sis Lenweri* infantry like a knife through butter.

But the surprise was short-lived. The enemy quickly learned to form a shield wall and fend off the beasts with their spears and swords. It was effective, and Kat realized she needed a better tactic. From her place on a low hillock, surrounded by Vard's Rangers and James, she sent out a plea for the hounds to push forward past the foot soldiers to strike at the cavalry. At least they could upset the horses and perhaps pull some riders from their seats.

It gratified her to see the hounds respond instantly and she winced as one of them took a flesh wound from a spear. The pain made her sick. She turned and retched, glad of her empty stomach. James was by her side in seconds, clutching her shoulders.

"Are you well?"

She must have looked a sight for his face blanched as she raised her visor to meet his gaze. "One hound has received a slight injury. I'll cope."

He held her gaze for a moment longer, then nodded and stepped away. Katrine snapped shut her visor and searched for her hounds once more.

They had fanned out, and she sent them a sharp reminder to stay in their groups, smiling as they instantly slid back into formation. They were already making an impact, leaping at the horses of the elves and spooking them. She flinched as a horse screamed after having its tendon torn in two. The poor beast went down, and five hounds leaped on the rider.

She turned her head away from the slaughter. Her next group of five pounced on a downed *Sis Lenweri* rider.

Images of fangs tearing throats and puncturing soft, dark skin poured back to her. No matter how hard she tried, she couldn't block them out. As she watched, a group of mounted enemy came to the rescue of the downed rider, brandishing swords and spears. Katrine gathered her magic in readiness to hurl a fireball to defend her beasts. In seconds, two head-sized balls of fire slammed into the enemy, blowing two from their mounts and blasting deadly fire into the rest. Her hounds were safe for the moment.

And then pain struck her again from close at hand. She searched the field, finding Dawngazer down, snapping at the *Sis Lenweri* who had leaned over and speared her with his sword. The fierce female hound, who was pregnant with the next generation, had a blade through her neck. As she watched, another rider used his horse to trample her hind legs. The hound snarled in pain, and Kat screamed. She went down on her knees, almost blacking out. Hands reached for her, James and… another.

"Kat," James said, "come back to me."

All she could respond to was the pain—searing, unbearable pain—pulling her under, sapping her strength. But she might save Dawngazer if she could only cast one fireball.

"Pull me up," she said through her teeth. "I need to see."

As the men did her bidding, she drew on the core of magic that remained. Eyes closed, she made it bigger and sharper, full of heat and destruction for those who would harm her hounds. Her eyes snapped open, and she saw the hated elves, unleashing her magic in a torrent of three balls that slammed into the enemy. With her last ounce of will, Kat directed the fireballs so they would miss her downed Dawngazer.

The elves attacking died, but the pain in Kat only ate at her harder. It was everywhere, crushing her to the ground. She felt her helmet torn off, and James's eyes appeared before her. She couldn't even raise her head, could barely breathe.

"I love you," she croaked, not even sure she spoke loud enough for him to hear.

* * *

James kneeled before Kat, her eyes staring as though already dead. The damned hound was doing this. The beast was still alive and in pain. She'd be the death of his woman. He had to do something.

Katrine rasped words at him, but he couldn't make them out. He pushed himself to his feet and ordered the rangers to guard her. Leaping from the hillock, he strode toward the struggling beast. The battle still raged around him, but the hounds had moved beyond their dead comrade, still intent on killing. The hounds and the devastating fireballs had given him the chance to approach the injured beast. With a last desperate glance at Katrine, panting on the hill, eyes glazed, James kneeled before the beast.

He could see she was the pregnant matriarch of the pack. Kat had been ecstatic when she realized the hound—Dawngazer, he thought her name was—was expecting. And she was far advanced, he could see.

Could they save her? The neck wound was nasty, but not necessarily fatal. The crushed legs were another matter. He winced as he carefully assessed them. Both feet and lower bones of the hind legs were trampled. She would never walk again.

But she held the future for the pack. Katrine screamed, a haunting, desperate cry that ended in a blood-curdling howl. She couldn't survive this.

James drew his knife and looked into the hound's pain-ravaged eyes. What he saw there was hate. Did she understand what he was about to do? If this beast could rise, she'd tear his throat out.

He removed his cloak and laid it over her head. With a prayer to the Goddess, he plunged his knife into her heart, accompanied by a last scream from Katrine.

James stood, retrieved his cloak, and, grabbing the hind legs of the hound, dragged her back to the hillock.

Kat was unconscious—or dead. His heart skipped a beat at the thought. It could already be too late for her. Panic seized his mind. He couldn't live without her. And then a chorus of threatening growls assaulted them. James spun to see nineteen snarling night hounds advancing on the hillock.

He swallowed hard, dropped Dawngazer's legs and threw himself down beside Kat. Her eyes stared straight ahead, and he was sure she had passed. But then he heard a low, rasping breath, and she blinked.

"Kat!" He shook her armored shoulder gently. "Come back to us. Call the hounds off." She didn't respond except to groan and take another shallow breath. He tried again. "Someone get a wineskin, quickly."

He patted her cheek gently as he waited for what seemed an eternity for his request to be fulfilled. Finally, a ranger shoved a wineskin into his hand. "Help me sit her up. And for all our sakes, keep an eye on those hounds." The beasts had advanced to sniff at the body of their matriarch, whining and snarling.

They raised Kat to a sitting position, and James steadied her head. Her breathing came easier in that position, but her head lolled to the side.

"Kat," he said, raising the skin to her mouth. "Drink this."

He didn't wish to cause her more pain, but she had to be told of Dawngazer's fate. How would she react? He closed his eyes, gathered his resolve, and opened them again.

He trickled a little wine into her mouth, and she coughed as it went down the wrong tube. Her eyes flashed open, the fear in them gripping him by the throat.

James waited for her to understand what had occurred. Her hand came up to seize the wineskin, and she took a large gulp. He wiped her face with a moistened towel someone shoved at him.

"Where is Dawngazer?" she croaked, rolling over to her hands and knees. James rose to a crouch, ready to defend her from the hounds. He saw the moment when she realized she had lost her beloved beast. A wail tore from her throat, and his heart broke. The hounds all howled with her, some growling and taking a step forward. They understood what had happened well enough, even if Kat didn't.

She shushed them with one glance, and they all sat on their haunches. She whirled to face him. "Who stabbed Dawngazer? Was it the enemy?"

He met her eyes, accusation and fear in them. He shook his head. "No, it wasn't. She was gravely wounded, beyond help, and her pain was killing you. I knew she'd never walk again, so I stabbed her through the heart, ending her suffering… and yours."

She slowly rose to her knees, and a ranger helped her to stand. When she could look him in the eyes she asked, blue eyes blazing, "Who gave you the right to make that choice? These hounds are mine—mine do you hear? No one decides their fate but me!"

James refused to be cowed or guilty about what he'd done. "It was her or you! I'd do the same again if faced with a similar situation. Don't ask me to live without you."

Katrine turned to the rangers on the hillock, effectively dismissing him. "Six of you will come with me. The rest can resume the fight. Dawngazer's body needs a proper burial." She replaced her helmet and mounted Demon with difficulty, then accepted the body of her dead hound.

James stood before her. "What should I do?"

She looked down at him. "Please yourself. I don't care."

CHAPTER ELEVEN

ALECIA fought with fierce determination for most of the morning, the fire in her belly lending her strength and endurance. Her ladies seemed to draw courage from her. Not once did she see Gorin, though she searched for him. If she could take down the elven prince or his father, they'd be much closer to victory.

Nearing midday, Alecia was close to exhaustion. Her concentration faded, exposing her to danger. Twice, Lyam had saved her from serious injury, and once Ramón had intervened, ordering her from the field. Grudgingly, she had obeyed, retreating to the northern gate for a quick break and a drink of watered wine before returning. They couldn't afford to allow the enemy any respite, though the *Sis Lenweri* appeared equally tired.

Since returning from her short break, Alecia had had flashbacks to her dragon dream, the one where the beasts swept from the north and attacked. Was it a warning? Pictures in her head kept jabbing at her, and she wondered if she should act on them. After all, what good were premonitions if you didn't use them? She finished her opponent and signaled for her ladies and Lyam to withdraw again. Lin had a nasty cut on her thigh that needed attention, and Kenna looked dazed. If they fought on in this condition, she might lose them both.

Besides, she wanted to climb the wall and watch for the dragons. If they attacked, she'd be ready.

"We just had a rest," Cretia said, a deep frown on her face. "I was just regaining my rhythm. That's important, you know."

They paused as the northern gate was opened for them.

"Two of you need wounds tending to," Alecia said, leading them through. "And I feel a dragon attack is imminent."

"Really?" Arelle said. "I'd give anything to try my hand at those exploding arrows. I didn't get a chance last time."

"Yes," Lin said.

Alecia placed her hands on her hips. "Not you, Lin. You're going to find Benae and get that cut fixed. Take Kenna with you. She looks like she could fall over at any moment."

Lin raised her brow, but, at Alecia's sharp look, merely frowned.

While Lyam accompanied Lin and Kenna to medical treatment, Alecia, Arelle, and Cretia gave their horses to stable hands and climbed the wall. They stood, staring over the battlefield. It was a sobering sight.

Though difficult to assess, Kain and Gwaethe's forces appeared to be struggling to hold their own. Faenwelar's army had reinforced Gorin's at just the right time, and the long marches had exhausted Kain and Gwaethe's forces. The Brightcastle and Wildecoast armies were doing a little better, but after the vicious fighting all morning, Alecia thought something had to give. They couldn't keep up that level of effort all day.

Her eyes swept over the eastern edge of the battlefield, finding the king's banner in the center of the field. That's where Vard would fight, but it was too far away to see individuals. Wildecoast had made quite a dent in Faenwelar's back lines, cutting through the foot soldiers and into the cavalry. And it appeared Wildecoast had more cavalry than the *Sis Lenweri*. She spotted the Cosara banner at the northern edge, and a few others of the prominent houses strung out along the line.

Behind the cavalry were the foot soldiers, an interesting tactic. Reserve cavalry and soldiers hovered behind them, and then the support wagons where Alique would be. She sent a prayer to the Goddess to keep all her friends safe, and a special prayer for Vard.

She turned and looked to the north. That was where the dragons would come from if they behaved as they did in her dream. While keeping a lookout, she approached Reese.

"Be on the alert, Ramar," she said. "I feel a dragon attack is imminent."

He laughed. "We are ready, Princess. But they only have two dragons left after our firestorm of yesterday."

She looked at him, eyes narrowed, and he sobered.

"Yesterday's dragon wasn't fatally wounded, Ramar, and two dragons could still inflict serious damage on us. So far, they've been cautious. How long before they launch an outright attack? If we push hard, Faenwelar may think it prudent to sacrifice his soldiers to dragon fire in order to gain an advantage."

He nodded and left to see to the preparations, placing all his archers and support crew on high alert. Alecia and her ladies stalked the battlements, watching for any sign of dragons approaching. They were joined by Lin, sporting a bulky bandage around her thigh. Kenna had been admitted, suffering from a severe headache. Alecia's heart sped at the news. She couldn't lose any of her ladies. They were like sisters.

Lin patted her shoulder. "She'll be well. Benae has seen to her personally, and she was resting quietly when I left."

Alecia nodded, taking a long, calming breath. She had to trust Benae in this. Then, over Lin's shoulder, she saw a speck in the sky. It appeared too big for a bird, but she might be wrong. Lin turned at the look on her face, and soon they all stared into the north as one speck became two, then three, and finally, four.

"Dragons!" Alecia called. "Four from the north!"

Heads snapped up from around the wall, and Reese blew four sharp notes on his horn. They all knew what it meant. Even on the battlefield, heads turned to the sky.

The dragons' appearance led to a frenzy on and off the wall. In the field, soldiers raised shields and drew cloaks around their bodies. Those not fighting sought cover in the trenches or retreated to the keep.

Alecia's heart went out to those trapped on the battlefield without protection. They had to save them.

As the dragons approached, she saw they were golden, green, red, and ... black.

Kain's words came back to her—that the black dragon's body had vanished. Unless this was another dragon, that beast had survived Kain's attack. Her body went cold, and then boiling hot. What did this mean for their war effort? They could attack the dragons, but how could they ever kill them? Would they forever live with the threat of these beasts?

She shook her head as they loomed closer, peeling off in different directions.

The green beast headed straight for the Wildecoast forces while the red and gold dragons veered west toward Gwaethe, Jacques and Kain. The black swooped further to the west and then climbed high into the sky. Her first duty was to chase those beasts away. The green was closest, so she chose that one to focus on.

"Reese! Get your archers to focus on the green. The other dragons are too far away." The elven leader nodded and sorted his teams with a few brief gestures. They moved smoothly into position.

Alecia kept Lin with her and sent Arelle and Cretia to watch the other dragons and attack if they could. She nocked her arrow, already loaded with the explosive, and focused on the green beast, mentally calculating distance time and elevation, and taking the wind into consideration. She might get three shots, if she was lucky. Perhaps only two.

Sighting along the arrow, she nodded for the assistant to light the wick, pulled the string back to her ear and released. The arrow flew true, striking the beast on the shoulder as it passed above her. It exploded, and the fore rider tumbled off, falling into the forest to the east of the keep. The aft rider scrambled into position and beat out the flames that had taken hold of the dragon's skin and wing. The green dragon screamed and a gout of flame released on those below. Both enemy and allies endured the blast of its pain and anger.

Alecia and her team nocked their second arrows, adjusted for distance and wind, which was coming from the east, and released their arrows. The dragon would be too far away for a third shot, so she lowered her bow to watch the darts fly. Two hit the beast, one on its left wing and the other on the right. She cried in delight as the huge attacker hovered in midair, screaming its pain and distress at the heavens.

As one, the defenders on the wall held their breath, waiting to see what the dragon would do. It gave one last scream and sped off to the northeast, flames still visible on its wings.

Alecia sought the red beast, which had veered south toward the keep. As she watched, fire arrows from the wall hit the red dragon. Its tail exploded with flames but otherwise it appeared unhurt. Then she noticed that no riders sat upon the creature. Surely there had been two before? There were always two riders.

She jogged over to Cretia, who watched the carnage, bow hanging from her hands.

"What happened?" Alecia asked. "The green beast has fled to the east."

"We got both the riders, but the dragon is unhurt except for its tail," Cretia said. "Though if you ask me, it has driven the beast mad."

Indeed, the red dragon flapped over the Selinore and Amitanian sections of the allies, screaming fury and fire at those below it. Banners were aflame and archers were shooting long bows at it, hoping to drive it away or at least blind it.

"What a mess!" Alecia said. "At least the *Sis Lenweri* appear to be faring equally badly. They've retreated to allow the beast to inflict less damage on their soldiers. We must do something!"

Alecia grabbed her bow, a handful of arrows with explosive attached and a pot of coals, then dashed down the stairs. She seized the reins of the first horse she came to and flung herself into the saddle, charging through the gate and down the road between the trenches. At the end of the dugouts, she drove her horse to the left, heading for the allied forces where the red dragon wreaked its destruction.

What she saw almost stopped her heart. Soldiers were on fire, and others were desperately trying to help their comrades with whatever they could. Suits of armor had become roasting pans for bodies trapped within them. Others had grabbed anything close to hurl at the dragon and still more actually had bows and arrows which they were risking their lives to fire. To say it was chaos was to fail in describing the utter devastation.

She quickly assessed the best place to stage her attack and dismounted. The dragon was concentrating on those immediately below it, fire eating up its tail and no rider to direct it. However, its actions were unpredictable, flapping first one way and the other. It could turn on her at any moment, especially once she fired her first arrow.

Swallowing terror she refused to give in to, Alecia set her pot on the ground, nocked the arrow, and dipped the wick into the glowing coals. The seconds the yarn took to catch a spark felt like minutes. Once done, she straightened and drew the string to her ear, pushing all thought of a premature explosion from her head. Aiming for the wing of the beast, she released the arrow. It exploded just past the creature, singeing the tip of the right wing.

The dragon appeared almost uninjured from her dart, but she had drawn its attention. The angry eye of the fire-breathing creature turned to her. Alecia yelped in fear as it sent a gout of flame at her. She was too far away for it to be more than uncomfortably warm, but that wouldn't last.

"Princess! What are you doing? Get out of here!" A female voice urged from her left. Hands plucked at her arm, but she shook them off. She was too busy nocking her next fire arrow and lighting the wick. When she looked for the dragon, it was so close it blocked out much of the sky. The sight froze her for a moment. and the hands tugged at her again.

She reefed her arm free and aimed at the gaping mouth that opened above her, ready to toast her… and fired. Several things happened simultaneously. The dragon let out a roar, closely followed by flame that swept toward her. Her arrow soared toward the dragon, missing the flame and entering the mouth. She saw it lodge in the roof of the cavernous mouth before someone knocked her sideways, a blast of heat slicing so close to her that her cloak caught fire instantly.

Screams came from behind as the dragon's fire hit others. Alecia rolled onto her back to put out the flames and removed her helmet, which had become too hot to tolerate. Her armor had saved her life, as had the actions of whomever lay beside her.

"Princess Gwaethe!"

The elven leader was the last person she had expected to see. The dark-skinned beauty wasn't looking at Alecia, but at the red dragon, which had a hole blown in its skull between the eyes and the nostrils. It was hovering above them, screaming its pain to the heavens, blasts of flame issuing from the hole Alecia had wrought.

Then it fell silent and looked down at her and Gwaethe as they lay prone. Alecia was certain the beast would roast them alive. Her eyes remained glued to the awesome beast, regardless. She held her breath as its reptilian eyes blazed down at her. It was waiting for something, but what?

Alecia, tattered cloak smoking and armor scorched, stood, pulling Gwaethe up beside her. If she was going to die, it may as well be on her feet, not as a groveling coward.

"Red Dragon!" she cried. The beast tilted its head, though it must have been in a world of pain. "Be gone from this battlefield. Go back to where you've hidden these past centuries. I wish you no ill, but will not permit you to plunder this kingdom."

Alecia wanted to close her eyes and pray that when she opened them, this would have been a horrible nightmare. However, Gwaethe's hand found hers, and it gave her strength to hold the dragon's gaze.

"Be gone, I say!" The beast turned its gaze to Gwaethe, and long moments passed before it gave one last roar to the heavens and flapped away to the north.

Alecia watched the dragon retreat, hardly believing her luck. Then she looked at the devastation the beast had caused. Elves and men lay dead, many killed by dragon fire. The same flame that Gwaethe had saved her from had killed dozens. Her borrowed horse had survived, smart enough to have galloped away when she dismounted. She walked across the blackened land toward her mount, determined to escape before the battle resumed. She must find Vard, and there were two more dragons to defeat.

Gwaethe was like a fly buzzing in her ear. She whirled to face the elven princess.

"I must leave you to finish here. Find Gorin and end this."

"You are insane, Princess Alecia," Gwaethe snapped. "What made you think you could fight that thing single-handed, let alone speak to it?"

Alecia shrugged. "It was worth a try. We failed to down the beast when it flew near the keep, and it was causing grief over here. I thought I could help."

"You risked your life for us," Gwaethe said, eyes wide. "You could have died."

"I prefer not to think about that. All is well." She looked around. "Well, perhaps not yet."

"The dragon will be back. It said so."

That caught Alecia's attention. "It spoke to you?"

Gwaethe nodded. "Its voice sounded in my mind. It said to tell you your courage saved you, but, next time you meet, the outcome may be different."

Alecia swallowed the bile that sprang to her throat. "I've made a powerful enemy, then." She was too tired to care at that moment. She turned to gather her horse's reins and remembered. "Thank you for saving my life. I won't forget the debt I owe you." She mounted and rode slowly away.

"There is no debt owed, Princess Alecia," Gwaethe called.

Alecia waved without looking back.

* * *

Kain was on foot, battling an elven commander gifted with the short sword when the dragons appeared. He tried to keep them from his mind, but their threat kept intruding. At the edge of his awareness, he knew when the green dragon fled, but the efforts of his enemy left little room for anything else. The elf's dark eyes had lit with an evil glee when the shadows of the beasts fell across the battlefield.

And then the golden beast had appeared, hovering high above and blasting his ears with a mind-rending shriek.

There followed three short blasts on a horn, and the enemy retreated, sliding back to the center of the battlefield, taking their injured and dead with them. All around him sucked in breaths many thought they'd never take. Why the reprieve when they had been hard pressed by their enemy?

Gwaethe's voice in his head made him jump.

We have defeated the red dragon! I come! I come!

The garbled message confused him. How had they defeated the beast, and why was she coming to him? To help him fight a creature that couldn't be killed? He'd seen that black dragon fly in then flap away. It had almost been the end of him, so distracted had he been. If not for the captain of his guard, he'd be dead.

Feeling more exhausted than he could remember being before, Kain drew his longbow and nocked an arrow, waiting for the golden dragon to attack. It was still too high to hit with any certainty. As he was gazing at the glittering beast in the sky, Gwaethe came to a soil-churning halt on her golden stallion and threw herself off.

She handed him three arrows fitted with explosive packs and wicks and held out a small pot. "You're one of our best archers, Kain. I know you can do this. Unlike the plain arrows, you can hit anywhere, and it will have an effect, as long as you at least glance the body or wings."

He scowled at her and then looked up at the dragon, which hovered above. Was it a little closer now? Why didn't it attack?

He nocked one of the explosive arrows to his bow and hefted it to judge the balance. Not bad. "How long do I have before this goes up in my face?"

"How should I know? I never fired one. But Princess Alecia brought these, and she is an expert. I would say they are suitable for the task. There are three with differing wick lengths. You have the one with the longest, so you should be safe."

Kain grunted. "Princess Alecia's invention paid off." He squared his shoulders and aimed at the dragon, which was indeed dropping toward them, its wings beating in a slow flap. "Light the wick."

Gwaethe approached with the pot and dipped the wick into it. "It's lit!"

Immediately, Kain brought the bow up sighted and drew the string to his ear, instinctively judging the distance and wind, as well as the movement of the beast. "Here goes nothing."

He released the arrow which flew straight at the dragon. Just when he thought he had the perfect shot, the golden creature moved its head to the side and shunted the arrow off course. As it did so, the explosive detonated, showering it with burning powder. It screamed, sending a deadly stream of flame to the ground, right where its own fighters would've been had they not withdrawn. Some of Kain's soldiers caught the side of the flame and rolled on the ground, trying to extinguish the fire in their cloaks and tunics.

He turned to look at Gwaethe, eyebrow raised.

"I did not say it would be easy. That beast has cunning the others did not, unless it was merely luck that allowed it to knock the arrow away."

He examined the dragon, whose rider had extinguished the flames on its head and neck. "Perhaps the riders have better control than I thought they did."

Kain nocked the medium-wicked arrow as the rider pointed at him. Standing feet apart, he shot the arrow, wick hissing and spitting, at the golden beast bearing down upon him. The arrow hit a glancing blow to the left cheek, bounced off its neck and exploded in the face of the fore rider.

There was no time for another shot. and Kain shouted at everyone near to take cover. He grabbed a shield from the ground and brought it up before him as the beast, totally unfazed by the latest explosion, barreled at him. The dragon's size made it ungainly. If he could wait until the last minute, perhaps he could sidestep enough to take him out of the direct path of the flame.

Kain made his choice, but the beast turned to follow his exit path, and he prepared for a roasting death. A buffeting wind struck him from the west, and he never felt the deadly blast. The black dragon took his place in the line of fire and sent back a blast of its own. It hovered mere paces from the ground, forming a barrier that protected Kain and many around him.

The golden beast, with no riders, hovered before the black, smoke rising from its mouth and head. The scales, formerly glittery golden, were now scorched black. Otherwise, it seemed unhurt. The black lunged at the gold, pushing it back a dozen paces, then lunged again. Perhaps this beast was on his side? Or did it just want the honor of killing him? An eye for an eye, literally. For it was indeed the beast he had shot, complete with a healed but empty eye socket. He shook his head in amazement.

Elrie, the black dragon said, the deep gravelly sound filling Kain's mind. *We meet again.*

Nugoriem? Kain asked tentatively.

Who else? I said we would again meet, and here I am.

So you can kill me and take your revenge?

Laughter echoed in Kain's mind. *Would you like me to send Hirova away?*

I would, but what would it cost me? Kain asked.

Merely some of your time. I assume, even though you live only a tiny span of years, you can afford this time, son of Orionkael?

Kain nodded. This had to be the strangest conversation he had ever had, apart from the last time he and the black had talked.

Nugoriem launched himself at the golden dragon, Hirova, spreading his wings and blazing fire at her. The golden dragon launched itself into the air, virtually backward, massive gold and silver wings lifting it beyond the threat and the battlefield within minutes. Soon Hirova was winging her way northward.

"Kain," Gwaethe called. "What is happening?" Her voice held a rare quiver.

"This is Nugoriem, the beast I thought I had killed. He has been good enough to defeat his friend for us."

"So he can have the pleasure of killing you?" Gwaethe asked.

Nugoriem's laugh boomed in his head, and he turned to Gwaethe.

"Would you mind watching what you say?" Kain said. "He can understand you. Try not to insult him further."

No, Elrie, that is your task, is it not?

The dragon landed on the battlefield and looked upon Kain from its great height. He tried to meet the serpentine gaze with equanimity, but it was difficult when he didn't know when he'd be fried.

"Gwaethe, get everyone to move back and tell them not to interfere. You might also send someone to the keep and ask for them not to attack this beast."

Beast, is it? Nugoriem said in his mind. *Once upon a time, elves and the great dragons worked together for the salvation of the kingdom people. It can be so again.*

You don't wish to kill me? To attack us? Kain asked.

You have the blood of Orionkael in your veins, elrie. I am curious to see if you also have the gifts of a dragon lord. What do you say? Nugoriem lowered his head and slid his right leg forward. It appeared as though he was making a step for Kain to climb.

Do you mean for me to mount you?

Step quickly, son of Orionkael, before I change my mind. Hold on tight. We would not want any nasty accidents.

Kain didn't need to be asked twice. He took a run and leaped onto the back of the black dragon, positioning himself on a flat, broad scale over the beast's shoulders. He gripped two slender protrusions that sprang from the base of Nugoriem's neck, as the dragon gave an almighty leap into the sky. Up they flew, Kain's stomach lagging well behind. Other than that, he quickly became accustomed to the motion of the beast as it flapped its great wings.

They took a circle of the battlefield, Nugoriem careful to stay high enough to avoid the arrows.

Viewed from this height, Kain could see several areas where they could take advantage of the *Sis Lenweri* strategies. He also spotted Gorin and Faenwelar.

Speak to the Lenweri *princess, dragon lord. Tell her where she can find her nemesis.*

Dragon lord? Did this magnificent beast really think he was worthy of the title? Or was this merely some elaborate joke? He quickly connected with Gwaethe, sending her instructions, and giving her Gorin's location.

I do not jest, elrie. You will be my rider and my partner, if you so desire.

But I almost killed you.

You have shown your worthiness in your actions then and since. It is not simple to bring down one of the great dragons. And you showed empathy toward me by allowing me to use your magic. I would be honored to travel with you.

Kain closed his eyes as the magnitude of this moment dawned on him. In that instant, he was truly reunited with Orionkael as he had never imagined. He believed he had stepped into his father's shoes before, but this was something he had gained all for himself. To think he had aspired to breed horses!

Riding a dragon and all that came with it? He could never turn *that* down.

He swallowed several times before he got his emotions under control.

You knew my father?

Yes, I trained him and Faenwelar. You are much like him.

I'd like to travel with you. It's more than I could have hoped for, as is this help you're providing.

They had completed another circuit of the battleground, still out of reach of the archers.

I never liked Faenwelar, and he told me untruths about the Lenweri. *I also discovered he attacked Orionkael, and my old friend later died. That kind of action should not go unpunished. He does not deserve to lead the elven race.*

In fact, Nugoriem said, *let us collect the leader of the* Sis Lenweri, *and you can demonstrate to him your suitability to lead your people.*

With those words, the dragon banked and swooped in a steep dive straight toward the banner Faenwelar fought under. Kain held on for dear life as the black dragon plummeted, then came to an abrupt halt just above the *Sis Lenweri* high prince's banner. The elves below gazed up at Nugoriem's underbelly, not fearful, as they presumably believed the dragon to be on their side. Kain smirked as huge black claws gripped Faenwelar around the upper arms and hoisted him off his horse.

Realizing he was in deadly trouble, Faenwelar struggled, cursing Nugoriem, but unable to do anything about his predicament. Then the black dragon rocketed upward, away from the enemy forces and the danger of an arrow attack. He need not have worried, for the *Sis Lenweri* were too dumbfounded at having their leader plucked from his horse to act.

Where are you taking him? Kain asked.

By now, Nugoriem was sweeping northward. The archery range appeared, and the dragon banked and swept down to a smooth landing, depositing Faenwelar in a heap in the center of the field.

Kain dismounted and strode to the enemy leader as the elf struggled to his feet and straightened his armor and weapons.

"We meet again, High Prince," Kain said, standing ready to draw his sword.

"Indeed!" Faenwelar snapped. His eyes stabbed at Nugoriem before landing on Kain. "What is the meaning of this?"

Kain indicated the black dragon. "It was Nugoriem's idea. Something about showing you who the proper leader of the *Lenweri* should be. I guess that means we need to fight each other. Draw your sword, and let's get this done." He drew his weapon and set his feet apart, knees bent, ready to move.

Faenwelar looked down his nose at Kain. "I don't battle inferior warriors. If your father couldn't best me, I doubt you can."

Kain didn't rise to the bait. "You'll fight, or you'll die." So saying, he launched at Faenwelar, surprised when the somewhat portly elven leader had his sword in hand and defending in plenty of time to parry Kain's aggressive attack.

Back and forth they fought, equally matched for all that Kain was half-human and Faenwelar's best years were behind him. The elf kept up a continuous stream of commentary designed to enrage Kain.

But Kain had trained with the best and fought without emotion, having blocked all external stimuli and become one with the sword. There was only one thing that mattered, and that was winning. He even forgot the great dragon behind him in the cut and thrust of the fight. If he sustained a few nicks, then Faenwelar wore just as many. The high prince of the *Lenweri* used emotion to feed his swordplay. Kain starved him of that.

There was a moment in the fight when Kain feared he'd lose. All energy suddenly drained from him, and his attention wavered. Faenwelar pounced, attacking him with a flurry of expertly aimed slices and stabs, which he only just deflected. Then the *Sis Lenweri* struck, sweeping Kain's feet out from under him. He hit the ground, and Faenwelar's sword swept down, only missing his neck because Kain rolled frantically to the side.

On your feet, Kain Arenil. I didn't fly you here to lose. Nugoriem's voice in his head jerked him out of himself, and he resumed his feet just as Faenwelar swung his sword upward. Kain had just enough time to parry the blow and returned one of his own, which sliced into the back of Faenwelar's calf. The elven leader went down, clutching his lower leg. He looked up at Kain with sudden fear in his eyes.

"You can still redeem yourself, Faenwelar," Kain said. "Swear fealty to me, and I'll allow you to live. I'm sure I can find some use for you."

Kain Arenil! Redemption is not possible. He lost his soul a long time ago. If you don't kill him now, he will cause you untold grief and threaten the peace so many have died for.

Kain ignored Nugoriem's suggestion, though the tone was more of an order. He didn't believe there was anyone who was irredeemable. The elven leader was an expert swordsman and an intelligent leader, albeit lacking in decency.

Faenwelar answered through gritted teeth. "I wouldn't swear allegiance to you under any circumstances."

Kain steeled himself to take the leader's life in cold blood and raised his sword. "For Orionkael," he said and brought the sword down on Faenwelar's neck.

It was a quick death, more than could be said for many of the elves the *Sis Lenweri* high prince had tortured. Even so, as Kain filled his lungs with the breath of life, his heart was heavy.

Turning his back on the body, Kain strode to Nugoriem, who was blessedly silent for once. He mounted the dragon, and they took to the air, winging their way back to the keep and the battle. Kain wondered when the day would end.

CHAPTER TWELVE

LL was chaos on the western edge of the battlefield. Gwaethe surveyed the enemy, who were only just reforming their lines after the black dragon drove off the golden beast. She would not have believed it if she hadn't seen the confrontation for herself. Alecia's bravery had also been a revelation.

Gwaethe looked around for Jacques and found him already organizing their lines, bringing the cavalry up for a last push.

Kain's forces were in disarray after he took to the skies, but she had witnessed the black dragon lift a struggling figure from the middle of the battle and dared hope it was Faenwelar. She had heard things about the high prince of the *Sis Lenweri*, and if they were true, Kain had his work cut out for him. Perhaps her brother would merely kill the enemy leader by dropping him from a height. However, knowing Kain, he would fight for the right to lead their people. In the end, that would be best—assuming Kain won.

She sent Jacques to lead Kain's elves and gathered her honor guard. If Kain was taking care of Faenwelar, it was time she did the same with Gorin. She knew where he was thanks to a quick message from her brother as he flew over the battle. Gwaethe spoke to her guard, outlining her plan. Of course, Syndra immediately disagreed.

"This is madness, Princess. You will get yourself killed. He is not worth the trouble."

Gwaethe drew herself up and stared Syndra down. "I could not hold my head high if I did not kill the elven scum. He is a blight on our people, just as Faenwelar is. Both need to be eradicated, and it is fitting that I deal with Gorin."

Syndra opened her mouth to speak, but Gwaethe threw up her hand. "Enough! You will get me to Gorin and see that none interfere. That is all." She turned her stallion and got her bearings. When she spotted Gorin's banner, she signaled her guard forward, Syndra grumbling under her breath.

Such was the disorganization of the *Sis Lenweri* forces at first that Gwaethe and her guards had much less opposition in reaching Gorin than she had imagined they would face. The dragons and their dismissal, along with the apparent desertion of the black dragon, *and* the carrying off of their ultimate commander, had created a valuable distraction. She was halfway to Gorin's banner before she faced any resistance. It helped that her soldiers had removed their *Lenweri* armbands before taking off.

But now the *Sis Lenweri* had gathered their wits and their troops, their faces progressively more determined as she pushed through their ranks. This must work, otherwise she might find herself cut off from her allies.

Gwaethe spied Gorin in the distance, seated on his white stallion, his banner held by a mounted elf. The bastard wasn't even fighting. He scanned the skies as if watching for the black dragon to return. Perhaps he thought Kain would lose, and Faenwelar would fly back in and save the day. She growled at the image.

Over my dead body!

Before she thought to alert her guard, Gwaethe had screamed a challenge and was galloping toward the unsuspecting *Sis Lenweri* prince. Syndra was the only one who stayed with her, swearing under her breath, but the others weren't far behind.

Gwaethe fought like a wild thing, using her stallion to shove through clumps of the enemy before they knew she was upon them, and allowing her short sword to clear any resistance.

Syndra was equally ferocious, howling like a wolf if Gwaethe was threatened.

They were only ten paces from Gorin when he noticed them.

Gwaethe pulled up in a spray of stones and mud and pointed her sword at him.

"Gorin! I charge you with taking my people prisoner and killing them in a manner which was cruel and abhorrent. I also charge you with flogging me until I was near death."

Gorin sneered at her, one slender brow raised. "It is the little *Lenweri* princess, come to accuse me of ruining her life. The truth is, Gwaethe Arenil, your family has failed to lead the *Lenweri* to prosperity, despite many decades of your rule." His gaze raked the skies again before it returned to her. "Where is Faenwelar?"

Gwaethe snorted indelicately. "I have no idea, but, if my brother is wise, he will dispose of your father, never to trouble this kingdom again."

She had tired of this discussion. She swept her sword in an arc, the signal for her guard to spread out and see that none interfered, then spurred her stallion at Gorin.

Gwaethe took him by surprise, and he barely drew his sword in time to parry her strike. A pity, she had aimed at his eyes exposed by the raised visor of his helmet.

Gorin slammed the visor down and sent his sword sweeping toward her, his greater strength almost cutting through her defenses. Her arm buckled under the pressure, but her stallion sensed her struggle. Jacques had trained the mount to respond to its rider's distress, and he had impressed his teacher with his aptitude. Now, it spun to bring her out from under her enemy's blade.

As she moved out of range, Gorin's voice mocked her. "Run away, Princess! You are outmatched."

His voice angered her, but she cooled her temper. She could not make wise decisions when mad. It was what he wanted, or perhaps he thought her incapable of beating him. She must succeed, and then her nightmares might leave her.

Gwaethe went in for the kill, determined to finish him.

Her stallion screamed a challenge as he hit Gorin's horse side-on with his broad chest. At the same time, Gwaethe sent a killing strike at her enemy's unprotected armpit.

With his leg trapped between the horses, Gorin's movement was limited, but he turned his chest to Gwaethe as her sword sliced at him. The blade glanced off the side of his chest instead of entering his body at the armpit. His own sword hit Gwaethe on the side of her helmet.

Gorin brought his blade down again, and she swayed, part rolling and part falling from her saddle. Hitting the ground hard, her sword flew from her hand. All that protected her was her stallion who had maneuvered himself over her.

Gwaethe rolled onto her feet, using her horse to pull herself into a standing position. Her head was spinning from the blow and fall, and it seemed as if two of Gorin now faced her. But he slumped in the saddle, clutching his left knee.

"Get down from your horse," Gwaethe panted, blinking to clear her vision. It didn't help. "Fight me on the ground."

"I am afraid I must decline, Princess. My leg is broken. If you want to fight, mount your stallion, and let us finish this."

Gwaethe stared at him, surprised he hadn't taken more advantage of her when she was vulnerable. As she pulled herself up on her horse, just as her balance was most precarious, Syndra cried out a warning.

About to throw her leg over the saddle, Gwaethe turned to see Gorin coming at her.

She halted her movement, standing upright in her left stirrup, and parried the attack, hoping her mount would keep her in position.

A precarious idea came to her. She remained standing in the stirrup, leaving herself exposed to tempt Gorin into a strike. He took the bait, striking at her again.

Pain lanced through her as his sword struck the leather plates over her abdomen, and then sliced her leg. But, gritting her teeth, she stabbed her sword into Gorin's groin, the blade landing true and sliding deep.

The forward movement of her horse pulled her sword from her enemy and carried her away from immediate danger. She watched as blood spurted from Gorin's leg, and seating herself, turned to watch the demise of her enemy. Her guard closed in around her.

"It is over, Gorin. You are as good as dead."

The elven prince raised his visor with what appeared to be the last of his strength. Gwaethe saw the fear in his eyes.

"Well fought, Princess."

With those words, Gorin tumbled from his mount and into the mud, his blood mixing with the dirt of the battlefield.

Syndra leaned close. "Can you ride? We are deep in enemy territory."

Gwaethe continued to stare at the body of her enemy, her head fuzzy, gut churning and leg throbbing. Was she going to die as well?

"The leaders of this uprising are dead or presumed dead," Syndra said. "We must retreat and request parley before more of us die. Do you agree, Princess?"

Gwaethe could do little more than nod as she was dragged to safety.

* * *

Alecia was seized by an urgent need to find Vard. Anything could have happened to him while she fought the dragons. She found her ladies and Lyam nearby, not surprised to see an angry light in her protector's eyes. Afterall, she had bolted, leaving them all far behind. It seemed her promise to be more mindful of her safety had not lasted long. They galloped back to the battle raging north of the keep. Finding Ramón, they helped him and his guard fight off a group of *Sis Lenweri* on horseback. She shouted in his ear.

"Have you any idea where Vard is?"

"No, and you're not going after him."

She gave him an icy glare. "You can follow me or stay out of my way." She heard someone, possibly Lin, snort.

Alecia hauled on her reins and turned Silver to the east. Vard would be there somewhere. With Faenwelar gone, the battle would soon end, and she must ensure Vard was safe. Already some *Sis Lenweri* had surrendered, but not all. Ramón retreated from the skirmish before them, and Alecia and her ladies followed.

"Look, Alecia," he said, "I must remain and see that the surrender goes smoothly. I suggest you stay here and wait for the King's Blade to find us."

She shook her head. "That's not happening. I don't need *your* help, but you can send some of your soldiers with me. I'd appreciate them."

If the situation had not been so serious, she would've laughed. Ramón was clearly torn between ensuring her safety and his larger duty of securing Brightcastle.

Not to mention the glory of being the victor.

She raised her brow as he considered his options.

"Alright," he said, blue eyes troubled, "I'll give you twenty of my soldiers and help secure the eastern border of the battle. Please be careful."

Alecia nodded. "Thank you."

She sat on Silver, her ladies and Lyam with her, as she waited for Ramón to assign the soldiers to her detail. Her fingers tapped the reins, teeth clenched as it took longer than she expected to pick out her guard.

Eventually, the guard leader reported to her, and they were off. She tried to steady her pace, but it was difficult. With each minute that ticked by, Vard might take a fatal sword strike to the chest. He was good, but in battle anything could happen.

They neared a small hillock, and Alecia detoured to it, trotting Silver to the top. Her ladies and Lyam followed her while the soldiers secured the base.

From that elevation, she surveyed the battle to the northeastern edge of the conflict, picking out banners as she went. There were few to see this far into the conflict. Many had been torn down and trampled under the horses and bodies.

At last, she saw her uncle's banner. As King's Blade, that was where Vard would fight.

"There it is!" she cried, but her heart seized at the sight of the melee that was happening in that area. Hardly any mounted fighting was taking place, which meant she'd have even more trouble locating her love. She stamped on the thought—both that the revelation boded ill, and that she'd thought of Vard as her love. This was no time for sentimentality. She was simply fetching her daughter's father.

Alecia memorized the landmarks, and they charged back down from the hill and toward the waiting battle.

It wouldn't be easy to break through to Vard, but Alecia had gained experience in the preceding days, and the enemy was in disarray. Losing Faenwelar and seeing the dragons chased off had slashed their spirits. They stayed in a pack, pushing their way toward the banner where she hoped Vard fought.

As they got closer, the *Sis Lenweri* defense intensified, as though determined to hold them back. Alecia gathered extra cavalry from the Wildecoast forces as she went, including Isiloe, Chandrelle, and a band of *Lenweri* warriors on ponies and horses.

"Isiloe!" Alecia cried, when she recognized the elven warrior. "Well met! Can you help me get to Vard?"

"Princess! You appear to have been dragged backward through a swamp."

"Never mind that! Come with me and bring your guard."

In a pack, they forced their way closer, those on the outside of the group hacking at the enemy when needed, but generally just pushing them aside until they got close to the king's banner. Then it wasn't so simple. The *Sis Lenweri* here fought like devils, and she lost several of Ramón's guard.

She spotted him! On foot, Vard laid about him with his short sword and his knife, his eyes golden as though he was partly transformed, bringing death to any who dared approach. With him were Samael Delacost, and a woman who Alecia took to be Lady Merielle Cosara, her brilliant red tresses poking out from her helmet.

The three of them took Alecia's breath away as they fought to keep themselves and each other alive. There were others with them, but none as gifted.

But, although talented, the *Sis Lenweri* outnumbered them. Alecia continued to push through the ring of battle toward Vard, a plan forming in her mind. If they opened one edge of the circle, then Vard and his friends could leap upon their mounts and be carried to safety. They must retreat anyway. The *Sis Lenweri* had lost already and must surrender, and she wouldn't lose more people than she had to.

She called to her companions. "Break through! Carry our friends to safety!"

With that, Isiloe gave an ear-splitting cry and spurred her horse into the *Sis Lenweri* before her. Alecia followed her lead, her sword bringing death to any who stood in her way. If she had been tired and filthy before, it was nothing to the dirt and fatigue and blood that caked her when she finally broke through and spied Vard. He ran an enemy soldier through, and their eyes met. The world seemed to stand still. She pushed up her visor, and his eyes blazed at her across the blood and bodies.

"Get up behind me!" she screamed, just as Isiloe and Lin joined her. She spurred forward, Silver's hoofs trampling the body of the enemy Vard had just run through. He was up behind her in the blink of an eye, his sword already sheathed, his arms around her waist.

"You're a sight for sore eyes, my love," he whispered against her ear.

Alecia gulped down emotions that would carry her away. "Hold on, this could get tricky."

She trotted Silver out of the circle of death, heading east where the fighting was lighter, where there were patches of clear earth. When they were free, she kicked her horse into a canter, determined to reach safety. A feeling of unreality came over her. How could Vard be seated behind her after months of being apart? Was this war really almost won?

She heard Hetty's voice in her head. *Don't get ahead of yourself, girl.* She turned her horse and looked back over the battleground.

Isiloe approached with Samael behind her, and Lin with Merielle. They were a disheveled looking bunch, that was certain.

Vard dismounted, and she missed his warmth behind her immediately. He helped her from Silver and stood looking down at her as if taking inventory.

"You arrived just in time, my love. It was getting a little tight."

Sam snorted. "We would've fought our way out of there, My Lord."

Merielle slid from behind Lin and more of those from the field arrived. "I was just getting warmed up," she said, removing her helmet and trying to tidy her hair.

Vard introduced them.

Alecia smiled. "I wanted no more death this day, My Lady. It appears the enemy is close to surrender."

Vard gazed out over the field. "They should be, but do they know that?" One of the nearby foot soldiers handed him a horn. He raised it to his lips and blew three short blasts.

Nothing seemed to happen for a moment, and then the allied soldiers began to disengage. Other horns echoed the three blasts from across the battlefield. Their soldiers trickled toward them, carrying or dragging their injured and dead. Tears pooled in Alecia's eyes as she watched them stagger past her, some with a salute or a ragged cheer for Vard and his heroes.

She slumped under the feelings bombarding her: exhaustion, grief for men and women who'd never laugh again, suffering and trauma. Each fighter who passed her took a small slice of her heart. She felt a hard arm around her waist, one that supported and comforted.

"Alecia, it's time to return to the keep," Vard's voice rumbled through her. "There are decisions still to be made."

She shook her head. "Where is Lyam? He was with me when we rescued you." She mounted Silver so she could have a better look over the field. Lyam's bay mare lay dead nearby, but there was no sign of her protector.

Vard joined her on foot. "My father was with you? I never saw him." He cast his gaze over the field then examined the horse. "She's dead and this is Father's sword." He picked up the bloody weapon and cleaned it on the cloak of a dead Sis Lenweri. "The mare's leg is broken, and her throat has been cut. Father must have put her out of her misery."

"Then where is he?" she asked, getting down off Silver and tramping across the field, beginning a check of every kingdom soldier she found, dead or alive. "He has to be here. He must be safe."

Vard followed her and turned her to face him. "Alecia, we'll find him. I'll organize a search. Just come with me to the keep."

"I won't leave him dead or injured out here. He saved my life, Vard!" She shut her mouth, unwilling to confess more of her dangerous exploits. Lyam must be safe!

Vard turned her and they walked back to Silver. He helped her up on her horse and Lin handed her a flask of wine. She drank deeply. The strong liquid burned all the way to her stomach and warmed her.

"Thank you, Lin. I needed that."

Vard looked up at her. "I promise I'll find Lyam. The word will be sent out. He can't be far away. If he were dead, there'd be a body." His words were optimistic, but his eyes told a different story.

Once Vard had found a suitable mount, Alecia, her guard, and the Wildecoast leaders made their way to the keep.

Along the way, she kept a sharp eye out for Lyam. It was clear that the halt in the battle called by the allies had been embraced by the enemy. The *Sis Lenweri* forces had retreated to the far northern edge of the battlefield. Most of the field had been cleared of injured and dead. A steady stream of allied soldiers and injured filed off the field and through the narrow northern gate into the keep. Those who were hale were directed to the western entrance which gave closer access to the city itself. She saw no trace of Vard's beloved father.

Alecia and her companions lined up to enter via the eastern gate, but the soldiers in line, seeing her, stepped aside and allowed her to enter before them.

The gesture humbled her, numbing the pain she suffered at Lyam's absence. She urged the soldiers with her to enter while she hung back to speak to as many of the fighters as possible. They were of all places and people—some were her own Brightcastle folk, but many were of Wildecoast, Amitania, or elven societies.

"Where is Princess Gwaethe?" she asked one *Lenweri* Ramar.

"The princess was injured in her battle with Gorin. She is being attended to."

Alecia heard an exclamation behind her, and Isiloe pushed through.

"You said the princess was hurt?"

The ramar nodded. "It is serious but not life threatening, Ramar Isiloe. I can take you directly to her should you desire it."

Isiloe nodded, and they both mounted her horse and cantered away. Alecia watched them go, praying that Gwaethe would be well. She was vital for the recovery they desperately needed.

It was a long time before she passed through the gate and into the forecourt of the keep, but she didn't regret spending time with those she had fought alongside.

Vard stuck by her side through all of it, quietly supporting her, lending her his strength. He had detailed one of his sergeants to mount a search for Lyam, though he must long to conduct it himself. Like her, he had wider responsibilities. She thought of Iona and wondered how her child fared. The poor thing had not seen the sun for days, Solomon too.

As Alecia broke through into the bustle of the castle forecourt, she moved aside to allow those behind her to advance. The chaos was overwhelming. Ramón stalked up and pulled her into a hug.

"You're alive!" he said, holding her away and assessing her. "Injuries?"

Vard growled. "I'll see to any injuries the princess has, Zorba."

Ramón's flinty blue eyes raked over him. "Oh, Anton! By all means, play the protective lover for the little time you're here. Sorry to have stepped on your toes."

Alecia was too tired to tolerate their jibes. "Enough, both of you! There are more important things to attend to than resuming your antipathy toward each other."

Vard grunted. "Agreed."

Ramón shrugged. "It's good to see you in one piece. You too, Anton."

"I've asked my people to camp south of the city, Zorba. All who are well, at least. Does that meet with your approval?"

Ramón nodded. "That would be appreciated, though we've made room for leaders and healers in the keep and with the nobles. Benae is clearing out one of the mess halls for a second hospital. You're welcome to send seriously injured there."

"Lyam Anton is missing, Ramón," Alecia said. "He was with us when we found Vard and then vanished. We discovered his dead mare on the battlefield. A search is being conducted but I'd be grateful if you could report this to Benae and Captain Estevot."

Ramón glanced at Vard. "I'm truly sorry, Anton. Your father has covered himself in glory during this battle. He will be missed."

"We don't know that he is dead, Zorba," Vard growled.

"Of course," Ramón said. "I'll see to the search personally and enquire of the *Sis Lenweri* when we speak with them."

"The surrender!" Alecia said. "What's planned there?"

"That's taken care of for now. I've sent Estevot to the *Sis Lenweri* with a document outlining the terms of their surrender."

"You've sent Estevot?" Alecia hissed. "Could you not have waited until someone more senior was available? Perhaps one of the Wildecoast commanders?"

Vard cleared his throat. "As leader of the Wildecoast Army, I would've liked to have been involved."

"You weren't here," Ramón said. "I thought it wise we dealt with the matter urgently. Don't worry, I had our best legal and military minds go over the document, including input from Lady Henrietta."

Alecia was mollified by that news, but not completely. "Our elven allies won't be pleased we left them out."

"No one will be pleased," Vard growled. "You had better hope this doesn't blow up in our faces."

"You'd like me to fail, wouldn't you, Anton?" Ramón threw back his shoulders and stood eye to eye with Vard. "You've never respected me."

Vard said nothing, but arched one eyebrow. A muscle in Ramón's jaw clenched, as did his fists.

Alecia forced her way between them. "Let us await the enemy's response before we tear each other to shreds."

"Indeed," Ramón said, flicking his gaze to Alecia. "The *Lenweri* will draft their own agreement with their brethren to end the civil war. That is beyond the scope of the document we created." His glare returned to Vard who gave a sharp nod.

Ramón was right. There were two issues to settle, that of the *Sis Lenweri* attack on Thorius and the elven civil war. The latter wouldn't be resolved today. She touched Ramón on the arm. "Where's Kain?"

He dragged his gaze from Vard after several long moments. "I don't know. Like most, I saw him fly off with Faenwelar. I await the outcome of that."

"Gwaethe Arenil killed Gorin," Alecia said. "She is wounded, but will live. It's to be hoped that Kain has disposed of Faenwelar too. Surely the *Sis Lenweri* can't have any enthusiasm for continuing this conflict if their supreme leaders are dead?"

"Let's hope not," Vard said. "Alecia, can I speak to you for a moment?"

Ramón waved her away, so she went with Vard as he led her to a quiet corner.

"We only have a moment, my love," he said, holding her hands, "but I wanted to assure you, I love you and would do anything for you and Iona. My offer of marriage still stands."

The breath left her in a gush, and she stood gaping, unsure of how his declaration made her feel.

Did she love him? Yes!

Could she now marry him? Only if it didn't stop her from being queen.

But was it right to deprive her daughter of her father?

She squeezed his hands. "I too wish for us to be united… but I must know the outcome of the succession. You think I have no chance, but my recent actions might have changed that. I genuinely believe I'm the best candidate for the role of kingdom leader. Being a woman shouldn't matter."

She watched his throat spasm and wondered what caused it.

"You're indeed the best candidate, Alecia. I've never doubted it. Can you win approval of the powers that will decide your fate? I don't know."

"You'll see, Vard. I'll make you proud. But first, we need to officially end this war."

She turned away as a great shriek echoed over the keep. All eyes looked upward as the black dragon cast a shadow that swept from the north and angled over the battlefield. Alecia shivered, straining to see if there was a rider. *There was!* But she couldn't see if it was Kain or Faenwelar.

Alecia released Vard's hands and ran to Ramón. "We must be there to witness this. Get your horse!"

Ramón barked an order at a passing groom and soon had three horses for them. They left via the eastern gate and cantered after the dragon. Nikolas Cosara and Josef Formosa were just preparing to enter, so they took them along. The leaders cast Vard angry looks, which he ignored. What was that all about?

Alecia kept her eye on the dragon as it swept toward the *Sis Lenweri* encampment. She still couldn't see who was riding it. Please let it be Kain. This would almost certainly be over if it was.

The kingdom leaders pulled up several hundred paces from the *Sis Lenweri* and watched as the dragon did two laps of the field. Alecia looked back toward the keep and saw that a contingent of *Lenweri* in their white armbands had emerged and gathered behind them.

The dragon landed in a great beating of wings and with an ear-splitting bellow. The man on his back slid off and turned to the allies.

Kain Jazara!

He waved a greeting at them. In the enemy camp, a small group of elves separated from the waiting crowd and approached. Estevot and his guard were with them. Perhaps he was a braver man than she had thought.

Kain stopped before Alecia and the others.

"Greetings friends," he said. "I present to you Nugoriem, the great black dragon, and a friend to the kingdom."

CHAPTER THIRTEEN

ALECIA was the first to curtsey to the beast, and the others bowed. Nugoriem lowered his head.

"Faenwelar and I fought," Kain said. "I killed him. I also heard my sister killed Prince Gorin. I'm here to make an offer to the *Sis Lenweri.*"

"What are the terms, Prince Arenil?" Vard asked.

"That they surrender and put aside their recent allegiances. That the *Sis Lenweri* cease to exist and that from now on, all are *Lenweri.*"

"Brightcastle has already offered a surrender document. Estevot has it." Vard gestured to the captain who stood with the enemy.

Kain nodded. "That's appreciated. Let's get this done." His gaze took in the elven contingent that had followed them from the keep. "Friends, please join us as our honor guard."

The elves closed in around the party of leaders, and they met the *Sis Lenweri* and Estevot on neutral ground.

At first, all was tense and silent, none wanting to speak the first words, perhaps lest they be the wrong ones. Perhaps Kain merely wished for the *Sis Lenweri* to offer their surrender first, so that, forever after, their movement was without force.

"Kain Arenil," the *Sis Lenweri* leader said. "I am Ramar Jupei, the highest ranking of the *Sis Lenweri* who can stand here."

Alecia was shocked at his words. A few gasps said others were too that no higher-ranking officer still stood.

"Greetings, Ramar Jupei," Kain said. "We come in peace, hoping for a settlement to this conflict."

"Have you defeated our leader, Kain Arenil?" Jupei asked.

Kain nodded. "I have. Nugoriem, the black dragon, witnessed the contest and will testify it was a fair fight. Faenwelar is dead."

"As is his son, Gorin," Jupei hissed. "Killed by your sister."

Kain nodded. "Princess Gwaethe has informed me."

"It seems I only have one alternative," Jupei said. "Those of us who lead the *Sis Lenweri*, including our elders, have agreed to surrender, effective immediately." He removed his sword and offered it to Kain, then stepped back. Others came forward and laid their swords at the feet of the kingdom leaders.

Next, Jupei took the scroll from Estevot and read from it.

"From this day forth, we, the *Sis Lenweri,* agree that the kingdom of Thorius belongs to the humans. It is for them to allow the *Sis Lenweri* access or not as they see fit. Let this day be the start of a new tolerance between our people."

Jupei took a quill and signed the letter, then blotted it and placed his personal wax seal. A few of the other *Sis Lenweri* leaders did the same. All the kingdom leaders present, including Alecia, signed their names as witnesses. They also signed a duplicate, and Jupei was handed this to keep. He bowed to the assembled allied leaders and took a step backward.

"We will withdraw to our home and build a new life." He looked at Kain. "Prince Arenil, you are welcome to visit when you can. There is much to discuss."

Kain shook his head. "I need assurances you will support me as leader of the *Lenweri*. There will no longer be a *Sis Lenweri*. Henceforth, all elves will be one people, never again to be divided."

Jupei frowned. "I'm sure you understand. This will need further discussion. To disband our faction without consultation would be wrong."

Kain's face reddened, but he held his temper. "I expect your people to fall into line with the *Lenweri* and accept me as king of all our people. Return to your homes and attend a meeting within the month—to be held in Amitania. You may send a party of up to thirty to negotiate. Don't disappoint me."

Jupei's jaw clenched, but he nodded and turned to leave.

"Oh—and Ramar Jupei," Kain said, "there will be a prisoner exchange for all those fit to travel. It will take place tomorrow, and it will be reciprocal."

Jupei nodded again, and left without further discussion.

When the *Sis Lenweri* had departed, Alecia approached Kain.

"I'm glad to see you in one piece, Kain."

He smiled at her, and she suddenly felt hopeful for the future. "I was fortunate to stay on Nugoriem's back, and also to defeat Faenwelar. Come, I'll introduce all of you."

They approached the huge black beast in a group, Alecia and Vard with Kain, and the rest just behind.

"Nugoriem, I present to you Princess Alecia of Brightcastle, and Lord Anton of Wildecoast. Also here are Admiral Cosara, General Formosa, and Captain Estevot."

All bowed to the dragon, and his voice rumbled in reply. "I am pleased to meet such esteemed leaders. I congratulate you on your victory and wish you well. Through Kain Arenil, I hope we can have a peaceful relationship."

Vard nodded. "If it's within my power, Lord Dragon, there will be many peaceful and productive years ahead."

Again, Alecia thought that a strange thing for Vard to say. Perhaps he was speaking on behalf of his dead king.

Well, it was time to get *that* issue resolved.

The dragon seemed pleased with Vard's words and dropped his head. Kain ushered them away from the beast, and they began their walk back to the keep. Kain accompanied Alecia and Ramón and stopped after only a handful of paces.

"I must fly with Nugoriem to check on my people," he said. "Can you please convey my apologies for the moment? I'll attend your court as soon as I can."

"Bring your sister to Princess Benae," Ramón said, "if she needs medical care."

Kain smiled. "I'll do so. I bid you a good evening." He jogged back to the dragon, and they launched into the air in a flurry of wings that kicked up detritus from around them.

Alecia smoothed her hair and laughed. "Remind me to stay further away next time Nugoriem takes off."

The men with her laughed politely, except for Vard, who merely offered her a warm smile.

Ramón spoke. "I'd like you all to join me for a feast on the morrow. I know there is much to do now, but perhaps by then we'll be ready to celebrate. In fact, I'd like to announce a full week of celebrations. That way, some of the injured may take part."

Alecia smiled. "That's a wonderful suggestion, Ramón. It's been long since we had anything to celebrate."

Privately, she wanted the succession dealt with immediately, but the people of the kingdom deserved the time to recover and mourn their dead.

Perhaps Ramón was becoming a worthy leader.

Vard caught her hand and pulled her behind the others a little way so they could talk in private. "Join me for dinner tonight?"

She smiled up at him. "I was about to suggest the same. I'll have a meal laid for eight o'clock, and you can play with Iona before she goes to her rest."

He raised her hand and pressed his lips to it. "Eight it is."

Vard bowed, mounted the horse he had borrowed, and trotted away. Again, Alecia spied angry looks from Cosara and Formosa.

She mounted her borrowed horse and rode with Ramón back to the keep, chatting about his plans for that afternoon. Alecia's first call would be to the basement nursery where her daughter and Solomon were.

"Come with me to see the children, Ramón," she said, as they left the horses in charge of the grooms. "You must have missed Solomon."

He sucked in a deep breath and nodded. "I really have. It's been several days since I laid eyes on him. Thank goodness for the nannies and Lady Henrietta."

"Indeed," she said.

They entered the keep, planning the feast and other festivities as they walked.

"Of course," Ramón said, as they entered the lower basement corridor, "the weeklong festival will depend on how our casualties recover and will have to be conducted around many burials."

Alecia had given this some thought. "Should we have a special memorial graveyard built for those we lost? The crown will pay the costs, will it not?"

"I think it is only right. I'm sure Wildecoast will help also. That reminds me, I must send ravens to the capital to advise them of the outcome of the war."

She nodded. "Let's see the children first, and then you can take care of that."

They found the door to the nursery, still guarded by two burly sergeants, and knocked. Hetty opened it and ushered them in. Her usual polished noblewoman's front had slipped a little with the recent stress, and Ramón eyed her strangely.

"You remind me of someone tonight, Lady Henrietta. I can't quite place it, though."

"I'm sure it will come to you eventually, Guardian."

Ramón appeared to dismiss his curiosity, and crossed to Solomon, who sat on Benae's lap. He kissed his wife's cheek and laid his hand on the child's head.

Alecia approached Iona, who was jumping up and down in her cot. She picked the child up and hugged her tight, Iona letting out a joyful squeal.

"She's missed you," Hetty said. "I'm no substitute."

Alecia smiled at Hetty through her tears. Just as well she hadn't visited Iona during the war, or she wouldn't have been able to leave.

She hugged her daughter until the child fussed, then settled her on her hip.

"How would you like to play with Dadda tonight, Iona? And have dinner with us." After a pause, she whispered. "And be a proper family for a change."

Hetty's sharp eyes studied her. "The war is won, and in our favor?"

Alecia nodded. "Yes. Both *Sis Lenweri* leaders are dead, Faenwelar killed by Kain Arenil, and Gorin by Princess Gwaethe."

Hetty's eyes widened. "Poetic justice. An eye for an eye, if you like."

"Gwaethe was haunted by Gorin's abuse when in Amitania, and Faenwelar killed King Orionkael. I'd say it couldn't have turned out better. And I met a dragon!"

"Then they really are flying our skies again?" Hetty asked.

"They are. There are four, and I think all are still alive. The one I refer to is the black dragon that was thought killed by Kain. Now it's his mount! One day, he must tell me how that happened."

Ramón cleared his throat. "Speaking of dragons, Alecia, it's one thing to shoot a fire arrow at them and another altogether to challenge one." He looked at Hetty. "Our princess here had a hand in chasing off two of the beasts."

Alecia felt her face heat and tried to look anywhere but at Ramón and Hetty. Her gaze fell upon Benae, who stared open-mouthed at her.

"I wish I had seen that!" Benae said. "Weren't you scared?"

Alecia laughed. "Terrified, but I didn't think, just acted."

Ramón snorted. "Where have we heard that before?"

Hetty tsked. "You have a child to think of. When are you going to understand the risk when you physically fight? This kingdom can't afford to lose you."

Alecia huffed. "I don't think many would agree with you, my friend, least of all Ramón and Benae."

Benae stood and approached her, handing Solomon to Ramón. She placed her hand on Alecia's shoulder.

"I agree with Lady Henrietta, Alecia. You have a greater value beyond fighting wars." She paused. "But I understand you want to prove yourself. Ramón has always been too quick to protect you."

Her words confused Alecia. Where was this going? Why would Benae now be sympathetic to her? Was it time to bury their animosity and move forward?

But that wouldn't be possible until they settled the succession.

"Nonsense!" Ramón said. "Ladies need to be protected, not exposed to violence and death. I'll never apologize for protecting them."

"You're not my father, Ramón," Alecia said, "nor are you responsible for me. And women know death and violence very well. We bear children, which is perilous. Remember how I almost died?"

He scowled. "And that brings us to Anton. Your savior on that occasion. But don't forget who it was who found the dog and brought him home to you."

"Ramón, not in front of the children!" Benae said.

Benae never enjoyed hearing about Ramón's quest to bring Alecia back from exile; about how he had tracked Vard down and brought him to Alecia in the nick of time to save both her and Iona. She would ever be grateful for that, regardless of how the throne was settled.

"It's fine, Benae," she said, "though I agree the children shouldn't be exposed to this ugliness. I can take your feelings about Vard. They'll never change. Just know, Ramón, that your friendship is valuable to me, no matter what transpires in the future."

He frowned at her. "Why would there be a time when we were enemies?"

Alecia noticed Benae chewing her lip. *She* certainly knew of reasons they might fall out and couldn't hide her fear. Was it crucial to her that she and Ramón be the Guardians of the future king? Solomon had no right to be the heir if she was correct in her suspicions.

It was so tempting to challenge them now, but she still needed the element of surprise.

Alecia drew a deep breath. "I've not yet forgiven you for the pain you caused my father in his last days." Her eyes slid to Benae, whose gaze was on the floor, her hands clasped before her. "But now isn't the time for misgivings. We have a victory to celebrate. You should send those ravens."

Ramón seemed reluctant to leave, but he nodded. He handed Solomon back to Benae, kissed her cheek, and left the three women.

"Lady Henrietta, please retire to my chamber. Benae and I thank you for your help with the children. You must long for rest and a bath."

Hetty nodded, curtseyed, and left the basement nursery.

"Benae, you must be exhausted," Alecia said. "Why don't we take the children back to their nannies, and you can enjoy a well-deserved break."

Benae touched her hair. "I must look a mess. I've barely changed clothes since this war began."

Alecia laughed. "I've changed, but not bathed. Dousing myself with liberal quantities of lavender water is no substitute for a bath."

Benae smiled. "I'll take Solomon back to his room, check some of the worst injured, and then wash this grime off. It will be welcome."

They left the gloomy chamber, chatting about their favorite bath salts.

CHAPTER FOURTEEN

ALECIA had bathed, washed her hair, and dressed in her favorite lilac gown. The new seamstress had made the dress, and this was its first outing. Millie had done her hair, and she sat before the mirror, applying her creams, eye liners, and blush.

All things considered, she was happy with her appearance. Luckily, not too many bruises marred her face, just an abrasion on her chin and a smudgy bruise beside her left eye. Hetty's special concoction, used in the past to mask injuries caused by mercenaries, easily concealed them. She smiled at her reflection, remembering how scared she'd been when confronting those men.

Now she was brave enough to take on dragons, not to mention lead soldiers in war. She never would've imagined a year and a half could transform her so completely. But her values were still the same, those her mother had instilled in her—care for people and justice.

She'd never again allow others to decide her fate, as her father had, and as Ramón was still trying to do. And truth be known, Vard would attempt it too. He had already proposed again and would expect an answer.

There was a quiet tap on her chamber door, and Millie went to answer it. Alecia followed and stood at the door between the sitting room and bedchamber, ready for a first glance at her lover.

Millie pulled back the door and curtsied.

"Welcome, Lord Anton. Come in."

Alecia's eyes roamed his lean form as he stepped over the threshold. His gold-flecked green gaze, like the seas at Wildecoast, trapped her, stealing her breath. They stood, staring at each other, forgetting they had company. At least Alecia did—Vard would never forget himself like that.

He wore his hair loose, but restrained with the customary leather band around his forehead. Fitted black breeches hugged his muscled thighs. She shivered at the memory of those legs squeezing her as they rode back together from the battle. A black tunic with silver piping emphasized his chest and lean waist, and his white undershirt brought out his deep tan. He was glorious to behold, and Alecia wished this moment would live in her memory forever.

Millie cleared her throat. "I'll be leaving if you have no further need of my services, Princess. It's good to see you again, Lord Anton. I'll ensure the food is delivered presently." She curtsied again and left the chamber.

Vard smiled, and Alecia's face heated. Why did she feel like a girl who had never been kissed?

"Would you like a goblet of mulled wine, Vard?" Without waiting for an answer, she crossed to the fireplace, poured the wine, and heated it with a poker.

When she turned to deliver the drink, she found him right behind her.

"Oh!" She stared up at him, their wine held in her two hands separating them. "Ah, any news of Lyam?"

Vard frowned, his glorious eyes clouding. "Nothing! Plenty saw him fighting at the end but not his wounding or death. He seems to have vanished." He swallowed hard. "War is always dangerous, but I never believed he would be taken from me so soon after finding him."

Alecia's heart cracked at the pain in his voice. "I'm sorry, Vard. Lyam and I had started to form a bond. He was an extraordinary man—like his son."

"Let's not believe the worst, my love. I have hope and so must you." He took the goblets from her and placed them on a nearby table, then clasped her hands. He raised one, then the other, and kissed her fingers. His actions entranced Alecia. Vard had become so refined over the last year. Had he grown beyond her?

"Alecia," he said, "you become more beautiful each time I see you. When you arrived at the battle today, I had never beheld a more glorious vision. Your eyes held a ferocity I'd not seen before. Your body a sureness that was new to me. My heart beat so hard I feared it would thump its way out of my chest. I had to concentrate hard not to fall prey to my enemy."

"I was there to save you, not to distract you!"

His brow rose. "As to the saving, I'm not sure I needed that, but the help was welcome."

Alecia shook her head. Her Vard was ever the proud man. He wouldn't take kindly to being rescued, and truth to tell, he might've been able to fight his way out of that mess.

She swallowed, remembering the fear that had gripped her at seeing him, yet being unable to reach him. It had been all too easy to imagine him being run through before her eyes.

"I love you, my proud King's Blade," she said. "You've come far since Iona's birth. I thank you for being such a wonderful support for my uncle, the king."

Vard smiled. "Beniel was a worthy king, and I was glad I could give him my loyalty. He truly appreciated it."

"Your Defender instincts never drove you to rid Thorius of him?"

"Of course not. He was a decent man."

Her heart ached at the thought that once Vard had been sent to assassinate her father. He hadn't because something had stayed his hand, whether it be his Defender essence or his love for her. Vard had kept her father alive, only to have him die of heart failure. If Jiseve had lived, they would now have had a king to step into Uncle Beniel's shoes.

"Do you think Father could've made a good king?" she asked, gazing up at him.

Pain swept across his face, and he swallowed hard. "Sometimes I find it difficult to believe you're his daughter. You're brave and good while he was self-centered and cruel." He studied her face. "No Alecia, your father wouldn't have made a good king." He looked like he wanted to say more, but pressed his lips together tightly.

She pulled free and walked to the fire, gathering her wine as she passed the table. Suddenly, she needed something warm in her belly. "You didn't know him before Mama died. Something inside him snapped. He was a different man. Sometimes I even think he hated me because I reminded him of her. His love for me was never the same after she left us."

Strong fingers folded over her shoulders and squeezed. She leaned back against his hard chest and laid her head under his chin.

"Alecia, my love, a father could only be proud of a daughter like you. And if he wasn't, then it was his loss. Let's not dwell on the past, but look to the future."

She sighed. "It's difficult to forget what has so recently passed. And, with losing Uncle Beniel, it has brought it all back." She turned to him. "How was it at the end? Did he have any last words?"

"There's a will and letters in Wildecoast."

"No," Alecia said, turning to face him. "I mean right at the end, before he took his last breath, what did he say?"

Vard swallowed as if what he had to say was painful. It seemed Vard *had* become close to the king. She was glad her uncle had had someone he could depend on.

"King Beniel was triumphant in the end. He fought Faenwelar, and I believe he would have been the victor. But his collapse on the field of battle meant that Faenwelar escaped."

She was silent as she imagined the scene. "And then? His last words?"

"I was with him," Vard said. "You can take heart from the fact that King Beniel didn't wish the throne to go to a child, or inexperienced Guardians, or anyone he couldn't trust."

She gazed up at him, hope bright in her heart. "He actually said that?"

He nodded. "Almost his exact words."

"Then he was coming around to the idea that his niece could rule after him? Did anyone else hear these words?"

Vard shook his head, a shadow dulling his brilliant irises. "No one heard except me, and I can't be sure what was on his mind." He cupped her face with his hand. "Do you think you have the support to make a play for the throne?"

"I only know one thing. I'm in a much stronger position than I was when I returned from exile. And knowing Uncle Beniel had doubts about the current players gives me hope that I can step into his shoes. Who else is there?"

Vard's jaw tensed. "Who indeed?"

There was a knock on the door. Two maids entered, bringing trays of food. Delicious smells wafted to Alecia, and her stomach grumbled. It was days since she had eaten properly without a great knot in her stomach.

"At last! I could eat half a cow."

Vard laughed as he joined her at the small dining table where candles had been lit.

"Let me bring Iona, and she can join us. Did you know she is eating some bread and cheese? Perhaps she can try something new tonight. Of course, she loves goat's milk."

Alecia fetched her daughter from the bedroom and sat her in the special highchair that Ramón had commissioned, along with one for Solomon.

Vard kissed his daughter on the cheek, and she squealed at the brush of his whiskers against her skin. "Dada!"

Alecia froze, and her gaze met Vard's stunned eyes. "That's her first word! She must remember you."

"How's it possible?" he asked. "It's been months since I've seen her."

"Dada! Dada!" Iona cried, thrilled with her new skill. Vard leaned over and kissed her again, and she giggled. That prompted them all to laugh. The child looked from one to the other, ecstatic at being the center of attention.

Alecia felt tears in her eyes. The thought of more moments like this was almost enough for her to forget her dream of being queen.

But being queen didn't mean she had to give this up. She could have it all, if only she made the right moves. Already Vard seemed to have come to her way of thinking if his words were anything to go by.

She sat down and handed Iona a sliver of bread, then dished up for herself and Vard. Lifting her goblet, she toasted. "To the future, and to our family."

Vard chinked his goblet against hers, and the warmth in his gaze reassured her that all would be well. More than well.

* * *

Nikolas Cosara had completed the inspection of his troops and now wanted to find his wife. Not having formal duties to attend to, Merielle had vanished soon after he saw her speaking with Ramón Zorba. That was after Kain Arenil returned on the black dragon...

Cosara found himself unsettled, and there was more than one cause.

Uppermost in his thoughts was Merielle's battlefield performance. The enemy had barely touched her. He had not fought alongside her except toward the end, but had kept a close eye on her; too close if the many nicks on his own body were any indication. He had been far too distracted, and it was a miracle he had survived.

But he *had* survived, and Ramón had allocated he and Merielle an extensive suite in the mansion of one of the higher-ranking lords in Brightcastle.

His troops seen to, he found the mansion and stabled his horse, then entered the house by the back door. The housekeeper greeted him and escorted him to the ornate staircase. From there a footman had delivered him to their apartment.

Without knocking, he entered, hopeful of finding Merielle there. He closed the door and scanned the darkened sitting room. A fire crackled in the hearth, but the room was empty. He prowled toward the bedroom door, poked his head around it, then smiled.

Merielle was in a large iron bath, rising steam rising infusing a lavender fragrance to the room. The smaller fireplace here was lit as well. Her eyes were closed, and there was a smile on her face.

"That had better be my lover," she said, eyes still closed.

He stalked toward her, bent, and kissed her lips. "As far as I know, I'm the only man who qualifies," he growled.

Her wet arm wrapped around his neck, and she pressed her mouth to his. He was soon lost in the wonder of her kiss. His questing tongue gained entry, and he explored her warm depths. She groaned, and the sound shot straight to his groin.

"You'll be the death of me, my love," he said, reluctantly pulling back.

"How so?"

"First distracting me on the battlefield, and then firing my lust after so long without. No man should be so tortured."

She held up one finger. "One, there was no need for you to worry about my safety." A second finger joined the first. "And two, when did arousal ever kill anyone?"

"Ask the former prince of this castle, and you'll find out."

Merielle blushed, and Nik's groin tightened further. If he didn't relieve the pressure soon, he'd disgrace himself. He disrobed, placing his clothes neatly over the back of a chair, and soon stood naked before his wife.

"I trust there are no maids expected?" he asked.

She smirked at him. "I made sure of it." Her expression sobered. "You're injured. Why didn't you say something?"

He couldn't take his eyes off her. "They're nothing. Besides, you can wash them for me… right now."

He stepped into the bath, and she made room for him, sitting up so her glorious breasts peeked above the water. The cooler air made her nipples harden. They weren't the only things that were hard. He sank beneath the water and groaned as the warmth crept over his muscles. Once fully in, he closed his eyes, luxuriating in the sensation of cleansing the water imparted.

He felt a cloth on his chest and opened his eyes to find Merielle on her knees, tending to him. Closing his eyes, he enjoyed her attention, moving the cloth from one area to another as she ensured all his cuts and scratches were clean. Some stung, but then she moved onto his manhood, and his eyes sprang open. Squeezing him gently, she laid her lips on his, and he thrust himself into the cloth.

"Ahh, I've longed for this." He reached up to cup her breasts, and she gasped. Breaking their kiss, he moved to her breasts, laving first one nipple and then the other. His hand moved between her legs, fingers exploring her sex then plunging deeper.

"Yes, Nikolas!" she said, thrusting on his fingers. She kissed him, and they fell into the rhythm of love until Merielle stiffened and cried out, her climax gripping her and not letting go. She collapsed against him, and he noticed the water had cooled.

"My love, let's get out of this bath."

Her eyes opened, and the love in their vibrant green depths transfixed him. How had he ever existed before her? He must protect what they had at all costs.

Nik climbed out of the bath, laid a blanket before the fire, then turned and helped her out. He wrapped Meri in a towel, grabbed one for himself, then led her over to the rug. Kissing her curves as he went, he dried every inch of her delectable body. He wanted her to be in no doubt of his love.

Last, he dried her hair, pressing his face into the luxuriant waves, her exotic scent transporting him to their first days in the cottage by the sea.

As he finished, Merielle studied him. She sat with a towel wrapped around her, red hair cascading around her shoulders and love in her eyes.

"You are already dry," she said. "Where is the fun for me?" She touched the gaping cut on his left bicep. "I will sew this for you."

He shook his head. "Hardly what I had in mind, my love. I'm going to take you to bed and make love to you until we're both exhausted."

Her eyes gleamed with excitement. "Oh, are you?" She held out her arms, and he pulled her up, lifting her and placing her on the bed. Without missing a beat, Nik kneeled before her and placed his lips on her sensitive nub. She grabbed his head and thrust up at him, and that was his undoing. He tried to make her climax again before taking his fill, but the days of abstinence had weakened him. Long before Merielle reached her peak, Nik plunged into her tight heat and lost himself in the maelstrom that only his wife could induce.

* * *

Lady Alique Jazara had gone past the point of exhaustion after days and weeks of battle, first in Wildecoast, and now in Brightcastle. But there was no one else sufficiently qualified when men and women were on the brink of death. She had sent the worst to Benae, and the others she tended in the makeshift tent hospital outside the castle grounds.

She desperately needed Kain and sent him messages. When those failed to produce her husband, she paid servants to search for him. All to no avail.

Now it was almost midnight. She sat at the end of the nearest bed, the wounded soldier in it asleep, and placed her head in her hands. It had been three days since she had a full night's sleep. In that time, she had barely eaten one meal a day. She vaguely wondered what her medical decisions had been like; how many mistakes she'd made.

There was a scuffle of feet at the opening of the tent flap, and someone cleared their throat. Whoever it was could approach her if they needed her, she thought vaguely. Her next experience was warm hands grasping her by the upper arms.

She opened her eyes and couldn't comprehend the face before her.

"Kain!" She flung herself into his arms and tears poured down her face. The endless days of fear and longing suddenly could no longer be borne, and she broke completely.

"My darling," Kain crooned, "it's alright. I'm here, and I'm never leaving you again."

She raised her head. Goddess! She must look a sight! Bad enough to be dirty and disheveled, but to cry as well? But she couldn't help it. It had been so unbearably difficult to be apart from him, not knowing if either of them would survive and uncertain about the future, even if they found each other again.

"You can't possibly say that, Kain," she sobbed. "You're a king now. At least that's what I hear. I've been expecting you all afternoon and night. Where have you been?"

He smiled and wiped the tears from her face with his cloak. "I've been looking for you. Each time I thought I'd caught up, you'd already moved on. And there have been other distractions." His face sobered. "We've lost many of our people, human and elven."

A sudden fear gripped her. "Gwaethe! Is she—?" Alique couldn't put her fears into words. Gwaethe was like a sister to her.

Kain smiled, and her heart settled its hurried pace. "My sister was injured fighting Gorin, but she's recovering, and he is dead."

"So much needless loss of life," Alique said.

"Indeed, but it wasn't our choice. If we'd left the *Sis Lenweri* to do as they pleased, that also would've been wrong."

She grabbed his face and kissed him hard on the lips. The action settled her nerves. It took her out of the grubby tent; away from the suffering to a plane where she could be joyous.

"I love you so much," she said, drawing back when the kiss threatened to become indecent. "Does this mean we can steal a moment for ourselves?"

He smiled. "Come with me. I have a chamber in the keep that will be perfect for this occasion."

He kissed her again and led her from the tent.

CHAPTER FIFTEEN

J AMES Tomel's heart had cracked in two the moment Katrine said those words. His chest ached with grief and longing to be with her. She couldn't mean it, could she?

But his wife was a strong and passionate woman, and her hounds meant so much to her.

More than me? He shook his head and breathed deeply, trying to still the panic. This couldn't be the end.

He hadn't spoken to her since she rode away from the battle. The hounds had followed, crowding between them so he couldn't approach. At least the Rangers, who'd accompanied them during the conflict, had protected her. Now she remained isolated in the tent she'd crawled into for more hours than he cared to count. He had ventured as close to her as he could get without being attacked by her beasts.

James placed his head in his hands and groaned. He played the events of the battle yet again, and couldn't see any other way he might have ensured Katrine's survival.

Well, if she wouldn't accept help from *him*, then he must find someone else to fix this. He looked around for a horse and, spying one close by, strode to it, mounted, and bolted for the keep.

The whole way there, James prayed to the Goddess that he could find the witch who was Katrine's mentor. Her name was Hetty, and his wife had visited the old crone in Brightcastle in the past.

He knew where she lived. If anyone could help, it was her.

No one tried to stop him from approaching the city, but, at the gate, soldiers were checking everyone.

He was stopped and asked to dismount.

"What's your business here?" A sergeant asked.

"I'm looking for someone. I hope she can help my wife."

"Your name?"

"James Tomel, Master Jeweler of Wildecoast."

The soldier studied him with narrowed eyes. "You don't look like a craftsman."

"Who does these days? I've been fighting, man. And each moment you delay could be the end for my wife."

"Bring her here then. We have healers."

James clenched his teeth. His marital problems were not this man's concern. "I can't do that."

"Master Tomel, my orders are not to allow anyone entry unless they can be vouched for. Is there someone here who can do that?"

"How should I know? Lord Vard Anton could, but I've no idea where he is. Or Samael Delacost, but he could be anywhere."

"Then you must wait until you can find one of them. Write a note, and I'll have it sent to Lord Anton. I believe he's at the keep." The man pulled out a parchment and quill, and handed them to James.

James huffed out a breath as those behind him grumbled at being delayed.

He scribbled a note to Vard, including details which would alert Vard it really was James at the gate, and handed it back to the guard.

"Please hurry." He turned and led his horse out of the way of the gate and the guards. He watched as the sergeant summoned a messenger who took the note and set off running.

If only he had thought to have Vard provide a reference for him, he could've avoided this. His heart beat a frantic pace as he imagined the mental anguish Katrine must be feeling. How could he be sure of her physical safety with those beasts so close? What if they blamed her, as well as him, for losing their matriarch?

He'd been waiting for over an hour and was lost in his waking nightmare when a large hand clasped him on the shoulder. Samael's smiling face, complete with a bleeding wound on his cheek, appeared in his field of vision.

"James, man," he said, clapping him hard on the shoulder. "It's good to see you. Where's Katrine?"

He swallowed hard, trying not to get his hopes up. "I don't know. I'm trying to get help for her. She's… fragile… and she won't see me."

Sam frowned, clearly not following his garbled explanation, but he knew Katrine well enough. "Vard sent me after he got your note. What do you need?"

"I seek a woman called Hetty. She might get through to Kat."

"Do you know where she lives?"

James nodded.

"Then let's go. You're free to enter the city."

James led his horse through the gates, which were still busy with soldiers entering, many of them injured. Sam mounted his horse, and the two of them progressed up the main street.

"Where's this Hetty?" Sam asked.

"Last time we visited, she was in a two-story cottage near Firedrake Alley."

After a few stops for questions, they found the alley, and James located Hetty's house. The building looked deserted, and no one came when they knocked.

"With the war, there's no telling where she went. Is there anyone who might know?"

"I think she was a friend of Princess Alecia's."

Sam looked at him skeptically. "Are you sure? No princess I ever heard of associates with someone who'd live here."

"I assure you it's true."

"Great! I just came from Vard who was with the princess. You're killing me with all this back and forward."

"Don't concern yourself," James snapped. "I can take it from here."

"What sort of brother-in-law would I be to abandon you? Besides, Esta would never forgive me if I prevented you from helping her sister. We'll go to the keep, and find the princess, and from there Hetty."

James nodded. "I appreciate your help."

They remounted and resumed their ride toward the keep, making slow progress because of the number of people on the street. It seemed the entire city was desperately trying to get somewhere other than where they currently were. Many were injured; everyone was dirty and bedraggled. He wondered when the city and the kingdom would recover.

"How do things stand for you now, James?" Sam asked. "I mean, you fell out of favor with the king for a while. Now he's dead, what happens?"

"Vard kept me close for appearances, but he cut me loose when we left Wildecoast. He didn't have time to spare for a disreputable master jeweler."

"I wondered what you did, but no one knew or was willing to say."

"Never mind. It doesn't matter now. All I care about is getting back to Katrine."

"Look, man," Sam said, "despite what your wife says, I'm not a bad person. If you got to know me, you might even like me. We could be friends."

James looked sideways at his companion. Despite his nasty facial cut, Sam had fared better than most in this damned war. His tunic and cloak were hardly damaged, and his blond locks were neatly tied back, beard trimmed. One day, he might even be respectable. But there was still a wall that prevented him from warming to Lady Esta's pirate lover. Even the thought of the two of them made his teeth clench.

"Possibly." It was abrupt, but as much as he could muster for the man with him—rather unappreciative of him, he knew.

They rode through the inner castle gate after Sam showed them his pass and dismounted at the steps.

"Stay here with the horses while I find the princess." Sam had a brief discussion with the housekeeper before entering the castle.

James shook his head. How had a bloody pirate risen to such heights while he, the king's former spymaster, had to beg for everything he got these days? It would end. It had to. He was still fuming when a feminine voice distracted him.

"Master Tomel?"

He looked up to see Princess Alecia on the steps above him, Sam beside her. He bowed low.

"Princess, thank you for seeing me."

Her eyebrows rose. At their last meeting, he had dismissed her.

"Master Delacost said something about you needing Hetty. Is it Katrine?"

He nodded jerkily. "She isn't well. I don't know how to help her."

"Have her brought here. I'm sure Princess Benae would see her, no matter how tired she is."

Again, he shook his head. "I can't get to her. She won't see me. I thought she might speak with Hetty."

Alecia smiled. "I hope you're right." She turned to Sam and spoke quietly to him, then looked at James. "I've just given Sam the instructions to where Hetty lives. You must guarantee her safety."

"Thank you, Princess," James said. "I won't forget this."

"Neither will I, Master Tomel," she said, turning away and re-entering the keep.

It looked like he owed her a debt. He wondered what form *that* would take. Knowing the nobility, it would come in the form of political support.

Sam cut his musing short as Sam spoke.

"Hetty lives in that house over there." He pointed to a fancy mansion three houses away. "Let's see if she's willing to help."

A maid showed them into a small parlor and fetched Hetty. She appeared quite different from when James had last met her. He introduced Samael, and they both bowed.

"No need for that," she snapped. "What's this? Katrine? Is she well?" She stood with her hand on the back of a nearby chair as if she needed support.

"She was injured in battle, but survived." James turned to Sam. "Could you wait outside for me?"

Sam scowled, but left as requested. Once they were alone, James continued.

"It's those hounds of hers. She used them in the battle. One was killed, and it was as if Katrine had the spear in her own body. She suffered along with it until the beast breathed its last. Afterward, she was in a bad way. Shock, she said."

Hetty nodded. "I've heard of such a thing in people who have a close connection with beasts. But did she recover?"

"Yes, but it happened again. This time the matriarch of the pack got seriously injured. Katrine was in agony. I thought she'd die, so I did the only thing I could think of to save her. The beast was dying anyway, so I stabbed it through the heart."

Hetty's eyes widened. "That would've taken courage. I hear they're terrifying."

James blew out a breath. "That doesn't matter. When I returned to Kat, I thought my actions had been in vain. But she was alive.

"Then she discovered what I had done, and now she hates me. She fled the field and holed up in a tent behind the battle lines, escorted there by some rangers. But she won't allow anyone close, and those hounds of hers are guarding her tighter than a mother lion protects her cubs."

He gripped Hetty's hands. "I must get to her, to check she's well, and explain why I acted as I did." He closed his eyes, gathering strength to go on. "I can't lose her, Hetty. Will you help?"

"What makes you think the girl will listen to me?" she asked.

"She respects you more than anyone. Perhaps you think she has forsaken you, but I assure you she hasn't. You're often in her thoughts. She agonized over refusing to step into your shoes."

Words that James had hoped would convince Hetty only made a cloud descend on her visage. She was difficult to read.

"There's no need to beg for my help, Master Tomel. I love that girl. I'm just not sure she'll listen to me." Hetty turned away, then again faced him. "Let me get my cloak and saddle a horse. Meet me in the back near the stable."

James let out a long breath. "Thank you." He followed the old woman out the door, and met Sam in the hall. "She's coming with us. We'll meet her at the stable."

Hetty was ready in no time. The three trotted back into the main street and took a right turn into the city. The crowds were just as thick, perhaps worse, and there was an unsettled buzz, as if no one knew what to feel about the end of hostilities.

James kept his eyes on those around them while Sam scanned the rooftops for danger. They should be safe, but the end of the war was only a few hours past, and there could still be elements determined to cause trouble.

They passed through the gate and moved into a canter, swiftly returning to the site of Katrine's crisis, then past it toward the Wildecoast encampment.

Many of the soldiers and support staff with the Wildecoast army remained in camp, but most knew Samael, so they had no trouble getting through the sentry lines. From there, it was a short ride to the tent Kat had sought as refuge.

Sam and James dismounted fifty paces from it. The shadows of the hounds lurked close to the tent.

A man raced up to Sam, wringing his hands. "Some crazy woman is in my tent. Are you here to deal with her?"

Sam smiled down at the fellow. "I know this is inconvenient, but the lady had a nasty shock and needs a while to recover. Do you have somewhere you can go for now?"

The man frowned, seeming torn between anger and sympathy. "Well, I'm a kitchen hand, so the cook may accommodate me for the night. But what about my things?"

James butted in. "I'll have them brought to you if you let me know where you are." He pulled a silver coin from his pocket and handed it to the man. "This is for your trouble. I'll try to have the tent back to you on the morrow."

The man bobbed his head. "Thank you." He pointed to a circle of wagons nearby. I'll be over there when you sort this out."

He trotted away, and James helped Hetty down from her horse.

As he did so, he scanned the area between them and the tent. He spied several rangers further out from the hounds. His heart eased. At least someone he trusted was keeping guard over her.

"How am I supposed to get past those dogs?" Hetty asked.

Sam tied the horses to a tree and joined them. "What dogs?"

James faced a problem. The hounds were a closely kept secret. Even Sam's wife, Katrine's sister, didn't know of their existence. He decided.

"I can only tell you if you swear to keep this between us."

Sam nodded and placed his hand over his heart.

"They're night hounds. If you look closely, you'll see them near the tent. They follow Katrine, and are almost impossible to deal with, certainly without further trouble. The reason Kat is in that tent is that she lost two of her hounds today. When that happened, she felt every bit of their pain. She has gone into shock. To save her, I had to kill the matriarch of the pack."

Sam whistled. "That's some heavy stuff." His sharp eyes flicked to his. "I don't suppose she thanked you for saving her?"

James slowly shook his head. "She said she never wanted to see me again."

Sam laid his hand on James's shoulder. "She doesn't mean it."

James snorted out a breath. "You don't know Kat as well as I do."

"Listen to me, James." Sam's hand tightened on his shoulder. "That woman loves you more than anything. Sure, she's hurting now, but she'll come to see you did the only thing you could."

"I hope you're right." James wasn't as certain as Sam. He knew Kat's enormous love for those creatures. "Let's get as close as we can."

The three of them walked to within twenty paces of the tent, waved through by the rangers on guard. Then one hound growled, and the others joined the chorus.

"Who's out there?" Katrine's thin voice carried to them on the cooling night air.

James went to speak, but Hetty's boney hand clutched his arm. "Let me."

He nodded, and she cleared her throat.

"It's Hetty, girl. I've come to talk with you."

James admired the old woman's brevity. Silence fell, only disturbed by the low growling of the beasts. Katrine murmured something James couldn't hear, and the hounds fell silent.

"You may enter, Hetty. They won't hurt you."

James longed to go with her, but clenched his fists and watched Hetty walk slowly toward the tent. She called out when she was before the flaps, and someone pulled them back. James saw a flash of dark hair before Hetty disappeared, and the canvas closed.

* * *

Katrine hardly recognized Hetty. She wasn't the wizened old witch she'd last seen. Now she appeared to be a noble woman, though somewhat disheveled. Gone was the crazy gray hair, replaced by an elaborate updo. Her clothes were rich velvet with pearls and beads, and her face wore only half the lines she'd last seen upon it.

"You're changed, Hetty," she said.

"Never mind that, girl," Hetty snapped and pulled Kat into a tight embrace. Katrine could feel the older woman trembling. Definitely not the Hetty she knew.

Kat returned the hug, then sought a little distance. "What brings you here?"

"Of all the silly questions! You're hiding in a tent in the middle of an army, your hounds scaring everyone away, and you ask me what brings me here?"

Kat's face heated. Hetty could always cut through her carefully raised barriers.

"I lost two hounds today, and it hurt; literally hurt like a hot poker was being thrust into my body. I thought I was going to die."

"That's all well and good, but tantrums are a luxury you can't afford."

Kat wrapped her arms around her body, tears threatening. "You don't understand!"

Hetty pointed a knobbly finger at her. "And don't you dare cry! The Katrine I know is strong. She doesn't push those who love her away."

"I didn't push you away."

What could this be about?

Hetty now pointed outside. "There's a man out there who loves you. He needs to see that you're well. And you've told him to stay away." She lowered her voice. "Do you really want that?"

Fury blazed through her and must have shown in her eyes, because Hetty straightened and rocked forward on her toes. Kat felt her gather her magic and had mixed feelings of triumph and regret. She didn't want Hetty to fear her, but it appeared she was respected, at least.

"He killed Dawngaze. She was heavily pregnant with the future of this pack." She took a breath, her chest tight. "How could he do that to her, knowing how much she meant to me?"

"I'll ask you a different question." Hetty's dark eyes stabbed at Kat. "How could he do anything else when he knew you'd be hurting? He feared for your life! Would you expect your husband to risk your health compared to a gravely injured night hound that was suffering?"

Katrine breathed out and closed her eyes. She knew the words Hetty uttered were the truth. James would've been terrified for her, but had he truly done everything he could for Dawngaze?

The thought of the pups that had died with her cracked her heart in two. She had sliced them from the dog's belly as soon as she reached safety, but could revive none. Tears threatened again, even though she'd already cried a sea of them.

Hetty inched closer and reached out a hand. The fingers shook, and Katrine looked up into her eyes. She frowned at what she saw there. Fear—and not a small amount.

"What has you so scared, Hetty?" she asked, finding it easier to focus on her friend than to examine her losses.

"Well, for a start, you looked like you would fry me to a crisp when I walked in. Then there are these hounds. I don't know what to think of them. They're too closely linked to you for your health and safety. And your husband… Did you not pledge to love him forever and a day?"

Kat nodded at the last.

"Have you fallen out of love so soon?"

Kat frowned and examined her heart. Beneath the fury, there was tenderness for James and passion still. "He doesn't understand me, Hetty. He doesn't see how important this magic and my hounds are to me."

Hetty snorted. "He pledged to stand by you, and he went into this with his eyes wide open. You told me how you made him work for your acceptance. Don't you think that maybe the Goddess sent you James to be your brake when you stepped too far? What would've happened today if he had not killed Dawngaze?"

She shrugged. "I may have died. It felt worse than the first time. When I said those things to him, I wasn't myself. I *do* care for him. I just don't know if we can go forward together."

Hetty growled. "Stubborn girl! You *need* a companion, someone who'll watch your back. Speak with him. He's gone through hell this afternoon. Tell him how you feel, and be honest."

Kat nodded, and Hetty patted her shoulder, then drew her in for a hug. "Remember, you chose James over being my successor, and that was only a few short weeks ago," she whispered before turning and walking into the night.

Kat watched her go, knowing deep in her gut that Hetty was correct. She had shamed herself this day and hurt James for no good reason.

How would she make it up? She went to the tent flap and stepped out. James stood in the dark, hounds between him and her. She growled at them, and they allowed him through.

He stopped before her, his handsome face creased with worry. He looked like hell—dusty, bloody, and exhausted. She took his hand and led him back into the tent. Once they were inside, she stepped close and wrapped her arms around him. Immediately, he hugged her tight, breathing out a shuddery breath.

As she laid her head on his chest, her heart settled to its usual pace, and she felt James's do the same. Once they were both calm, she looked up at him.

"I'm sorry. I didn't mean what I said earlier. I do care. I love you, James."

Tears carved a path through his dusty face. "Kat, I thought I'd lost you. I'm sorry for the death of your hound, but she was dying, and I couldn't lose you. It was the only thing I could do to protect you." His eyes hardened as he gazed down at her. "I'd do it again if I had to. You must understand that. If it's something you can't accept, then so be it."

She softened as he confessed, watching his face as it flicked through anguish to strength and truth. "I can accept it. Hetty has helped me see you may be the only savior I have. Perhaps this is the role you were sent to me for, as protector and the voice of reason. I can't be objective with my hounds. I'd sacrifice myself for them."

He nodded. "Can you truly accept that I may have to do this again? And do you think they can tolerate me after what happened?"

"I'll speak with them and make them see that if I'm to continue to be their guide, they must accept you. Otherwise, perhaps they must find another master."

He pulled her close. "I can't tell you how glad I am that we're okay. I have a long and happy life planned with you, my Kat."

He kissed her, and the rest of the pain and hurt that she'd felt since turning her back on him faded away.

CHAPTER SIXTEEN

JACQUES paced outside the chamber in the manor house Gwaethe had been moved to when the battle ended. He resented Kain stepping in and taking over. As Gwaethe's husband, surely it was *his* duty to see to her comfort and well-being. He tried to dampen his anger at his brother-in-law, but it was a battle he wasn't winning. His wounded pride urged him to speak with Kain and ensure the man kept his rightful place.

Tuthariel was in the room with his love. He'd sent Jacques out to give him room to examine and treat his patient. There was another who didn't know his place.

Damn! He was in a lather of frustration and resentment, despite their victory and the news that Gwaethe would be well!

His wife had killed the devil who'd tortured her and butchered her people. Ever since her abuse by Gorin and subsequent imprisonment in Amitania, she'd harbored demons he couldn't exorcise, no matter how he cared for and loved her. He hoped this day was the end of that.

The battle had left him feeling inadequate.

Gwaethe had covered herself in glory while he'd played only a small part. Oh, he had killed plenty of the enemy, taken his share of injuries, and his strategies had helped. But he felt flat.

And Gwaethe's "rescue" of him still had to be discussed. Finally, when she had needed him most, he'd been unable to reach her; he'd had had to rely on Syndra to retrieve his love before Gorin's guard turned on her.

Even though Gwaethe wouldn't agree with his assessment, he'd failed to make a significant impression in this war. He must find a way to lay these feelings of failure aside.

Before this conflict, he and Gwaethe had been restoring Amitania to its former glory. Perhaps returning to their project would bring him contentment.

There was still much to do, but they had made huge inroads into the project, a joint venture between elves and man. Gwaethe and he had been married, and they were creating a life together—a miracle considering elves and humans rarely joined their souls. He blamed her father for starting the trend, as the former king had fallen in love with a human woman and produced Kain.

The door before him opened, and Tuthariel appeared. "She is improved, Jacques Vorasava. You may enter, but do not stay long. The head injury is making her confused, and she has lost much blood from the wound to her thigh."

"But she *will* fully recover?"

The healer nodded. "I believe so." He turned and walked silently down the hall.

Jacques entered the room, shaking his head. Tuthariel's words hadn't settled his fears. He closed the door behind him and turned to find Gwaethe in the giant fourposter bed, eyes closed and dark skin pale.

Quietly, he crossed to the bed and took her hand. Her breath came easily, which settled the pounding of his heart, but he needed to speak with her.

Eventually, her eyes opened, and, for a few heart-stopping moments, it seemed she didn't recognize him. Her brow wrinkled, and her gaze swept the room before coming back to rest upon him.

"Jacques?"

He took a deep breath and smiled at her. Thank the Goddess!

"Who else would dare hover over you like this, my love?"

He squeezed her fingers. He didn't dare come closer for fear of hurting her cut leg and bruised abdomen. And the Goddess only knew how many other bruises and scrapes she'd received. She had the habit of being attracted to the hottest battles, which caused endless fear and distraction for him.

She groaned and closed her eyes. "Everything hurts." Her eyes flashed open again. "We won?"

He smiled. "We won. Our casualties are massive, and we'll be burying the dead for days if not weeks, but the *Sis Lenweri* have surrendered."

"I should be seeing to our people." She looked around again. "Where am I?"

"A manor house was allocated to Kain and his army leaders. He had you brought here rather than let you lie injured in a tent on the field."

Her eyes bulged. "He did what?"

Jacques shrugged. "I knew you'd want to stay with your people and tried to tell him, but he wouldn't listen. At least Tuthariel could see you sooner here. All the injured are being moved to treatment rooms within the city. There's no need to feel guilty."

"But I should be with my people." She tried to sit up, but gasped and clutched her head.

"Rest." Jacques stood and gently lowered her back against the pillows. He bent over and kissed her on the lips. She clutched his shoulders when he would've pulled away.

"Where are you going?" she asked.

"There's much to do. I'll be back later to see you, and, if allowed, I will spend the night here."

"Now there's an offer I can't pass up," she smiled.

Jacques shook his finger at her. "There'll be none of that. A few chaste kisses is all we'll share this night, and perhaps for another few." He kissed her again. "I'll find Isiloe and send her to you."

"Please do. I love you, Jacques."

"And I love you, Gwaethe, more than I ever thought possible." He walked to the door and turned. "Listen to your healers and stay in bed."

She smiled at him and nodded, then waved him away. "Go now, and you'll be back sooner."

He laughed as he left. Perhaps everything was alright after all.

* * *

Ramón knew a burning desire to check on Benae. Damn the message he must send to Wildecoast! But he understood his duty as Guardian of Brightcastle and would not give the former queen any cause to find fault with him. He and Benae would need everything stacked in their favor. He had heard the muttering of some nobles recently, and there was much that could go wrong.

Entering the raven coop anteroom, he scribbled three… make that five… notes on small strips of parchment and took them with him into the next room, which held the birds.

The raven keeper was there, feeding his birds and talking to them as if they were children. As a young boy, Ramón had loved the raven coop. Nowadays, the smell put him off. He wrinkled his nose as he waited for the keeper to finish.

The man turned and bowed. "Guardian, you honor us with your presence."

Ramón held up the parchments fluttering in his fingers. "I have good tidings for Wildecoast, and wanted to inform the queen as soon as possible."

The man reached for the parchments, and Ramón handed them reluctantly across. He had thought he'd fix the messages to the birds' legs himself, but perhaps that was unnecessary. Instead, he watched the keeper do the task he'd undertaken for more years than Ramón had been alive. The birds seemed genuinely affectionate toward their carer, which was just as well. They could be savage if threatened. He recalled the day he tried to pat one and got a nasty peck on his little finger that almost resulted in the loss of that digit. He still had the scar to prove it.

"Master Rafino," Ramón said, "I trust the birds should reach Wildecoast unmolested?"

The old man smiled. "Some of them will, perhaps all. There are those who like to interfere with the birds for sport, and others who strive to intercept the messages. Sending five is wise, My Lord Zorba. At least one or two should reach their destination."

His words did little to settle Ramón's fears, but their message wasn't as important as the previous ones when the war still raged. All would be well.

He watched as the five ravens were sent through the raven slot and winged their way east. "I'll leave you to your supper, Keeper," he said and hurried from the wall.

It was a ten-minute trip from the raven coop to Benae's apartment most days, but this afternoon, the journey took forty long minutes. Everyone wanted to ask him something, from where the overflow of injured should be taken to where and when the dead would be prepared for burial, and a myriad of questions only Benae or one of her helpers could answer.

He promised to get solutions for the most urgent of issues before the end of the day. The less pressing matters could be addressed on the morrow. There were other queries about the housing of soldiers, which he passed to the relevant sergeants in charge.

Even the chancellor wanted a word with him about the celebrations due to start tomorrow. By the time he made it to Benae's suite, his head was buzzing to the point of overwhelm.

He knocked and entered, walking into a darkened anteroom with a cozy fire in the grate and candles lit on all the stands. It took his eyes time to adjust to the dimness. When they did, he found Benae in the bath.

"That's a sight for sore eyes," he said, crossing to her. She looked up at him, her glorious green eyes dull.

"I had to do this. I know it's indulgent and very few will enjoy this luxury tonight, but I couldn't go another single step without this rejuvenation."

"There's no need to explain, my love," he said, leaning over and kissing her lips. "You've worked just as hard, perhaps harder than anyone else these last days and weeks. I know the weight of responsibility for the health of others weighs heavily. I fear you have many more days of it ahead."

She nodded. "There's much to do. We have hospitals overflowing with wounded and sick; there are medicines to make and herbs to harvest."

Ramón placed his finger on her lips, and she fell silent. "This time is for you, Benae. You don't do yourself any favors by dwelling on all that's ahead." He clenched his teeth at the messages he must deliver. They could wait until his wife had bathed and eaten. "I don't suppose there's any chance you'll stay here with me this night?"

She smiled. "After we dine, I'll return to the hospitals to attend to the most seriously injured and help with any problems that have arisen." She scrutinized him. "As I expect you will, my dear."

He smiled and raised a brow. "As much as I'd like to rest, I too must return to the walls and make sure the peace holds, even between our allies."

"We're a fine pair." Benae reached to take his hand. "Do you think anyone will notice all our hard work?"

Ramón scowled. "We don't work to get noticed, but for the good of the kingdom and especially Brightcastle. Now the king is dead, our duty is even more important. I'm sure Piotr will be here presently to present his claim to the throne."

"Do you really think so? Surely Solomon's place is secure."

Ramón drew a deep breath. "I wish that were true. However, Solomon is an infant, and we'd be foolish to assume. He must be protected, and *we* must be ready for anything."

Benae bit her lip. "Piotr could be a threat. Do you also think he may petition for the position of heir to the throne, or worse, seek to control Solomon?"

Ramón shook his head. "There's no telling what he'll do. Anything is possible. If it really was Piotr who organized the attempt on Beniel's life at Jiseve's funeral, he could try to murder Solomon."

Benae gasped, her hands flying to her throat. "He wouldn't kill an innocent, surely. It's one thing to murder a king, another to harm a child."

"We must hope the man has enough scruples to stop at taking the life of a baby, but we must also guard our son with everything we have."

Benae fell silent. "It's such a mess. Sometimes I wish I had never left my kingdom and my estate."

Ramón kneeled beside the bath and drew her to him, placing a kiss on her cheek. She didn't seem to notice. "How are things in Tylevia?"

"Much better now we have resolved the war with the *Sis Lenweri,* I suspect. My estate has had some trouble with them, but Jiseve sent soldiers to protect the farms, and, when he died, I left them there. The weather has been kind, and the crops bountiful all over Tylevia."

Ramón didn't miss the wistfulness of her tone. "Perhaps when all is settled in Thorius, we'll travel to your homeland. We can pay our respects to the king and visit your estate. We should've done so before now, but there was never time."

He cheered silently as Benae's eyes lit up. "I'd love that. Perhaps we can take Solomon, and he can see where his momma was born."

Ramón smiled. "Perhaps. I'm sure he'd love it."

"When will the festivities begin?"

"I intend to start tomorrow and continue for a full week. That way, anyone who's too ill to take part now may be well enough later in the week. On the seventh day, we'll have a grand ball, and the populace will enjoy a street festival." He paused. "And then we will have a hearing and announce the next king."

Benae looked at him, fear in her eyes. "Let's hope those with the power will support Solomon, as the king wanted."

Ramón leaned forward and kissed her lips, his hands on either cheek. "We can't allow any other outcome, my love."

CHAPTER SEVENTEEN

THE week that followed the *Sis Lenweri* surrender was the busiest of Alecia's life. That was just as well. It gave her little time to worry over what would happen when the nobles met to discuss the future of Thorius. Sometimes she longed for the simple life she'd enjoyed on the farm during her exile. She even ran into the Andras in the street one day as she helped with the housing of those who had arrived in Brightcastle.

They were enthusiastic in their greeting and had heard tales of her bravery on the field of battle. They invited her to visit the farm and bring Iona. Alecia agreed, but, privately, she doubted that could happen any time soon. There was too much to be accomplished. She also noted their lack of a mention of Vard and wondered if that was because of their distrust of him, or out of fear that they'd offend her.

Of the man himself, she saw little. She steadfastly told herself that was because he was as busy as she was. As King's Blade, she could only imagine the myriad of details he must attend to.

For one, there were the army commanders who demanded daily briefings. She knew Vard would want to oversee the deployment of his soldiers.

He was also sending some of his force back to Wildecoast, perhaps up to half of the able-bodied soldiers. They were becoming a drain on Brightcastle's strained resources. However, the commanders wanted to allow their men to celebrate the victory to their fullest extent, and that meant they wouldn't be pulling out until tomorrow.

On top of all his various duties, Vard would be searching for his father. Her heart ached that he should lose him again. Guilt over her part in his loss hounded her night and day. He must be alive, or they would have found his body. A rather intrusive inner voice reminded her that Lyam was a new Defender and as such the lack of a human body wasn't conclusive evidence that he was still amongst the living. Yes, Vard had much to occupy his thoughts and energies at present.

For her part, Alecia had personally checked every wounded man in their hospital wards and her ladies had volunteered to search the dead. The only other possibility was that Lyam had been taken by the *Sis Lenweri,* but the prisoner exchange hadn't revealed Vard's father either. It was a deep and troubling mystery.

Tonight was the culmination of a week of festivities. The keep was hosting a ball, and the main street of Brightcastle a festival. She smiled as she recalled Vard's request for a dance to be set aside on her card. She hoped for more than one. *No!* She was determined there would be *several* dances with her love.

Now, she had her wardrobe doors flung open and was gazing at the choice of gowns for tonight. She shook her head, having never agonized over her raiment this much before. The dress must befit a future queen of the kingdom without being so ostentatious that she upset the noblewomen.

In the end, she settled on the last gown she had had created for her by the keep's gifted seamstress, Isadore Bellemont. It was a deep purple satin, overlaid with purple lace upon which was sewn the Zialni crest in silver thread around the hem, on the bodice and the sleeves and around the modest neckline. She adored the gown, and its color was perfect to offset her eyes. Teamed with her mother's tiara, which sported amethyst gems, she was confident she'd impress without scandal.

The moths battering her stomach had her puzzled. Were they the result of anticipation at seeing Vard, or perhaps worry over how she'd negotiate society tonight? After all, she must convince as many of the nobility as possible that she would make a suitable queen without saying so outright. And there was the chance that her cousin Piotr would show his face and cause trouble. Both Ramón and Vard seemed to think this was a real possibility.

She huffed out a noisy breath. So much was still undecided. Had she really thought the end of the war would be the end of her worries?

Of course not! It was merely a step toward a new future when she might realize her dreams—a life with Vard and queenship of this magnificent kingdom that she loved so much. Her heart cracked at the memory of her father and uncle.

She had lost so much in the last year or so, and yet here she was, still fighting for her place and her people.

There was a knock on her chamber door, and Millie appeared at the door to her bedroom.

"I'm here to help you dress for the ball, Princess. Have you made your choice of gown?"

Alecia sighed. "Yes, the purple satin and lace will do nicely."

Millie clapped her hands. "I hoped you'd choose that one. It has the perfect blend of beauty and distinction—just like you, Your Highness, if you don't mind my saying so."

Alecia smiled. "Thank you, Millie. I don't mind at all."

* * *

Vard paused just inside the door to the ballroom, surveying those already gathered. Instinctively, he knew Alecia wasn't present. His gut churned at the news he must deliver to her; that he was the heir to the throne of Thorius. There was no version of that announcement where he could imagine her reaction as anything other than fury. He just hoped he could prevent it from spoiling their relationship. They were stronger than that, surely?

He would answer that question with a resounding "yes" except for the times he'd let her down, had left her alone—the last time with an infant to raise.

Had she forgiven him for that yet? He doubted it.

And now he must inform her he held the position she had coveted all her adult life, that of the supreme ruler of the kingdom. He didn't want it, but Alecia may not see it that way. She may only see another betrayal by the man who professed to love her.

He sighed and slipped into a quiet spot near a pillar where he could observe the crowd and the servers. Closing his eyes, he drew in a long breath and allowed a partial morph into the wolf, sending his senses of smell, hearing, and his sixth sense into the large room.

What came to him had his hackles up, for the snatches of conversation he heard were of uncertainty over the kingdom leadership. They aimed more than one word of anger and distrust at him.

His hackles rose further as he tuned into Formosa and Cosara, their heads together in a far corner.

He only caught snatches of their talk, but his name was mentioned several times. At least no one else was with them. However, he couldn't be sure who else knew his secret besides them. They likely wouldn't support his claim to the throne, but who *would* they support?

As Ramón's cousin, Formosa might throw his weight behind Solomon's guardians, Benae and Ramón.

Cosara was kin to Queen Adriana so perhaps he would support whomever she sponsored. That could well be him.

If it came to a choice between him and having an infant on the throne, guided by untried Guardians, he'd have to step into the role of king just to ensure the safety and peace of Thorius.

He had the strongest claim, having the parchment containing the king's last wishes, but he didn't want it. Vard shook his head. Beniel had known he was handing him a poisoned chalice and had done it anyway. Some days, he cursed the man.

And then there was Piotr, who was yet to show his face. It had been a week since the end of the war, more than enough time for Alecia's cousin to arrive in the city. None of James's spies had any inkling of where the man might be.

He shook off the chaotic thoughts in his mind and again scanned the room. Before he could reach his wolf self, a beautiful woman in a green and aqua sheath stopped before him.

"Lady Merielle," he said, bowing.

The flimsy folds of the gown exposed her cleavage and floated behind her in a short train. Gold bands gathered the waist and encircled the elbows, the sleeves flaring out in wings that reminded him of flying fish.

"You'll be the toast of the ball in that gown, I'm sure."

She smiled. "Do you think so? It is unconventional, clinging to my form as it does, but the colors are marvelous. I had to have the fabric when I saw it."

Vard noticed that golden discs with sapphires in their centers encircled her waist, and the elbow cinches were gold cloth decorated with pearls. More pearls adorned the bodice, forming the outlines of seashells and coral. The effect was astonishingly beautiful, but foreign. He wondered again about Merielle's origins.

He smiled at her, casting a quick look over her shoulder to make sure Nikolas hadn't noticed his wife talking to his nemesis. Unfortunately, he spotted the admiral scowling in his direction. Well, he might be an idiot, but he wouldn't allow Nikolas Cosara to dictate his friends.

"Don't worry, Lady Merielle. I applaud you for forging your own path, both on the battlefield and in the ballroom."

She beamed at his comment. "You are too kind. How can I ever thank you for teaching me to ride and fight?"

"Seeing you blossom into a warrior is thanks enough, My Lady. You have definitely formed your own style of fighting, and it's devastatingly effective. Can I also warn you that your husband is on his way over here?"

She pursed her lips. "I suppose he is looking daggers at you?"

Vard snorted with laughter. "Oh, I think it's gone beyond mere daggers."

She giggled. "You always make me see the humor in a situation."

Sobering, she continued. "Nikolas informed me that your father is still missing. I wish you luck in the search for him, Vard." She turned as Nikolas stopped beside her. "Hello, dear."

Nikolas kissed her on the cheek. "You're magnificent, my love. That gown is perfect for you." His eyes flicked to Vard. "King's Blade, you're positively regal tonight. Did you polish your buckle or some such?"

Vard quirked a brow at him. "Thought I had better present myself for the occasion. My position within the kingdom is tenuous, now that the king has passed over."

The admiral's eyes narrowed. "Let's not talk of such things this night. We can leave those discussions for the morrow." The musicians struck up a lively tune, and Nikolas took Meri's hand. "Would you do me the honor of dancing with me, my love?"

Meri looked at her husband with a mixture of delight and trepidation that sparked Vard's curiosity, but she took his hand, made her apologies, and the couple walked off.

As he watched them join the other dancers, Sam arrived.

"Good evening, Vard. No princess on your arm?"

Sam looked far from the brutish pirate, with his beard neatly trimmed and dressed in knee-high boots, black velvet breeches, and tunic, and a pristine white shirt. All trace of the weariness that had cloaked him after the battle was gone, but he sported a healing scar on his left cheek.

"Alecia hasn't yet graced us with her presence." He couldn't admit to Sam his desperation to be in her company that night after avoiding her all week. This night would be a chance to spend some time with his love and pretend that all was well in the world. "How do *you* fare?"

"I'm homesick for Wildecoast and my wife. Esta would've loved tonight. She's always ready for a dance. I don't suppose you'll reconsider allowing me to return with the forces leaving in two days?"

Vard looked down into his goblet, which contained watered wine as usual; nothing stronger for him. "I'm sorry, but I still need your support." Sam was another person Vard should've confided in long before now. Perhaps it was time. "Come with me to the balcony."

He strode toward the doors leading out to the garden, Sam following. He closed the doors behind them and moved over to the stone balustrade that bordered the area.

Sam's eyes were wary, and he wore a deep frown. "What's up now? Is it Nikolas? Are you going to tell me he's causing more trouble for you?"

"No, but I have something to tell you. It changes much."

Vard searched for his next sentence and came up with nothing.

"Vard!" Sam snapped. "Just tell me."

"The king made me his heir before he died."

Sam's eyes bugged out, and his throat bobbed in a gulp. He opened his mouth to reply, but snapped it shut, turned, and strode to the other end of the balcony. As he gazed out into the darkness of the garden, Vard slowly approached.

He placed his hand on Sam's shoulder. "It will send the kingdom into a spin when the nobles hear this."

Sam turned to him. "You're telling me. Wait—something makes sense now. Nikolas and Formosa know about this, don't they?"

"I was forced to tell them or face a mutiny on our way to Brightcastle." Or he could have compelled them, but he had no desire to get into the habit of doing that.

Sam breathed out. "So, you're the new king."

"Keep your voice down, Sam. I don't want anyone else knowing until they must."

"But… you're the king. Of course, you must tell the nobles and the military. You should already have informed them on the day the king died. Why didn't you?"

Vard ground his teeth. "I had my reasons, one of which was that I didn't wish to take focus away from the battle. I was the King's Blade, in charge of his forces. It changed nothing."

"I'm not sure that's true, but I can see your reasoning. What do you need me to do?"

"Tonight, I want you to stay close to Nikolas and Formosa. See if you can get any sense of their plans, and let me know if you hear anything."

Sam nodded. "Yes, Your Majesty." His lips curved in a smile as he replied.

"And stop that!"

Sam chewed on his top lip. "I'll do as you say, and also hold my tongue." He saluted and made his way back indoors. After a few moments to steady his thoughts, Vard followed.

Back inside, many more revelers had arrived, including Alecia. She stood by the food table, an older woman on one side and Lady Linnet on the other. Vard stood transfixed as he took her in.

Her gown was of the deepest purple with silver Zialni crests embroidered at hem and over the bodice. Sheer purple lace formed the sleeves, and the design emphasized her figure while giving her a queenly appearance.

He sucked in a breath. If nothing else told him, that dress conveyed loudly that Alecia was still bent on gaining the throne. She even wore a coronet on her head with purple amethysts twinkling in the light of the candelabra. He dragged his attention away from his love to examine the faces of those around her.

Many appeared to have noticed Alecia, and their expressions varied from wary to somewhat hostile. Others approached her, exclaiming over her appearance. Men and women hovered close, waiting for their chance to speak with the battle princess.

Vard backed into a corner to observe Alecia's interaction with those around her. The older woman detached herself from the group and made her way to Vard. Something about her was tantalizingly familiar.

Her gray hair was pulled back in a stylish chignon and her dark eyes highlighted with kohl. A silvery grey silk gown covered her form from the lacy neck to the ground and the sheer sleeves partially covered her hands.

It was the hands which gave her away at last—hands he intimately remembered as she healed his injuries after the assassin attack.

"Hetty!" he whispered. "*You* are Alecia's advisor? *The* Lady Henrietta?"

One pruned white brow arched. "Very well done for you to notice, King's Blade. You're the first to catch on, though I've seen Lord Zorba looking at me strangely."

Vard folded and unfolded his arms. He was glad to see Alecia with Hetty to support her, but still worried the witch had another agenda. She was far too secretive for Vard's liking. Then again, didn't they all have secrets?

"Congratulations on your victory," Hetty said. "What will you do now?"

"That will be for the nobles to decide, tomorrow hopefully. I want this over and done with, so the kingdom can move forward."

She eyed him with calculation. "Where do you see yourself in that new order?"

He frowned down at her. "I might ask you the same. You appear to have done well enough for yourself. Has Alecia offered you a permanent post?"

Hetty dismissed the question with a flap of her hands. "It's to be hoped that she's in the position to fulfill her dreams, My Lord." Her gaze sharpened. "I imagine you no longer should be called King's Blade, as the man who promoted you is dead."

Vard opened his mouth, an angry retort ready, just as Alecia strolled up, her lady behind her.

"Vard!" She grasped his hands and kissed him on both cheeks. "Where have you been these last few days?" As she dragged his head closer, she whispered in his ear. "Leave Hetty alone!"

Her eyes blazed lilac fire just as they did when they made love, but, this time, it was anger that ignited them.

"Hetty can look after herself," he murmured. Louder, he said, "You look wonderful, Alecia, but then you always do." Close up, he spotted the lines of weariness around her eyes and yellowed bruises on her chest and neck which powder hadn't been able to conceal.

She scoffed, her eyes roaming over him and appearing to like what she saw. He admitted to taking extra care with his attire this evening. His dark gray tunic boasted embroidered silver wolves over the shoulders and covered a spotless white shirt. Breeches of soft black calf skin tucked into matching boots completed his ensemble. A new leather headband, carved with a central wolf's head, encircled his forehead. The wolf had amber chips for eyes. He had finally shaved off his two-week-old beard, and knew he looked better than he had in weeks. But would he be enough for her?

"I look forward to our dance this evening," she said. "In fact, I'm free now." She grabbed his hand, made her apologies to the ladies, and led him to the floor. The musicians were just finishing a lively jig and moved into a waltz. Vard praised the Goddess for her benevolence. He pulled his partner close and took a deep breath of her glorious scent.

"You really are more beautiful than I've ever seen you, Alecia." He pulled her close, not caring what anyone else thought. She relaxed into his arms, for once not trying to steer him around the floor. The eyes gazing up at him were mildly annoyed.

"You appear somewhat disconcerted," he said, guiding her around a group of laughing lords, two of whom wore bandages.

"Can you please put Hetty out of your mind?" she asked. "I'd like to keep her identity secret for a little longer, and I can hardly do that when you openly argue with her." Her fair brows moved hypnotically with the force of her words.

He looked over her head at Hetty who stood against the wall, Lady Linnet beside her, glaring at Vard. "You might want to speak to your friend about that. She's looking daggers at me."

Alecia huffed out a breath. "Really! I don't know how I deal with this. I'll speak with her too." They danced on. "Have you found any trace of Lyam?"

"No." It was his biggest failure this week, that he had found no sign of his father. "And I've spent every spare minute searching. He seems to have vanished into thin air."

"I'm so sorry. Don't give up hope. Lyam is a survivor."

"That he is, my love. "Now," Vard murmured into her hair, "let's put aside our worries and enjoy being together. It's been so long since we danced like this." He tightened his arms around her, and the distance between them vanished. It transported him back to the night of her betrothal ball when he first held her in his arms, succumbing to the force between them he could never conquer.

Alecia sighed, not in frustration this time, but in enjoyment. "I was thinking this morning that the last weeks had been fraught with danger and worry of one type or another. It's good to have one less problem to solve—meaning the elven conflict. If only we could have lasting peace in the kingdom…"

They danced on, Vard enjoying the press of her body while he waited to hear where her last sentence would lead.

"You were saying?" he asked.

She shook her head. "It's folly to think all our problems will just vanish. They'll continue to occur. That's what life is."

"One difficulty after another," Vard murmured. "Are you prepared for the acclamation tomorrow? Do you intend to put yourself forward?"

He didn't know what to hope for. If she had given up on her dream, it would be easier for him, at least initially. He wouldn't face her ire at securing that which she desired.

But he deluded himself. Alecia *would* be angry, watching him attain that which she had longed for.

She'd see it as a betrayal.

"I do," she said, eyes half closed, her body relaxed against his. "Lady Henrietta has worked tirelessly this week to shore up support for me."

"And your exploits on the battlefield speak for themselves, my love. Everyone is talking about them. I wouldn't be surprised to hear songs being composed in your honor."

She blushed. "If that's what it takes to secure my place on the throne, I must bear it."

"I sincerely hope your dreams come true, Alecia. You'll make an exceptional queen."

And she would. He just hoped she got there on her own merit, and his claim to the throne wasn't upheld. But he'd step in to ensure that

Thorius was well-governed. He shook his head, closed his eyes, and pulled his love close once again.

Tonight was for enjoying the moment. Who knew what tomorrow would bring?

* * *

Alecia stood near the entry doors, ready to greet the remaining guests who were fashionably late. The dance with Vard had heated her blood and confused her. He seemed as unsettled as she was this night, and she didn't understand why. Was it his conversation with Hetty? She smiled. Perhaps it was being close to her, Alecia, after all this time. Her wayward thoughts were curbed as James Tomel and his wife approached.

Katrine was resplendent in a simple gown of embossed royal blue satin overdress with a paler shade of blue underdress. The royal blue was a perfect match for her eyes. The cinched waist showed off her curves and generous bosom to good effect. She wore her hair in a simple twist with blue sapphires set in silver at throat and ears. Alecia envied the simplicity and beauty of her friend, if she could be called that after such a brief acquaintance.

Katrine curtseyed and turned to her husband, who had already bowed.

"Princess, I'd like to introduce my husband, James Tomel, Master Jeweler to Queen Adriana." She faltered at the last words. "Oh, I imagine that's now a dated title."

Alecia stepped into the breech. "Nonsense. Master Tomel, I'm delighted to officially meet you. My aunt has excellent taste in all things, and I'm sure she'll still have significant influence at court. You have no cause to fear the future."

Katrine and James exchanged a look which Alecia couldn't interpret, then they smiled at her.

"You're most gracious, Princess," James said. "I certainly hope to continue my association with your family. And I thank you again for your help last week."

"You are most welcome. Please enjoy the festivities," Alecia said, ushering them through.

Next in line were Jacques Vorasava and Gwaethe Arenil. The *Lenweri* princess wore a silvery green gown of elven design with elaborate embroidery around the scooped neck and upper arms. The dramatically full sleeves were lined with exquisite filmy material Alecia had never seen before and matching green slippers peeked from below the hem. Jacques helped arrange the short train, which also featured embroidery.

"Welcome, Princess Gwaethe and Lord Vorasava," Alecia said. "I'm glad to see you recovered, Gwaethe."

Gwaethe smiled. "*Almost* recovered, my dear husband would say."

Indeed, Jacques had his mouth open to say something, but smiled ruefully instead. He wore black leather breeches with a bronze shirt and tunic, and a short cloak attached to his shoulders. His boots had curious broad cuffs and extended to his knees. Alecia thought him very stylish indeed, if a little flamboyant.

"Princess Alecia," Jacques said, bowing and then raising her hand to his lips. "May I congratulate you on vanquishing those dragons? I'm told the exploding arrows were your idea. Bravo!"

Her face heated. She really must control her emotions better. Besides, there were more important matters to discuss. She stepped closer to the Amitanian rulers.

"Can I count on your support tomorrow?"

"You have a strong case, Princess," Jacques said, "and we have long been your friend." He looked at his wife. "I think we can say we will do all we can to support you."

Gwaethe nodded, and Alecia smiled, though his words were hardly cause for celebration.

"Thank you both. Please enter and enjoy our hospitality."

High Prince Kain Arenil and his wife Alique stepped through the door as Alecia was puzzling over Jacques's remark. She wiped the confusion from her face and smiled.

"Congratulations, Prince Arenil, soon to be king of the *Lenweri*," Alecia said, curtseying to Kain. He bowed back, laughing at her words.

"I am yet to be crowned, Princess. I think your accolades can wait."

"Nonsense, Kain," Lady Alique said, drawing Alecia's gaze. Alique looked to be supporting her husband in his role as elven ruler, if her gown was any clue. She wore a dress like Gwaethe's, although Alique's was sky blue and silver. She appeared very comfortable in her role as wife to the new elven king.

"Lady Alique," Alecia said, "I don't know what title to give you. Can you assist?"

A cloud rolled over her face. "I have yet to discover one that fits. Certainly, I can't claim the role of queen, being without elven blood."

"Surely that's for the *Lenweri* to decide?" Alecia asked.

Kain tipped his head to the side and eyed his wife. "I told her that, but she insists on remaining in the shadows."

Alecia narrowed her gaze at the beautiful healer. "You wish to be free to continue your life as you wish. I can understand that. I'm not sure it will be possible."

"The last weeks have shown me I can't live without Kain near me," Alique said. "But I don't wish to bore you with my troubles. However, I'd like to return to Wildecoast for a time to check on the injured and pay my respects to King Beniel. I'm so sorry for your loss, Alecia."

She nodded. "Thank you. I've barely had time to allow it to sink in. I assume tomorrow's hearing will bring it all too readily to life."

Kain gripped her hand and stepped closer. "You can count on my support tomorrow, Princess. If you should need someone to stand up for you, I'm your man."

Alecia gulped down emotion that threatened to choke her. "Thank you, Kain. That means much." She gathered her composure. "Please go on into the ballroom and enjoy yourselves."

The handsome couple passed into the crowd. Alecia was pleased to see there was only one more arrival to greet.

"Ramón!" She stepped close and kissed him on each cheek. His eyes widened, as did those of Benae beside him. She was immaculate in a red, black and silver gown with lace cuffs at her elbows, and a ruby choker.

"No need to make a fuss, Alecia."

Ramón ushered Benae forward, and Alecia kissed her on each cheek as well.

"You look much restored, and that gown is splendid, Benae."

Benae smiled, but appeared guarded. "Thank you, and the same to you. I love you in purple. I think we're both wearing Isadore Bellemont's designs."

Alecia inclined her head. "She's wondrous, and will be a wealthy woman one day."

"Alecia," Ramón said, "we're sorry to be so late. There was a last-minute fuss over Solomon's guards, and neither of us wanted to leave him. I hope it hasn't been too onerous welcoming our guests?"

Alecia's heart lurched. "Of course not! Solomon is safe?"

Ramón took her hand. "Your care for your infant brother is so touching. He is well. I just needed to check the papers of an additional guard. All was in order. Can't be too careful."

Alecia swallowed the fear-filled reply that rose to her lips and drew in a deep breath. "I agree. Solomon is precious. He is a target until the succession is announced; perhaps even after."

"What do you mean by 'perhaps'?" Benae asked, her tone sharp. "Solomon is the king's heir. He'll be declared king and we, his Guardians. There can be no other outcome."

Ramón placed his hand on her arm. "Be at peace, my love. Alecia meant nothing by her comment. Of course, Solomon will be king. No one can challenge him."

Unless someone can, Alecia thought.

Or unless he's killed tonight...

"Just ensure the child is safe, Ramón," Alecia said. "He's precious to so many."

She watched them enter the room, Ramón's head close to Benae's, as if soothing her. Soon enough, a crowd of excited partygoers hid them, but Alecia remained troubled.

Tomorrow would be a precarious day for them all.

CHAPTER EIGHTEEN

THE day of the acclamation dawned fine and cool. Alecia had been up before first light, unable to sleep, and now she paced before the fire, seeking inspiration for the day ahead. As a result, her mind was now completely scrambled, and she had worked herself into a dither. Why did she wish for this position, anyway? It might only lead to grief and come between her and Vard. What if he didn't wish to be married to the queen?

Just the fact that there were no longer queens in Thorius should've persuaded her to set aside her ambition. But Alecia had never been one to give up without a fight. This time would be no different. She went through the options for the position once again.

The logical choice was Solomon, as Uncle Beniel had declared him the heir. The next in line was Piotr, the son of her father's dead younger brother. She hoped Piotr stayed well away, but it was unlikely. And then there was herself, Alecia Zialni.

She was an adult, albeit female, and would give everything in her heart, mind, and body to step into her uncle's shoes. But the king had refused outright to consider her. It had hurt, and still did.

She stalked across the room and back again, then across and back again for good measure.

Placing Solomon on the throne was insanity when she was here, ready to embrace the position. At least she could be made regent until her brother was old enough. That would give her a chance to show the nobles and military what she could do.

Perhaps that was another option she should suggest? Her as regent? With Vard at her side, who could doubt their suitability?

But there would be many who wouldn't trust Vard, even though he had been named King's Blade. She had heard the nasty comments. Goddess, she still heard people say Vard had kidnapped her, and then complain about how he had escaped without punishment. Some people never forgot.

She sighed. She'd just have to walk into the acclamation, and hope and pray that the Goddess was on her side!

Alecia had again agonized over the choice of dress for the event. It was even more critical than last night that she get it right. In the end, she had decided on a silver-gray gown similar to her purple ballgown in design.

The Zialni crests around the hem, waist, and bodice were of embroidered red and black thread. She'd been tempted to splash out with a bold red, black, and white design like her battle cloak, but knew that Benae would likely choose that color scheme. She must stand for all things Zialni without being ostentatious.

There was a knock on the door, and Millie went to open it, Iona in her arms. Her daughter reached for Alecia as she was carried past. Her heart broke as she realized she couldn't cuddle Iona that day. She must maintain her immaculate appearance and not show up to the acclamation with grubby marks on her gown. The things she must sacrifice for this opportunity! And there would be more in the future. Her heart quailed at the thought.

Again, she wondered why she wanted this.

Hetty stood without, waiting for her.

"Is it time?" Alecia asked, her jaw clenched.

"It is, Princess," Hetty said, her dark eyes studying her protégé. "You look just right. Lady Linnet awaits us downstairs. Come, we don't want to be the last to arrive."

Hetty turned away, and Alecia sighed and kissed Iona on the cheek. The child screamed as she walked from the room and closed the door. This would only get harder if she got her wish.

She pushed motherly sacrifices from her mind and caught up with Hetty.

"Are you certain you're ready to give everything to this cause?" Hetty asked.

Alecia hesitated. "How can I know? I've watched from a distance as Uncle Beniel governed, and as my father managed Brightcastle. It's not the same thing."

Hetty's brows shot up. "You had better decide, and quick. This isn't for the faint-hearted. The sacrifices will be many. But you can do it if you're certain you want to."

"They probably won't choose me," she grumbled.

Hetty stopped and pulled Alecia to face her. "I won't waste my time helping you if your attitude is going to be wishy washy. Decide *now!*"

"Keep your voice down, Lady Henrietta," Alecia hissed. "This can still go horribly wrong."

A male throat cleared behind them. They stared at each other, then turned toward the interloper. It was Admiral Cosara.

He had dressed for court with even more care than the night before. Alecia spared a moment to admire his appearance before she greeted him.

"Admiral, what a delightful surprise to find you in this corridor. Can we help?"

His brow rose. "I was hoping you could direct me to the room which is being used today for the acclamation. I fear I'll run late if I don't get directions."

He was an imposing man indeed. Alecia wondered what issue he had with Vard for the dozenth time. Would she ever know?

"Certainly, Admiral. I believe the large audience chamber is the venue you're seeking. Lady Henrietta and I could show you if you would care to join us."

He nodded and bowed at first to Alecia, then Hetty. "I'd be very grateful, Princess."

He took Alecia's arm, and they headed down the corridor with Hetty following. Seeing a page up ahead, Cosara hailed the young man and appointed him Hetty's escort. Alecia admired the gesture. It had been awkward walking with Hetty trailing behind.

"Thank you, Admiral," Alecia said. "That was thoughtful."

He nodded as they resumed their walk. They chatted about Brightcastle and its people and industries as they went. Cosara was polished for a sea-faring man, though, as Adriana's cousin, he would have picked up his smooth manners around the court.

"Your wife is delightful, Admiral," Alecia said. "Her gown was astonishingly beautiful last night. Will she be joining us today?"

"She was still asleep when I left. It was rather a late night, and she danced for most of it."

"I hope to see her so we can get better acquainted," Alecia said.

At those words, he cast her an odd look, then smiled. "I imagine you have much in common, both having the heart of a warrior. Your skills on the field of battle are being spoken of throughout Brightcastle."

"As are Merielle's, Lord Cosara. You must be proud."

He grimaced. "I suppose you could say that, although I'd rather know she was safe."

Alecia nodded. "I imagine so, but Merielle has a calling. She's extraordinary."

He huffed out a breath. "Princess, you don't know the half of it."

Alecia would've loved to pursue that comment, but they had arrived at the audience chamber. She was announced as she entered, as were Hetty and the admiral, and they went their separate ways. She put the admiral and his exotic wife out of her head and studied the room. Hetty stood beside her, and Linnet joined them.

"They have allocated you a seat at the front on the far side, Princess,' Lin said, pointing discreetly. Alecia followed her finger and saw several nobles and heads of guilds seated near her allotted position.

She wondered if they were sympathetic to her or not, or perhaps a mix. She certainly saw no one she could be certain of. But it didn't matter where she sat, only who stood with her. She hoped Hetty had gained enough support.

She and her companions moved to their seats and were greeting those around them when Ramón approached.

"Morning Princess," he said, appearing uncomfortable. "I must advise you that Lady Linnet can't attend this acclamation. Only members of the nobility may be present and certainly can only vote if they're nominated and approved."

Alecia's heart kicked up. Her hands began a faint tremble, but she steeled herself. "Good morning, Guardian. Lady Linnet *is* a member of the nobility. She has every right to be present and to vote."

"That's a matter of opinion," Ramón said, turning to Lin. "My Lady, I'm afraid you'll have to leave."

"This is outrageous!" Alecia wouldn't be silent, no matter how much Ramón shushed her. "I'm legally able to promote my advisors to the nobility, and that's what I've done in Linnet's case. She has been a countess for some months and has land. You will not treat her like this."

Ramón's throat bobbed, but his eyes were hard as flint. "Don't let this get ugly, Alecia. Some attendees have complained."

Alecia stood so she could survey the hall and looked out over those assembled, which included Vard and Samael Delacost. She pulled Ramón to the side.

"Vard is here with Samael Delacost. Why is the ex-pirate not being evicted?" She felt terrible drawing attention to Samael, but she wouldn't be disadvantaged like this!

Ramón sighed. "Delacost is merely here as Anton's security. He has no voting rights or speaking rights."

Alecia felt like rolling her eyes, but a future queen simply didn't lower herself to such gestures. "Linnet stays. I can't think why there have been complaints. If you don't wish for there to be a scene, go and speak with the complainants. Tell them Lin is a bona fide noblewoman." She paused and met his eye. "She is at least as legitimate as the admiral, who I believe was made a nobleman and given lands by the queen." It paid to know one's history, both recent and ancient.

Ramón paled. "The admiral is also here as head of the naval forces, as you should well know." He sighed. "I'll speak with them. This is a needless distraction when we have more urgent matters to decide." He stalked off, waggling his fingers as he left the hall. Several nobles along with General Formosa, followed him out.

Alecia took a seat and motioned for Hetty and Lin to do the same. A few deep breaths helped to calm her racing heart, and she folded her hands in her lap, trying at least to appear unflappable. She was anything but. She must bring her thoughts back to the matter at hand.

A low rumble went through the hall, and Alecia turned to see a priestess approaching the thrones at the head of the room. Not only a priestess, but the high lady herself, clad in flowing black robes.

Alecia managed to stifle a gasp. This was really happening and somehow, she must conceive a way to not only be nominated but win the vote! She looked at Hetty, who sent her a look of such warmth and belief that some of the butterflies in her stomach settled. *Have faith.*

The high priestess stepped up before the thrones and cleared her throat.

"Good morning. May the Goddess be with you on this momentous day."

Those assembled made appropriate responses and slowly quieted.

"I believe the Guardians are yet to join us, so we will await their presence before I continue." She took a seat on the largest throne, a sign that she took the place of the king until a new one could be declared.

Alecia prayed it would be settled that day. Her mouth was dry, and she wished she had a flask of watered wine with her. She practiced relaxing her jaw and deep breathing. Hetty reached over and stilled her fingers that clawed at the fabric of her gown.

"All will be well," she whispered.

Alecia nodded, but didn't see how her advisor could truly believe her own words. She'd like to have blind faith in the Goddess to ensure that her plans came to fruition, but what if the Goddess had other ideas for Thorius?

At last, Benae and Ramón entered and took their seats on smaller thrones on either side of the priestess. Josef Formosa and the others who had left with Ramón returned and took their seats, none looking pleased. Ramón's jaw was tight, and Benae's forehead wrinkled. At least it appeared Ramón had prevailed, and Lin wouldn't have to leave. She sighed deeply and looked at her friend, who smiled.

Alecia closed her eyes and prayed to the Goddess for inspiration and strength. She hadn't finished before the voice of the priestess disturbed her meditations. She sighed, opening her eyes, a little more prepared for the ordeal than she had been before.

"This is a grave undertaking," the priestess was saying, "and none of us should take lightly the appointing of the next leader of this kingdom. We must look deep into our hearts *and* consider the wishes of the former king, Beniel Zialni." She paused, closing her eyes and lifting her arms, her lips moving in silent prayer. Then she lowered her arms, and her gaze swept those assembled.

"King Beniel Zialni, after the death of his brother, Jiseve, took steps to install his widow, Benae Zialni, and Lord Ramón Zorba as Guardians, both of Brightcastle and of Jiseve's unborn son. He gave Benae the title of Princess. It is clear that King Beniel had high regard for both his sister-in-law and for Ramón Zorba. It appears he trusted them to raise the heir to the throne of Thorius, and, in that role, govern the kingdom until the true king could come into his majority."

There was general murmuring and muttering, a mix of assent and dissent. By Alecia's reckoning, many of the Wildecoast nobles and military were wary of the Brightcastle Guardians, and so they may well support her. She hoped so, for her base was mainly Brightcastle nobles, and she by no means had all of them on her side.

"I call Lord Ramón and Princess Benae to the floor to speak on behalf of Solomon Zialni."

Ramón and Benae stood and made their way forward while the priestess resumed her seat. Ramón took a moment to compose himself before beginning.

"The day of Jiseve Zialni's funeral will stand as one of the darkest days of my life; of *our* lives. I don't think my wife and I are alone in our feelings on this subject. Many of you respected the prince. His brother, King Beniel Zialni, certainly believed Jiseve was the best choice of successor. It was the logical flow of things, and, indeed, Jiseve fathered a son who was guaranteed to take the throne if he lived to be an adult."

There was murmuring and nodding around the room.

Alecia sat frozen as she debated if she should reveal her deep suspicions.

Solomon was not Jiseve's son. He had no claim to the throne of Thorius. She dearly loved him, but there was no way she would allow this farce. She went to stand, but Hetty caught her arm.

The old woman had a fierce grip for her size and age. "Wait!" she muttered.

Alecia pretended to be shifting her position and relaxed back against the seat.

Benae stepped forward. "Since dear Beniel made us Guardians to protect Brightcastle in place of Jiseve, and to see to the raising of his nephew, it is clear that the king trusted in our aptitude for the role. This is what the king intended—for Solomon to inherit the throne and for Ramón and me to act as his advisors until he can do so in his own right."

A voice carried from the back of the hall. "If this is so obvious, why are you belaboring the point?"

Alecia turned to see Piotr Zialni striding down the side of the hall on his way to the front. He stopped before the Guardians and faced the crowd.

"I say show us the document that states that the babe Solomon Zialni is heir to the throne, and that his mother and step-father are his nominated guardians and administrators of the principality of Brightcastle," Piotr said. "*That* must be the first step. Then ask yourselves, did Beniel Zialni intend for these two to oversee the entire kingdom? *I think not!*"

Alecia listened, her heart in her mouth. Why couldn't they get through this day with no interference from Piotr? "He will ruin everything, and his evil plans will succeed," she hissed.

Hetty grabbed her hand again. "We don't know that Piotr had anything to do with either your father's death or the attempt on the king's life at his brother's funeral. Cool heads, Princess."

Alecia drew a deep breath, held it, and let it out. It was better to remain silent, at least for now. *Watch and wait…*

The priestess stood. "Who are you, Sir?"

Piotr drew himself up. "I am Piotr Zialni, nephew of Beniel and Jiseve Zialni, and heir to the throne of Thorius."

His words threw the room into an uproar.

Many of the attendees were on their feet, shock and anger clear on their faces. Most had heard the rumors regarding the prince's death and the assassin at the funeral. Some appeared fascinated by the appearance of the king's nephew, as if they wanted to know more.

Perhaps that was just what they needed, Alecia thought.

She stood. "Cousin! I welcome you to this acclamation. It has been long since I saw you." She came forward to stand beside Piotr and kissed each cheek, then stepped back.

Piotr bowed deeply before his cousin. Alecia thought her face might crack with the strain of keeping it pleasant when she wanted to scratch his eyes out.

The priestess cleared her throat. "Evidently, you have a claim to the throne. Please explain why you believe this gathering should choose you over Solomon Zialni."

Alecia stepped to the side as Piotr faced the crowd.

"Clearly, I'm a grown man, while Solomon, charming as he may be, and of a pedigree that could not be denied, won't be able to rule in his own right for decades. None of you can think that is preferable to the alternative of having a mature Zialni on the throne. At the very least,

I could govern in Solomon's place until he's ready. These Guardians might run Brightcastle satisfactorily, but the entire kingdom? As well as caring for one child and perhaps more? I don't think that's suitable. Can we take that risk in this era of significant change and with a war only just behind us?"

As Piotr spun his tale of suitability, Alecia tried as hard as she could to appear calm and unflustered. If Hetty's shaking of her head was anything to go by, she wasn't succeeding. How dare Piotr claim the throne of Thorius when she, Alecia, was here, the first child of Jiseve Zialni! It was criminal that she couldn't walk straight in and take the position.

A strident inner voice told her that Beniel had never considered her as heir. It just wasn't right. What had Piotr ever done to prove himself?

Worse, some of the folk in the audience were nodding at her cousin's words, including Josef Formosa, who held a great deal of power in the capital. She had no choice but to challenge Piotr regarding the rumors of his involvement in her father's death and the attack on the king.

Alecia stepped up beside Piotr.

"Tell me, cousin," she said, her voice ringing through the hall. "Where were you when my father died? It was sudden, and many thought he'd been poisoned. There's still no definitive answer on that, despite the esteemed Doctor Monive declaring natural causes."

Piotr raised a brow. "I was far away when my uncle died, just as you were. I couldn't have killed him directly, and I didn't order anyone to act against Uncle Jiseve. As his physician pronounced, the prince died of natural causes. I'd rather not say any more here to spare the memory of your dear father."

Alecia drew close. "You care not for the memory of my father," she hissed. "You never visited him when he was alive." She raised her voice. "And what of the assassination attempt on King Beniel the day of Jiseve's funeral? Since you're here, this is the perfect time to lay any rumors to rest."

"I wasn't in Brightcastle on that day," Piotr said.

Jacques stood. "Forgive me, my prince. I investigated the assassination attempt, and several witnesses came forward to testify they saw you in the city on the day of the funeral. The witnesses were trustworthy." He sat.

Alecia drew a deep breath. "Cousin, what do you say to former Lieutenant Vorasava's words?"

Piotr had paled, and his jaw was tight. He took several moments to compose himself. "This will make me look guilty," he said in an apologetic tone, "but as I wasn't invited to the funeral, I didn't want to attend and cause a scene. I still wished to pay my respects, however, so I watched from a distance. I had nothing to do with the assassination attempt."

"But it was the perfect way to attain the throne!" Alecia said. "I don't believe you're innocent, and I won't stand for you on the throne of Thorius."

Piotr smirked. "Seems like you have no say in the matter, cousin."

Alecia swallowed fiery anger in favor of icy calm. It wouldn't do any good to stoop to his level. Besides, he was correct in that she had little power. How could she swing this in her favor?

She turned to the assembled guests. "Lords and ladies, military heads. I don't believe this man is fit for the position of King of Thorius. Questions hang over his suitability on a moral level, and what has he ever *done* to prove he could govern this kingdom?"

The priestess nodded. "That is a fair question, Prince Piotr. Can you prove your fitness for the office of king? Have you had training in the governing of a kingdom? Do you have a suitable wife on which to get heirs? Can you show the kingly qualities of ethics, selflessness, and bravery?"

Again, Piotr paled, but to his credit he turned to face the assembled guests. "I can't say I've had the perfect training for the role of king. My father died when I was fifteen, leaving me to grow into a man with only an old servant for guidance. Mother taught me courtly skills such as table manners and dancing, and how to treat a lady respectfully.

Before he passed, Father taught me the sword, history, and how to respect my fellow man."

Alecia battled the urge to roll her eyes yet again. Piotr sounded so normal and so… "nice". But when she looked at him and talked with him, she got a bad feeling in her gut. He may not seem capable of the crimes she had accused him of, but she didn't trust him.

She looked at Vard and raised her brows. He gave a slight shake of his head. Did that mean Piotr was lying?

Piotr continued. "I'm yet to marry, but have sired several bastards which proves I can breed. As for kingly qualities, I'm humble, I speak the truth, and I was brave enough to come here and put myself forward for the position of king, even though I know many of you think I'm a monster. You should be able to see that I'm not."

Alecia stifled a snort at the "humble" comment. He clearly didn't know what that word meant, and she had a hankering to show him. Unfortunately, it appeared his words were soothing the crowd and convincing them.

The priestess stood and stepped up beside Piotr on the other side to Alecia.

"Lords and ladies, military leaders and members of the elven and Thorian royal families. I humbly submit that you should now show to me your vote, by raising your hand, if you are willing to accept Piotr Zialni, prince of this realm, as a candidate for king."

There was a loud buzz in the room as many discussed the declaration.

The priestess clapped her hands, and they quieted. "Can I have a show of hands if you believe this man should be allowed to stand for the position?"

Formosa's was the first hand that shot up, then Melanis Stenmore's. As Alecia watched keenly, more and more hands were raised until she estimated more than half had agreed. The priestess and one of her acolytes counted, and she waved the hands down.

"It is decided. Prince Piotr Zialni shall be permitted to stand for the position of king. He shall also be allowed to petition for the right to be regent to Solomon should the child be successful in gaining the throne."

Clapping broke out in the hall as those who had voted for Piotr celebrated. Her cousin descended the stairs and shook hands with Formosa and many others while Alecia ground her teeth. Benae and Ramón whispered frantically together from their thrones on the stage.

Ramón stood abruptly and strode forward. He clapped loudly and waited while the room quieted. Piotr raised his brows at the Guardian.

"Prince Zialni," Ramón said, "Please take a seat. I have something to say." He looked at Alecia and gestured for her to be seated as well. She took a chair close to the front. It was time to make her own decisions and not be constrained by Hetty. As matters escalated, the battle queen inside her fought for freedom.

Piotr frowned, but did as asked. It didn't surprise Alecia to see him sit beside Formosa. Was there perhaps some deal between the two men? She had heard of him lurking around the Wildecoast court of late. Ramón couldn't be happy for his cousin to be supporting Piotr.

Ramón waited for the room to be still, then spoke. "It seems I can't stop Piotr from his tilt at the kingship, but I'd never allow him to be granted control over my… over Solomon."

Alecia caught her breath. Ramón had almost called Solomon his son. Certainly, he might feel close to the child, might even think of another man's progeny as his own, but, clearly, he hadn't meant to slip like that. Her gut heaved, and her heart pounded. She must defeat both Solomon and Piotr if she wanted her dreams to come true. And that would mean discrediting them or beating them in a vote.

She could discredit Solomon, or thought she could. But *would* she do it? How might that affect her relationship with the child and his parents? Did it matter? Did she need Ramón and Benae if she was to be an effective queen? She firmly believed it was better to build bridges than destroy them. Piotr she couldn't discredit unless she uncovered more information. He'd have to be outvoted.

While Alecia's mind worked frantically, Ramón's words dropped into the assemblage like a stone into a pond, causing ripples that became ever larger.

"As Solomon's guardians, appointed by the king himself, we're best placed to care for and advise the lad as he comes into his majority. And Piotr will be involved over my dead body."

Piotr shot to his feet, Formosa's hand gripping his forearm.

Ramón took several steps toward Piotr before the priestess's voice stopped him.

"You will not do violence in a holy acclamation, My Lord. I have noted your feelings. We will vote on the position of king, then the other matter can be resolved if required."

Ramón clenched his jaw and nodded abruptly at the priestess. He stalked back to his throne, where Benae was on her feet, glaring at Piotr and the priestess in equal measure. Alecia felt more than a moment of sympathy for Benae. She wouldn't be putting Iona's future in the hands of her cousin, no matter how reasonable he seemed.

But she had more concerns to deal with than the Guardians' fear of Piotr. There was about to be a vote, and she hadn't thrown her hat into the ring. She lurched to her feet and strode back up the stairs to the side of the priestess. She turned to address the crowd as Nikolas Cosara stood up from his seat.

The priestess appeared ready to roast them on a spit. And she could do it. In her position as high priestess, she was answerable only to the Goddess.

"Princess Alecia! I must insist you be seated while the vote is taken," she said, pointing to Alecia's chair. "And Lord Cosara, we are about to vote on the matter of king of this nation. Take your seat!"

Cosara didn't comply, but pushed his way past those seated beside him and exited the row. He strode to the priestess, bowed at her and at Alecia, and faced the audience.

"I can't allow this farce of an acclamation to continue without bringing something to your attention."

Vard shot to his feet and strode to Nikolas's side.

"Hold your tongue, Admiral." He caught Alecia's eye, and she was stunned at his pleading look. "Princess, can I speak with you?" He engaged the priestess. "My Lady, we need an adjournment immediately. There's an urgent matter I must discuss with Princess Alecia."

If the priestess was angry before, she now appeared furious. "Lord Anton, you insult this acclamation and the people in attendance by bringing your private matters before it. If you have anything to discuss with the Princess Alecia, do it after we finish here."

Vard bowed deeply to the priestess. "I'm your humble servant, My Lady, and I take no joy in causing this disruption, but I must speak with the princess. Now."

The priestess shook her head. "No. This is most irregular. And Lord Cosara, you will be seated immediately. There must be no further disruptions."

Nikolas's eyes narrowed as he stared down at the holy priestess.

Just as Alecia thought he'd accede to her wishes, the admiral grabbed Vard's wrist and raised it above his head.

"Lords and ladies, heads of gilds and military, meet your new king!"

CHAPTER NINETEEN

THE uproar that descended upon the meeting was nothing to the tumult and confusion within Alecia. All breath left her body, and black spots danced before her eyes. She could barely see as she staggered toward the nearest chair.

Benae's emerald eyes appeared before her, and a hand guided her to safety on one of the thrones. No sound came to her that made any sense, just the roaring of the blood in her ears. Her body was icy, and prickles raced over her scalp.

Someone thrust a goblet at her, and she latched onto it, its warmth distracting. The aroma of herbs and wine drifted up her nostrils, and she took a large gulp of the drink, focusing on the warmth as it spiraled down into her stomach,

Alecia opened her eyes. She hadn't even realized they were closed. Suddenly she felt a ninny and certainly not the brave battle queen she strived to be. She handed the goblet to Benae and pushed herself to her feet. Vard appeared before her, golden flecks rioting in his irises.

"Alecia, I can explain everything," he began.

"You'd better be quick about it, Vard. What does he mean— 'meet your new king'?" She waited for his reply, her stomach threatening rebellion.

His failure to meet her eyes, the tightening of his jaw, and his hands scraping through his dark locks did nothing to ease her fear.

Something had him under great pressure, and she was frightened to hear the truth.

"We need privacy, so I can explain."

While he turned to address the priestess, Alecia wanted to scream "just tell me now". She didn't, but how she restrained herself, she didn't know.

Hetty and Lin joined her. She appreciated the comfort their presence brought.

The hall was in an uproar; the priestess clapping her hands to bring them to order, but being ignored. The admiral sent a piercing whistle through the echoing space and slowly those present quieted.

Vard bowed before the priestess. "I humbly request an adjournment, so I can seek counsel. I suggest we break for refreshments and gather again in an hour."

Alecia tried to read Vard's intention in his words and his body. All she could hear were the words that Nikolas had uttered; all she could see was Vard's reaction.

Somehow, what Nikolas said must be true.

But if it was, why was she only just being informed, and in public?

The priestess nodded, and Ramón pushed his way through to the front. "Refreshments are available in the small audience hall. Please enjoy them for the next hour, and we'll continue this afterward."

As he spun, he grabbed Vard's elbow. "You have some fast talking to do to get yourself out of this, Anton."

Vard tore his arm from Ramón's grip. "You know nothing of it. Keep your threats to yourself." He returned to Alecia and gripped her arm. For the sake of propriety, she left it there. "Alecia, I ask you to hear me out before you unleash your anger. Come with me to the anteroom, and I'll explain everything."

She gritted her teeth as she accompanied Vard to the room behind the audience chamber. A small crowd followed them, but when Hetty asked if she needed support, Alecia shook her head and slammed the door on those gathered outside. She spun to Vard, squinting in the dull light provided by two candles which was the only illumination in the small space used for quick exits from meetings and as a changing vestibule.

"You promised to explain—well, I'm waiting."

Rats gnawed at her gut at the thought of what she might hear, but she tried to ignore her fear.

He drew a deep breath. "It all started the day of Beniel's death. No, before then. We enjoyed a relationship as close as king and servant could get. Your uncle trusted me, I think because he knew you did."

Her nose twitched, and she huffed. "That might overstate things a little."

Vard flinched, and she hardened her heart against his obvious discomfort.

"As I said, he trusted me. He also knew he was going to die. Twice he discussed the future, his fears over the Guardians, and asked me if I believed they could run the kingdom. He considered choosing someone else as his heir. I thought he might select Piotr, or perhaps even Cosara, as he is cousin to the queen."

His throat bobbed in a spasm. "After the battle with Faenwelar, King Beniel collapsed, and it was clear he was dying. He bade me remove a letter from his coat." He paused as if the next words were ones he'd rather not utter. "The parchment was a letter declaring… declaring me his heir."

Alecia sucked in a ragged breath and choked on her spittle. As she gasped for air, Vard stepped close and patted her back. Once she could speak, she put some distance between them.

"So, you're telling me you're the king? You're telling me *now*, after all the time you've had to announce this? Clearly Nikolas knew. Who else?"

"Formosa, and Queen Adriana… and Samael Delacost. That's all."

She shook her head. "Now I understand the new animosity toward you from those men." She turned her back on Vard and paced back and forth across the small room. Her mind flopped about like a stunned fish, unable to understand the situation she found herself in.

No! She understood alright. *Her* uncle had handed Vard the one thing she craved above all others. Fury swept over her, and she stopped before the man she should've been able to trust.

"Why didn't you tell anyone else?"

He sighed. "It changed nothing, and the war was a greater priority. The *Sis Lenweri* threat was on our doorstep. I knew if I declared the contents of that letter, all hell would break out. The only reason I told Formosa and Cosara was because they threatened mutiny on the march here from Wildecoast. It was the only way I could think to secure their support in the war."

"And once the war was won? You should've gone public with your news then. You should've told *me* at least!"

"I know how it must look. That's why I wanted to speak urgently with you."

"When you realized Nikolas was going to expose you. That doesn't count! You've had an entire week."

"I'm a coward. I've wanted to tell you so many times, but always found an excuse. How could you not be furious at what had fallen into my lap?" He paused. "I don't want it, Alecia. I want you to have the throne, the crown, the kingdom—all of it."

She folded her arms, anything to hold herself together. Just when she thought the months and years of betrayal were over, he did this. He had known how it would look, and it had terrified him enough to keep quiet.

"I looked at the options for the throne. Solomon and his guardians…" He shook his head. "I can't see them running Thorius in these troubled times." He fixed her with a pleading gaze. "Piotr is my worst nightmare. None of what he said was the truth. We can't trust him." He gripped her hands where they lay on her crossed arms. "I thought perhaps if I had the power, I could see that it passed to you."

"Typical! You think I can't win the throne on my own."

"No! That's *not* what I meant. You know it's not that simple. I saw how much opposition there was to a woman on the throne. Your own uncle couldn't stomach it. But I hoped you might sway the people, convince them to accept you as queen."

"And what would you have done with that letter from Uncle Beniel?"

"I would have burned it and every copy there is. Alecia, I see how you've grown, and I know you're the right person to heal this kingdom and take us into the future. I'd be proud to stand by your side."

His words left her without speech. He was proud of her and thought she could assume the role of queen. Now if she could only convince the members of the acclamation.

"You really think I'm worthy? And you'd support me? Because in the past you've told me there was no way I could succeed."

He unfolded her arms and wrapped them around him, then drew her close. "I was a stupid man. You should have no trouble believing that. Finally, I understand this is your rightful place. If I can help you attain it, I will."

She pulled from his grasp and stalked away. "How can that ever be? You have a letter from the king naming *you* his heir. You're his clear successor, and everyone knows it now, or they soon will."

He followed her across the room. "Some could see the king naming me heir as a desperate move by a man in his last days. It *was* insanity."

She shook her head. "Do you really believe that? You were there at the end. Was Uncle Beniel of sound mind?"

He frowned. "There are times I've wondered if he was… to write that letter naming me. But no, I can't in honesty say he was demented."

Alecia placed her hands on his cheeks. "You'd make a wonderful king, and my uncle saw that. He realized *you* were the king we needed. You've guided us through this war to victory."

Vard shook his head. "I did little but follow Beniel's wishes. *You* did much more than I did. Rather, this victory was a community effort. Our forces were fractured, but so were the *Sis Lenweri*. In the end, the Goddess blessed us with success."

Alecia dropped her hands. "Ever the humble servant."

"I'll take up a kingly mantle if I must, but it's not what I want. What *I* want is you and Iona and more children. I wish peace and prosperity for this kingdom, and I can help you deliver that. Alecia, you deserve to be queen. Beniel was mired in the past. That's why he didn't see the truth."

"And Adriana? What does she think of my uncle's wishes?"

He snorted mirthlessly. "She thought to continue her reign as queen with a new husband."

Alecia stared at Vard. "That's rich. How dare she try to steal my man and the father of my child! She'll be lucky if I ever speak to her again."

"Don't be too hard on her," Vard said. "She had just lost her husband. I believe that was grief talking."

"Adriana has long had her eye on you. And she's still young enough to have children. It would be her perfect plan."

Vard pulled her into his arms. "Do you forgive me? My only crime is not telling you sooner. I should have, I know, but I hoped I'd never have to reveal our rivalry."

"Silly man," she said, before placing her arms around his waist. "I forgive you, but you must be honest from now on."

He nodded. "How do we ensure you gain the throne, my love?"

Alecia drew a deep breath and let it out, feeling more optimistic than she had for a long time.

"We do it together, as we've always achieved anything worthwhile."

Alecia opened the door and called Hetty and Ramón into the small room. Hetty hustled in, all spikiness, and chilled the room with her disdain. She wasn't best pleased to have been left out. At least she had stayed. Moreover, she carried a tray with bread, cheese, and wine.

With her came Ramón, his blue eyes stormy. "What's the meaning of this, Anton? Is it true?"

Vard scowled at him. "We aren't obliged to take you into our confidence."

Ramón lunged at Vard, and Alecia stepped between them, placing her hand on Ramón's chest. "Cool yourself," she said, "this won't help."

His look could've killed Vard had it been a knife. Instead, he retreated to the wall where he leaned, jaw clenched, glaring at Vard.

"This isn't Vard's fault, my friend," Alecia said. "He is legitimately the king by the hand of my uncle himself. "

Hetty's brows shot up. "King Beniel invoked the Choice Law?"

Alecia nodded. "He did. It appears he was concerned about Ramón and Benae being able to run Thorius. He made a change at the end and told Vard with his last breath."

"That's preposterous!" Ramón started toward Vard again, but Alecia held her hand up.

"It was the king's will," she said.

"I'll challenge it. Solomon will have his legacy."

Alecia fixed him with a stern look. "Are you sure?"

Ramón snapped a look at her. "What do you mean?"

She raised one brow. "Are you sure the throne is Solomon's legacy?"

When Ramón remained silent, she knew her suspicions were correct.

"Ramón, *you're* Solomon's father, not Jiseve. There isn't a drop of Zialni blood in that child."

Ramón's mouth fell open, and Vard stared at his rival, then at Alecia.

"So, it comes down to a battle between the two cousins," Vard said.

Ramón spun. "What do you mean? There's no way I'm stepping aside for anyone. Piotr tried to kill King Beniel and came a damned sight closer to killing me. I took a bolt for the king, and this is how he repays me?"

Ramón was furious, and Alecia could somewhat understand his emotion. But that didn't make it right.

"When my uncle made you guardian over Solomon, he did so under the assumption Prince Jiseve was his father. That's not the case. Respond to my accusation, or I'll make it public."

Ramón's eyes widened, but Hetty forestalled him with her words.

"Yes, Lord Zorba. I would hear your response, and I imagine others present would as well."

Ramón huffed and spluttered, turning to walk around the perimeter of the room, his eyes flicking here and there, not resting anywhere for long. Finally, he returned to Alecia.

He released a long breath. "You're right. I *am* Solomon's father."

Alecia folded her arms and waited for an explanation.

He shook his head. "It isn't what you think, or not only that. Benae wanted to protect her son and saw this as the best way to do so. She also wanted to ensure that her husband continued to protect and fund her estate and people."

"Did my father know that she was pregnant?"

He shook his head. "Benae was determined to wait before telling him, so that down the track, it would be more believable that Solomon was his. He would come a little early, but that's not uncommon. When Jiseve died, she saw no reason to change her plan."

"You were happy for the kingdom to believe your child was Prince Jiseve's?" Vard asked, scowling heavily.

"I don't expect you to understand, Anton," he said, "nor do I care what you think. I love Benae, and she begged me to go along with her plan."

Alecia's heart ached suddenly at the thought that Solomon wasn't her brother. But it didn't matter. She'd always love him.

Ramón squared up to her. "Does this have to come out? I don't know what it would do to Benae."

Alecia considered his question.

If they didn't expose Solomon's parentage, some would still wish to support him, and he would forever be a target for assassins. He deserved the chance to grow up knowing his father and having a normal life.

Alecia placed a gentle hand on his arm. "Ramón, I think we must. Some will want to support Solomon, even though my uncle signed a more recent declaration naming Vard. We have to set things to rights."

"You call that man becoming king setting things to rights?" Ramón sneered at Vard. "I wish that assassin had done away with you when he had the chance."

"Ramón!" Alecia snapped. "I know there is no love lost between you, but there's no cause for that." She narrowed her eyes at her friend, trying to see the intent in his gaze, but it was just too dark.

She reached for Vard's hand. "Can you wait outside, please? Tell them we'll be out soon."

Vard nodded, cast Ramón a warning glance, and left quietly.

"I tell you, Alecia, he'll be the death of you, and you can't see it."

"That's enough!" She raised her hand, index finger pointing in the air. "I don't intend to stand here and discuss Vard with you. I thank the Goddess every day that you brought him back to me when I needed him most. And because you did that for me, I'll grant you the boon of explaining to the acclamation what has occurred. You may speak to Benae first and decide how much you'll reveal."

He shook his head slowly. "I never thought you'd treat me with such disregard. You call yourself a friend..."

"You owe it to your son to stand up and declare yourself his father. My uncle never would've placed you in this position if he had known Solomon was not Jiseve's. Therefore, you're in this situation through deceit."

She paused, trying to keep her anger under control.

Ramón stared at her, his eyes swirling with a good deal of anger of his own. "May I go?"

A small smiled curved her lips. Finally, some respect.

"You may, and I hope you'll thank me for this one day."

He turned to go, but she stopped him.

"Ramón?"

"Yes?"

"I have one more question. Please tell me you had nothing to do with the assassin in the garden on the night of my betrothal ball."

His jaw tightened several times before he raised his chin and spoke. "I cannot."

With those words, he left.

Hetty joined her, a skeletal hand gripping her forearm. "Princess, are you well?"

Alecia drew in a large, bracing breath. "Oh yes, my friend. Finally, I know the truth of Solomon's parentage, and Vard's wounding. Both are laid at the feet of someone who I thought I could trust. He had his reasons, and I still care for him, but I don't regret what I've done this day."

* * *

Vard stood against the back wall of the chamber the acclamation was being held in, Samael by his side. The ex-pirate was distracted by his wife who had arrived while Vard and Alecia were closeted in the anteroom.

Vard wasn't sure if he was glad of Esta's presence or not. Her personal vote could be against him and Alecia. Apparently, though Brightcastle had been ignorant of his elevation, the news was already all over Wildecoast.

Esta had heard it from Adriana herself, and the former queen had sent Lady Esta as proxy for her. The lady had pursed her lips when she greeted Vard. He suspected she would not vote for him, thus canceling Adriana's vote. He shook his head as speculation threatened to scramble his brain. Alecia could have all this political intrigue and be welcome to it. Honestly, he didn't know why she wished to be queen.

He sighed. Alecia was noble, kind, and truly good. She wished to be monarch to see her people flourish. She was the right person for this task, and he knew it. However, it would make their lives unendingly difficult.

He straightened from his slouch against the wall as Alecia and Hetty returned from their conference. Their eyes met across the room, and Vard felt the contact; like a cord had snaked out from her and bound him. He nodded, and she smiled.

"It looks like we're back in session, Sam," Vard said. "Stick close."

The high priestess saw Alecia and strode to the stand.

"I welcome the Princess Alecia back to the acclamation. And I also see the Guardians are in attendance." She nodded to Alecia, then to Benae and Ramón. Benae's face appeared carved from stone, and Ramón was pale. Their day had certainly taken a turn for the worse.

The priestess cleared her throat as she waited for those mentioned to be seated.

"I hope this session will be free of the strife we suffered during the first. You will remember Admiral Cosara had declared Lord Vard Anton, King's Blade, the heir to the throne of Thorius."

Her words again brought muttered exclamations and curses. Vard kept his eyes on their convener, though he felt the weight of their stares.

She held up her hand. "That will be enough of that. I wish for this to be decided before day's end." She turned to Vard. "You will explain, Lord Anton."

Vard walked to the front of the room and stood beside her. He related the story exactly as it had occurred while those in the hall listened with rapt attention.

"I never wished for the position, nor lobbied for it. The king was nervous about the Guardians' ability to cope with the running of the kingdom. He was searching for another option. I was astonished when he showed me the parchment."

"Can I inspect it, My Lord?" the priestess asked.

Vard pulled a parchment from his tunic. "This is a copy. The original is safe elsewhere." He handed the document over. "You'll see the queen has verified it."

The woman examined the paper and nodded. "This appears legitimate. I expect those voting will want to see the original. Is that possible?"

Vard nodded. "I can fetch it."

"And you would accept the position of monarch as King Beniel wished?"

He hesitated. "I don't wish for the position, but I'd accept it to ensure the kingdom is run with fairness and ethics."

"Then I don't see there is much point in voting," the priestess said. "The king's later proclamation supersedes Prince Solomon's nomination. Are there any who disagree?"

A chorus of voices echoed around the hall. The woman again held her hand up. "One at a time!"

"Lord Zorba?" she said.

"I have two things to say. One, I don't wish Vard Anton to rise to the position of king. I don't trust him. If he is king, I can see only trouble for Thorius." He paused, appearing in distress. "I also want to announce that I declare Solomon Zialni my son, by blood."

The uproar caused by Zorba's declaration was deafening. He grew pale and several of the footmen stepped closer to the crowd. To his credit, the Guardian raised his chin and squared his shoulders.

The priestess's mouth dropped open. She appeared to struggle for words. Alecia stepped forward, placed her hand on the woman's arm, then took her place. She clapped five times, allowing her gaze to rest on the rowdiest attendees. The hall gradually quieted.

"My friends," she said, her voice carrying to the farthest reaches of the room. It had to be Hetty's sorcery that allowed the feat. "Lord Zorba has been a loyal servant of Thorius, especially since he came to Brightcastle. I would like to thank him for his efforts. It isn't easy to administer a principality, and he has done so with dignity and bravery. He also conducted himself on the battlefield with distinction."

She fixed her lilac gaze on her friend, and he bowed to her. Many of those present clapped.

"However, it seems that Prince Jiseve Zialni, did not father the child, Solomon. He isn't eligible to attain the position of king by his birth."

"How can we be sure?" someone called.

"My Lord," Alecia said. "You only have to look at the child to see who his father is. But the boy shouldn't be the object of scrutiny. He was put forward as heir through no fault of his own." Alecia looked at Ramón. "Is there anything more you have to say, My Lord?"

Ramón nodded. "I apologize for misleading the subjects of Brightcastle regarding Solomon's paternity. It was a joint decision made by his parents, with many things to consider. Benae and I withdraw as Guardians of Brightcastle, and we withdraw our son as contender for the throne."

Ramón bowed to the assembly and joined his wife at the back of the room. It had been hard on them, if Benae's tears were anything to go by. Vard wondered if they would recover from their disgrace. He turned back to Alecia, who had stepped aside for the priestess.

"Thank you, Princess. With the withdrawal of Solomon Zorba, we have no need of anyone to act as regent. Can I have more opinions on Lord Anton as king? He was, after all, put forward by King Beniel himself."

Piotr stood. "Vard Anton is not a member of the family, and I believe he influenced my uncle when he was vulnerable."

Vard held his tongue.

"Does anyone else wish to voice an objection?" The priestess raised a brow.

Formosa stood. "There's no way I'd tolerate Vard Anton as king. His past is shrouded in mystery, and there's a rumor that this was a plot organized by the queen so she could marry Anton and keep the throne."

His words pushed a wave of shock around the hall.

The priestess's gaze rested upon Vard. "Lord Anton, please come forward and speak to this accusation."

Vard gritted his teeth and strode to the podium. He waited for the uproar to calm down. There was confusion and outright hostility on many faces. *Dammit!* He didn't want the position, but must handle this carefully, or Piotr would inherit.

He held up his hand for quiet. "My fellow citizens, I know how this must confuse and upset some of you, perhaps most of you. I never expected the king to grace me with this position. However, the accusation that this is a plot by our former queen to keep control of the throne is fantasy."

Formosa shot to his feet. "I have it on very good authority that's exactly what the queen proposed to you in a private meeting."

Vard eyed Formosa. "Oh really? Do you see our widowed queen here? No! She is where she should be, mourning her husband and taking no part in this choice."

"Lady Esta is her proxy," Formosa said. "Let's ask her who the queen bid her vote for."

Vard turned his gaze on the general after partially morphing into the wolf. "I don't intend to ask Lady Esta to betray her confidence, but it's no secret that the queen is a supporter of mine. She has the right to vote in this acclamation as there's more than one candidate. That doesn't mean we colluded to achieve this outcome. My heart lies elsewhere."

At his words, there was another buzz of discussion in the crowd, and Alecia's cheeks flamed, though she met his gaze with a challenge of her own.

Vard looked at the priestess. "My Lady, I give you my solemn word and pledge that the position I now find myself in was nothing to do with a plot by the queen. King Beniel was in his right mind when he put me forward as his heir. I don't welcome it, but must accept it. As to what the queen expected, that's her business."

The priestess nodded. "I accept your word and believe it is the truth. It appears this acclamation is to be decided by a vote between Vard Anton and Piotr Zialni."

Piotr surged to his feet along with several supporters, most of whom came from Wildecoast. There were cries of "outrageous", "criminal" and "disgraceful".

The priestess threw up her hands and grimaced at the unruly protesters.

Along with Piotr's supporters, another voice echoed through the hall.

Jacques Vorasava's deep tones cut across Piotr's angry ranting and the cries of Formosa's cronies, pulling everyone's eyes to him as he strode to the area before the thrones.

"This is untenable," he snapped. "Excuse me, High Priestess, but I must interject. There has been a grave omission here this day, especially as Solomon Zialni… ahh, Zorba, has been removed as heir to the throne of Thorius." He paused as his eyes swept the hall. Vard did the same, wondering what the man was doing.

"What do you propose, Lord Vorasava?" the priestess asked, appearing relieved that someone had calmed the hall no matter his aims.

Vorasava took a deep breath, as if he prepared to dive off a cliff into an uncertain sea. "I propose another candidate to rule Thorius. It seems to me that with Solomon's removal, there's no one we in the western part of the realm can confidently vote for. Piotr brings with him rumors and suspicions, as does Vard Anton. One is of the Zialni family, and the other is not; one is a commoner, and the other noble. Both are shrouded in mystery."

Vard folded his arms and scowled at the man. He knew little about the former lieutenant now married to an elven princess, except that he, Vard, had aided Vorasava when he had almost died.

However, the man had created a blended community where elven and human had come together in peace. His perspective might be interesting.

The priestess huffed, and those gathered shuffled in their seats, muttering. Some appeared outright hostile.

"Really, Lord Vorasava," the high priestess said, "I hardly think we need more options, and I can't imagine who else would have the qualifications."

Vorasava quirked his brow. "I nominate Princess Alecia Zialni."

If Vard had thought the hall unsettled before, he'd been mistaken. Those gathered erupted, some cheering, but most howling Vorasava down. He stood, shoulders back and chin up, his eyes cold and mouth a sharp slash in his face.

Vard was somewhat impressed. He must talk to this man, especially if he ended up king. But first, they must resolve this situation.

He returned to the front of the hall and held up his hand. Possibly anticipating more excitement, those gathered quieted quickly.

"Friends, let us hear Lord Vorasava's thoughts on this," Vard said, catching the eye of the priestess. "That is, if Your Holiness has no objection?"

The woman threw out her hands. "Oh! Please go ahead, Lord Vorasava. Far be it from me to see this matter settled quickly and peacefully." She stepped back and folded her arms.

Vard indicated that Vorasava should continue.

"Ladies and gentlemen, we of the western realm differ from you of the coast. We want a candidate we know and respect. It seems to me that King Beniel has clouded this issue with his two most recent choices of heir. I don't think it will hurt to consider his niece as queen."

"Then let her marry Vard Anton," someone called from the back.

Vorasava continued. "Princess Alecia has long been the people's champion, both common and noble. She is loved in Brightcastle and beyond. Recently, she has distinguished herself in battle. Indeed, if I were to nominate one person who changed the course of this war more than any other, it would be Alecia Zialni. She inspired the fire arrows which enabled us to stand against the dragons and, alone, drove off two of the beasts."

There were a few calls of "hear, hear" from the audience, and when Vard looked, many were nodding.

The priestess interrupted. "And what of the law that says there will be no ruling queens in this kingdom?"

Vorasava shrugged. "Who am I to judge? The Goddess is female, and you are her high priestess. Why should the monarchy be any different? If there is to be a vote by the acclamation because there are currently two candidates, why not make it three?" His eye swept to those assembled. "Or do you wish to accept the document that claims Vard Anton as the heir?" His words fell on stunned silence.

Many appeared confused. It seemed the acclamation would stall with nothing decided.

Vard spoke to the high priestess. "My Lady, what do you advise? We need your wisdom this day."

The woman grimaced and huffed out a breath. "I call Alecia Zialni, Princess of Brightcastle."

Alecia walked slowly to the area before the thrones and bowed to the priestess.

"Princess Alecia, do you accept the nomination made by Lord Vorasava?"

Alecia's eyes went wide, and she swallowed loud enough for Vard to hear.

"I do, Your Holiness."

"Then I agree you should be able to take part."

The priestess walked back and forth across the area between the thrones and those seated. Finally, she turned to the audience.

"I decree there should be a three-way vote. Each voter must write their choice on a card and place it in a box. If there is a clear winner, that is one candidate receives more than fifty percent of the vote, that person becomes our monarch, and we will support them." She sighed. "If there is no clear winner, the candidate with the least votes will step down, and we shall vote again on the remaining two."

Piotr spoke. "Can we vote for ourselves?"

"The candidates are permitted a vote for whomever they chose," the priestess said. "We have exactly one hundred and eleven people in this hall eligible to vote, and twelve of you carry proxies. That makes one hundred and twenty-three votes, and believe me, I will ensure there are no more." The priestess paused to glare at those assembled. "But first we must hear from Princess Alecia."

Alecia bowed again and faced the audience.

"I'm humbled to be nominated for the role of Queen of Thorius. This kingdom is dear to my heart, as are its people. If elected, I swear to be a fair and ethical ruler. I will not allow the persecution of people for their talents or beliefs. I'll work to end hunger among the common class and review the legal system to be fairer for all.

"In partnership with our healers, I'll improve the health system and see to the building of hospitals, both human and elven. I will work with the elven people in a spirit of cooperation and understanding. And I will ensure that the throne facilitates trade between people and kingdoms, free of exorbitant taxes.

"I believe in Thorius and its people, and I will always support them, no matter the outcome of this acclamation."

Though the speech was humble, at its end many stood and applauded, especially those who lived in Brightcastle. Several were nobles, and Vard noted Alecia had said nothing to make them believe they'd lose their comfortable lives.

Vard applauded and basked in the admiration that was being shown to his love. She'd indeed make a magnificent queen.

The high priestess stepped forward as Alecia retreated to her place beside Vard. He longed to offer her the words of praise that gathered in his heart but didn't want the court to believe they colluded any more than some of them already did.

"Now, honored guests. You have heard from each of the contenders for the throne of Thorius. Please take a sheet of parchment from the tables in this hall, write the name of the candidate of your choice, and place it in the glass bowl in the alcove. Those of you who have agreed to be proxies for another may have a second vote according to the wishes of your sender. If their chosen candidate is no longer available, then you may make a choice for them, based on what you believe their preference would be."

Her words caused much hesitation amongst those who had proxies to cast, including Lady Esta, who wore a deep frown. Vard didn't envy her. He joined the line at a nearby table and cast his vote, only hesitating briefly before writing the name on his parchment.

When all had completed the task, the priestess and her assistants sorted the votes into three piles and counted them all, including the total number of votes. Then the high priestess returned to the podium.

"I thank you all for the efficiency you have shown in this task. The total number of votes is one hundred and twenty-three. That is correct." She paused, her gaze examining the crowd, then falling on each of the candidates. Vard fought the growl that battled to escape. The high priestess certainly knew how to manipulate a crowd.

"Now to the other numbers. We have a clear loser, and no clear winner." Vard watched Alecia's shoulders slump just a little. He clenched his jaw and concentrated on the priestess who continued.

"To avoid influencing the second and final voting round, I will only announce the loser. After the ballot, all the candidates and any advisors may peruse the voting cards and validate them. For now, you will trust me."

"The losing candidate is…" She released a deep sigh. "Piotr Zialni."

Piotr's gaze was fixed straight ahead as Alecia cast a hasty look in Vard's direction. He frowned at her and gave a slight shake of his head. His worst nightmare had eventuated. As much as he had tried to avoid it, he must battle Alecia for the position, a position he didn't want. But it was worth it to see that Piotr failed. And he could vote for Alecia, hoping that would help her cause.

Piotr approached the priestess and bowed to her, saying some quiet words. He presented himself to Alecia, then stopped before Vard.

"I wish you luck, Lord Anton, in the vote, and in the future, especially if you're successful." The surly prince sneered at him and strode away. Vard sighed. If he wasn't an enemy before, he certainly was now. No prizes for guessing what the man had said to Alecia. She appeared pale and frowned deeply.

Hetty and Linnet approached and spoke to her until the priestess clapped her hands.

"There has been a slight complication," the priestess said. "Prince Piotr has declined to take further part in the voting, allowing for the unlikely event of a tie. I pray to the Goddess this count will lead to a conclusive result. I invite you to vote for either Lord Vard Anton or Princess Alecia Zialni. Proxies, if your candidate has been excluded, you may change your proxy vote for the final round along the lines of whomever you believe your principal would have chosen. I know this is difficult, but please give it your close consideration."

He met Alecia's lilac gaze and nodded at her. She returned the gesture. Vard would have given anything to hold her close and reassure her she'd be queen.

As they lined up for the second vote and completed it, the setting sun cast orange light through the thick glass windows on the western side of the hall.

Vard found himself almost as tired as he would have been after a physical battle. It wouldn't bode well if they declared him king. Fingers crossed, it wouldn't come to pass. After voting, he returned to the floor before the thrones and Alecia followed. They stood facing the audience, watching as one by one they made their way back to their seats.

"Good luck," Alecia muttered quietly.

"You won't need luck," he whispered back, hands clammy with sweat and trying to ignore the fine vibration of his nerves.

The priestess and her aides again retired to count the votes. She returned, again examining both Alecia and Vard, as if judging whether they had made the correct choice. Then she faced the silent audience. An errant wind moaned through the cracks in the stone walls, and light from the setting sun cast everyone in bronze.

"Good people," she said. "I thank you all for your patience, and the attention you paid to your task today. This is a momentous day for Thorius. We have voted for this man, chosen by King Beniel to succeed him, and this woman, Beniel Zialni's beloved niece. I believe our former king would approve."

Vard was not so sure of that. Beniel would have been livid that Piotr put himself forward and dismissive of Alecia because of her gender.

"Now to the count. One hundred and twenty-two voted in this round. Thankfully, one of our candidates achieved over fifty percent."

Vard's shoulders relaxed under the weight of the announcement, and then immediately stiffened. They couldn't have voted for him, could they? The choice *had* to be Alecia. She was ethical, brave, and strong, and yet wise well beyond her years. Besides, she actually wanted the position. He sent a quick prayer to the Goddess, even though the count had already taken place.

The priestess opened her mouth—then paused.

* * *

Alecia couldn't believe she was this close to her dream. One of them would be monarch once the priestess made the announcement. She didn't dare hope it would be her. Vard could do the job, and her uncle had wanted him, not her. Beniel had dismissed her without a second thought even though he knew she longed to be queen. She shook her head. *Stupid! Have some faith in the people. You've done your best to show them you can do this; that you will work for them no matter who they are.*

"I can announce," the priestess said. "That the next leader of the kingdom of Thorius, by a margin of twenty votes, is… Alecia Zialni!"

A gigantic cheer went up, and Alecia found herself surrounded by supporters and advisors. She tried to look for Vard, but couldn't find him. Never mind, he'd be happy for her, and they could speak later.

She was the queen!

She, Alecia Zialni, a mere female, had gained the throne.

Tears filled her eyes and every emotion she had bottled up over the last weeks returned to swamp her. She allowed herself to be guided out the door and to a modest reception room where food and drink had been prepared for a celebration. It was all too much, and she wished she could escape to get her emotions under control. But this was her lot now. Hetty brought Iona to her, and fresh tears filled her eyes. She smiled as she cuddled her daughter.

"That's better," Hetty said. "You deserve this, My Queen. Since you were a little child on my knee, I knew you were destined for greatness."

Alecia nodded. "I remember. I just wish Vard could be here."

Hetty smiled. "He will be, Alecia. He's just allowing you your moment."

Ramón and Benae approached.

"Congratulations, Alecia," Ramón said, "or, rather, Your Majesty." He bowed deeply then kissed her on each cheek. "I hope we can still be friends."

A part of her wondered if that was because of her new role. Another wanted his friendship to continue. She would need as many friends as she could find.

"Of course, we're still friends, Ramón, though we need to discuss this afternoon's revelations."

Ramón drew Benae forward. "And what of my wife? Now that the dust has settled, are you willing to call her friend?"

Alecia looked at Benae. "Honestly? I don't know. Benae has been at the center of much of the recent trauma in my life."

Benae blushed. "I won't beg for your acceptance, Alecia. Nor will I plead for your forgiveness. And I won't apologize for seeking Jiseve's hand in marriage, or for falling in love with Ramón. I tried to be a good wife to Jiseve, even though I begged to be released from my commitment." She paused. "I guess the only thing I'm sorry for is pretending Solomon was Jiseve's because it hurt the man I love." Her emerald gaze sought Ramón, and she pulled him against her, whispered words on her lips.

Alecia waited for the tender moment to pass. "Despite my misgivings, I wish you the best, Benae. We'll talk soon."

They moved off to be replaced by several nobles who gushed over her. They were the ones Hetty had lobbied on her behalf. She would have to watch them, ensuring they didn't overstep, but Hetty could help her.

Nikolas and Merielle sought her company, reserved congratulations on their lips. They might have voted for Vard, but were gracious. Master James and Lady Katrine were similarly aloof. It hurt a little, as she had thought Katrine was becoming a friend. Never mind, she was queen now. It was time to set old allegiances aside and create new ones. She couldn't appear biased for or against certain people, especially the power brokers who had voted this day.

Samael escorted Lady Esta to her side.

"Princess, this is my wife, Lady Esta Aranati. Esta, your new queen."

The woman before her was beautiful in the classic sense. She smiled, her caramel eyes warm. "Congratulations, Princess, or should I say Your Majesty? Though I didn't vote for you, I'm excited that we now have a queen!"

Alecia laughed at her honesty, though her husband shushed her. "It's quite alright, Samael. I admire your wife's honesty. I hope I can live up to your excitement, Lady Esta."

What an astonishing woman, to have married a pirate! She must ask them how that came to pass… later.

They moved off, and a procession of nobles and guild heads came next. It didn't take long for Alecia to wish for escape. Hetty appeared.

"Excuse me, Princess," she said. "There's someone who wishes to speak with you urgently."

Alecia's tired mind didn't wonder who, just rejoiced in the chance of escape. She followed Hetty to an adjoining chamber which was used as a dressing room.

Vard awaited her.

His smiling face and open arms beckoned. She walked straight into them, releasing a long sigh as he pulled her close.

"This is all I need," she said, pulling back to look at him.

"I wish that was the case," he said, smirking.

"I'm sorry you lost." She kissed the corner of his mouth tentatively.

"No, you're not."

"You're not either." She licked the groove of his neck.

"No, I'm not. I'm happy you got your wish. Now can you grant me mine?"

The pulse at his throat beat erratically as he said those words as if he was unsure of her response. It gave her a clue as to what his wish might be. Nothing easy, but a lifelong commitment that would be more difficult in the public eye.

But it didn't matter.

"Would you marry me, Vard?"

His quick intake of breath told her she had the question correct.

She gazed up at the man she loved, the one she had chosen to run away with all those months ago. His love for her shone from eyes fully golden with desire. Suddenly, she couldn't wait to be married to him.

"I'll marry you, Alecia. I'll be your champion and your protector, and I'll always have your back."

"And what about worshipping my body, making love to me whenever I demand it and siring my children?" She smirked up at the surprise in his gaze. Yes, she had changed these last months.

"That too, my love. All that and much more."

And with that promise, he kissed her until her toes curled, and she forgot she was now the Queen of Thorius.

EPILOGUE

ALECIA waited in the anteroom of Brightcastle Keep's chapel. Her nerves hadn't ceased buzzing over the last two weeks since being voted heir to the throne. In moments, they would crown her Queen of Thorius. She smoothed the simple crimson gown she wore under her Zialni battle cloak, then fingered the Zialni tiara. Taking a breath, she closed her eyes and tried to chase the nerves away.

"It's too late for second thoughts now, Princess," Hetty said, her sharp eyes focused on Alecia.

She lifted her chin. "I have no second thoughts, Lady Henrietta, but I wouldn't be human if I wasn't nervous."

Alecia adjusted the hood of her cloak again, wanting the garment to sit just right. She and Vard had brought the regalia from Wildecoast, arriving last evening after a hurried farewell to King Beniel. Former queen Adriana had traveled with them to Brightcastle for Alecia's coronation. A dozen rangers had guarded the royal objects of office overnight, holding a vigil in this very room.

The high priestess and four of her acolytes entered. Hetty and Alecia bowed low before the holy ladies, receiving nods of acknowledgment. The priestesses crossed to the regalia and lifted the orb, scepter, rod and crown while the high priestess stood before Alecia.

"It is time, Princess," she said, turning to exit into the chapel. Her acolytes followed with the regalia.

The holy women would carry the royal objects throughout the chapel, so that all guests could view them. Alecia would follow on their heels, a sign that she was a servant to the Goddess and the people.

Hetty awaited her at the door. Once she passed that barrier, she would be on display. At this moment, she'd rather face a dragon than the leaders of her kingdom. But she must endure it.

Alecia drew another deep breath and joined Hetty, who opened the door and ushered her through. Alecia's eyes swept the chapel and spotted those carrying the regalia already halfway down the first aisle. She stepped out, talking deep breaths and concentrating on the holy psalm sung by the priestesses. Once she had steadied her heart, she allowed her gaze to fall upon those she passed.

Walking with practiced sliding steps, she turned her head to the right, smiling at Admiral Nikolas Cosara and Lady Merielle. They held hands, a sight not common in the chapel. Meri was resplendent in an aqua sheath, and a simple chignon tamed her bright red hair. The admiral nodded, but spoiled it by scowling.

Vard's friend Samael and his wife Lady Esta sat behind. While Sam smiled broadly, Esta's brow was troubled.

Both James and Katrine nodded to her, their brows also wrinkled as though they shared concerns about the kingdom's future. Doctor Mosard, Wildecoast royal physician, inclined his head respectfully. General Josef Formosa, splendid in his ceremonial uniform, scowled so deeply Alecia was glad no guests could bear arms in here.

She skirted the second grouping of guests on that side, comprising Wildecoast nobles and guild heads. None showed joy at her elevation. It seemed she had much work to do if she was to win over those who held power in Wildecoast. Was her inclination to rule from Brightcastle a mistake? These people needed to be exposed to her to persuade them of her suitability.

Alecia cast the thoughts aside and concentrated on the moment as she headed up the next aisle and across the middle.

Elora and Rasalar, who had recovered from her head injury, stood to her right and Commanders Magbalar and Leovaris on her left. All regarded her with approval, even Ruven, whom she had struggled to impress at their first meeting.

Her heart lifted. Elven endorsement wasn't essential, but it would help ensure a peaceful future between their two peoples.

Crossing the center aisle and moving into the chapel's left side, Alecia cast her eye over the Brightcastle heads of the army to her right and the Wildecoast army commanders to the left. All were respectful, though, again, those from the eastern city regarded her with less enthusiasm. In the next section, on the far left, Brightcastle's guild leaders and minor nobility surrounded her. They all smiled and nodded, raising her spirits.

Then it was up the far left of the chapel, past the remaining Brightcastle lords and ladies and Doctor Monive, Brightcastle Royal Physician, and across the front. Proceeding down the central left aisle, she was confronted with former Queen Adriana, Ramón and Benae, and Jules Estevot to her left. Her warm feeling evaporated as she thought of her scheming aunt. Benae and Ramón always brought mixed feelings, though her heart softened when she saw their child, Solomon.

She continued through to the back and turned up the central aisle. The regalia had reached the front of the chapel and now lay on the altar. The high priestess waited, her acolytes positioned to each side.

All in the chapel turned to watch as their new queen completed her march. That aisle had never felt so long, but Vard's golden gaze drew her on. He must have partially morphed into the wolf to appear so fierce. It gave her courage, and she smiled.

To her right, her elven friends—Isiloe, Melandrach, Gwaethe and Jacques, and Kain Arenil with Alique—beamed. What a fitting way to end this procession!

Finally, she reached the holy priestess and turned to face the congregation.

"Welcome, one and all," the high priestess said. "Today we crown our new queen, Alecia Zialni."

"Goddess! Bless the Queen!" the audience said.

Alecia stepped forward, removed her tiara, and gave it to the high priestess, baring her head before she spoke to her people.

"Thank you for showing trust in me. I promise to govern faithfully, with justice and mercy. I will uphold the words of the Goddess and ensure that her people never forget her."

At her words, Vard, Ramón, Nikolas Cosara, and Jacques Vorasava exited their seats and strode to the front. Alecia had nominated these lords to represent the breadth of Thorian leadership, accepting that although they may not all have voted for her, they were men of integrity. Perhaps some would question Ramón's presence, but she hoped it would bridge the gulf that lay between their families.

The four men retrieved a canopy while the acolytes positioned the coronation chair facing the altar. Alecia removed her battle cloak, laid it over the back of the chair and sat. The lords held the canopy above her, angled so that none in the congregation could see.

Alecia shivered without her cloak. She felt exposed in the thin gown and under the eyes of the holy priestess and the Goddess, not to mention the burning gaze of her love. She closed her eyes and prayed for wisdom and courage. The priestess ripped her bodice a little to bare her chest then anointed her with holy oil on hands, breast and forehead.

The holy anointing hymn, sung by a dozen novices, echoed in the chapel, and Alecia rose from the chair, still hidden by the canopy. Oil dripped down her forehead, its fragrance reminding her she had pledged dedication and devotion to her people through accepting this office. She felt it slide between her breasts and shivered. *All will be well.*

Alecia pulled herself from her musing and looked up into the face of the former queen, Adriana. Her aunt's gown was also crimson, and she held the royal cloak, most recently worn by her husband, Beniel Zialni. Her lips thinned and emerald eyes narrowed as they looked upon her niece, but she held out the robe. The acolytes took the cloak and placed it over Alecia's shoulders. When Alecia again sought Adriana, she was gone.

The canopy was removed, along with the coronation chair, but the holy priestess bade her stay facing the altar. Each of the acolytes fetched one of the royal regalia and handed them to Alecia—orb, scepter, and rod.

The holy lady nodded, and Alecia turned to face the congregation, allowing her eyes to sweep across them without really seeing individuals. The high priestess lifted the crown and then nodded to someone at the side of the chapel. Two men carried a covered object which Alecia knew was her new throne.

The older man was Kain's stepfather, and the younger his stepbrother from Wildecoast. Her heart filled with joy that these men had fashioned the new Queen's Throne. Their eyes glowed with pride, and, when Alecia looked at Kain, his grin said everything. They shared a smile, and she nodded at the new leader of the *Lenweri*.

Master Jazara pulled the cover from the throne amid gasps of amazement. It must be truly splendid but, as it lay beside her, she couldn't gaze upon it. She sighed, stepped forward so the throne could be maneuvered behind her, and sat. It was comfortable with a padded velvet seat.

The high priestess held the crown above her head. "Behold the royal crown and your new queen, Alecia Zialni." She turned and placed the crown on Alecia's head. It sat perfectly, though she felt its weight keenly, along with the responsibility. "May the Goddess protect and guide her!"

The congregation surged to its feet amid clapping and cheers. She plastered a smile on her face and let herself 'see' all of them, the happy and the fearful, the sad and the hopeful.

Lastly, she looked at Vard, his eyes shining with love and pride. He held Iona, who was dressed for the occasion and wore a silver tiara. Her little hands clapped along with everyone else. Then her face reddened, and her high-pitched scream tore through the chamber.

Alecia felt her own face heat with embarrassment, but Vard calmly placed the little girl on her feet. She toddled to the stairs, went down on her hands and knees, and climbed the carpeted steps to her mother.

Alecia placed the valuable scepter and rod beside the throne, and, leaving the orb in her lap, lifted her daughter. Iona immediately reached for the pretty relic, and Alecia held it for her to admire. Someone in the congregation laughed, and soon all joined in, or at least smiled at the spectacle of the toddler sitting on her mother's lap.

Alecia smiled too, gratified that the congregation had seen this as amusing and not offensive. She stood with Iona and smiled at her new subjects, lifting the orb so it caught the light and cast a rainbow of sparkles throughout the chapel.

This last move delighted those assembled, and they clapped and cheered harder.

Vard ascended the steps and took Iona, giving Alecia a chaste peck on the cheek, and the three of them basked in the glow of acceptance at last.

Well, acceptance might have been too strong a word, but they had taken a large step forward that day.

That night, after a long afternoon of celebration, Alecia and Vard took supper in her chambers. All had assumed there would be a ball that evening, but the new queen had declared a week of festivities culminating with the coronation ball and street party. Her exhausted staff were enjoying a night off after preparing for her coronation. This evening was for their little family. Iona was tucked in bed, and the handsome man with her had eyes for her only.

And what glorious eyes they were. It seemed Vard couldn't contain his animal urges this evening. His irises kept flaring in a disconcertingly golden display.

She had asked him to marry her and, now she was queen, preparations would begin for their wedding. It would be the grandest celebration seen in the kingdom since the marriage of King Beniel and Queen Adriana. The thought of the former queen sent a wiggle of unease through her. Adriana still harbored feelings for Vard, not to mention a desire to rule beside him.

No matter. Once they decided where they would live, she could settle Adriana in the other city, never to trouble them except for state visits.

She nodded, and Vard raised an eyebrow.

"What has you so pensive, my love? This should be a carefree evening."

She huffed out a sigh. "I was thinking of Adriana. And of where we should live. I detected animosity, or at least suspicion, from many of the Wildecoast nobility and officers, today. Perhaps my inclination to live here is not the most inspired choice. If I were to make Wildecoast my home, as have the kings of the past, those eastern people would get to know me. Hopefully, that would settle their fears."

"You *could* do that," Vard said. "It's your decision, Alecia. However, you said you wished to follow the tradition of the queens of Thorius and make Brightcastle your home."

"But is it wise? Will it be a continual reminder of the divide between kings and queens, of east versus west?"

"Must you decide now?"

He leaned across the table and kissed her, his lips distracting with their silky softness, demanding her attention be upon him and only on him. He pulled away, his eyes flaring golden.

"It seems not," she breathed, wondering how she would resist him another month until their wedding.

Vard stood and pulled her to her feet, weaving an arm around her waist. He danced with her to music only he could hear. "I was proud of you today. I thought my heart would burst."

"My heart almost did," she said, laying her forehead on his chest. He smelled of forest and musk and the soap he had bathed with. "I'd fight dragons and night hounds rather than go through that again."

"Lucky you don't have to be crowned more than once."

He looked down and tilted her chin up, so her eyes met his. She couldn't look away, nor did she wish to. This man was all she needed in a husband, and, in four weeks, he would be hers.

His lips descended, capturing hers, gentle yet demanding. She invited him in, content to lose herself in him this night, rather than abstain from such pleasure. He carried her close to the edge, but when she would've fallen over, he drew back.

"We made a pledge, remember?" he asked.

Alecia groaned. "I'm regretting that promise. What's the point when we've made love so many times in the past? Take me now!"

He smiled tenderly down at her, his fingers caressing her cheek. "I know you are worth waiting for, my love. Another month won't kill me, and it won't harm you either." He placed one more lingering kiss on her mouth. "If I don't leave now, our pledge won't last the next five minutes." With a last kiss on her hand, Vard slipped from her chamber.

Alecia closed her eyes, missing him already. And then she smiled, hugging herself with anticipation. With all she had to organize over the next month, time would fly.

The future held much promise, and she could not wait for them to be husband and wife—forever.

THE END

GLOSSARY

Places

Kingdom of Thorius (Thor- ee- us) – the kingdom of men which encompasses the King's seat of Wildecoast and the Prince's seat of Brightcastle, along with many smaller towns

Wildecoast (Will – dee – coast) – city perched on the top of a cliff overlooking the sea on the east coast of Thorius; climate is mild but windy

Brightcastle – large inland town surrounded by forests and farms, three to four days ride west of Wildecoast

Amitania (Am – it – ay – nia) or *Elvandang (Elle – van – dang) in elvish* – the deserted city north of the Usetar Mountain Range in northern Thorius; once a thriving city and now home to elves and humans under the leadership of Princess Gwaethe Arenil and Earl Jacques Vorasava

Usetar Range (You – set – ar) – the mountain range running across the northern parts of Thorius

Selinore - the forest home of the peaceful Lenweri, in the mountains north of Brightcastle

People

Lenweri – the elven people who are tall and elegant with black skin and pointed ears; live in mountainous forests north and west of Thorius, in places encroaching onto Kingdom lands; also known as dark elves; they welcome males and females in their fighting force

Sis Lenweri – the faction of dark elves that wishes to take the kingdom of Thorius back from men; only males are welcome in their fighting force.

Defender – a race of shapeshifters who are created to defend those in danger; they sense those in need of their help; a Defender can shift into animal form and the ability is inherited through family lines; when they shift back into human form, they retain their clothes from before the shift; their gifts may include the ability to compel others to do their will.

Guardian – a person or people appointed by the king to oversee a part of Thorius.

Ranger – an elite force trained to fight and track to the highest proficiency; may include females.

Characters

Princess Alecia Zialni (Ah-lee-sha Zee – al – nee) – the King's niece and daughter of Prince Jiseve Zialni who once ruled in Brightcastle and was next in line to the throne. Alecia's story began in **Princess Avenger** and continued in **Princess in Exile**

Vard Anton – the love of Princess Alecia's life and a shapeshifting Defender; once army captain of Brightcastle in **Princess Avenger** and his story continued in **Princess in Exile**

Iona Izebel Zialni (Eye-own-ah Is – zee – belle Zee – al – nee) – Alecia and Vard's daughter, born while Alecia was in exile; she has inherited her father's Defender gifts; she is five months old when **The People's Princess** begins

Benae (Ben-nay) Zorba – Princess of Brightcastle and joint Guardian with her husband Ramón Zorba; she was once married to Prince Jiseve Zialni (now deceased) and has given birth to his child; Benae can heal with her mind and has a close relationship with her stallion, Flaire. Benae's story was told in **The Lady's Choice**

Ramón Zorba – Lord of Wildecoast and once squire to Prince Jiseve Zialni; now joint Guardian of Brightcastle with his wife Benae; brother to Lady Alique Zorba. Ramón's story was told in **The Lady's Choice**

Solomon Daire Zialni – son of Benae Zorba and Prince Jiseve Zialni (now deceased); an infant of three months when **The People's Princess** begins

Hetty (aka Lady Henrietta Guiote) – mysterious ancient woman with magical powers; once Alecia's governess and nanny; declared a witch by Prince Jiseve and sentenced to death but rescued by Alecia

King Beniel Zialni (Ben – ee – elle Zee – al – nee) – King of Thorius; lives in Wildecoast; older brother of Jiseve Zialni and uncle of Alecia Zialni; married to Adriana

Queen Adriana Zialni - wife of the King; lives in Wildecoast; Alecia's aunt

Piotr Zialni (Peter Zialni) – son of Beniel and Jiseve Zialni's younger brother; next in line to the throne of Thorius (his father is dead) after Solomon, unless King Beniel or Alecia have a son

Izebel (Is – zee – belle) – a previous warrior Queen of Thorius from centuries ago, when females could rule; Alecia's idol; her daughter Daphini was the last queen of Thorius

Gwaethe (Gway-eth-a) Arenil – Lenweri princess, daughter of King Orionkael Arenil, who was murdered by High Prince Faenwelar of the Sis Lenweri. She has a golden stallion with silver mane and tail called Rassar which means Sunbeam; her love story was told in **Elf Princess Warrior**

Jacques Vorasava – Captain in the Brightcastle army. Jacques is tall with dark hair, beard and moustache; he has an olive complexion; he is married to Gwaethe Arenil and is now an Earl, and their story was told in **Elf Princess Warrior**

Doctor Damald Monive – chief physician in Brightcastle Keep; presided over the inquiry into Alecia's father's sudden death when he was married to Benae

Millie – Alecia's maid who also helps out with Iona's care

Melandrach (Mel-on-drac) Arenil – brother to King Orionkael and uncle to Gwaethe and Isiloe; a hermit who lives in isolation in the remote mountains above Selinore; he is also a Defender and becomes Vard's mentor

Lyam Anton (Lie-am) – Vard's father who has been missing for over fifteen years; he is now a Defender and can shift into hawk or bear

Katrine Aranati (Kat-reen Ar-an-arti) – sorceress and younger daughter of an impoverished farming estate south of Wildecoast; older sister is Esta Aranati; once a smuggler called Lady Star; heroine of **The Master and the Sorceress**; now mistress of the night hounds

James Tomel (James Tom-elle) – master jeweler and oldest son of a farming family; lives in Costa; hero of **The Master and the Sorceress**; spy master for King Beniel

Esta Aranati – Katrine Aranati's older sister; she is head of the Aranati estate and was once a smuggler known as Lady Moonlight; heroine of **The Lady and the Pirate**; married to Samael Delacost

Samael Delacost – once a pirate, was captured by Nikolas Cosara, admiral of the King's Navy and is now sworn to obey the admiral or spend the rest of his life in prison; hero of **The Lady and the Pirate** and now married to Esta Aranati

Merielle – mermaid who has become human; she has vibrant red hair and is not familiar with the ways of Thorian people; heroine of **The Lord and the Mermaid**; good friend of Esta Aranati

Lord Nikolas Cosara (Nikolas Cos-arra) – Admiral in the King's Navy; he is cousin to Queen Adriana and the hero of **The Lord and the Mermaid**; he is married to Merielle

Alique (Ah-leek) Jazara nee *Zorba* - beautiful blonde healer, married to Kain and brother to Ramón; cousin to General Josef Formosa. Her story was told in **The Elf King's Lady**

Kain Jazara – once general of the Thorian army, he has discovered his father was Orionkael Arenil (past elven king); he has taken up leadership of the peaceful Lenweri; he is married to Alique Jazara and is hero of **The Elf King's Lady**; half-brother to Gwaethe Arenil; son of Orionkael Arenil, the murdered elven king; has a black horse called Snow

Josef Formosa – promoted to general of the Wildecoast army after Kain Jazara was forced to resign; he is cousin to Ramon and Alique Zorba

Alecia Zialni's lady guards –

Linnet Perfore – Alecia's second-in-command; talented scout; tall redhead; gray eyes

Cretia – the planner of the group; blonde with baby blue eyes

Arelle – the peacekeeper; inspired by Alecia to learn weapons; black hair, blue eyes

Kenna – scout and fierce warrior; hyperactive; brown hair and eyes

Jules Estevot (Jewels Ess-tee-vow) – captain of the army in Brightcastle; has blond hair and ice-blue eyes

Reid Vetta (Reed Vet-tah) – Master goldsmith in Wildecoast and Esta's betrothed for a short time

Doctor Achan Mosard – Physician to the king in Wildecoast

Master Dunnet – Vard's man servant

Elora Arenil (Elle-Aura Arenil) – King Orionkael's widow and Gwaethe's mother

Isiloe (Iz-il-oe) – Gwaethe's cousin by Orionkael's sister- unlike most of her race, Isiloe is short with white hair and pale blue eyes. She is a captain (Ramar) in the elven army

Chandrelle (Shan-drel) – Isiloe's sister; tall, dark elven woman with long dark hair; warrior

Exmund - Jacques's aide and corporal in the Brightcastle army; youngest brother of James Tomel, hero of **The Master and the Sorceress**

Elvor Faenwelar - High Prince of the *Sis Lenweri*; enemy of Gwaethe and the humans

Niel Gorin Faenwelar – of the *Sis Lenweri*; Elvor's son

Rasalar (Raz-a-lar) – Isiloe's mother; sister to Orionkael and Melandrach; once a soldier and still trains recruits

Sergeant Dodlan – second in command to Jacques in his trek north and remains with him in Amitania

Master Jenkin – Brightcastle weapons master

Tyra – Benae's maid- stocky, blond; helps with healing

Julli (Ju-lee) Dovara – Alique's maid; gifted helper and healer; not a great horsewoman; gentle and caring

Alia Kelsis – the elven woman who leads the female Sis Lenweri in Selinore

Ruven Magbalar – Sis Lenweri soldier rescued by Gwaethe and became a loyal supporter; he is now elven army commander in Amitania

Théoden Leovaris – Sis Lenweri soldier rescued by Gwaethe and became a loyal supporter and captain of her guard

Vortek Cruzen – Defender who trains with Melandrach

Soma Nuran – a mercenary Alecia convinces to help enlist dissenting army conscripts

Night hound – a beast the size of a wolf, with short grey, black or red hair, heavy snout, and stumpy ears; the eyes are red; there are six toes on each paw and the back feet have retractable cat-like claws, huge and razor sharp; have not been seen in Thorius for at least fifty years

Nugoriem – the black dragon; name means 'eternal fire'

Elven terms

Alen – Lord

Gir – Sergeant

Ade – Corporal

Ramar – Captain

Saleh – attack

Elrie – half-blood

ABOUT THE AUTHOR

Bernadette Rowley is a lover of epic fantasy who is a veterinarian by day and an author by night. She is currently published in the genre of high fantasy romance with nine books and a box collection, all set in her fantasy world of Thorius.

When she was a young teenager, an aunt gave her a copy of The Sword of Shannara by Terry Brooks and Bernadette has lived in various fantasy worlds ever since. The author who has influenced her writing most is Robert Jordan (Wheel of Time series). It's no surprise that her chosen genre when writing romance is fantasy.

"I can see these settings so vibrantly in my mind and hope my readers can too."

But Bernadette has no desire to spoon-feed her readers by laboriously describing her fantasy settings. She would rather the reader use their own imagination.

Along with sword and sorcery, dashing heroes and stunning heroines, this author includes strong healing themes in many of her books - an element which is central to her everyday job.

"When I started writing the Queenmakers Saga, I never imagined my day job would force its way into my stories as it has."

And of course, there are animals, especially Bernadette's beloved horses.

Bernadette lives in Southeast Queensland, Australia, where she enjoys a great coffee, walks in nature and catching up family and friends.

CONNECT WITH THE AUTHOR

Website: www.bernadetterowley.com
Subscribe to the Bernadette Rowley newsletter and
get a free map of the world of Thorius

Facebook: www.facebook.com/bernadetterowleyfantasy
Twitter: www.twitter.com/bt_rowley